PRAISE FOR
LARRY BROOKS

and *Bait and Switch*. His name is Larry Brooks. The guy has a slick tone and a crackling, cynical wit with lots of vivid descriptions (of both interior and exterior landscapes), and the sparkling figures of speech dance off the page and explode in your inner ear. Though as modern as an iPad 5S, he is truly and remarkably Chandleresque. He's dazzling. Check out his new one, *Deadly Faux*—it's sexy, complex, intelligent; a truly delightful novel with more plot twists than a plate of linguine swimming in olive oil."

—James N. Frey, author of
How to Write a Damn Good Novel, for *Deadly Faux*

"An absolute must read, *Deadly Faux* is guaranteed entertainment. In Wolfgang Schmitt, Larry Brooks has created a wisecracking protagonist who is witty, resourceful, intelligent, and, most surprisingly, vulnerable. Brooks plunges Wolf into a seemingly unwinnable caldron involving Las Vegas casinos, the mob, and femme fatales, then turns the heat up high. I finished *Deadly Faux* in one sitting, couldn't put it down, and can't wait to read the next book. Step aside, Nelson DeMille and Stuart Woods—Schmitt happens!"

—Robert Dugoni, *New York Times*
bestselling author of *The Jury Master*, for *Deadly Faux*

"*Deadly Faux* is a fast, fun read with plot twists I did not see coming and a satisfying ending."

—Phillip Margolin,
New York Times bestselling author of *Sleight of Hand*

PRESSURE POINTS

PRESSURE POINTS

A NOVEL

LARRY BROOKS

TURNER

Turner Publishing Company
424 Church Street • Suite 2240 • Nashville, TN 37219
445 Park Avenue • 9th Floor • New York, New York 10022
www.turnerpublishing.com

PRESSURE POINTS

This is a work of fiction. All the characters and events portrayed in this book are either products of the author's imagination or are used fictitiously.

Cover design: Glen Edelstein
Book design: Glen Edelstein

Library of Congress Catalog-in-Publishing Data
Brooks, Larry, 1952-
 Pressure points / Larry Brooks.
    pages cm
  ISBN 978-1-62045-459-6 (pbk.)
 I. Title.
 PS3602.R64437P74 2013
 813'.6--dc23
                                    2013024447

Printed in the United States of America
13 14 15 16 17 18 19 0 9 8 7 6 5 4 3 2 1

For my teachers,
Laura and Nelson

"Every day man crucifies himself between two thieves—fear of tomorrow and regrets of yesterday."
—Benjamin Disraeli, 1804–1881

Acknowledgments

The author would like to acknowledge the continuing efforts of those who kept him focused and sane in the writing of this book: my beautiful wife, Laura, who lovingly understands and cares for all my pressure points, and to whom this book is dedicated; my son, Nelson, for keeping me centered and smiling; Dan Slater, a much appreciated editor with a vision; Mary Alice Kier and Anna Cottle at Cine-Lit, agents with the patience of angels. I would like to thank my family for their enthusiastic support—Bev and Dick, Sybil and Lester, Tracy and Eric, Kelly and Paul, Lynn and Scott, who I hope will read this one. Special thanks go out to Kathy Q-P, George, Ernestine, Gary, Bruce, Jane, Travis, and all the other folks at PSI. You have changed my life.

This is a work of fiction, and the names used here are in no way intended to describe actual individuals, living or dead or anything in between. You may think you know who you are, but it's not you, I promise.

While this novel depicts activities that take place at an entirely fictional personal growth seminar, they are in large part figments of the author's imagination. For purposes of dramatic context, the seminar experience described in this book has been taken to extremes and should not be construed as representative of the proven techniques employed by the human-performance industry. The author encourages anyone seeking to expand and improve their life to step into the journey, be it at church, in books, or perhaps at a seminar . . . before it steps on you first.

PRESSURE POINTS

BOOK
ONE

RESENTMENT

Prologue

It was the echo of gunfire that kept him running. His body had long ago abandoned hope, pushing on faith alone through a fog of pain and fatigue. Logic screamed that this was pointless, while another voice whispered it was all a lie. Both were old friends that had served him well, and like Jesus on his fortieth desert night, he was tempted.

But neither voice was real. The gunshot had been real. The echo of it was real.

And so he ran. For his very life, and for those left behind. He knew that precious little time remained, and what was left was as critical as it was dwindling. Everything he had ever learned or believed or dreamed was at stake. He was out of options, down to a final chance that, win or lose, would be his statement to the universe.

It was his time. He had come full circle.

It is not paranoia when they are really out to get you.

When they are right on your ass, downwind of the scent of your blood, closing fast.

Whoever the hell *they* are.

He ran all through the night's relentless downpour. Low branches whipped his forehead and cheeks until they bled. He could feel his heart pounding in every extremity of his body, his vision clouded by sweat and rain. Both elbows were bloodied from a fall when his foot caught an exposed root, sending him skating wildly across a patch of decaying leaves. Leaping over a rotting log, he felt his right ankle turn impossibly inward, and the ensuing bolt of pain seized his leg like a pair of gigantic hands twisting with the enthusiasm of a gleeful sadist. But he had no time for this or any other distraction, not on this night, when, one way or the other, his past would finally and conclusively catch up with him.

From that past he summoned his God and pleaded for mercy. No deals this time, no hollow promises in exchange for salvation. Just simple mercy. For it, he had only his humility to offer. Things would be different if he survived. He would be different. And he could never go back. Not after all this.

He ran well past the point at which he would have assumed he'd give it up. His mind was consumed with every step; there was no world beyond the trees, no business that mattered other than moving forward. When he was unable to run another step, he would collapse to his hands and knees, taking cover as he desperately gulped down air, listening for some audible trace of a pursuer. It was in these quiet respites that truth descended, and in that truth, made clear after a night as prey, he found his last and best hope: success, like failure, was nothing more than a choice. It could be willed into being.

All his life he had been succeeding on instinct while he steered clear of obstacles. He was a master of the low road. Underachievement had come so easily, and now, it was time to pay. He would have to survive on sheer will alone, here in the frigid night on the high road, where survival and success were one and the same. Where mediocrity dies.

A wall of blackness suddenly appeared in front of him. His body was weightless as he ran full out, his legs unresponsive as he attempted a sudden stop. There was nothing to grasp as he fell forward; the soft ground below him had vanished. He tucked his shoulder and rolled, landing hard on his back. He bounced between protruding roots and fallen branches as he tumbled down a steep embankment, finally landing on the smooth rocks of a riverbed. He was immediately conscious of an absolute penetrating coldness, and his mind wrestled with it until he realized he was lying in a shallow but urgent stream. Mountain water, not long removed from the ice from where it came. The only other sensation he could perceive emanated from his twisted ankle, which was throbbing angrily in the frigid water.

Just a few breaths, a moment to summon his will. To remind himself that he was no longer mediocre, that mercy was forthcoming. And then he would go on.

He crawled from the river on his hands and knees, then struggled to his feet. He wouldn't last long now, not soaked like this. After a few steps he realized the ground had changed into something smooth and hard and black. He lowered to his knees, feeling it with his hands.

He had found the road.

He walked for what seemed like hours, but no cars came. The faster he walked the warmer he was, so he summoned what strength remained to save himself from a cold death.

Somewhere along the road he thought he heard a voice, barely audible over the roar of the river behind him. A moment later he heard it again, calling his name, and knew this was not his imagination.

The earliest hues of dawn had turned the trees into black cutouts framed against a blanket of pale pink. The road snaked ahead in a dark path of open space, dissolving into the treeline. After a moment, coming into focus against the trees, a shape seemed to float into view, looking down. A faceless ghost, materialized from mist, with a smile as cold as the water that had moments earlier enveloped him.

The ghost said his name again. It was a familiar voice,

calm and pleased with itself, and only then did he recognize the face. And because it was the last face he expected to see, a face that couldn't possibly be here, he concluded he was already dead.

He closed his eyes and gently sagged to the pavement, waiting for what was next, at peace with the knowledge that he had given everything and that there were no more choices remaining.

1

Early on in the life of every fledgling advertising agency there comes a day of reckoning, a cold and inevitable moment in time when ultimatum and bluff collide, nose to nose like heavyweights in a stare-down of career-defining proportions. The ultimatum is, almost without exception, issued by the fickle hand of client whim or the shifting winds of creative vogue. Times change, shit happens. The client who loved you yesterday suddenly wants new terms, a new team, a new look and feel. You thought—because they told you so as recently as yesterday—that the look and feel you'd been providing them with was looking and feeling just fine, yet without warning, an e-mail arrives from someone in the client's purchasing department whom you've never met, informing you that you are no longer cutting their creative mustard. That you might just possibly, in fact, suck.

The respondent bluff, again almost always without

exception, is that of the agency scrambling to stay alive. New deal? Name your price. New account team? Already on board. New look and feel? Talk to us, we are creative whores, we have absolutely no pride. Because at this point in the agency's pubescent biography, this suddenly fickle anchor client is the only game in town. All the agency's chips are on the table, and every job is at risk. At the end of this day of reckoning one of two realities remain: hope or layoffs.

Anchor clients are grown, not stolen. And like children, their departure is inevitable and cold.

Such a day came for the advertising and marketing agency known as Wright & Wong, a Seattle firm the trade rags had dubbed the hottest creative shop in the world of Internet commerce and all things digital, during the week between Christmas and New Year's Day. Their largest client was coming in to fire them from the account.

Ben Wong, the cofounder and sole equity principal at Wright & Wong, was reportedly off golfing in Scottsdale that week with a group of other young CEOs, who had formed an alliance of sorts that for all intents and purposes appeared to be founded on the love of golf. Wong hadn't been seen or heard from since the agency's annual holiday bash, which this year, because of pressing project deadlines, was held in the lobby with a boom box and thirty-two chickens from Boston Market. So today, responsibility for the agency's fate was in the capable if not completely willing hands of Brad Teeters, Mark Johnson, and Pamela Wiley, the firm's biggest remaining cheeses-in-residence when it came to such details as clients, gross profit margins, and the vaporous mental state of the creative staff.

The client in question was nothing less than The World's Largest Microprocessor Company. Their standard corporate vendor agreement—or CVA, the political football at the heart of today's scrimmage—stipulated that at no time and for no reason whatsoever shall the agency use their name in any outside communications or marketing materials. When Wright & Wong's team leader for this account, Brad Teeters, had asked how they were supposed to respond to a simple and reasonable question such as "So who are your largest clients?," he was told that he could use the term "The World's Largest Microprocessor Company" as long as the company name itself was neither spoken nor printed. Because the linkage between this description and the actual name of the company would likely appear at the one-hundred-dollar level on *Who Wants to Be a Millionaire?*, no rationale was provided nor asked for.

The whole contract controversy began when a new copywriter in W&W's creative department used the hallowed client name in a press release about a design award the agency had just won. This innocent transgression caused a suit in the client's Silicon Valley procurement department—known to the rest of the world as "purchasing"—to hyperventilate. He called an emergency meeting, at which it was concluded that it was time to put a choke hold on Wright & Wong by implementing the terms of their key vendor relationship model, or the dreaded KVRM.

The gist of the KVRM went something like this: "Agency will forgo any and all markups on outside direct expenses incurred in serving The Company; agency will pass all outside costs, including materials, subcontractors, talent, and other costs, directly through to client as incurred; agency will not be entitled to retainer fees and will bill on a project basis according to client-approved specifications; agency will pass through any standard media placement discounts directly to client, thereby billing media placement on a net basis only . . ." and so on. Basically, it was indentured servitude.

To top it off with a nice little personal touch, the KVRM stipulated that the copywriter who'd implemented the travesty be terminated forthwith. A little blood from the neck of a twenty-three-year-old copy rookie would make this $75 billion corporation whole again.

Mark Johnson, Wright & Wong's CFO and Controller, desperately wanted to tell The World's Largest Microprocessor Company to go fuck themselves. In the first draft of his responding memo, he'd used the word *bullshit* eleven times, three of them in all caps. Pamela Wiley, corporate

Creative Director and reigning design queen (from hell, depending on whom you asked), sided with her minions and was insisting that Wright & Wong resign the account, preferably with a big eat-me grin on their faces. That left Brad Teeters, Vice President of Client Services and the guy who took over the account five years earlier, holding the bag. It was he who had edited Mark's memo into presentable form, complete with capitulation and regret, throwing yet another wrench into the already gummed-up works of their relationship.

At ten minutes before eleven, Mark Johnson and Pamela Wiley joined Brad Teeters in his office to go over any remaining details and vent their final wrath before putting on an appropriately warm but immovable game face.

"Is *this* why we get the big bucks?" said Mark as they sat down in the chairs facing Brad's desk. This was the one and perhaps only thing that linked them as comrades-in-arms: money. More accurately: the lack thereof. The injustice of its selective distribution and ultimate migration into Ken Wong's pocket. The three of them had recently joined forces in issuing a list of demands to Wong, whom they were making rich while their own technology-weighted 401K plans were seesawing in a downward death spiral with nauseating velocity. But their strategy to take over the business was another story. Today they had to *save* the business first.

Mark Johnson was, as he liked to describe himself, a man of color. Not exactly black, but certainly not the token white guy in the accounting department, either. No one at the agency knew for sure, but you could envision his mother as a Bible Belt Miss America and his father as a bourbon-smooth Motown backup singer. His hair was tightly cropped, and he had a sort of Malcolm X thing going with his wire-rimmed glasses. Long, graceful limbs gave him a walk that seemed to defy gravity, and you could easily imagine him dancing sooner than you might imagine him going ten rounds.

"I tinkered with the proposal," Brad said, looking down at a pile of neatly bound folders on his desk. He was being polite—he'd been up until three-thirty last night rewriting Mark's response to the KVRM. Because so many of the criteria for a continued relationship with The World's Largest Microprocessor Company were financial in nature, Johnson had asked for and taken the first cut at the counterproposal. What he'd turned in was a suicide mission from page one.

Mark Johnson's eyes narrowed to slits. "You mucked around with my proposal, you arrogant prick." This was as pissed as Mark ever got.

"That would be *our* proposal," said Brad, allowing a proper shade of smile to accompany his response. "I don't think telling the most successful company in the history of the electronics industry that they don't seem to understand the basic theory of commerce in the U.S. economy is our best approach here, do you?"

"Well, obviously they don't." Mark shifted in his chair, busted. Nowhere on the geography of his perfect mocha features was there a trace of humor or humility.

"It's a tone thing," said Brad. "I just added a little spin. It's what I do."

"Mark's right," Pamela chipped in, her expression impatient. "This is America—we have a right to do business in a manner that *keeps* us in business. What, we're supposed to sign up for this piece-of-shit contract and break even, just for the privilege of working with them? Somebody has to call them on their bullshit."

Pamela Wiley was the firm enigma. It was as if there were secret goings-on outside the office that remained beyond anyone's understanding, variables that conspired and arranged themselves in ways that defined Pamela's mood for the day. Most days she was either chilly or, like today, simply unbearable. Pamela was attractive enough if you could get beyond her expression, which was often tight and distant, as if concentrating on something urgent, like her plant collection. Then again, she was simply brilliant at what she did and completely without compromise in her dedication to it, and this bought her a lot of slack at Wright & Wong. She wore her hair short and salon perfect, with a conservative sense of business fashion that was uncommon to her profession as a graphic designer. She kept her copy of *Glamour* right under her copy of *Lithography Times*.

"So," said Brad, his own impatience permeating his voice now, "let's all count to three and fall on our swords. Let's be dead freaking right about this." His grin announced his sarcasm.

"That's not what I'm saying," she said.

"That's not what I'm saying, either," chimed in Mark. "But let's not kiss their ass like everyone else. Let's give them a realistic response that shows we won't take it up ours."

Brad issued a dismissive chuckle. "How about we lighten up, okay? I've got it handled. I just added some . . . finesse."

"Gee, I feel better now," said Pamela with the same sarcastic smile Brad had shown.

"I worked my ass off on that thing," added Mark. Brad could see stress around his mouth and in the way he was sitting rigid in his chair.

"I know, and it's great work. You drove the lane, set up the play . . . now you dish to me for the slam. Trust me on this." Brad's basketball metaphors were as famous as they were despised. Most of the time, like now, they were resolutely ignored. He wasn't sure if his coworkers didn't know or didn't care that he had played college basketball, but the effect was the same, and for years it had quietly eaten at him.

"Trust you?" said Pamela, shaking her head slightly. "Right. Last time I looked, you were still in sales."

"Last time I looked," said Brad, "it was my account. Any questions?"

There weren't. Mark and Pamela shot each other a familiar look as they got up and left the office. Brad watched them go, believing in his heart that everything would turn out just fine.

2

The World's Largest Microprocessor Company sent two emissaries to wrestle Wright & Wong to the ground on the third business day after Christmas. They were from Procurement, which also meant they knew nothing about how the advertising business worked. Brad knew the profile: mid twenties, MBAs from respected California schools, no more than three years under their belts, and flush with all the clout that a $75 billion name gives you. Today's duo fit the profile perfectly: a young man who looked like a refugee from a Kenneth Cole ad and a very young woman whose defiant expression just dared you to try to ask her for ID. Smug hellos in the lobby, a deliberate and quite tangible scent of we've-got-you-by-the-balls behind their obligatory smiles. Pamela and Mark handled the greeting, while Brad attended to some last minute detail of preparation.

Actually, Brad simply liked to make an entrance. It was because of his height. At six-foot-seven he knew he made an impression. Even though he didn't need to, he made a subtle production out of ducking under the top of the doorway as he entered, a radiant grin igniting the room, his hand already extended as he took command of the space with power-forward strides. Everything about him was impressive but calculatedly nonthreatening: a nice but not too flashy suit, hair a little messy but appropriately hip, a handshake that was just a touch too strong, as if he couldn't help it.

"Well then," Brad said as everyone settled in, already knowing that this opponent would not fall easily, "let the sucking up begin."

No grins, not even a smirk. Small talk was aborted when the young woman eyed the pile of proposals waiting in the center of the table and said, "May I assume you've prepared a counterproposal? The KVRM is really quite cast in stone, I'm afraid."

Mark shot a look toward Brad. "Well, to be honest, we've reviewed the contract *terms,* and we have some questions. May I?"

Mark was reaching for the proposals when Brad put his hand on top of Mark's.

"Actually," Brad said quickly, "I'd like to start, if I may." Mark froze for a moment, then reversed his motion as he lowered himself back into one of Ken Wong's $1,200 leather swivel chairs.

All eyes fixed on Brad.

"First of all, thanks for coming here today. We're honored to be counted among the key vendors for The World's Largest Microprocessor Company."

The acknowledgment issued by the clients was both smug and obligatory.

"And I'd like to thank Mark for all the work he's put into this. He's the primary author of the document and, I must say, its strategic champion. I think you'll like what he's prepared for you today."

The girl consulted her notes and said to Mark, "You're the administrative guy, right?"

"CFO," replied Mark, his eyes suddenly diverted but

his voice a little too sharp. Brad used the moment to notice Pamela glaring at him as if he'd eviscerated her cat.

Hearing Mark's tone, Brad jumped in quickly. "As the senior account professional and accountable party, I'd like to overview our document, which isn't really a counter-proposal per se. Think of it as an expansion on what you've proposed in your KVRM, working toward a mutually satisfactory account model."

Pamela just about slid off her chair. Everyone in the room noticed, but somehow she managed to keep quiet. Brad smiled in acknowledgment, then plowed into his well-rehearsed oratory.

In a nutshell, he basically agreed to everything the KVRM demanded. The World's Largest Microprocessor Company had Wright & Wong right where they wanted them. It was their way or the highway. With a phone book full of upstart agencies and hungry competitors who would kill for this account, there was really no other way to proceed. *That's* how much, Brad assured them, Wright & Wong loves this account. No more markups, no agency media discount, the financial kimono is hereby open for all to see. Slide the tab across the table to us. We'll make it work.

Pamela got up and left the room without a word about halfway through Brad's presentation. Mark never moved a muscle except for closing his eyes, a fist jammed against his teeth so hard you could see the flesh turning cadaver white. Both clients noticed, but Brad waved off the distraction with a serious nod of his head that said *I'm where the buck stops, pay no attention to the guy behind the curtain.*

Brad opened his briefcase and withdrew a copy of the proposal. "This is our signed copy, notarized as you requested. Ken Wong apologizes for his absence today, but he's away on business." His smile was impossibly genuine, yet somehow humble in the face of capitulation. They would make it work. You win.

"Are there any questions?"

There weren't. As the collective body language began to shift in anticipation of departure, Brad reassumed the floor by saying, "There is one more thing on our agenda, however."

The girl raised her eyebrows as everyone settled back into their seats.

"The KVRM specified that we would terminate the writer who used your name in the press release."

"I'd assumed that has been handled," said the girl.

"It has. We've pulled him from your account."

Her head cocked slightly in confusion. "He wasn't terminated?"

"He violated your rules, not ours," said Mark gruffly.

Brad grinned patiently. "We understand your feelings about this, and the writer has been reprimanded and re-assigned. But he will not be terminated."

The clients exchanged the requisite moment of indignation and jotted notes to themselves before moving on to a short list of other business that was important only to people who worked in Procurement.

When the meeting concluded, Brad politely suggested lunch, but as he expected, the busy young clients respect-fully declined. Mark quickly shook hands and bolted, the first to leave the room. In his case, it was more an escape than an exit.

"Can I give you some feedback?" said the young man as he put on his overcoat.

Brad nodded eagerly. One always nodded eagerly at this request from a client.

"Figure out who on your team is in charge, and run with that. Your politics were showing today, and it's bad form."

ANOTHER Brad Teeters habit was a brisk hike around the block following client meetings or staff interactions that contained any discernible amount of head butting. He em-barked on today's stroll with a bit of extra pep in his step—the meeting had gone precisely as he knew it would. As he rounded the final corner, he spied Pamela standing near the door, sucking the last stubborn carcinogens from her post-meeting cigarette—a habit as predictable as Brad's walks. When she saw him approach, she deliberately flicked the butt in his direction, shook her head disgustedly, and re-entered the building.

This is going to be fun, he thought.

Mark and Pamela, still reeking of her nicotine break, were waiting for him in his office. Mark was pacing, hands in his pockets, eyes fixed on his feet. He didn't look up as Brad entered or as he sat and put his feet up on the desktop.

Mark stopped pacing, stared at him a moment, then said, "Please tell me what the hell you were thinking."

Brad's smug grin stretched from ear to ear.

Pamela and Brad looked at each other with can-you-believe-this-guy shrugs. It was clear that neither of them could.

Brad grinned as he shrugged. "Where's the trust? Where's the love?"

Mark began rubbing his temples as he looked at the ground between his expensive Ecco loafers. Brad almost felt sorry for him.

Pamela took the baton. "It isn't that you just plopped a turd into the punch bowl of common sense, Brad. I mean, God knows I have no clue where all that came from or what you intend to do about it. It's the 'fuck you' to Mark and me that concerns us. Mark busted his ass on that proposal, and you go off without telling anyone and change everything to God knows what and don't even talk to us about it! How am I supposed to go into the trenches with you after this?"

She stopped. Not because she was finished, but because the smirk on Brad's face was sending her blood pressure into the red zone.

"Are you done now?" asked Brad.

Pamela looked away toward the windows, and Mark, who had raised his eyes to watch Brad's reaction, allowed his gaze to drift toward the door. Brad used the moment to open his drawer and withdraw a piece of paper, which he slid toward them.

Mark grabbed first, his forehead etched into an ever-increasing divot as he studied the document. Pamela leaned in, saw what it was, then leaned back as if it were infectious.

"What's up with this?" was what Mark said.

It was an invoice in the amount of $900. Brad was billing The World's Largest Microprocessor Company for the one-hour meeting they had just concluded: one man-hour times three hourly rates, plus the hour Brad spent with the wayward writer discussing the name-dropping sin.

Brad leaned forward and consciously erased all trace of humor from his expression. It was time to rescue their pending partnership, which was floundering on the precipice of oblivion.

"Two things," he began. "First, I will never, and I mean never, let you guys down. Which is why the viability of our partnership is stronger and more exciting now than ever, which I hope you'll realize in a moment. Hell, you guys just proved to me how much you need what I bring to the ballgame. And frankly, your lack of confidence pisses me off. How dare you think I'd put that or any account in jeopardy, or do anything remotely destructive where either our client or our relationship is concerned? I deserve better, and you know it . . . because you deserve better."

He paused long enough to gauge their response. They had already assumed the subtle body language of acquiescence.

"Which, I might add, is precisely what your document would have done, Mark. Those little purchasing pukes would have spit you out and stomped on the wet spot if they had read it your way. Which, by the way, is the second thing." Brad turned to Pamela. "Did you even read it?"

She shook her head without looking up at him.

Mark, perhaps in an attempt to rescue Pamela, held up the invoice with a quizzical look. "Just tell me what the hell is going on."

Brad allowed his smile to reassume its throne. "Here's the deal," he said to Mark. "You obviously don't know shit about agency contracts."

Brad was correct in this assumption. Wright & Wong had grown up as a project company, doing business one contract at a time. The nuances of agency retainers and the subtle treachery of billing for client services was new to all of them.

Brad turned to Pamela now. "And you don't know shit about the business side of this industry. Lucky for us, I do, on both counts. It was all there in the KVRM. All you had to do was see it and grab it, but you were both too busy pissing your pants. It's boilerplate for their ad agencies. We've been billing like a contractor instead of an agency. They're just asking for the old agency shaft, kids, so let's give it to them, whaddaya say?"

"Your holier-than-thou shtick is getting a little old," said Pamela.

"Really? Here's a new shtick. What's your hourly rate as Creative Director?"

She winced, as if the question surprised her. "One fifty."

He turned to Mark. "And what's your hourly rate as CFO?"

"Don't screw with me."

"I'm not screwing with you. Answer me."

"There *is* no hourly client-billing rate for a CFO. You know that."

Brad leaned back, once again lacing his fingers behind his head. "There is now," he said.

Pamela and Mark exchanged yet another lost look. Brad allowed the moment to pass before continuing. "Market rates, sports fans. Account-service billing. I'm talking industry-standard practices, something of which you have no clue and this company is about two decades behind in implementing. Our client is asking us to grow up, join the big boys, and bill them for every minute we spend on them. Creative Director rates are three hundred an hour at Chiat-Day and Weiden, and as of today they're three hundred an hour here, too. Last month we put in a collective four hundred sixty hours kissing their asses. I know because I analyzed the timesheets. You know how much that is at a senior account executive rate of two fifty an hour and an account supervisor rate of one seventy-five? I'll tell you how much that is—it's almost ninety grand! Ninety large, kids, which from now on we get to bill each and every month."

He watched the wheels grinding into motion behind their eyes.

"*Comprende?*"

A slow Machiavellian grin was emerging on Mark Johnson's face. Pamela saw it happen, which only confused her further.

Mark leaned forward, staring at the invoice. "We jack up our rates across the board, we implement time sheets for the account staff, we track copying and faxing, we record mileage, we log telephone time, we bill for administrative time . . . hell, we act like lawyers."

He turned to Pamela, the grin in full bloom as he pantomimed shooting a free throw and said, "He shoots, he scores."

Pamela shook her head in genuine disgust.

"You go back to your cubicle," said Brad, "and draw something amazing. That's why we're here, you know, even talking to clients like these. Because of you. Not because I'm so charming and Mark here is so pretty. You, Ms. Wiley, are the juice, the jazz, the product . . . leave the nuts and bolts to us. We're your partners. You can count on us."

Mark stood and extended his hand. "I guess we owe you an apology."

Instead of shaking, Brad swiped a sideways high-five. "You did good work on the proposal. Every question you flagged was legit. It's just that sometimes the ref is calling them tight, and you've got to play a different game. They call it crunch time."

Pamela rolled her eyes as they turned and left the office. "God help me," he heard her say from behind the wall.

Watching them leave, Brad was immediately struck by an old and unwelcomed feeling, a whisper in the back of his mind that this self-assumed role as corporate savior wasn't nearly as much fun as it used to be, or as it should have been. Nothing like hitting a jumper at the buzzer for the win, something that never happened in that career, either.

A moment later Pamela stuck her head back around the corner and added in a whisper, "I still think you're an asshole . . . partner."

BEFORE leaving for the day, Brad made a point of stopping by the cubicle of the young writer who had inspired this travesty of corporate mistrust. He knew the kid had been mainlining Mylanta all morning long, and had noticed him lurking in the periphery when the two client representatives arrived and later as he, Mark, and Pamela kibitzed. He already knew he was off the account, but there was more at stake here than his next assignment. As one of Pamela's direct reports, Brad wasn't completely confident that the young man's anxiety would be properly addressed. The guy was a legitimately insecure rookie copywriter, after all, and Pamela was, well, Pamela.

Brad's instincts had been right. Pamela hadn't said a word to the guy about the outcome of the meeting. The young man's eyes were moist as he simply nodded, unable to mumble a coherent thank you to Brad's assurance that at Wright & Wong, the choice between doing the right thing and kissing the client's unreasonable ass was an easy one, and that the box the clients had brought with them to ferry his head back to their salivating lawyers was returning empty.

Whether it was true or not, it was the least he could do. The aforementioned *right* thing to do. And he would be rewriting some lame brochure copy the kid had generated in his present state of emotional dysfunction, and this would quiet the ensuing whine.

3

In its earliest incarnation, the notion that Brad, Mark, and Pamela should wrestle the business away from Ken Wong's exclusive grasp actually belonged to Brad's wife, Beth, spoken in a moment of post-coital bliss.

Brad and Beth were motionless in each other's arms, Brad behind her in the spoon position that was their ritual following her riding him to release from the top. It was the only way she could come, always twice, once before and once after his own orgasm. He couldn't remember the last time they'd varied this routine, but he certainly wasn't complaining. Once in the saddle, with her eyes clamped tightly shut, Beth was selfish and hungry—interesting qualities in a lover, from Brad's point of view. She was also adroitly quiet, her orgasms arriving with gasps instead of screams. For those few minutes she was someone else, anyone he wanted her to be. As for him, he was rendered *convenient*, as if he were, indeed, someone else. It was a compelling stew of intimacy and distance, and it hadn't cooled in the four years since their marriage.

When they were finished, she stroked his arm tenderly and whispered, "I'll take good care of you." She'd said this the first time they'd ever made love, in this precise position and at the exact same moment. Their lovemaking had assumed the comfortable predictability of ritual, and with these words the ritual was rendered complete.

They were quiet for several minutes tonight, listening to one of the movie soundtracks they always played when they had sex.

"He's screwing you, you know," was what she said.

Beth knew what she was talking about when it came to Ken Wong. The two had worked together for several years at The World's Largest Microprocessor Company, and when Wong and his friend Peter Wright ventured forth to start the agency twelve years earlier, Beth had gone with them as the firm's first bookkeeper and all around handyperson. She was, in fact, instrumental in hiring Brad away from Weiden and Kennedy in Portland, the behemoth Nike agency that had also, once upon a time, taken a ride on the Microsoft train. When Microsoft bailed—theirs was a substance-over-style culture, precisely the opposite of W&K's cavalier Just Do It approach to life—Brad and his high-tech savvy became a free agent who knew a ground-floor opportunity when he saw one.

That was nine years ago. Brad and Ken Wong had set out to conquer the digital world, sharing rooms on the road, flying coach, downing thousands of microbrews and lattes while writing business plans on cocktail napkins, faking it when they didn't have a clue and taking no prisoners when they did. They were an effective if not harmonious pairing—Wong wasn't a marketing guy, he was a visionary with contacts. A technocrat with style. Brad, on the other hand, had the gift of chemistry.

Peter Wright remained behind in those days to run the production side of things. Like Wong, he was a programmer by training, and, as if it were a proven prerequisite for the job, had the personality of a shoe box. Consequently, nobody wanted him within winking distance of a client, most of all Brad. It was an ongoing debate as to which milestone in the company's history had been the primary catalyst in its rise as an industry player: Peter Wright's mysterious death or Brad's subsequent emergence as the primary liaison for the firm's anchor account. The two were inexorably linked, though Brad had silenced any cynicism with his track record.

One took one's breaks where one found them, dead or alive.

Beth's resignation from the firm just prior to her marriage to Brad had also been the source of spirited coffee-room debate. Her first marriage to an attorney had dissolved three years earlier, widely reputed to have had something to do with her extremely close relationship with Wong. Whether they were simply good friends or co-dependent allies or covert lovers was never clear, but there was no question that Beth pulled the agency's strings from backstage, financially speaking at the least. When Mark Johnson was brought on board to fill the newly christened position of CFO, Beth's status in the pecking order and her relationship with Wong quickly went south on the same train. The bank had insisted on the hiring of a new CFO shortly after Peter Wright's death because of the ensuing mess of settling the estate and the void left at the senior-staff level. As an inevitable result, Beth and Mark had never warmed to each other, and the outcome was clear long before it was announced. Beth was history.

Cause and effect had always been interchangeable elements of the rumor mill at Wright & Wong, so when Beth resigned shortly after her relationship with Brad flared, tongues wagged and eyes rolled. Beth's story was that she didn't want the pressure of a romantic relationship at work, and love got the nod. Mark's story was that Beth couldn't handle her subordinate role in the company's financial management and, by implication, that she resented the fact that the bookkeeping standards she had kept had tumbled out the window the day he arrived. Wong had no story, adding fuel to the assumption that he and Beth simply couldn't coexist in a post-affair environment. He was, after all, the guy who'd hired Mark, and he'd been something less than stable since his partner's demise. The kittens in the office had a field day with it all, and Brad sensed the presence of Beth rumors of legendary proportions still haunting the halls. Four years later, with Brad emerging as the heir apparent to the top job, Beth's status as a financial visionary was cemented forever, if not in the accounting department, then in the vicinity of the water cooler.

But while Brad's paycheck had indeed grown commensurately with the agency's evolution to the point at which all the toys and vacations were well handled, the fact remained that Ken Wong was now worth something on the order of $25 million, while Brad had a faltering 401K just shy of a hundred grand and a savings account still years out from breaking into six digits. As his wife had suggested, he was indeed getting screwed. From behind.

Beth first brought this economic injustice to his attention about a year ago. Brad had been too busy making Ken Wong rich to see the big picture, and since the agency's success was the barometer of his own achievement, he'd never really thought of it that way. The fact was, the prospect of Ken Wong ever sharing ownership of the agency in any form, the agency built largely on Brad Teeters's back, had simply not come up. Brad wasn't sure whether to be ashamed that he'd never broached the subject or pissed at Wong for holding his cards close since Peter's death, with no intention of sharing the wealth. Beth assured him he should embrace both with equal degrees of suffering and guilt.

Like a conductor waving the wand of fate before an orchestra of seemingly random events, two things got Beth's attention, which she used as fodder to build her case to Brad. The first was the announcement that the agency was moving, heading uptown from its humble beginnings in a warehouse near the now-defunct Kingdome stadium. The new building was to be gutted and refitted with a labyrinth of Plexiglas walls framing cubicles and connected by balconies hanging from massive cables, adorned by lush indoor plants and pretentious art and metal sculptures and science-fiction lighting appliances, all set against ancient industrial brick walls, which were to remain pristine. It was modeled, someone later suggested, after the movie *Disclosure,* in which Michael Douglas gets screwed, too.

On the fourth level, Ken Wong had designed himself a private office with its own elevator, a one-eighty view of Puget Sound, seventeen hundred square feet of travertine marble floor covered with a $10,000 handmade Tibetan rug, a private bathroom with shower and sauna, and a kitchenette with granite counters. The next largest office was Brad's, a mere two hundred square feet with a view of the parking lot.

Wong was a genius at getting rich quietly, clandestine behind the mountain of praise he heaped on his appreciative key employees.

The problem, the thing that got Beth's attention at the time, was this: the agency would not be the owner of the building. Ken Wong would. He would lease it back to the agency at a monthly cost in excess of seven times their current rent, with a monthly net cash flow to himself of five grand a month and an equity upside rumored to be in excess of $4 million within five years.

Meanwhile, Brad and Mark and Pamela and everyone else at Wright & Wong would have their 401K, replete with the company's whoop-dee-do fifty-cents-on-the-dollar matching fund.

Beth knew as much as anyone that Ken Wong hadn't worked an eight-hour day at the agency in five years and couldn't give you three client names if his vintage wine collection depended on it. He liked to brag that he hadn't taken a day of vacation in twelve years, when in fact he'd taken no less than eighteen *weeks* of vacation in the last twelve months, many under the guise of business seminars at places like the Grand Wailea on Maui or at the Plaza in New York. Wong hadn't touched a project, read a proposal, reviewed a script, or talked to the company's accounting firm since his partner committed suicide and Mark Johnson came in to cover his ass.

Ken Wong was a great guy, no argument there, but he had checked out.

At Beth's insistence, Brad called Mark and Pamela to his house—the only such invitation in all the years they'd been working together—for what turned out to be an all-night, alcohol-fueled commiseration. Beth actually led the discussions, her role being that of counterpoint to their we-can't-do-this-to-Ken sensibilities. This, in turn, set into motion a series of meetings with various species of lawyers and advisors, also attended by Beth, clandestine "what ifs" with trusted clients and the submission of proposals to three local venture capitalists, all leading to a six-page document that was left on Ken Wong's chair one monumental Friday afternoon just before Veterans Day weekend.

The proposal was simple: let us buy a ticket on the gravy train, or we're leaving. And by the way, if we leave, we're going to start our own agency, and we're going to take all of Wright & Wong's existing clients with us. And they'll come, too, because they've never met you, and they trust *us*. Despite how it sounds, this is neither unfair nor unprecedented, just as you say your own purchase of the new building was neither unfair nor unprecedented. To quote Ken Wong himself, this is business. An offer was on the table for the purchase of seventy-five percent of Wright & Wong's stock, grandfathering half of the market value to the three buyers for "sweat equity" accumulated over the course of their employment, the rest to be paid with private financing. Or, if Wong preferred to leave, they'd cash him out completely at seventy-five percent of full market value, sweat equity be damned. His call.

Wong sat on the proposal for a month and a half, never mentioning it, presumably taking it to his cadre of lawyers and posse of misinformed friends, most of whom had founded and actually ran technology-based companies of their own. Wong belonged to a group of young CEOs who met monthly on their respective corporate dimes in places like Grand Cayman and Fiji. Their advice for their colleague was simple and, from their point of view, ridiculously obvious: fire the ungrateful bastards, and do it now.

But Wong, to his credit and the great surprise of everyone, knew better. Ken Wong wasn't the man his protective friends, salivating lawyers, and ambitious senior executives thought he was.

He wasn't even the man Beth thought he was. Not anymore.

4

Ken Wong smiled as he wondered what they'd think if they knew he was more nervous than they were. It was four minutes until the appointed hour of two o'clock, and he could imagine the three of them somewhere on a lower floor of the building, huddled quietly away from curious ears as they pumped each other up. He looked about his cavernous office with its contemporary leather furniture and absurdly expensive signed and numbered prints and shook his head as he put himself in their shoes.

So much had happened in the last six months. These people who would take his company from him had no idea how it felt to be Ken Wong. Not now, facing what he faced.

Everything was about to change. Beth coming on board, Brad's hiring, landing the Big Account, Beth leaving, Peter's suicide . . . today would be one of those milestones, he mused, and it made him smile. It was high time for another change. Because of what he'd been through in the last six months, Wong gradually realized that he'd forgotten to build a life for himself along the way. Each night he drove his leased Mercedes home to a lavish but lonely condo overlooking Lake Washington within eyesight of Paul Allen's estate, usually after too much food and yet another quiet serenade from a bottle, the vintage, like his loneliness, growing more exquisite with each passing year. Along the way, despite women who'd smelled his wallet and friends who coveted what his experience as a magazine-certified Internet pioneer could teach them, he'd always been alone. He'd done it all alone, with a little help from his colleagues in the CEO group. He *was* his company, and that was all that he was.

Brad, Mark, and Pamela entered his office after a cursory knock. They didn't look at Wong as they filed in like defendants entering a courtroom, assuming their customary seats at the thick glass conference table.

Wong watched them for a moment but, to his great surprise, had to look away. He was his usual natty self, his custom-made, $300 Francesco Smalto shirt right off the drycleaner's hanger, his hair short and jelled, brushed straight forward as if it had been styled at the Forum in Rome. His features were sharp, his Asian eyes quick and birdlike. He was half Chinese and half Indian, lending him a presence that took on depth with his GQ sensibilities—a mover and shaker who could kung-fu your ass all the way to the bank. This intensity and lean physicality demanded notice and, from Brad at least, respect. Mark regarded Wong as more frail than fearsome because he knew how much Wong depended on him to understand the business he owned. For Mark, the intellect of a man defined the man. As for Pamela, her boss was largely invisible, an irrelevant necessity.

They would not meet his eyes because they believed he had deserted them and, in doing so, had somehow betrayed them. But they were wrong. The betrayal, he knew and they suspected, was now theirs. And it was time to teach them a lesson.

Before beginning the meeting, Wong stepped into the

alcove of his office where the kitchenette was located. He opened the refrigerator, withdrew a green bottle, and took it back into the office, where he gently and with great panache placed it in the center of the table. It was a fine Moët & Chandon from the late eighties, purchased in honor of some revenue milestone that the agency had long ago left in the dust. He'd bought it simply because he liked the Queen song in which the champagne had been immortalized.

"Well, it would certainly be easy to read something into *this*," said Brad, as usual the first to set the tone of a meeting. In turn, Mark and Pamela relaxed, allowing their awkwardness to dissipate, leaving only their smiles.

Wong's smile in return was subdued. "Thanks for coming," he said, looking up to make eye contact. "Let me begin by offering the three of you my sincerest apologies."

He waited a moment, reading them like a stock ticker at the moment merger news hits the air.

"You've been busy," Brad finally said. "We understand how it is." Try as he might, he wasn't able to eliminate the possibility of sarcasm from his inflection. And as he said it, he pictured Beth's expression of disapproval; she was often impatient with his softening of moments, preferring the sometimes harsh light of the truth.

Wong grinned with parental patience. "Oh, I'm not apologizing for making you wait for my response to your proposal." He let them squirm a moment more. In the joust that was their routine of late, he always enjoyed the silences. "I'm apologizing for putting you in a position in which you had to *make* such a proposal to me. *That* apology is long overdue."

Now it was Mark who leaned forward, uncharacteristically taking the floor. As usual, he was the only one wearing a tie, worn today over a crisp white shirt. Of the three, Mark had the most daily contact with Wong, usually concerning financial and banking issues. In all of his years at the agency, he'd never heard Ken Wong apologize for anything.

"But you did put us in this position," he said.

"I know that."

Brad looked at Mark quizzically, then back to Wong. "Could you say that again? Just in case I'm hearing things."

Wong had to force his smile. "I'm saying that bringing the three of you into the equity side of the business is justified and long overdue. I apologize. And I intend to make it right."

Brad grabbed the Moët & Chandon and hoisted it to arm's length. "Well, I'll sure as hell drink to that."

"Perhaps," said Wong, not allowing the smile of the previous moment to deteriorate even a little. The desired effect—seeing the three faces before him freeze and then go slack—was immediate and gratifying.

Brad placed the bottle softly back onto the table.

After a moment, Mark said, "I was really hoping we wouldn't play games here."

Pamela shot him a look. "Jeez-louise, let the man talk! What'd you think, he'd just *sign* the damn thing? Let him negotiate, for shit's sake!"

"We've already negotiated," shot back Brad, definitely not playing games now. "And our terms are nonnegotiable. I thought we made that clear."

"Crystal," said Ken softly.

The three exchanged confused glances.

"I don't understand, then," said Mark. "What's up with all this?" He was referring to the champagne and the cryptic apology.

Ken shifted in his chair in a way that was, after a decade of meetings with these folks, an obvious precursor to an approaching monologue.

"I am troubled by what I see. I watch the three of you, listen to how you speak to one another, and I ask myself, do I really want to turn my business over to them? Cutting each other off, getting testy before testy is warranted . . . assumptive, full of both justifiable and misplaced pride . . . we've all got *context* with each other, you know? In a partnership, we'd have to do better than that, don't you agree?"

He paused, but no one had anything to offer in the way of answer or interruption. So he continued, facing Pamela.

"You . . . you're so sure that an injustice is at hand that you're defensive and hacked off before the bell sounds. I've seen you suck the energy out of a room before the coffee is poured. How can you join this partnership when you don't trust your partners? What have we really done to make you so angry at us? What have *they* done?"

A weight descended on the room. Ken Wong had never spoken to them this way. Perhaps he, too, had acquired a taste for the harsh light of truth.

He turned to Mark now. "And you . . . why is it that you've worked hand in hand with me, almost on a daily basis, for what, five years now? And you've never once suggested that we just go grab some lunch together, other than the ones I've instigated? When was the last time you asked me about my weekend, or even how I was feeling? In fact, why is it that you eat alone every day, when there are over a hundred people out there who don't know who you are, who look up to you and wish that they could get just a moment with you? Don't underestimate the power of relationship in this partnership you're considering, Mark. With us and with them."

"I don't underestimate it."

"Maybe not. Maybe you just undervalue it."

"I don't undervalue it."

Wong looked parental with a sad smile. "We could talk about defensiveness, too, if you want." His voice was gentle and therefore powerful.

"And, Brad, I'll be damned if I can figure *you* out at all. You've got everything it takes to run a company, and yet you don't run one, and you blame *me* for that. Who is *really* to blame, is what you might want to look at. Who created your life? Me? I wonder if you really believe that."

Brad squirmed. "I don't really think this is—"

"Hold on," shot back Wong, his tone suddenly sharp, especially for him. His power had always been written on his business card, rarely conveyed in his voice. "Just don't say anything, okay? Just listen for a change, okay?"

He looked at them each in turn, his eyes moist. This was definitely new territory for their boss, and they all processed an explanation of the same general essence, one that gave them a sudden new hope that they dared not show in their expression: Ken Wong was scared. They had him. First he had apologized, now he was going for his inevitable pound of flesh. They had forced this moment from him like a president resigning on television before the nation. It was certainly about time, but it didn't make it any easier for the man on the spot. Each of them, in their own way, gave birth to a moment of empathy for Ken Wong, and they respectfully assumed the posture of some-one about to listen carefully.

Wong gathered himself. "I know what you people think of me. Oh, I think you *like* me well enough . . . God knows we've been to hell and back with Peter and all, and we've had some good times and accomplished a lot. I give you credit for valuing all of that, to whatever extent that you do. But I also know you don't *respect* me. You won-der where I am when I'm gone, you resent the fact that you're doing the client and creative work, and you don't understand what the hell *I'm* doing. You wonder why I don't play the company game, why I don't use the very systems I've created, and you assume I think I'm above all that because I own the place. That's understandable. Per-haps you think I'm doing nothing at all. I don't know. I'm pretty sure you've run the numbers in your head and have decided—somewhat legitimately, I admit—that you resent my supposed wealth, which is only of the paper variety, I assure you."

Wong paused, noticing that each of them, in their own way, was trying to wear as soft an expression as possible. Brad's face even had a shade of shame to it; then again, with Brad, one never knew.

Mark went for the water, and the room silenced as the sound of tumbling ice and pouring fluid filled the room. Everyone listened to the muted clicking in his throat as he swallowed.

Wong smiled through glassy eyes. "You think I've gone off the deep end." He paused. "Maybe I have."

Wong now poured a glass of water, everyone closely

watching the ritual. Every sound seemed heightened, the world moving in slow motion.

Wong gathered himself. "I will accept your proposal," he said. "But I have a condition."

Brad started to speak, but froze when Wong held up his hand.

"My condition is neither a counterproposal nor a negotiation. If I were you, I'd think of it as . . . an opportunity. A privilege, perhaps."

All three feigned openness, shifting in their chairs, mustering smiles, nodding slowly. Let's get on with it, lay it on us. You've just changed our lives, the least we can do is hear what you have to say.

"Last summer I had a life-changing experience," said Wong. "Since then I've had several, in fact, but that's another story. While you thought I was off playing on a beach or wasting agency money on some useless convention, whatever the hell you thought, I was attending a class . . . a seminar. Maybe you've noticed something different about me since then, maybe not. You have to seek before you can find, and frankly we haven't seen that much of each other lately. But things are different now. I'm different. I see the world through a new lens. A very clear lens. Which means, I see your proposal differently than I might have in the past."

Wong noticed that they seemed to agree with what he was saying, with their raised eyebrows and subtle nods, and he wondered if they were just blowing smoke. It didn't matter though. It was time to hammer it home.

"My condition is that you attend this seminar yourselves. All of you."

He watched those politely agreeable faces melt into confusion. He watched their eyes meet, Pamela and Mark waiting for Brad to respond.

"You want us to attend some seminar, and that's your condition for agreeing to the proposal?"

"That's correct."

"And you have no issues with the proposal other than that?"

"Actually, I do, but they don't matter right now."

"I think they do matter," said Brad.

"All right. I will agree to the price you have offered, and the terms. My only change to the proposal is that I will sell you the entire ownership share of the agency. I want out. I'm retiring. I'm gone."

The smile returned to Wong's face, this time with no emotion or tears. It was genuine amusement watching the faces of Brad, Mark, and Pamela as they struggled with their response, barely able to hide their glee, mindful of the need to appear shocked rather than delighted, perhaps even concerned. But they had just won the lottery, and they were bursting with delight.

"The agency will be yours," Wong said. "And at a price that splits the difference between your sweat-equity price and true market value, which you so generously offered should I choose to leave. Think of it as a win-win proposition. But you have to go to the seminar first, and you have to graduate. Otherwise, the deal is off."

Wong allowed another moment to pass.

"There is one more thing," he added. "About the seminar, I mean."

All three acknowledged with expressions of agreeable patience. Wong made a bit of a pageant of getting out of his chair and leaning one hip on the corner of the glass conference table.

"My final act prior to resigning will be to name a new CEO, based on careful consideration of each of your qualifications and experiences. And on one other piece of input, which I assure you I will evaluate and weigh as heavily as anything else."

No one else seemed eager to ask, so Mark said, "And what would that be?"

Wong smiled. He allowed his eyes to drift for a moment, then he snapped them back, focusing on Mark. "On your performance at the seminar," he said. "As the person paying the tuition, I receive a detailed report and analysis of your experience."

The three of them fired quick looks at one another.

"Wait a minute," said Brad. "I don't mean to be the voice of dissent again, but if the agency will belong to us, then we should all be involved in selecting a new CEO."

"It's not yours yet," said Wong.

"Yeah, but—"

"Nothing happens until the seminar has concluded. At that time I will select a new CEO and sign your proposal, effectively selling you the agency. Then I will retire. That's the deal. You can do anything you want after you own the stock."

Brad made his own little production out of taking a deep, impatient breath, slouching into his chair. "Seems a little autocratic, don't you think?"

"Life is often autocratic."

Brad rolled his eyes. "I don't understand how a week of psychobabble in some contrived environment will tell you anything you don't already know about us."

"I assure you it can, and that you will," answered Wong.

LATER, marching down the stairs after the meeting toward their respective offices on the lower floors, Mark said to Brad, "It's all crap, you know."

"What do you mean?"

"This sudden I-care-about-you-I'm-going-to-save-you approach. It's bullshit."

They walked a few more steps, having lost Pamela to the women's restroom.

"He won't sell his business to us," said Mark. "He'll die first."

Brad nodded very slowly. He was thinking the same basic thing, but with a bit of a twist: Wong would sooner kill them than sell the company to them or anyone else at a price below market value.

5

NEW YORK CITY

40 Days Before The Seminar

It certainly wasn't the first stretch limo to pull up in front of the newest high-rise in Midtown. Construction was at the finish line, and the ribbon cutting would take place in a month to accommodate the mayor's wife's social calendar. Some of the tenants had been showing up unannounced to approve their decorator's choices, and some did so in limousines. This was, however, the first one that Chaz—the security guard handpicked by the building manager to man the main entrance—had seen that brought with it a woman like *this*. Could be a movie star, a little past her prime but still able to seduce any lens that happened to point her way. The guy with her was short, though quite handsome for a middle linebacker. Neck like a bridge foundation. His navy wool overcoat and Bally loafers would run Chaz a month's pay. Chaz watched the guy fumble with a large golf umbrella as the woman unfolded from the car in what seemed like slow motion.

Neither smiled as they arrived at Chaz's position behind the semicircular kiosk that formed the centerpiece of
the cavernous lobby. The woman didn't look at Chaz, just
as she hadn't as much as glanced at her escort. She wore
sunglasses; Chaz liked it when women wore sunglasses, especially mature business-bitch women on a rainy day. It
smacked of attitude, and attitude always rang his beeper.
She adjusted her collar and seemed to be admiring the
smoke-gray marble as her escort leaned in and said,
"Seventy-seven" with an impatient voice, glancing at his
watch as he did so.

The guy had the bluest eyes Chaz had ever seen, man
or woman.

Chaz hit a switch on the panel in front of him to un-
lock the elevator, then pointed the way, wondering who
they might be, knowing he'd be best served by quickly for-
getting they'd been here at all. He'd been doing this a long
time for the same faceless employer, and that's what you
did in this business: you forgot what you saw.

THE room was completely devoid of furnishings or wall
coverings. Soon it would be a conference suite with a
hardwood table from Brazil and thirty leather chairs cost-
ing three grand apiece, but today it was filled only with
the odor of new carpet and paint. One wall was entirely
glass, offering what would be a northerly view toward
Central Park were it not for a gauntlet of lesser buildings
along that particular line of sight. Taking in this view,
hands clasped behind him, was a completely bald man
wearing a nondescript suit and casual shoes. He remained
motionless when the door opened behind him, as if he
didn't hear.

He watched their reflection in the glass until they
were within arm's reach before he turned, hand extended.
The woman's greeting was politely businesslike without the slightest trace of warmth, and the younger man
avoided his eyes as he shook hands with an apathetic grip.
He already knew who this guy was: the boss lady's son.

Nepotism made him nervous because it was too often a smoke screen for incompetence, especially in this business.

The bald man started to say something clever about their surroundings but stopped himself, realizing any prospect of small talk was over. He'd already explained he was in the midst of moving and that the meeting would be compromised by a lack of furniture, which was already more than the woman cared to know. He was nothing if not perceptive, which was how he'd survived this long in this nasty business. Either they would bite, or they would pass. That's how it usually happened, and everyone in the room knew the rules. So far, she had always liked what he was able to do for her.

He reached into a briefcase at his feet and withdrew a file. He opened it and handed it to the woman. A photograph of a man, naked from the waist up, was paper-clipped to the inside over what appeared to be a résumé.

"Subject is forty-five, a little young for your purposes, but credible. Six-one, one eighty-eight, nine percent body fat. Alternate for the Canadian Olympic boxing team in '84, fourth-degree black belt in tae kwon do in '91. Exceptionally high IQ, admitted to NYU, studied theater, didn't graduate. Reads Nietzsche, and he's a practicing Buddhist when he's not working. Uncharacteristic profile for a boxer . . . rumor has it he just liked to hit people. No priors, still a Canadian citizen, though he's spent most of his career in Europe. Been in the business for the last twelve years."

He looked up from the file. "He comes highly recommended."

"Available in our time frame?" asked the woman, studying the chiseled physique of the man in the picture as she listened.

"Actually, he's not. But, for the money you're offering, strings can be pulled."

She looked up at him. "I'm sure they can." Their eyes remained fixed. The younger man seemed to notice and disapprove.

"Have you even studied the profile?" the younger man asked, a trace of irritation in his voice.

It occurred to the bald man that he'd like to throw his diminutive guest with the Paul Newman blue eyes—had to be contacts—through the plate glass, wondering how long it would take to plummet nearly eight hundred feet down to West Forty-fourth Street. The image made him grin.

"Something funny?" asked the younger man.

"Oh, indeed. I think it's funny that you would ask me such a question after my record of performance." He shook his head and turned to the woman now, saying, "He's new at this, isn't he?"

"Answer the question," said the woman. Both men froze, an effect she knew she could create with the proper tone. Sharp, like a spike heel to the throat. "We have a particularly specific client for this one. This one must be . . . without compromise."

The man collected himself quickly. The deal hung in the balance, and the deal, not past or present resentments, was all that mattered.

"Thoroughly. As I always do. Subject is proficient in small weapons, manual explosives, and covert surveillance electronics. Special Air Guard, the equivalent to our Green Berets or Navy SEALs."

"Exposure?" she asked, flipping the résumé to the second page.

"Not a problem, at least for your purposes. Like I said, he's been working in Europe—that and his background make him . . . ideal."

The young man shot his mother a withering look and said, "The exposure issue is critical to our client."

The bald man tapped the photograph. "Trust me. This is your guy. He's perfect. And he will cost you. Twice what we agreed."

"That's a dangerous premium," said the woman, her voice again bearing the smooth implications of a razor blade.

The bald man raised an eyebrow, tried to look amused. This always came up at this point in the discussion, and it always went away.

"As usual, I encourage you to look elsewhere."

The woman returned the subtle amusement as she placed the file into her valise, then withdrew an envelope and handed it over to their host.

"I'll need to meet him."

"That can be arranged. On his turf, however, circumstances as they are."

"Agreed. I'll need the others, too," she said. "The usual team."

"Of course."

She shook his hand, then turned to go.

At the door the young man paused and added, "Let's go kill some people, eh?"

"Right," said the bald man, his expression deliberately blank. As the door closed, he tapped the envelope against his lips, shaking his head.

Then, his voice barely audible even to himself, he said, "Fucking wackos . . . "

6

It was two days after Ken Wong had issued his ultimatum about the seminar, and Brad had yet to share the news with Beth. This was risky, because the buyout proposal was Beth's baby as much as anyone's. He knew what she would say. Perhaps this was why he was particularly quiet on this evening, though he knew he had to be careful when he was like this, because Beth had a nose for the silences, and once she caught the scent, no secret was safe. So he moved through the evening at a subtle distance, ready to write off his distraction to fatigue if challenged. He also tossed in just a shade more affection than normal to deflect suspicion, though it met with a cold reception that told him she wasn't about to be duped.

He watched his wife as she sat at the computer preparing their taxes, stricken by the notion that he was about to rock her world with the news of Ken Wong's pending retirement. She would be ecstatic, she would want to dance in tiny circles. Nothing would be the same after she knew.

And yet, while he recognized his reluctance to tell her, he wasn't completely sure *why* he hesitated, why he didn't just charge through the door and announce that the CEO position was at hand and that the buyout would happen after all. But there was that one small, irrational detail, rapidly working its way up to a bona fide hitch: he'd have to tell her *all* of it, and in his case all of it included the confession that he had no interest in attending Ken Wong's little seminar. Not for all the chocolate in Hershey, PA.

And so he watched, like a ghost standing in a corner. And in watching, he considered his life with startling clarity. Once, while staring at the shelf full of unread books and CDs that never got played, he caught Beth looking at him, saw her look away quickly, granting him his space. There was a time when such a glance would have come with an accompanying smile, but not tonight. Not lately, in fact.

In the middle of the evening Beth got up and left the room without so much as looking at Brad. It was an announcement that she knew something was up, that he wasn't fooling her, and that he'd best get around to it soon.

In his solitude Brad thought about the past.

They had begun working closely on billing challenges with the microprocessor account soon after Peter Wright's death, all proper and respectable, and the chemistry between them quickly heated to a boil. Over what eventually became daily lunches they talked about advertising and basketball and great movies and cheap food and religion and family values and the sad state of popular music and sculpture and the unfathomable beauty of the world out there. How amazing, she had said, to meet someone who noticed it, too. Beth was the wild one, the perfect counter to his measured decisions. Brad was the solid one, the perfect anchor to Beth's drifting ship. She shared the fine print of her failed marriage, about the death of intimacy, and how intimacy was the music of her soul. How amazing, she had said, to be intimate again, without it hinging on sex. They began building castles and trading dreams, burying some, resurrecting others. Most of all they laughed, and on more than one occasion they cried. When Mark Johnson arrived to threaten Beth's role in the company, which occurred at the point in their new relationship at which they had to acknowledge the brewing chemistry, Brad had been her saving grace, walking the line between comfort and an adult's understanding acceptance. And on top of everything, Brad didn't care about the Beth and Wong rumor. She denied it, and that was good enough for him. Hell, even if it was true, he said, it didn't change anything, and that was good enough for her.

One of the beliefs they shared, even before it was true for them, was that best friends make the best lovers. After a year they began sleeping together, mastering the art of language as an erotic aperitif. She was beautiful and spunky, with thick auburn hair worn in a different style every time he saw her. He liked that, appreciated her seizing of every moment. Her eyes flashed caution, like a great cat, but her smile made proximity safe, and the contradictory combination was fascinating for men and women alike. She was fire, and sometimes the heat was comforting. He fell hopelessly, impossibly in love long before he would admit it, and on complete impulse one night in the rain on the pier, shortly after her resignation from the firm, he asked her to marry him.

Now, four years later, Beth was perceivably if not dangerously distant. The perception was several months old and it was subtle, but subtle winds scream like tornadoes in a marriage that had known only passion and unity. They had weathered a few storms in their four years together: Beth's inability to find satisfaction in a handful of aborted positions in various accounting offices, her decision to leave the world of dollars and cents entirely, her stint as a housewife during which the marriage nearly imploded, and her latest flyer on a multilevel marketing opportunity pushing nutritional supplements and change-your-life dreams. He had tolerated it all, though this latest "career" was pushing his limits—it was all about downline recruiting and had very little to do with health—and in each case she had confessed her frustration and naiveté. In these moments of vulnerability she expressed her appreciation for his quiet support and rock-solid grasp on reality, both tempered with his patience. These forged fires had made them stronger, which was why this most recent hint of matrimonial chill was all the more alarming and difficult to define.

One thing, however, was very visibly on the table and not open for discussion in the Teeters household: Beth wanted out of the middle-class neighborhood and all-American rut in which they lived. She wanted equity money, to live on the hill with the big boys, and she had married a man with the talent to give her that, talent she didn't possess. He sensed that this was the source of her distance, the unexplained delay in the buyout process looming over each six o'clock inquiry about his day. Yet it was something he couldn't acknowledge because it resided at the very epicenter of their recurring emotional tremor: that being Beth's reliance on Brad to make their dreams come true.

He knew this was serious because it had crept into their bedroom. Their sex had always been a separate reality; it was based on something that couldn't read or write or balance a checkbook. Brad saw the dreamer come out when they made love, a woman longing to howl at the moon. He wasn't sure if they were lucky or simply sexually compatible, but this was one area in which mere settling was not enough, and until recently they had continued to explore while fending off the demon of familiarity. Though he would never confess it to a buddy in a locker room, Brad wanted no other woman on the planet, and his fantasies all featured his wife in the starring role. She could be, do, and say anything he wanted, and no matter how mysterious her silences or incomprehensible her withdrawal from the professional life she had pursued so doggedly, this made it all okay. Let them all wonder, because he *knew* what a treasure he had married.

While he knew he loved her more than he could fathom, he wondered why it was so hard to tell her so. Not long ago he had used the leverage of too much red wine to confess his inability to express himself in this regard, and she had laughed it off and hugged him, explaining simply that he was a guy, this is how guys are. Pressing her lips to his ear, she whispered that she knew how much he loved her by the way he fucked her, and this was enough.

But it wasn't enough. She expected him to see through the lie and give her what she needed.

It was time to talk, and both of them knew it.

He went to bed unusually early, thinking about just that, trying to pass the time with a paperback unfinished from his last airplane ride. He watched his wife undress before she slipped under the covers naked, turning off the light in the same practiced motion. He already knew that sex was not on the evening's program; his introspection had nixed that possibility before his coat hit the hanger.

"Something's on your mind," she said moments after they had stopped adjusting their body positions, finding just the right contour to their accustomed spoon profile.

He didn't answer at first. But he knew he must—they kept nothing from each other, especially when one chanced to reach out in this way. To deny her his thoughts was to violate the perfect rhythm of their trust.

"Just work," he said, pulling her tighter, feeding off her warmth.

"Whatever you decide, you know I'll back you."

This brought him up onto an elbow. She, in turn, rotated slightly so that he could see her soft smile in the dim light, with not a trace of smugness or sarcasm evident. It was as if she knew everything, and for a moment he considered the possibility that someone, perhaps Wong himself, had confided in her. But this was Beth's way, the wisdom of an old soul, her understanding of the power of waiting safely in the pause. In that instant he realized the depth of his dilemma, because he knew his resistance to Wong's puzzling seminar ultimatum was, in fact, his own demon, his nobody-tells-me-what-to-do knee-jerk reaction to anything remotely smacking of authority. That particular inner child, he knew, needed a good ass-kicking for sure. If it weren't for Beth, there would have been no buyout proposal, and without the proposal his shot at the CEO spot would have taken a different form, certainly at a different time. She was *involved*, there was no getting around it. And now, here on the doorstep to the next level of his career, he was suddenly hesitant and secretive, blocked by his own train wreck of emotional baggage. This was her dream as much as it was his, and her dream was fraught with contradictions: her complaining about his traveling and the long hours, the weekends, her frustration with his inability to relax, his moods, her need for more of him than the job permitted him to give to her. All of this would get worse when the top spot was his, and yet she wanted it so much it hurt him to admit his own insecurities about it. The very thing she longed for would be the very thing that would challenge rather than simplify, compound rather than solve. Looking into her eyes, seeing the unconditional love and support reflected there, he understood the contradiction.

She didn't want it because of the status and the money. She was prepared to fight the good fight, to suck it up. She wanted it for *him*, as much as she wanted it for them.

"I know," he whispered, kissing her on the cheek, letting it linger.

She seemed to sense his need to finish putting it all in its proper and neat little box before he could talk about it, so she patted his arm and closed her eyes, gently returning her cheek to the pillow. He watched her for a while, an angel in shadow. Only after she smiled slightly without opening her eyes, knowing he was watching, did he kiss her cheek once again before flopping to his back on his own pillow.

Screw Wong, and screw his damn seminar. Something was not right here. Ultimatums were flying around like elbows at a Lakers-Blazers game. Everyone was posturing, considering the right moves for the wrong reasons, making the wrong choices for inarguably noble ones. Things needed to calm down, sort themselves out. There would be no more ultimatums in this game, not on his court. If he had to, he'd talk the others into simply walking away with him and building their own agency from the ground up. Although they'd prayed it would never come to that, they all knew that it still could. He'd do this his way, the only way he knew, the only way that worked.

It was long after midnight before he finally fell asleep.

7

As Pamela Wiley turned her leased Acura into the parking lot of her condo complex that same evening, she realized she couldn't remember a thing about the drive home. She'd been on autopilot from the moment she left the office, replaying Ken Wong's words from two days ago about her absence of trust and her unhealthy view of her new partners. It was all true, and it had a bitter taste going down.

She wanted to talk about it, but there was no one to call, only names in a book she'd misplaced, their numbers long faded from memory, their faces still youthful in her mind. Even her ex-husband's face was still twenty-five years old, still shaking his head as he walked away one winter day six years before. No family, only resentment and regrets where birthdays and holidays should have been. A call to someone at work would become the goof of the year, the Pam-ism of all time, and tonight her pride was still stronger than her need for company. Her last date had been . . . well, she couldn't remember a last date, per se, only the infrequent connection in a bar, her hardness dulled by alcohol and loud music, screwing with a serious urgency bordering on anger. Some liked it like that, some didn't, but none of them liked *her* all that much, based on results. Her unexplained post-coital tears usually sent them bounding out the door, shoes in hand.

Her husband had hated that, the tears that came after sex, not letting him get up until the room had cooled. He kept asking what was wrong, when he should have been asking what was right.

All the lights in the condo were off. Ambient streams of illumination from the parking lot were clouded by the slowly drifting waves of her cigarette smoke, which filled the room and reminded her of dreams. Even those were gone. Sure, there was the buyout thing with Mark and Brad, but that was simply business, a vanilla and inevitable evolution of things conducted between people who really didn't give a shit about each other. In the spare bedroom was an easel and a drawing board, upon which her dreams had died a lonely death, left to wither while she chased down her career. Her husband had hated that, too, how it represented her maniacal devotion to "her art." He was a freaking bartender, a college fling gone too far, for shit's sake, so what did he know? She lived now to sketch logo comps and manipulate brochure layouts on computer screens, more an arrangement of metaphor than the art of her childhood, more digitizing than design. Her job now was wrangling egotistic writers into submission to her ideas, nursing young design talent toward her vision, kissing the collective client ass at every turn. And she was good at it.

She realized she didn't care about anything at all tonight. Not about the buyout or being the CEO or whether Ken Wong remained or shipped out to Bali. This was it, the bottom of the barrel, and it was dark down here. She only knew she had to hold on, that the ship was pulling out and, thanks to Brad, she had a ticket. God bless him for that, the prick. Wherever it landed, it was certainly better than here, than now. She had to care about *that* tonight, and nothing else.

Maybe Wong was ahead of the game, with his sudden enlightenment and his truth-speaking and his ridiculous little seminar. Maybe it would usher in whatever was next, and who was she to question the master plan?

Maybe, as Wong had said, the seminar had already begun.

Before turning out the light Pamela opened the drawer of her dresser and withdrew the .357 Magnum she kept there for peace of mind. Her husband had bought it for her—in an act of cluelessness that defied understanding, the guy had actually asked for it back three years after the divorce—but she didn't associate it with him, didn't allow the memories to ruin her relationship with it. It was her friend, her protector, and her comfort, things he never seemed to understand.

She turned the safety off and returned the gun to the drawer, as she always did before turning off the light.

THIS was a night Mark had been dreading and had put off until now, two weeks after his father's funeral. A hungry realtor had sold his father's house on the first offer, and the place needed emptying. It was an old house in a neighborhood now considered "charming" by first-time home buyers. And it was full of ghosts. As the executor of his father's affairs and with his brother, the asshole attorney, back in St. Louis suing HMOs, it was left to Mark to go through everything, to sell what furniture he could and donate everything else to a surprisingly picky Salvation Army. By midnight he had succeeded only in exhuming boxes from closets and the attic, their contents now spread before him on the floor, a lifetime of documentation awaiting extinction. So far he had thrown nothing away, losing track of the clock as he ransacked all that remained of his parents' time on earth.

He was surprised and moved to find his mother's presence so quietly preserved in these boxes. He found her jewelry, worthless but for the private memories they conjured: his mother dressing for work, primping for church. There was a purse and a single pair of shoes, no doubt something sentimental that his father simply could not part with. She had been a beautiful woman, even as she slowly turned yellow from the kidney disease that would take her, always smiling gently as if she knew what you were thinking. Mark recognized the subtle scent that was wafting up from the boxes, his mother's scent, a musky perfume, as if she had quietly floated through the room to plant a kiss on his forehead.

Perhaps she had.

His father's possessions did not fall into the category of memorabilia, had not been edited and lovingly stored by a grieving partner. His father's things were all in use, expecting their owner to return and put them back into play. Everything was just as he'd left it the day he died—dead from a heart attack before he hit the ground after falling from his stool at a video-poker emporium—toothbrush on the counter next to a tube of Crest with the cap lost, a half-used roll of toilet paper on the floor instead of in the wall dispenser, the bed unmade, the morning's newspaper bearing the date of his death in a pile next to the back door, the fridge full of beer and frozen chicken dinners.

Unlike to his mother, Mark realized he wasn't sure what he'd say to his father if one last chance to say goodbye miraculously had been offered. They were proud men, and this defined their exchanges. The two of them had an arrangement, one based on the choice to keep the family unit intact rather than on any real desire to share each other's company. Mark's father had recently retired from his job as a county employee, a supervisor in the highway maintenance department. He drank, smoked cheap cigars, and most of all he complained: the assholes who ran the city, the criminals who ran the country, the racist pigs who lived uptown, the stupid niggas who lived next door, the flaming computer nerds who were taking over everything and not a black man in the bunch, the ignorant kids who hadn't learned anything from his generation, a generation that put it all on the line for them and this is the thanks they give, the demise of good jazz, the death of Dr. King. At the end of their time they'd shake hands, like brothers, a ritual with which Mark never felt completely comfortable.

Going through a box of old photographs he'd never seen before, he wondered what they would do if his parents could go back, if they could rewind the tape and lay down a few new tracks. He wondered if things would be different or if their lot in life had been written, as they thought it was.

He thought of Ken Wong and the seminar that just might change everything. He knew Brad was pissed off and resentful of what he perceived to be an ultimatum, but Mark knew better. Hell, Mark knew Wong better than any of them. He had seen the changes in him of late, felt the vastly different energy, as evidenced by his tone in the meeting today. This seminar was an opportunity, nothing short of a gift they could not yet comprehend. This would be a chance to be different, to take some risks.

A sudden heaviness in his eyes reminded him of the hour. And that he had no one to go home to.

It was in that moment that Mark decided he would attend Ken Wong's seminar, whether the others went with him or not.

Almost immediately he felt the physical effects of his decision. It was like electricity, centered in his abdomen, coursing through his nervous system with a particular attraction to the skin on the palms of his hands. He didn't like how it felt, didn't like what it meant or the fact that he was inexorably subordinated to it.

It was fear. An old friend inherited, he believed, from his father.

8

Brad was more conscious than usual of everything around him as he entered the office the next morning. He was reminded of that old *Twilight Zone* episode in which the guy drops and breaks the magic stopwatch that could freeze and unfreeze all time and space, allowing him to move through the world unseen and thus able to examine every nuance of things otherwise taken for granted. Normally, upon entering the building, he was in such a twit over some detail that couldn't wait that he seldom stopped to smell the Starbucks. The place was a zoo, actually, but clients loved it like this. When they were being shown around, they were like kids on a field trip to the creative factory. Stand back, or you might get beaned by a stray idea or, on a bad day, bitten by a copywriter.

It was the damn seminar. It had him noticing everything.

The last thing he expected this morning was to find Mark and Pamela waiting for him. He'd never seen them in the building this early. Both had upped the fashion ante today, a little crisper and more chic than normal. He could sense they came in peace, perhaps in search of his counsel, which he was always happy to provide.

"Somebody help me, I'm being ambushed," he called out as he took his seat.

"So," Mark began, sitting on the corner of Brad's desk. Pamela had assumed one of the chairs angled to the side. "We going camping together, or not?"

Brad just rolled his eyes. Of course the seminar was their agenda of the day.

Pamela seemed confused. "You don't think he's talking about anything like that Outward Bound shit, do you? I don't do tents, guys, I gotta tell you right now. No fucking tents."

"I heard it was a week in a Quonset hut in Tibet," said Brad, leaning back. "You shall find enlightenment in the shadow of the Great Mountain."

"I'm serious," replied Mark. "What are we gonna do?"

They exchanged looks, each waiting for someone else to take the lead.

"How about you?" asked Brad, posing the question to Mark.

Mark nodded very slowly, as if confirming his thoughts to himself before he spoke them. Finally he said, "I say we go."

"Sure you do," said Brad lightly. "You want the CEO job so bad you can taste it."

Mark grinned, but not because it was all too true. It was a "bite me" grin, with its roots back to his falling out with Beth and, therefore, with Brad. If it weren't for the Beth thing, they might have been friends, or at least warmer than the room-temperature relationship they maintained now. Mark understood that Brad had to support his wife's version of the truth, and it was fine with him as long as it didn't pop up in nasty little comments like that one.

"It's not a big thing, really," said Mark. "And when you think about it, the main reason to not go is nothing more than our own bullshit."

"And what bullshit is that?" asked Pamela.

"Our reaction to what we perceive to be a power play. It's simple. We resent it, so we resist it. We resent Ken, so we resist him."

Brad noticed Pamela's mouth tighten as she chewed on this.

"I don't know," she said. "Kind of freaks me out."

"That's exactly why you should go," said Brad. When they both looked at him as if he'd just insulted her religious beliefs, he added, "Hey, that's what Ken would say to you. Think about it."

"Maybe you should think about it," said Mark softly.

"Listen to you guys!" said Pamela. "He really got to you!"

"Perhaps the seminar has already started," said Brad, going for his best Ken Wong imitation, and bringing a chorus of rolling eyes.

"You'd go if we both went, though," said Mark to Pamela. "Right? I mean, if the deal depended on it, you'd go."

She froze a moment, then slowly nodded without looking at him. "Yeah. I'd go. That's what partners do."

Mark, nodding with her, turned to Brad and said, "Guess it's in your lap now."

"That certainly sucks," replied Brad.

Pamela was nodding with an ironic elevation of her eyebrow. "That's what partners do."

Mark added, "Do the math, Brad. A week at a seminar, or we go out on our own."

They all ran the familiar math in their heads. If they took fifty percent of Wright & Wong's gross revenue with them within the first year, including the chip account, they'd need forty bodies from Day One. Considering a billing float of sixty days, a ten-thousand-square-foot lease with a five-year clause, twenty PCs and three new design stations, network software, new letterhead, phones and fax—even if they freelanced audiovisual production at first and outsourced media buys, they'd need a half million dollars in angel money to hold them for three months. All without any of them taking out a dime to live on. After that, it was a roll of the dice.

"What the hell were we thinking?" mumbled Pamela.

"It can be done," said Brad. "We've been over it and over it."

"Yeah, it can," said Mark. "But do you want to put your neck in that noose? More than you don't want to go to Ken's seminar? Seems like a no-brainer to me."

Brad looked earnestly at both of them, then slowly shook his head. He allowed his gaze to drift, as if he was thinking.

"I don't know," he said after a moment of staring at the same window Pamela seemed to have adopted. "I really don't know."

He could sense his two partners exchanging looks, unsure of its context. He watched them depart, noticing that Pamela was hesitating at his door.

"What?" he said as he looked up at her.

"Yes, you do," she said.

"Do what?"

"Know."

Her smile appeared in the instant before she left.

9

Mr. Bradley M. Teeters
10015 E. Slater Court
Bellevue, Washington 98009

Dear Mr. Teeters:

Congratulations on your decision to attend The Seminar, to be held February 7-13 of this year, at our facilities in northern California. We are confident you will find your time here to be both challenging and rewarding.

Enclosed you will find material which pertains to your preparation for your time with us. In order to receive full value from your investment of time and money, we highly recommend that you review these materials carefully.

Also enclosed is a list of policies, rules, and regulations. Again, we recommend you study this material prior to arrival, so that your uncompromised attention might be focused on the curriculum we have planned for you.

And finally, there is a liability waiver for your review and signature. A signed and notarized copy of this document must be in our possession prior to your arrival. A stamped envelope has been provided for this purpose.

"Any idea that is held in the mind, emphasized, feared, or revered, begins at once to clothe itself in the most convenient and appropriate physical form that's available."
—*Andrew Carnegie*

Again, congratulations.

Warmest regards,

Richard Phillips
Georgia Bass
Facilitators

The envelope was waiting for him on the kitchen island. It was late, and Brad was just coming down from the frustration of sitting on a runway in San Jose for two hours with no explanation. He had been summoned to an all-day meeting hosted by the marketing department at The World's Largest Microprocessor Company—its quarterly graphics standard browbeating—followed by a six o'clock account review by the swell folks in the procurement department. It was his twenty-sixth day-trip to the Bay Area so far this year, his twenty-fourth airport snack bar dinner, and the fourteenth time he'd arrived back home from this itinerary after midnight.

The envelope was as thick as a government contract. Curiously, it had been opened. He wasn't sure if it was this fact or the assumptiveness of the cover letter that caused his cheeks to flush.

Brad dropped his briefcase and laptop bag to the floor and slid onto a stool to investigate further. The reading list caught his eye first—*Think and Grow Rich* by Napoleon Hill, *The Road Less Traveled* by M. Scott Peck, *The Art of War* by Sun Tzu, and about ten other titles. He'd have to consume three books a week until the seminar began in order to, as the cover letter suggested, receive full value on the investment of his money and time. He half expected the instructions to further stipulate that these tomes were to be absorbed while seated in the lotus position.

Right, Ken, I'll be sure and pick these up right after I finish reading Chicken Soup for the Chump's Soul, *which I've been studying for the last nine years.*

One glance at the instructions and he realized this might take awhile.

The heading read: "Rules of Order at The Complex." They were simple and clear and very close to qualifying as fascist: no alcohol; no drugs other than prescriptions; no cellular or digital telephones; no pagers; no radios, CD players, or other portable electronic devices, including televisions; no computers; no incoming or outgoing telephone calls; no incoming or outgoing mail or packages; no books, magazines, or reading material other than those included on The Seminar reading list; no short pants; no suits, ties, or formal business attire; no leather-soled shoes; no athletic equipment; no water bottles; no chewing gum, candy, or mints; no promotional or solicitous material or activity, pertaining to either business or religious beliefs; there will be no running on the property; there will be no sexual interaction on the property, including masturbation; there will be no profanity used on the property; there will be no hostile or violent physical contact between teammates and/or instructors; anyone departing The Complex prior to the conclusion of The Seminar will be responsible for their own transportation.

At the end of the list, the final entry read: *there will be no refunds.*

At the bottom of the page was an assurance that emer-

gency-contact information and instructions regarding
transportation and logistics would be forthcoming.

"You gotta be shitting me," Brad said aloud.

Next, he leafed through the thickest document of all,
the legal-liability waiver. It was thirty-four pages in length,
with print approximately the size of lint. Brad turned to a
few random pages, noticing that each one seemed to repeat
the same words in familiar-sounding combinations and fa-
vored bloated legalese, such as "to wit" and "heretofore"
and "antecedent."

He said the word "bullshit" out loud, and nearly
jumped out of his skin to hear a voice behind him say,
"What's bullshit?"

Beth was buttoning up her robe and yawning.

"You opened this!" He held up the envelope.

"Is that a question or an accusation?" She clearly
didn't like his tone and returned the volley with equivalent
mustard on it.

"I don't mind, I guess, but why the hell would you do
that? You never open my mail."

"I didn't open your mail."

"Then who the hell did?"

She stared at him, her eyes gradually narrowing. He
looked away, realizing that he'd been an ass.

She looked away, too, as she said, "I was coming down
here to welcome you home and give you a hug."

"I'm sorry. Really."

The silence continued for a precarious moment in
which it could have gone either way. Then she looked back
at him, a forced smile in evidence.

"Let's start over. Welcome home, sweetheart."

They embraced, and he held her a little tighter than the
situation would have otherwise warranted. With her face
pressed into his neck, she said, "The envelope was open when
I took it out of the box. I don't know how it happened."

They parted, and his smile was sheepish.

"What is it?" she asked.

"Special delivery from the Twilight Zone."

"The seminar thing you talked about."

A few days earlier he had finally broken down and told her about Wong's ultimatum. He had positioned it to her as an inconsequential issue, just another example of Wong's power-playing from the other planet he'd been living on since Peter Wright's death. Of course Brad wasn't going to go, so there was no reason to discuss it further.

Until now.

"They seem to think I've signed up." She took the letter from the pile and read it. "You should read this shit," he said, holding the rest up slightly.

"Should I?"

"Not really. No point."

"Because you're not going."

He pursed his lips, sensing that her question held more weight than the context of this nocturnal chitchat would have called for. For an instant he realized he didn't believe her about not opening the envelope.

"Not a chance."

She nodded, her eyes drifting. Then, obviously making a decision, she leaned in, kissed him again, and said, "Come to bed, then."

"You're disappointed."

"No, I'm not."

"You want me to go."

"Of course I want you to go. For more reasons than you think. But you have to do this your way."

He pondered what this might mean for a moment, then said, "Do I?"

Her smile appeared again. "Don't you always?"

Then she pivoted on her slipper and disappeared into the shadows of the house.

"Do I?" he asked himself quietly, staring down at the envelope.

HE didn't go directly to bed. Instead he plugged his laptop into the phone jack in the kitchen, got online, and began to pepper the Yahoo! search page with words, hoping to link up with something that would at least give roots to an otherwise all-too-mysterious situation. The return address on the envelope had been a post office box, and there wasn't a telephone number in sight. Northern California was a big place. The company, if it was even a company, didn't have a name; it was referred to only as "The Seminar" in the materials. It was like naming your poodle "Dog." The only other thing of note on the page was a logo—a really lousy one, at that—shaped like a diamond and rendered in a three-dimensional image, like a thick, twisted bar made of chrome.

The more he thought about it, the more uncomfortable he became.

Entering the keyword "complex" on Yahoo! yielded 1,537 associations, the first of which was the Kennedy Space Center Complex, followed by a roster of colleges, laboratories, and biogenetic white papers. Strike one.

He tried "human performance industry," having heard Wong use the term with Mark. This yielded four entries, none of which even closely resembled his target, and one of which linked to an impotency clinic. Strike two, big swing and a miss.

"EST" yielded 162 outcomes, almost all of them acronyms for companies and chemical compounds. The word "forum" yielded 250 hits, all of which were "Chats and Forums" from the Internet community. He even tried the word "Lifespring," the only related program he could dredge from his waning memory of a time when some of his more youthful and lost friends went off in search of the meaning of life.

Four links, foul balls all, each a nickname for unrelated things.

And finally, he typed in the word "seminar." Thinking for a moment that he'd found hope, he discovered twenty-seven different categories of seminars, everything from investing to achieving extended tantric orgasms. He spent ninety minutes digging through it all, with nothing to show for it.

Swing and a miss, strike three. Game over.

When he went to bed, Beth curled against him as she

glanced at the glowing digital clock, which was closing in on 3:00 A.M.

"Find anything?" she mumbled.

"Nada," replied Brad as he worked his face into his pillow.

"I have a question," she said. This immediately raised his adrenaline a tick or two, since in their marital experience this announcement had been the harbinger of many a long night.

"I'm not going," he mumbled, trying to sound as tired as he could.

"Then," she paused, as if scanning for just the right words, "why is it that you've just spent half the night searching for something that would convince you otherwise?"

She held her head an inch off the pillow, as if listening. This lasted for only a few seconds before she seemed to collapse back into the softness of it and didn't move again for the longest time, her breathing quickly slowing into the heavy rasp of sleep.

Brad, however, stared at the glow of the digital clock until five.

10

Brad was floored when he saw that Ken Wong was already at his desk at a quarter to seven the next morning. His intention had been to stage an ambush, the crowning touch of which was to have been sitting in Ken's $5,000 high-back leather chair with his socked feet up on the desk when the boss arrived. Insolence of this ilk was a recurring reminder that Brad knew where Ken came from, that you couldn't fool him with all the Mont Blanc bluster and rushing off to airports, that they both knew who made whom.

Wong was already sitting at his desk, head down. Soft music—with what sounded like chanting in it—came from a thousand-dollar portable Bose tabletop sound system. Wong didn't look up, though Brad knew his presence had been detected.

Brad slipped the cover letter from The Complex under Wong's nose.

"Nice tie," said Brad.

"Good morning to you, too," said Wong, only glancing briefly at the letter before he leaned back in the chair Brad had looked forward to commandeering.

"You're in early," said Brad as he sat down.

"Pile of legal toilet paper due yesterday," said Wong.

"Oh, are we being bought out?"

"Estate stuff, actually." Wong wasn't exactly smiling.

"Got a minute?"

"Of course."

"This came to the house yesterday." He indicated the letter with his eyes. He noticed that Wong didn't look down at it in response. "I'm a little confused."

"Of course you are."

"You enrolled us already?"

"I did."

"But we haven't agreed to attend."

"*You* haven't agreed to attend."

"The others have?"

Wong nodded.

"And you just assumed that I would."

"Oh, I'm not sure you'll attend the seminar at all." Wong finally cracked a smile, a bit fatherly in nature. "In fact, while I hope you do, I'll be rather pleasantly surprised if that happens. But it was a safe assumption to get the ball rolling. Meaning, I was up against a deadline, and there was nothing to lose."

"But you said it was an all-or-nothing proposition. That we either went as a team, or the deal was off."

"That's not what I said."

Brad raised his eyebrows and drew a deep breath, pivoting slightly in his seat. Wong remained perfectly motionless, all knowing eyes and smug wisdom.

"Let me refresh your memory," said Wong. "I said the buyout deal depended on all of you attending as a team. Which means, if one of you decides not to attend, then the deal, as proposed, is off."

"Right. So you're assuming we're all going, then."

"No, I'm not. If one of you decides not to go, we make a new deal with a new team. I will name a new CEO from among those that do go. There will be no buyout, but there will still be the need for a new CEO, because the company will remain viable and I still intend to retire."

Brad felt his face growing warm. "That's not what you said."

"That's not what you heard. But it is what I said."

Brad pursed his lips and nodded slightly, consciously keeping his eyes on Wong's now. "This is bullshit, you know."

"That's your perception."

"You dismantle our leverage by hanging a CEO title out there if one of us will abandon the others and stay on. That's manipulative and—"

"That's business."

"Is this what you learned at your little seminar?"

Wong grinned, considered a comeback, then changed his mind.

Brad had to look away, commencing a moment of silence.

"What are you feeling right now, Brad?"

"Excuse me?" Brad felt himself go rigid as a goalpost.

"What's going on for you right now? You want to storm out of here? Tell me off? Maybe get up and kick my ass? Who's driving the Brad-mobile right now, you or your old programs?"

"My old *what?*" Brad held on to the armrests to prevent himself from launching at his boss. To make matters worse, Wong wore what Brad assumed was an amused smirk, a bona fide shit-eating grin, as if all of this was a calculated move that was working far better than expected.

"I'm not trying to provoke you," said Wong, again fatherly.

"The hell you're not!"

"No, you're making up a story that suits you right now. Amazing how we do that, to make ourselves right about things."

"You're a smug bastard sometimes, Ken."

"Too true. But right now I'm just calling it like it is. Honestly, I'm sorry that you're upset."

"Just cut the EST shit, okay?"

"Maybe you should come back and see me when you calm down."

Another pause, another deep breath. Brad had always been aware of his ability to recognize shards of truth fighting against the current of his temper, and this was one of those times. God, he hated it when Ken Wong was right.

"This seminar of yours," Brad said, changing the timbre of his voice to one of contemplative caution. "What's up with that? I mean, all of a sudden there are these ultimatums and weird demands. I don't get it. You don't need someone else to tell you who should and shouldn't be the CEO around here."

"I agree. But perhaps you do."

"Pardon me?" Brad drew a deep, controlled breath.

Wong put on his reading glasses and leaned forward to scan the cover letter from The Complex. Then, without looking up, he said, "There was a time, not too long ago, actually, when I thought you would be the next CEO of Wright & Wong, that it was a foregone conclusion. But now"—he looked up at Brad—"I don't think you're ready."

Brad nodded, trying to keep his face expressionless. "Okay."

"No, it's not okay," countered Wong.

"What am I supposed to say to that? Gee, thanks, Ken, it's been swell making you rich, and I'm glad it all worked out?"

"You're very bitter about that, aren't you?"

"Don't have to be David Copperfield to figure that out."

"And now, you get to resent me because of what I just said, about you not being ready to be the CEO. You can go home, tell Beth what a judgmental asshole I am, spray a little venom around the office, maybe take Mark and Pamela to lunch and accelerate the plan for your new agency."

Brad squinted. "You bastard." Wong had essentially squashed that option with the CEO incentive.

"Maybe you should go cool off."

"And just what am I supposed to do with this sudden revelation? Go make some cold calls?" He paused. "I don't know what I think."

"I do." Wong's voice was soft, sympathetic.

"Yeah? Then why don't you tell me. Tell me what I think."

"You think you're the victim here."

Brad didn't say anything to this. He just let his mouth fall open and bounced his head a few times, as if the weight of his jaw caused the elasticity in his neck to test itself.

Wong's smile grew even more patient. "You think something is being done to you, that it's unfair, that it sucks, and that there's nothing you can do about any of it. That life sucks, you check out, and that's the way it is. Am I close?"

"I can't say anything. Anything I say plays right into what you're saying."

"See what I mean?"

"See what?"

"There's your victim program again."

Brad managed a grin of his own, just to show that he was on top of his anger.

"You don't think I can hack it, do you," said Brad. "This seminar of yours . . . you think I'm afraid I'll fail and that I'm covering my fear."

"No, I think you're playing victim. That's all. Just that."

"You think you can goad me into going by pushing my buttons or maybe by appealing to what you think is some overamped sense of pride and machismo, that I'll go just to prove you wrong. But you know something? That's not it. And it's not going to work. I'm not going anywhere, and I'm not backing off from the proposal. You do what you have to do, I'll do what I have to do."

"We all have our choices, don't we, Brad?"

"Yeah, Ken, we all do."

Brad pursed his lips and shook his head slightly, the grin long gone, trying for his own flavor of fatherly disapproval. Wong just smiled, though a bit sadly, as if watching a son march off to war.

Brad got to his feet and walked to the door. His pace was important now: too fast and his anger would announce his defeat, too slow and he was copping an attitude. And so he sauntered, trying to appear thoughtful.

Brad stopped at the door to lob a final volley.

"Just ask yourself who is being proactive in this deal. Who put it together, who stepped up. Even who was here this morning to break it down with you, do the hard work, ask the tough questions. Then ask yourself who should be the CEO."

Wong was already nodding. "I've been doing just that. It's not half as clear as you think it is."

Brad shook his head in disgust as he turned to leave. Wong chose that moment to say one more thing. "Will you think about something for me?" he said. There was no mistaking the sincerity now. After nine years together they had developed the ability to shed the tough moments like rain.

"All right."

"You think about this: both Mark and Pamela called me at home last night, to talk about the letter and the intro packet. Both of them apologized to me for the late hour, but they were as confused as you, and they wanted to hit it head-on. They wanted to understand. So they listened." He paused. "You weren't the first with this, Brad. You were the last."

They kept their eyes locked for another moment. Then Brad turned and walked toward the steps a little quicker than he would have liked.

AFTER lunch, long after Brad had calmed down and run through every conceivable comeback he wished he had made and every possible action he was tempted to take, he stopped by Mark Johnson's office, trying to appear spontaneous. Mark, whose shirt was as glaringly white as Wong's but with an accountant's dull tie, was drilling his PC keyboard with the intensity of a legal secretary.

"Been to any good training seminars lately?" said Brad.

Mark looked up, started to say something, hesitated, then spoke with a serious countenance that did not remotely match Brad's. There would be no commiseration today.

"You should know that I told Ken I'm going," he

said. There was a challenge in the way his eyes held their ground, like a martial artist who knows that power resides in the countermove, not the offense.

"Wonderful," was all that Brad could muster.

"Pamela is going, too."

Brad nodded. "I recommend you don't drink the Kool-Aid."

"We hope you'll come with us."

"Really. I would think a two-horse field pays better odds than three."

"It's not about the job, Brad."

"Right."

"Not for me, it isn't."

Mark held his gaze for a moment before he returned his focus to his keyboard, entering numbers with a frightening proficiency.

11

The Cucina Cucina restaurant in Kirkland wasn't exactly all the rage among the area's high-tech intelligentsia, but it was on a prime chunk of Lake Washington shoreline, and on the rare Seattle day in which the sun made an appearance, it was as good as it gets, sans pretension. Beth and her "upline" manager—the network marketing term for the person who signs you up—sat at a window table with the best view in the place, facilitated by a ten-dollar tip slipped to the twenty-year-old part-time hostess, who had never encountered such a thing in her seven months working here. Rich Dobson was that kind of guy, quick with a ten spot for anyone who might be of service, the more onlookers the better. It mattered not in the least that it was pouring down rain today and that the wind was whipping the water into a cappuccino froth; Rich had an eager new recruit to impress, and, what the hell, life's too short for bad tables.

Beth was nervous about this lunch, and for several reasons. Her first inkling of anxiety had arrived earlier that morning as she stood in her closet, conscious that the choice of outfit held more importance than she'd expected, that she wanted to look both powerful and attractive, unsure which was the stronger need. This was her first "periodic review" since the huge box of nutritional-supplement samples had arrived on her doorstep, and while she had indeed talked several relatives and a few friends into buying a bottle or two of DHEA, she knew this wasn't what the game was about. The business was all about signing people up to work under you, and this was all that Rich Dobson would care about today. They could be selling YMCA spaghetti-feed tickets for all he cared, and considering he'd been involved with Amway, Herbalife, PrimeAmerica, and several other multilevel "strategies" in his ten years in "the business," he certainly knew what worked. He would cut her the appropriate amount of slack today for not having enrolled her first downline salesperson, but he would be disappointed, and that was what made her nervous. After too many new career start-ups to count since leaving Wright & Wong, Beth was starting to doubt herself, and it was important to her that she come out strong. At their first meeting Dobson had told her he could tell a winner when he saw one—she'd called a telephone number handwritten on a sign nailed to a pole reading, "Earn Five Grand a Month Working at Home"—though he hadn't asked for a résumé or a reference. It was all first impressions, he had said. She hadn't signed on with any illusions—Beth had given up on illusions years ago—but she was curious, she had a friend making serious money doing something similar on the Internet, and there was something about Rich's enthusiasm that made her decide to take a risk. Maybe this could work for her, too. Her friend was dumb as a parking meter and driving a Beamer.

The other reason Beth was nervous had to do with Rich Dobson himself. With one glance she knew he was a player, a man who looked in the mirror every morning and then looked again. He wasn't blessed with any significant physical gifts—average height and build, just another face in the crowd—but he made the most of what he had with his Italian clothes and his cruise-ship jewelry and a fifty-dollar haircut. The man reeked of confidence and the facade of money, and in her quietest moments Beth knew this had been part of it for her, a stark contrast to the accountants and office managers with whom she'd worked since leaving the agency. Financial statements didn't care what you looked like. They robbed her of a natural advantage she'd been able to exploit at the agency, the opportunity to play hormonal workplace politics. Upline managers like Dobson cared very much what you looked like, and if she played him right, she could become his favorite repository for an ongoing stream of downline leads. She knew enough about network marketing to know that if you hooked on with the right upline manager, a real pro who understood that the care and feeding of his downline organization chart was his meal ticket, success would be orders of magnitude easier to achieve. She'd sell the products, and once Rich realized his help was required, he'd feed her a steady stream of enlistments, people like her who'd seen the posters on a pole. Rich Dobson would be the ideal upline for Beth, because with one conversation Beth had his number.

Which was why her outfit was critical today. She selected a black suit with fuck-me heels and a significant quantity of gold jewelry. Straight from the executive suite of a Beverly Hills cosmetics conglomerate. Classy, with just a hint of bitch. It was one of Brad's favorites, too.

"You're perfect for this business," Rich blurted out after a few minutes of awkward small talk. She'd already confessed her hesitation to recruit anyone to her downline quite this soon, and he'd quickly taken away her anxiety with the assurance that nobody did it this fast, that it took time to get familiar with the program and the product. Confidence would come, and he could tell that confidence was one of her finer assets.

"I mean, look at you . . . you're the goddamn profile, you're what this product and this company are all about."

Beth blushed. "I've never taken a supplement in my life," she said. "Vitamins. I take multivitamins and Echinacea."

"So? Just don't go there. I mean, don't *lie*, for chrissake, I'm not saying that, but don't volunteer it, either, know what I'm sayin'? They'll assume you've been taking this stuff for years. I mean hell, just look at you!"

His eyes worked her up and down the way a car buff eyes a Testarossa.

"Besides, it's not about product, it's about enrollment. You understand that, don't you? How this business works?"

Beth nodded sheepishly. She was positioning herself at his feet with wide-eyed sincerity.

"I know I can sell anything I believe in," she said. "I believe in nutrition, and based on what I've read, I believe in these products."

"That's good enough for now," he said, already digging into the salad that had arrived while they talked. "I can get you started on your downline organization, until you master the pitch. You can come with me on appointments, listen to how I do it. You're bright, you'll pick it up. And there's training available, all kinds of books and seminars."

Beth visibly shifted when she heard the word.

"Seminars?"

"Tons. Personal shit. People in our industry eat that shit up. It works, too." He wasn't afraid to speak with his mouth full, and she had to look away.

"My husband is going to a seminar next month," she said, picking at her own salad. "Some kind of human-performance improvement training at a ranch in California. His boss is making him go."

"No shit? Brad, right? Listen, I've been to a bunch of 'em. They rock. Not to worry, he'll love it."

"He's not so sure."

"Nobody ever is, that's why they work. I mean, if you had your shit together, you wouldn't need to go, right? Everyone thinks they have their shit together, so there's always resistance at first. Not that Brad doesn't have his shit together. I'm just saying."

"I know what you mean."

"It's not like the old days with EST and Lifespring and all that consciousness stuff. I mean, they don't lock you in a room and make you hold your water and get naked and scream at your mother. They used to do shit like that, make you jump off bridges and face your deepest fears, but people died, and things changed. Like, as in overnight. This one seminar, they refused to let some lady take her asthma medicine, said it was all in her mind. Lady died right there in the room, and that was the end of that seminar company. Lawsuits up the yin-yang. All those programs sort of developed from the same source back in the sixties: Alexander Everett, William Penn Patrick, Werner Erhard, all those guys, they all used to study together. It's like a network deal, everything going today is basically a downline of one of their programs. You know what EST stands for?"

Beth shook her head, her own mouth full. She was concentrating on keeping a straight face, watching the way Dobson got on this roll. His problem wasn't a lack of charisma, it was a lack of class.

"Erhard Seminar Training, swear to God. Erhard's not even his real name. John Paul Rosenberg, guy couldn't get arrested before he became a guru, you believe that? Heard of The Forum? Very big these days, probably the biggest. Run by his brother, not many people know that. Lifespring is history; they're the ones with the dead bodies and the lawsuits. Anthony Robbins used to teach NLP until he figured out he could make more money selling it than teaching it. He's walking proof of the pudding: if you can think it, you can do it. But it's all cool, like I said, I've been to a bunch of these trainings, and they really do rock. Changed my life, I can tell you that."

"I'll be sure and tell Brad," she said.

The mention of Brad's name caused Rich Dobson to shift in his seat, his energy shifting along with him. "He approve of this? Of the program?" He motioned to the company brochure on the table next to him.

Beth chewed her food, in no hurry to answer, knowing

this was a moment that would define how they moved forward together. She had no intention of crossing any lines with the dashing Mr. Dobson, but she had to play this card with a careful hand, because his continued interest in her success would be the key to making this work. And based on her research, the five percent who did, in fact, make it work were doing very well indeed.

"Brad lets me do my own thing," she said with just the right twinkle in her eye.

He smiled back, nodding as he ripped the French bread into halves, placing a piece on her plate.

"We're gonna be good together," he said. "I mean, I can feel it, you know? You have a way with people, they trust you, and that's what this business needs. People others believe and trust. I drive a new Mercedes-Benz, and I work less than twenty-five hours a week, mostly having meetings with incredible people like you. That's how I do it, and it's how you'll do it, too."

He took much too large a bite of the bread, smiling as he chewed.

Beth raised her wineglass and offered a toast.

"To our success," she said, holding her glass aloft.

Dobson, hurrying to swallow the bread, did the same.

"To success," he said, his mouth still full. "Whatever it takes."

LATER that night, when Beth was fighting back second thoughts carried on a renewed wave of doubt, this comment kept coming back to her. *Whatever it takes.* Based on what her instincts were telling her about Rich Dobson, he would indeed do whatever it took to get what he wanted, no matter what lines it crossed, no matter whom he had to step on in the process. Like her, Rich Dobson had never taken a nutritional supplement in his life. She doubted he'd ever been to a seminar, either.

She told Brad the lunch had gone well, that Rich Dobson was totally committed to getting her up and running, and that she was very pleased thus far. She could tell Brad was skeptical, but the way he hugged her and told her he hoped she was right reminded Beth of why she loved him and why he deserved the top job at Wright & Wong. And, while the two were very much entwined, she needed to make her own mark, too.

Whatever it takes.

She wouldn't walk away just yet. She could get past the lack of class; the Mercedes and the Rolex were classy enough to hold her attention. She wasn't exactly sure why, but something told her it might be interesting to play this one out for a while.

12

Brad lost count of the number of times over the course of the weekend that he asked Beth if something was wrong. It was one of those weekends when nothing specific was scheduled, allowing them to catch up on errands and backlogged mail and other assorted minutia. Each time he asked, the barely perceptible chill in her response was harder to handle than any full-on manifestation of resentment. Her unenthusiastic and, after a while, impatient tone of denial simply added to his frustration. The vicious circle was complete when she finally grew tired of his inquiries and displayed a more tangible attitude from that point forward.

It was as if she was letting him stew, amused by his unrest, like a parent watching a child pitch a ridiculous fit. She could have taken his anxiety away with a single smile and an earnest hug, but her low-key response to his paranoia had what he perceived to be a mean edge to it, without the slightest shred of empathy, and it pissed him off.

On Sunday night, as the television news was signing off, she said, "You realize we've been fighting about absolutely nothing at all."

"I thought we've been fighting about your complete and utter willingness to let me stew in my own shit."

"I'm sorry you had a bad weekend, but I wish you'd stop trying to blame it on me. It's your stew, sweetheart, not mine."

Brad clicked off the television using the remote, and the bedroom was now as dark as his mood. Everything in his head waiting to be said had already been outed during the weekend, and he knew he was on the verge of rekindling the fire of her frustration with him. So he turned on his side and closed his eyes, knowing sleep was still hours away.

After a moment he felt her kiss him on the cheek. Nothing more was said until morning, when her mood seemed to have changed back to normal.

MONDAY morning at work. What a way to recover from a weekend in domestic purgatory. It was like trying to recover from a hangover with a stiff shot of paint thinner.

He was on the telephone with a client when Pamela stepped into his office. She placed a note on his desk: "Ken's office, ASAP." She didn't smile as she turned and disappeared.

Brad wadded up the note and concluded his call. Then he deliberately killed another five minutes before heading for the stairs.

Mark and Pamela were sitting at Wong's conference table when Brad arrived. Wong was at the kitchenette pouring himself a cup of coffee from his private stash of Starbucks' finest, provided hot by a catering service each morning.

With one look Brad knew where to sit. A thick notebook was waiting on the glass tabletop before an empty chair. Mark and Pamela had identical notebooks in front of them, though theirs remained untouched and unopened.

As Brad took his usual seat at the conference table, formalized over years of meetings here, he immediately noticed that his name had been imprinted onto the cover of the black-vinyl book. Under his name was the logo of The Complex, the same one he'd seen on the introductory letter of a few days earlier. The book was twice as thick as the legal disclaimer, which Brad had still not studied at length.

Wong returned to the table with his steaming mug of coffee and a smile that was a little too peppy for Brad's taste this morning. The mug had the same logo on it, and Brad wondered why he'd never noticed it before.

"Welcome to the seminar, ladies and gentlemen." His eyes went to the books in front of them. "What you have here are some evaluations and questionnaires, which I think you'll find kind of fun to fill out. I suggest you take this off-site today, since they require your full attention. Have the completed workbook back by five for FedEx."

Brad smirked. "I've got a proposal due tomorrow, a shitload of letters to write, a birthday present to buy for the assistant to the EVP of marketing at Boeing, a haircut at four, and a creative briefing in ten minutes. I fly out on Wednesday for the Weyerhauser sales meeting, and I've got to make my own reservations because we account managers don't have our own secretaries, thank you very much."

"Drop by between emergencies and you can have some of my bonbons," said Pamela.

No one said anything for a moment. Wong broke the tension by offering, "We're all busy, Brad."

They just looked at him. And just to piss him off, they were all smiling.

BRAD took his notebook from The Complex to a nearby shopping mall and commandeered a table in the food court. He ordered a burrito from Taco Time and took out his pencil. Then he stared at the cover without moving for nearly ten minutes.

This was the moment. Every time he'd told himself or someone else that he wasn't going to attend Ken Wong's seminar, a little voice whispered that the jig was up, that he could fool some of the people with this false bravado, but he and his inner child knew better. All the noise had nothing to do with the seminar at all. It had to do with power and control, ironically two of the things Brad knew he might understand better with a seminar or two under his belt.

But now, here in the mall, there was no one around to impress. It was just him and the notebook. Filling in the blanks would commit him to nothing, and it would keep him in the game. Like a disapproving father who sneaks into the back of the church to witness his daughter's marriage to someone too much like himself, Brad opened the notebook and began to read.

He'd always enjoyed taking tests and kicking the shit out of the toughest of brain teasers, beating the clock, beating his classmates and coworkers to completion, competing for the highest score, usually winning. Once, in a fit of self-confidence disguised as boredom, he'd sent off for a Mensa qualifying test, but he never returned the completed examination, which was more difficult than he'd anticipated. There was also a thirty-five-dollar entry fee, and he couldn't rationalize belonging to Mensa at any price. It was still in his file cabinet at the office. He never told Beth or anyone else about his brush with genius.

Leafing through this material from The Complex, he recognized the first section as a basic IQ test, similar in many ways to the Mensa exercises. There were ninety questions to be completed within a forty-five-minute time limit. But the first question Brad addressed was self-imposed: how the hell would anyone know if the time limit had been observed? He pondered that one a moment and concluded that the test was designed to be impossible to finish without guessing at some answers and that anyone who aced this baby was revealing themselves to be in the bottom quartile of personal integrity.

Some were hard: *Which of the five is least like the other*

four? Copper, silver, brass, gold, lead. Shit. Brad selected gold—it was the only one of the five Beth would accept on her birthday. (On the way home it occurred to him that the answer was brass; the others are simple metals, while brass is an alloy composed of two metals. Everybody in Mensa knew *that.*)

Some were impossible, to wit: *Using a single and unbroken line that winds through the structure, inside and out, bisect every line segment in the following diagram without crossing any single segment more than once.*

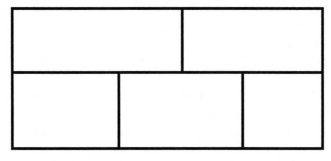

Brad filled six pages in his day planner with failed attempts before deciding it couldn't be done.

The next section focused on a smorgasbord of math problems, which Brad sailed through thanks to the calculator on the left-hand side of his business card wallet. His favorite: A lizard has a head nine inches long. The tail is equal to the size of the head plus one-half the size of the body. The body is the size of the head plus the tail. How long is the lizard? With thanks to Mr. Botkin, his high school freshman algebra teacher, this one took him seven minutes and the backside of his Taco Time napkin, which he folded up and put in his pocket for future reference. What the napkin didn't show was Brad's answer: seventy-two inches. One big mother lizard.

He fetched another burrito and dove back into the booklet. He worked for two hours without a break, realizing—somewhat begrudgingly—that he was having a good time.

Section Seven was a series of open-ended essay questions designed to push buttons, such as *Who is your hero,*

and why? List everyone to whom you feel you still owe
an apology, and everyone who owes you one, and why.
Which one of your childhood dreams do you still hold
dear, and to what degree has it come to fruition? What
was the last thing you stole? How are you most like your
father? Define God. What is your deepest and most recur-
ring fear in life? If you could be someone else, who would
you be, and why? Which religions have it right, and which
have it wrong, and why? List everything you've ever re-
gretted doing or not doing. How will you spend the rest of
your life? What do you stand for?

Each question had its own blank page of writing space.
It took Brad nearly three hours to complete Section Seven,
and when he did, he realized that he had completely lost
track of time and that his hand was throbbing.

He left the mall at ten to five with a headache and an
inexplicable pit in his stomach. He didn't remember his
four o'clock haircut until morning.

MARK Johnson spent the afternoon in the lobby of the cushy
Madison Hotel, several blocks away from where Brad was
doing the same work on the same set of questions. Sitting on
a couch in the deserted piano bar, it took him ninety minutes
to finish the first six sections, and that included reviewing
all of his answers. He didn't have to wonder how he'd done,
because he knew he'd nailed every problem, every word as-
sociation, and every mathematically inspired diagrammatic
relationship, not a mistake in the lot. He'd taken and passed
a Four Sigma qualifying exam a few years ago—now *that*
was a test. This was grade school by comparison.

He allowed himself an hour break for a walk and some
lunch, but he was unable to finish his sandwich because of
his eagerness to get back to the tests.

Some of the afternoon's material were no-brainers.
His hero was Nelson Mandela, and in his view the only
societal group worthy of harsh opinion was the fraternity
of lawyers. He'd forgiven his parents their humanity and
regretted, on their behalf, being neither white nor black. Al

Gore and "W" had both embarrassed the nation. Men, in general, were asses. He wished he were in love. There was no one he would kill, given the chance, and no one he could think of deserved to die, though several names came up as he considered the question. Most religions have it both right and wrong, mostly wrong.

One question caused him to ponder an answer more than others. It was the question about fear. He feared failure more than anything else in the world. The waste of his gift, the plundering of his potential. The fear of disappointing his father. The fear of being black. The hesitation—hell, it was fear—to be white. The terror of rejection. The fear of not knowing how to be like everyone else and simply blending in. He just didn't know how. But now, having committed it all to paper, he realized this was not true. These were all fears, indeed, but not his greatest fear, his supreme nightmare.

What he really feared was that someone would confront him with his answers. That he'd be exposed as a coward with no answers at all, no longer able to hide behind his intellect. This fear alone was reason enough to stay away from this or any other seminar. He feared having to be real with someone he didn't know, which was almost as terrifying as being real with someone he did.

His intellect was all that he had. Other than what he knew in the depth of his vast intelligence, he felt nothing at all. He was empty, without dreams, without love or hope.

What the hell was happening to him? It was just a seminar, for shit's sake. That's all it was. A lousy seminar.

FOR some reason Brad wasn't at all surprised to see Pamela sitting in Ken Wong's chair when he arrived at five fifteen. Pamela was the last person he'd normally expect to see perched there, which was precisely why it made sense today—the world had gone mad, so of course Pamela was pretending to be the boss.

She looked up at him, then down at her watch, and said, "Five minutes and I'm outta here. Where's Mark?"

In front of her was a Federal Express box with one end open wide. She held out her hand, into which Brad placed his completed workbook. She stuffed it into the box and again looked at her watch.

"He has three minutes."

As if on cue, Mark entered the office, obviously out of breath.

"The CFO is in the building," she said.

Mark handed his workbook to Pamela, who slid it into the box and began to seal it up. Brad and Mark exchanged looks. Though it was a little thing, Pamela had seemingly taken charge. Something about her radiated palpable assertiveness.

"You're really into this," said Brad.

Pamela didn't look up. Still smoothing the adhesive flaps together, she grabbed her purse and moved quickly toward the door. The FedEx office and its unforgiving afternoon deadline was two blocks away, and she had seventeen minutes.

"You have no idea," she answered.

"Tell us," said Mark, and everything stopped. Brad wasn't sure if the room froze because his request was delivered so earnestly that it was interesting or if Pamela interpreted it as sarcastic and was preparing to level the Pamism of all time directly between his eyes.

Her glare was guarded. She was waiting for some clue that the request for elaboration was sincere. She'd gone home to work on this because she could smoke and the coffee, while marginal, was free. She hadn't anticipated how the process would affect her. And because of how it had, she wasn't in any mood for their usual patronizing crap.

"Let's see," she said, holding up her fingers to tick off a forthcoming litany of points. "I was reminded that I'm shitty at math, and the verbal section might as well have been written in Latin. I realized I don't even have a hero, everything I ever wanted to be when I grew up is now a pipe dream, my parents disliked me even more than I disliked them, and who I want dead is longer than my Christmas-card list. I haven't been in love in years, I'm agoraphobic, nobody likes me, and the worst part is, I'm relieved, I still believe in God but I must have really pissed him off, I'd be anyone else if I could be, I'm addicted to nicotine, I'm gaining weight, my cat is neurotic, I have no idea what I stand for, and when I look out at the rest of my life, I . . ."

She stopped. It was obvious she was building up to something she couldn't control, just as it was obvious she was doing everything in her power to avoid the moment.

"Screw this," said Brad. "This is so full of shit. Let's tell Ken to take his seminar and his company and shove 'em both into the same dark little crevasse."

Suddenly Pamela's eyes ignited, and she turned on Brad. "No, you shove it! You're the one who's full of shit, Brad." She paused, her chest heaving for an instant. "I'm just thankful someone cares enough about me to give me this chance."

"Pamela, I . . ."

"Let me finish! Do you have any idea how often you interrupt people? Maybe you should think about sharpening up your own pencil, mister, instead of finding something wrong with anything that isn't your idea and, worse yet, might just put you in a situation in which you are not in complete control of things."

Brad raised his eyebrows and inched backward, his hands coming up as if to deflect a blow. He noticed that Mark wasn't looking at either of them. His smile was involuntary, and as he pasted it on, he knew it was the wrong mask for the moment.

"Well, you certainly don't need a seminar to express yourself," he said. "Good quality in a CEO."

"Fuck that and fuck you, and you're damn right I don't." She paused. "I need it for a lot more than that." A second pause, then, "I'm going. And I'm excited about it."

She tucked the box under her arm and moved toward the door. She turned back and said, "I hope you're going, too, by the way, and not because I want to hang out. Because whether you know it or not, you're in need of some quality time on the funny farm as much as I am. Only difference between you and me is that you'd never admit it—to yourself or anyone else. And that's sad."

Brad blew out a breath, expanding his cheeks in a bal-loonlike fashion and trying to get Mark to respond with similar mock outrage. But Mark wasn't looking at him. Mark wasn't outraged, he was embarrassed.

"Guess she told me," said Brad.

As Mark got up to leave, he said, "Maybe we should both pay attention."

13

18 Days Before The Seminar

Ken Wong sat on four boards for small high-tech start-ups, all in the Seattle area, each of which had some of his money on their balance sheet. He was also a member of three executive growth teams, the Make-A-Wish and Special Olympics Executive Advisory Councils, two very overpriced chic health clubs, and the local Rotary. When he was in town, a day did not go by when he was not called upon by an aspiring entrepreneur with a hot new online idea and a desperate need for capital. Wong rarely invested in these schemes, but he obviously liked the idea of supplicants sitting at his feet as he dispensed sage advice, so the proposals continued to come.

He was in one of these meetings when the intercom interrupted. It was Tanya, Wong's personal assistant who doubled as the company receptionist.

"Sorry, Ken, you have a call."

"I'm still in my meeting, Tanya."

"I know, and I told her that, but she insists."

A little alarm went off inside his head. He knew who it was.

"Excuse me," he said, and left the room.

He took the call in an empty conference room on his floor.

"Ken Wong."

"I need to see you."

He was right about the caller. The alarm in his head was suddenly louder.

"I'm in a meeting."

"Excuse yourself," said the woman.

"I have meetings all afternoon."

"Cancel one. I need an hour."

He started to protest but changed his mind. He knew better than to argue.

"Where and when?" he asked, studying his watch.

"Three. You know where."

The line went dead, and he hung up the phone, shaking his head.

He did indeed know where.

DURING the walk through the Pike Place Market to Kells Irish Pub, he remembered how he used to feel doing this. They had selected this location because of its distance from the Bellevue-Redmond high-tech center and its preponderance of tourists, among whom he and the woman had been rendered invisible as they cuddled over their drinks, whispering and dreaming. Yet it was defensible in the event someone saw them, much more so than a lonely park or an obscure parking lot. It had been their standard rendezvous point in the early days of their relationship, which soon became the appetizer for a few hours alone engaging in unspeakable acts in his condo overlooking the lake, where he still lived alone.

They had been coworkers at The World's Largest Microprocessor Company, where they had played mind games with each other for years before they crossed any lines. She'd left the company with him when he founded Wright & Wong, and the games continued for several more years before escalating into a full-blown affair, concurrent with her own marital unrest. It had lasted three years, right up until the world shifted on its axis and Peter Wright was found dead in his home, which was followed by her adept skill at saving his ass from Wright's family. Nothing had been the same since then, especially since she'd married one of Wong's senior executives.

He saw her sitting at their old table. It had always been their ritual: she arrived first, always at the same table, with her drink already under way. He liked the visual, the way she dressed just for him, always dramatic in something tight and black. He had called it her New York look, and it used to make him crazy.

"Welcome to New York," he said when he saw her, kissing her cheek in greeting. She corrected him, saying that her black suit was more California hip than New York chic.

Just like the old days. A page from the scrapbook of secrets he'd whispered in her ear all those years ago. He wondered what she wanted now.

Sitting down, he glanced at his watch. "I don't have much time."

She grinned smugly as she sipped from what looked like a glass of cola, adorned with a lime. That, too, was part of the routine, since her going home to a suspicious husband with alcohol on her breath wouldn't be prudent. They had been so good at deceit. Today, though the new husband was much less suspicious than the discarded one, the cautions remained the same.

"How have you been?" she asked. Her smile said she was deliberately mocking his request for quickness and efficiency.

"There's a lot going on," he replied.

"So I hear."

"I bet you do. Care to share any covert intelligence from the other side of the negotiating table?"

It was not lost on Wong that Beth was Brad's advisor and primary motivator in the process of crafting the buyout proposal. At first it had felt like a major betrayal, because for years Beth had been on the inside of so much of Wong's thinking and dreaming. But times changed: Peter died, Beth saved the day, their relationship crumbled, and Beth finally divorced that asshole silver-spooner she called a husband, all within a year's time. They had remained friends at first, but when Beth fell in love with his star account manager, marrying him within a year of her divorce, that, too, went away. He sincerely wished them well from the outset, secretly relieved that the emotional and financial roller-coaster ride that was inherent to intimacy with this woman was finally over. It was this relief that allowed any residual bitterness to be kept at a safe and quiet distance and to keep it out of his already strained relationship with Brad.

Since—and because of—his own seminar experience, he had completely and gratefully let her go, along with so many other poisons to which he had been addicted. And there had been many, the strongest of which was guilt.

"Actually," she said, "I'm here to listen. You're going to tell me what's up with this seminar thing of yours, and then I'm going to save your ass. Again, I might add."

"You don't need to remind me what you've done for me."

"We'll see, won't we," she said, eyeing him coldly as she sipped her drink.

Wong shifted and made a tiny grimace. "What makes you think something is up with the seminar? You're paranoid, you know."

"Because I know you. And because they called me. They want to meet with me."

He just stared.

"I see that doesn't surprise you," she said.

"The more they know about Brad, the better job they can do with him. Who better to tell them about Brad than you. Standard procedure." He shifted again, avoiding her eyes for a moment. "I don't want my company run by people who aren't ready."

She took a sip, setting the glass down gently. "Do you want anything?" There had been no sign of a cocktail waitress; that much hadn't changed here at Kells, either.

"Listen," said Wong, ignoring the question as he leaned in. "Let's cut to it, okay? You're obviously here after something more than me."

"Nothing personal," she retorted. "It's pretty simple, really. You want Brad to go to your little seminar, and actually so do I. I think it would be wonderful for him and might help our relationship, if it's what I think it is."

"It is. And much more."

"It's the *much more* I'm concerned about."

"You don't trust me at all, do you?"

"Just protecting my husband," she said.

"The mother lion," he said, remembering that her tendency to mother and protect had come up before between them, in ways they no longer discussed.

"So let's talk about what you *don't* want. You don't want Brad and the others waltzing out the door with your business in tow. They could ruin you, you know."

"So they say. Perhaps we'll see."

"Don't bullshit me, Ken. Remember who you're talking to."

He grinned. "How could I forget?"

"I can make him go, you know."

"I have no doubt."

"What you don't know is, he's leaning the other way. Trying to talk the others into pulling the plug right now, to hell with you and your seminar ultimatum."

"It's the ultimatum part of it that pisses him off, am I right?"

"That's part of it."

"All the more reason he should go. Risking potential ruin on such foolish pride . . . he's in need of a little emotional and intellectual tune-up, wouldn't you agree?"

"Absolutely. And I can make it happen. You get to keep your equity intact, and I get a polished and healthy new CEO for a husband."

"Perhaps."

"You know he's the only choice to replace you."

"Maybe. Frankly, Pamela may be a better choice."

"You're kidding."

"Not at all. It's a creative company, it should have a creative leader. Nothing wrong with a little eccentricity at the top, either. Keeps people hopping."

"She's certainly qualified on that count."

"Don't underestimate her. Or Mark, either."

Beth shook her head, turning her eyes away for a moment. When she looked back, she said, "You and I and everyone else knows Brad's the best choice for your job."

"He has to go to the class, or it won't happen."

Now it was Beth's turn to squirm a little.

"Like I said, I can *make* him go," she finally said. "Or I can keep him from going, and they all walk. You know what I'm saying. It's you who is risking ruin here. Even more than us."

"You're saying you saved me once, you can drown me now."

"Your words, not mine."

His smile was poker-perfect. Then he said, "I was right. You haven't changed."

She just smiled back, taking another sip.

"You want something from me," he said.

"I want you to tell me what's up your sleeve with this seminar business, and don't think for a moment that I don't already know that there's more to it than jumping off a pole and discovering God. Just tell me what this is all about, and I'll make it happen. For all of us."

"And just how, might I ask, will you do that?"

Her face suddenly changed. It filled with mock surprise.

"Of all people, you shouldn't have to ask."

"You can be a real bitch, you know that?"

"We both know that, don't we?"

His gaze drifted toward the windows, as if he didn't hear, to the busy Post Alley outside, streaming with umbrellas. Something had shifted with her last remark, and she allowed him his moment of contemplation. Or, perhaps, she was simply enjoying watching him squirm.

"You owe me," she said softly.

*   *   *

HE told her about the seminar. He'd been coaxed into attending by his CEO buddies. He talked about the transformation he'd experienced there, the recognition of his own limits and demons. He told her about his defining moment, the experience of running for his life through the forest, and how the certainty of death meant an unavoidable confrontation with what was true about his character.

He confessed that it was the seminar that had finally, once and for all, allowed him to put his time with her behind him. To forgive himself for everything he'd done.

He told her enough to convince her that his motivations in forcing his three key executives to attend the seminar were both pure and heartfelt and that any agenda hidden here was the secret hope that somehow they would fail, that they'd realize they were not prepared for the risk or the responsibilities of leadership at all. That they'd change their minds. And in doing so, he could then sell the business for what it was worth, instead of the dime-on-the-dollar blackmail scheme they were ramming down his throat.

This confession, the revelation of this self-serving facet of the ultimatum, seemed to allay her suspicions. She knew there was something more than altruism afoot, and now that she'd heard him say it, she seemed satisfied. It was his humiliation before her that she'd come to hear, and she would go home with it tucked away in her memory for later use. Beth kept everything and, eventually, used it all.

But because Wong knew Beth so well, he didn't tell her everything. For her own good, and Brad's.

14

Beth was dreaming of drums. Someone was downstairs, beating a huge bass drum in a simple but erratic rhythm. As it grew louder, she reached her hand over to touch Brad's hip, a nighttime comfort they had cultivated together. Her eyes popped open when she did not find him there. She sat up. Two things were wrong: Brad was not in bed next to her, and the drumming had not been a dream. It was still pounding, and it was coming from outside.

She got out of bed and went to the window, already knowing what she'd see. Lights from the driveway solved this little mystery, and when she looked out, her only surprise was that Brad was wearing just a T-shirt in this cold weather as he shot baskets in the driveway. It was almost one-thirty in the morning.

She didn't know whether to smile or cry. He hadn't used the basket he'd so lovingly bolted to the garage in over a year. It had always held a special place in her heart, if not his, a symbol from his past. She knew it hurt Brad to have his most cherished memories, even his badge of identity, so hidden from the world, which cared not in the least that he had sat on the end of the bench at Washington State University for three varsity seasons or that two of his eighteen total season points in his senior year had come in the form of a turnaround jumper over the outstretched hands of Sean Elliott when he was at Arizona. He had always intended to be a coach, and here he was kissing the collective ass of the digital brain trust for a living.

Watching him, she felt she was stealing a private moment from a little boy, and she couldn't help sensing that her little boy was hurting. They'd had one of those distant evenings, with him asking her several times between the quiet spells if something was wrong. She'd said no, and each time he'd reminded her of their earlier discussion, about his feeling that she milked these moments to elicit just this response, that he had to pay some sort of dues before she'd get real with him. She just smiled and said nothing was wrong, and the silence commenced again until he tried one more time.

Tonight, he had been right. Something was wrong. Or at least, there was something she didn't want to tell him. Either he was brilliantly perceptive, or she was really bad at acting as if nothing was wrong.

And she knew better than that. In fact, her acting had been perfect thus far.

She grabbed her robe and went downstairs.

She opened the screen door and stepped out onto the driveway. He didn't look over at first. Instead he pumped in a few sweet jump shots from the top of the key. He hadn't lost much over the years, she thought. What a shame men leave their games behind. Except for golf, of course, which seemed to be a requirement of aging. So far Brad had escaped that addiction.

Brad pretended not to see her. He'd shoot, fetch the ball, shoot again. Nearly a minute passed before they made eye contact, though just for a moment. Brad, it seemed, had a lot on his mind tonight, and Beth correctly assumed this was about something more than her chilly approach during the evening.

The day had gone down as one of his worst at work. At a video shoot, the on-camera talent was wearing the usual wireless lavaliere microphone as he delivered witty on-camera narrative about how the client's new printers would revolutionize an industry that everyone knew was beyond revolution. During a coffee break, somebody forgot to turn the microphone off, so the client and the entire crew were treated to the amplified sound of the actor urinating in the men's room while he told another crew member that the script was crap and that the client looked like she hadn't been "properly fucked" in years. The client, who Brad agreed looked precisely that way, immediately pulled the plug on the production and stormed out of the studio with a commitment to introduce Wright & Wong to their legal department.

Then, just to make the day complete, Brad returned to the office to an e-mail from Pamela telling him that another client in a major division of The World's Largest Microprocessor Company had requested a different account manager. It didn't matter that he had landed this piece of business himself and was the only person on staff who knew anything about it. The client's agency liaison had been delegated downward to a still-wet-behind-the-diploma business-school grad with a Razor scooter in his trunk—his name was Chip, swear to God—who thought his company needed "younger blood" on their marketing team.

So here he was shooting hoops in the middle of the night, trying to impress his wife with the fluidity of his shooting touch. The fluid had thickened a bit over the years, but it still poured smooth and true.

"Still got it," said Beth, taking a seat on the step, clapping her hands.

Brad didn't look at her. He took the ball on a bounce, pivoted, and launched a little jump hook, which swished as planned.

"You're mad at me," she said.

He still didn't look back, but he smiled. "No. I *was* mad at you, but now I'm just pouting."

"Works every time, doesn't it?"

"You're out here, aren't you?"

"Might have something to do with the fact that I can't sleep with a Harlem Globetrotter in my driveway."

Brad grabbed the ball, palmed it with one hand, took a carefully measured step, and leapt high into the air. The attempted dunk bounced off the back of the rim, and as he landed, something in his lower back yelled that he shouldn't consider trying that again.

"You're still my hero," she said. "Even if you can't dunk."

"I can still dunk."

He took the ball and palmed it again, but this time he laid it softly off the board. Beth didn't say anything, recognizing the moment as touchy.

After watching him make a few more shots, she said, "There is something I want to tell you."

"Wonderful." Swish, from the free-throw line.

"Hey, at least I'm out here trying to get this over with."

"And thank you so much for the pleasant evening. I don't know if being right makes it better or worse."

"I'm sorry, Brad. I have to think things through sometimes."

He put the ball under his arm and looked at her. "So tell me."

"I had lunch with someone today."

He nodded, waiting for more.

"A man."

He stopped nodding as an involuntary grimace spread across his face. He said, "Just say it all at once so I don't fill in the blank spaces with a bunch of shit that will ruin this conversation before it begins."

She knew exactly what he meant. No games. No coyness. None of what he liked to call her "feminine deceit," which he made clear tended to drive him up the wall.

"He's from the seminar company. I didn't tell you because he asked me not to. And it made sense to me, based on what he said about the program. So I decided to honor his request, but I'm shitty at hiding things. You should be happy about that."

"I'm thrilled."

"I mean, I can't get away with anything."

"How tragic for you." He turned back to the basket, firing up a shot. Brick.

"Don't you want to know more?"

The tone of his answer was further along the path toward the inevitable explosion than she'd anticipated. "Don't mess with me, Beth. Not now."

"Okay, okay. Listen, I didn't *do* anything wrong, okay? The guy called me a few days ago and said he'd like to interview me. Said that I could help them create a world-class seminar experience for you by helping them understand more about you. Lunch was his idea, and I didn't tell you because I knew you'd be upset."

She had met him at the same Cucina Cucina in Kirkland where she had lunched with Rich Dobson. Only this time there were no sexual politics, however innocent, though the guy was certainly handsome.

"You knew I'd be upset, but you did it anyway," said Brad, still not looking at her.

"You're twisting what I say again . . ."

"What a gal." Brad was dribbling the ball harder than normal now, his eyes focused on the rim, his face tight.

"I thought I was helping. I'm sorry if I messed up."

"Was he good-looking?"

Her tone changed, an acknowledgment that he had hit the target. "Yeah, as a matter of fact." She pictured those incredible blue eyes across the table from her. Too bad they belonged to someone so short—the Lord was cruel with His blessings sometimes.

They locked eyes for several seconds.

Brad cracked first. "I guess I asked for that," he said.

"I guess you did."

He fired up a shot. "I'm sorry. Let's not go there."

"Let's not."

Another shot, a layup with Brad's hand up next to the rim. "I'm not signed up for their seminar."

"Oh yes, you are. You just haven't quit yet."

He stopped again and looked at her. "Quit? The damn thing hasn't even started!"

She smiled, and he didn't like what he saw.

"Oh, I think it has," she said.

The truth of that comment initiated a silence between them in which Brad resumed his shooting rhythm, as if he were alone. As if none of this bothered him at all. Except he couldn't make a shot go in.

"So what did he ask you?" he finally said.

"I can't tell you that."

He stopped one more time, facing her. He was clearly tired of the running game and was ready for a full-court press.

"I promised him I wouldn't."

"You *promised* him?"

"That's right."

"Well, isn't that sweet. You promised him, and even if your husband is upset about it, you're on the other team. Wonderful."

"I gave my word, Brad."

"To hell with your word." He had now just stepped over the line.

"Maybe you should think about what you just said," she offered.

"Maybe I should."

She got to her feet, barely suppressing the urge to say the words that were suddenly burning on her tongue. She was dangerous in these moments; she could deliver the truth like a Nolan Ryan brushback.

As the screen door closed behind her, she heard him call out.

"Beth! I'm sorry . . ."

She stopped and turned back to the door. Something about his tone made her stay. She stared at him through the screen, the six-foot-seven little boy in his T-shirt, scared and alone in the driveway with his dead dream and a ball tucked under his arm. Watching the world race past him, while the foothold he thought was so safe was crumbling beneath his Nikes.

Emotion welled up behind her eyes, and she bit at her lip to hold it at bay. She felt his gaze on her, stripped of all bullshit now.

"I don't know what to do," he said.

She smiled, putting as much warmth into it as she could muster. God, she loved this man, with his intentions so pure and his mechanism so . . . male. So predictable. He was such a product of his environment, so much his father's son, so self-sufficient and proud. He was absolutely clueless as he chose his own helplessness and confusion. In the face of fear, he was clinging desperately to what he thought was the masculine thing to do, and it was pulling him beneath the waves toward an inevitable doom.

Women mess up their lives in other ways, with the little games they play and petty insecurities that make them settle. But this is how men do it.

Good thing for him, she thought as she mustered the requisite emotion for the moment, that she was here for him. To see what he couldn't see, to accomplish what he could not do. Whatever it takes.

"Yes, you do," she said, the tears appearing now. "Yes, you absolutely do."

15

8 Days Before The Seminar

Brad hadn't seen Ken Wong in over a week and had not talked to him since the day he handed off the seminar workbook. So it was a genuine surprise to see the CEO today, especially on his turf. He couldn't remember the last time Ken came down to visit him in his office just, as he put it today, to chew the fat. Brad noticed Ken had a fresh tan, a little pink around the eyes, and wondered where he'd gone this time on the company nickel. That would be partially Brad's nickel, by the way, which made it all the more infuriating. Lots of business waiting to be had in Antigua, by God.

Brad looked up from an ad he was rewriting. He tried to smile congenially, but immediately knew it didn't work. Ken Wong had always been a mind reader.

"Orlando," said Wong.

"Pardon me?"

"You're wondering where I've been, where I got the sun. Orlando."

"So how was Mickey?"

"Mickey's getting old, needs a new gig. I can relate."

"Maybe he should go to your seminar, find himself."

Wong smiled. He'd been ready for anything Brad could throw at him, and it was an easy deflection.

"Glad you brought that up, actually."

"Bet you are."

"You going?"

Brad stared at the copy in front of him, tapping his pen. "I don't know yet."

"Well, that's better than no-fucking-way, I suppose."

"Beth wants me to go." Brad looked up. "You have anything to do with that?"

Wong narrowed his eyes, wondering if this was bait or bluff.

"Of course not." A moment later he added, "How is Beth, by the way?"

"Beth's fine." Neither man wanted to stay on this subject any longer. This was how it came up, in short obligatory punches, because to ignore it was to honor the rumors.

"Mark and Pamela are in, you know," said Wong.

"Ah, peer pressure. It sucks, actually. And it doesn't work."

Wong stiffened both his position and his expression, calling a halt to the sparring. "Why do you think I want you all to go? Honestly, what do you think this is all about?"

Brad bit at his lip for a moment. This was an important answer, and he didn't want too much attitude to screw it up. If Ken got a lot out of his seminar experience, that was great. But he didn't have to cram it down their throats just to validate himself.

"So you can create a successor in your own image."

"You really think that?"

"Not really. But it's all I could think of. Actually, I think you're a control freak and you just can't bear simply handing over the keys. You don't mind me being honest, do you?"

Ken's smile was that of a chess master who already

had his arms around the endgame. "Wouldn't have it any other way."

"You learn that at your seminar?"

"That, and a whole lot more. You want to know what I think?"

I know what you think . . . you wish I'd get hit by a bus . . .

"Now, how do I honestly answer that? Yes, Ken, please tell me what you think."

"I think you just can't bear submitting to someone else's leadership, especially when it puts you out of your comfort zone. I think you're the control freak, and you can't tell the good guys from the bad guys anymore."

"Thank you, Doctor Laura."

Wong rolled his eyes, but just barely. "You know I've already paid your tuition. I would think you'd have considered this, that maybe dragging your feet might cost me money here."

Brad nodded slightly, slumping involuntarily. He knew that the others had discussed this with Ken at length, making him look precisely like the inconsiderate schmuck Wong was calling him now.

"I owe you an apology, then. You're absolutely right."

Wong's grin returned. "You don't owe me anything. The money is not at risk. Just think about it, okay?"

"I know, welcome to the seminar, yada yada yada."

Wong slapped his knees, signaling the meeting's conclusion. He paused by the door, freezing for a moment as if remembering something. This lasted several seconds before he turned back to Brad.

"There was an experiment at a university. A behavioral-psychology class took a wine bottle, one of those big magnums you see on display in restaurant lobbies but never buy, and they used vacuum technology to put a banana into it."

"Was it a good year for bananas?" asked Brad.

Wong grinned, honoring the crack, then went on. "Then they brought in this monkey, one of those cute little guys like an organ grinder has. The monkey hadn't been fed in a while, which was an important part of the experiment. So of course, when it saw the banana in the bottle, it reached down the neck and grabbed on and tried to pull it out."

Brad nodded. Ken seemed pleased that he had refrained from his usual sarcasm.

"Of course, the banana with the monkey's fist around it wouldn't fit back up through the neck of the bottle. All the monkey had to do was let go, pull his arm out, and that would be that. But you know what? He wouldn't let go of the damn banana."

They stared at one another. Finally Brad asked, "So what happened?"

"The monkey died. Starved to death with his hand in the bottle, still holding the banana."

Brad was the first to look away a few moments later, his face flushed.

"I won't mention the seminar again, Brad."

When Brad looked back a moment later, Wong was gone.

THAT night an envelope with a familiar logo in the return-address corner awaited him. It was the travel instructions for the seminar. An e-ticket had been booked for him, reserving a seat on a late-afternoon flight a week from tomorrow. The destination was Medford, Oregon, which was about forty miles north of the California border on Interstate 5. He'd passed through it a few times, once when driving twenty miles farther south to Ashland to attend their famed Shakespearean Festival. Beth's idea, of course. Once in Medford a bus would take him to a motel—curious, a motel instead of a hotel—and the next morning the journey to The Complex would take place, presumably by bus, since the instructions didn't say otherwise. There was a list of suggested clothing and toiletries. All writing or note-taking supplies would be provided. Curiously, there was no mention of the long list of rules found in the earlier correspondence.

Brad read the document while standing in the kitchen, his overcoat and hair dripping wet. He felt his body tense, well aware that his tactile sensations were growing more sensitive as he read. He used to feel just this way right before a game. Part fear, part thrill, part self-doubt. He loved the feeling then, though he wasn't sure how he felt about it now.

Brad folded the instructions up and put them in his coat pocket, hurrying because he could hear Beth coming down the stairs. She had brought in the mail so she was aware that it had arrived, but Brad wanted to see if she'd ask him about it.

She didn't.

The electric feeling prickling his skin didn't go away all evening.

16

A few days later Brad took the Rules of Order at The Complex and the legal disclaimer from the seminar to his lawyer, a personal friend who nonetheless charged him $250 an hour to squeeze in a little business between reminiscences of the old days playing basketball in the City League. In his mind Brad thought of him as Monopoly Man because the guy looked a little like the cartoon guy on the Chance cards in a Monopoly game. So it made Brad grin when the lawyer described the disclaimer as an "iron-clad get-out-of-jail-free card" and advised him not to sign it under any circumstances. Perhaps because there was time remaining on the one-hour clock, he then offered up his strong personal opinions about seminars and cults and the religious right wing. When Brad asked him if he'd ever been to a seminar like this one himself, Monopoly Man said no, he hadn't, and the session abruptly concluded.

*   *   *

BETH had gone to bed early, taking her *People* magazine with her. When Brad came in, she was asleep with the magazine on her lap, her face peaceful, almost as if she was smiling. Brad stood over her for a moment before switching off the light, which of course woke her up.

She didn't say anything. She just rolled over, ready to accept Brad into the contour of her back as he assumed their ritual spoon position for the night. Brad slipped under the covers and assumed the position, absorbing the warmth of her body. He knew she was still half awake as he put his lips close to her ear.

"I made a decision today," he said.

"That's nice."

"I mailed the disclaimer to California."

"That's nice." A moment. "What disclaimer?"

"For the seminar. I'm going."

She didn't move. But the pace of her breathing changed immediately and dramatically. He waited to be sure she had all the time she needed to offer a response, then decided the ball was definitely still in his court.

"I've given it a lot of thought," he said.

Now she rolled over and simply looked at him. Her face was concerned, as if he'd just suggested they buy a sailboat and leave for Bali in the morning. She was waiting to see if this was real.

"If I had caved right away, it would have been for all the wrong reasons, you know? I mean, it would have been about the CEO thing, about not being run over by Mark and Pam. Even about pleasing you."

"Well, I'm glad you're not giving up having to do things your way."

"Ironically, after all this, I am doing it for you. That's the main reason, I think."

"For me?"

"I think so."

"Then I think you should reconsider."

Brad smiled, then kissed her on the forehead. "You don't understand what I mean."

"Do you?"

He grinned as he nodded. "My resistance to going was starting to feel, I don't know, ridiculous. Like the kid at a school dance who won't dance. I was that kid, you know. Nothing about this has any rationale. It's all a product of my attitude, and I realized that my attitude is keeping me from a lot of opportunities."

She just stared at him, as if this wasn't enough.

"And Ken seems to have gotten a lot out of it, too," he said.

"What's that have to do with me?"

"I see you growing. I'm blown away at how you're growing as a person. You're leaving me in the dust, sweetheart. Did you know that's one of the main reasons women leave their men? Because they outgrow them."

"Who told you that?"

"Read it in *Cosmo* at my dentist's office."

She smiled. "You go because you want to go. Not for me, not for Ken or anybody else. Just you."

"I am," he said. "That's the paradox, you see. By doing this for you, I'm doing it for me. Because I get to keep you, I get to play in your league. And I want that. I want that very much. More than any CEO position."

They kissed. It was deep and sensual, yet not overtly sexual. Not yet, at least. This was connecting. This was endorsement.

Between kisses he whispered, "Please don't tell me the seminar has already started."

She grinned, rolled onto her back, and pulled him on top of her. "I don't think I need to," she said.

He froze. "See? You're way ahead of me."

"You have no idea. Now make love to me before I leave you in the dust in bed, too."

He did, and it was different. The rules had somehow changed. It was like their first time together, a little scary and incredibly exciting. Intimacy was the ultimate aphrodisiac, and simply by giving in to the seminar, they were already rendered more intimate. He wondered if everything would be different now, and he realized that, while energized by the prospect, he was also afraid. Because different was not necessarily better. Different could be anything at all.

They lay in each other's arms, spooning, Beth curled into the warmth of him. "I'll take good care of you," she said, stroking his arm as she always did, and he kissed her on the top of her head, as he always did.

Long after Brad had fallen into a deep and peaceful sleep, Beth lay motionless, her eyes wide open, her brain on fire with the possibilities.

17

2 Days Before The Seminar

Perhaps the perspective of the condemned man is the same as that of the newly liberated one. Maybe the world looks the same to one who knows that the day is his last as it does to one given a clean new slate. Heavy stuff, but it filled Brad's mind on this, his last day at the office before leaving for The Complex. Everything took on a fresh new meaning from the moment he entered the building. Like a psychic suddenly awakened from a coma, Brad perceived hypocrisy and egomania and insecurity all about him, installed in the walls like bugs in the Soviet embassy. The employees were fish, swimming in a sea of interpersonal bullshit, and like fish they were completely unaware of the water in which they swam. Bad water, sick fish.

Somebody desperately needed to clean the aquarium at Wright & Wong.

The day dragged on and on, made all the worse because Brad couldn't focus on his work. At the end of it he stood on the mezzanine and surveyed this world. He remained there for about ten minutes, completely motionless.

He wondered if he'd be back or not. If anyone would notice either way. Or if he'd realize that he was, in fact, the king of this domain and that his rightful throne as CEO awaited.

Let it rip, he thought as he left the building, looking forward to his last evening alone with his wife.

But he would have to wait. Beth would be forty-five minutes late for their dinner date and, when asked, would offer no explanation or apologies.

MARK was the last person to leave the office on that Friday night. This was unusual, since creatives were often found at their desk well after nine o'clock next to a pizza carton and a few empty beer cans. (Unspoken agency rule: beer was totally cool after six, grounds for firing before five, a gray area in between.) Tonight Mark felt like a mother leaving her kids in the hands of a senile aunt for a week. He had to anticipate everything: blank templates for weekly data summaries, a childishly obvious list of action items—known as "ARs": Action Required—for his administrative minions, arrange for sufficient cash to cover the check drafts he'd put on a timetable for the week, e-mails to bankers and insurance reps and the 401K guy and the janitorial service and everyone else who considered him their entry portal into the land of Wright & Wong. Maybe he should lay out Wong's underwear while he was at it.

It struck him that to an outsider he would appear to be a really important cog in this little machine. A Cheese. The man behind The Man.

If they only knew. There was only so long he could hide behind the sheer magnitude of his intellect. His time had run out, the growth of the agency was flushing him from the weeds. It was an old story, and it was about to happen to him: guy succeeds at something that comes easy, gets promoted into a highly visible position of responsibility that requires people skills and charisma and a butt-load of courageous tact, and after a while it's obvious there's been a terrible mistake made here. That's when he tanks. He fails valiantly, and when they reluctantly send him back into the familiar trench from which he came, his relief is much stronger than any sense of shame.

Mark felt the urge to simply bypass all the pain. Check out of the partnership and the CEO race and the seminar right now. That's what the smart money would do, and he was nothing if not smart. Because if he already knew he was destined to take a tumble when his head slammed against the glass ceiling, how long would it take for everyone else to get it?

He was a bean counter. Shut up with all this CEO garbage and let him *be*.

He was supposed to meet his friend, Mandy, at ten for a drink at a downtown watering hole. She was pretty and fun to be with, and best of all she was busier than he was. It had been two weeks since they'd seen each other, and he hadn't even told her about the seminar. What would he say about it, anyway? I'll be out of town at a self-improvement retreat? I'll be off working on my self-respect? Mandy was into German cars and name-label leather and French food—she'd laugh him all the way to the discount mall. She was his first relationship, such as it was, since his fiancee had called things off, confessing at the eleventh hour that he bored her to tears, nothing personal. That had been two years earlier—she moved to New York to become a model; last he heard, she was working in a bookstore—and he still kept her picture in his dresser drawer, facedown.

Mark called the bar and left a message with the doorman for Mandy. Interesting—the guy seemed to know just who she was. He wasn't feeling well, he'd call her tomorrow. Tomorrow he'd conveniently forget, and so would she. Which was why Mandy was the perfect girlfriend for Mark.

As he walked to his car in a horizontal rainstorm, Mark realized precisely why he'd signed up for this thing, and why he was suddenly looking forward to it. He was looking forward to it being over, to having his cowardice

and his introversion confirmed by outside experts, allowing him to gracefully and quietly go back to his spread-
sheets. Then the pressure would be off, and he could coast,
ride the Wright & Wong wave all the way to easy street.
Ken Wong would certainly make it worth his while, because Ken Wong was helpless without him.

So were Brad and Pamela, for that matter. Mark's ass
was covered any way it went down.

When he got home, his stomach betrayed him, and he
spent the better part of the night in the bathroom. As he
lay on the floor awaiting the next round of retribution,
he heard his words echoing off the tile walls, and they
sounded an awful lot like his father: Be careful what you
wish for, boy, because you just might get it.

Yeah, and fuck you, too, Dad.

PAMELA always froze with momentary terror when her
doorbell rang. The fact that this was a Friday evening at
the dinner hour made the sound all the more intrusive.
She was putting the final touches on her outfit for the evening—tight black dress, new Donna Karan pumps, and a
little touch of slut to her eye makeup; might as well go out
and kick up her heels and just maybe get laid on her last
night before the impending week-long confrontation with
herself—when the bell sent a shiver up her spine.

She was speechless when she opened the door and saw
Beth standing there, a sheepish smile on her face that acknowledged the moment as one that required a quick explanation. For the four years of their acquaintance since
Pamela had joined the firm, they were about as cordial as
strangers in a crosswalk.

"Beth," was all she could say, her smile forced. She
wasn't sure how Brad's wife knew where she lived, which
made this little surprise all the more curious.

Beth's smile evolved from shy to courageous as she
said, "Hi, I'm glad I caught you."

A frozen moment of awkwardness passed before
Pamela snapped herself back to reality by saying, "You

want to come in?"

"No, I'm going to meet Brad . . . looks like you're meeting someone yourself. You look great, by the way."

Pamela looked down at her own body, flush with obligatory disagreement.

"No," she said to Beth, *"you* look good. Like a future CEO's wife."

"Actually," said Beth, as if she didn't comprehend the comment, "I just wanted to stop by and wish you luck next week. I think it's great that you guys are doing this."

Pamela felt a tug of emotion—how sweet. How . . . out of place.

"I have a feeling I'll need it," said Pamela, nodding her thanks.

"You'll do great. Listen, I was thinking—you'll need someone to take care of your cat and water your plants for the week."

Pamela was famous for both—her cat was made immortal to the staff at Wright & Wong due to dozens of photographs Pamela had pinned to her office cubicle walls, and her penchant for indoor horticulture had been a topic of conversation at office parties for years. Her condo looked like the Raintree restaurant at the mall.

"Well, I was going to have my neighbor—"

"Nonsense," said Beth. "I know what I'm doing where plants are concerned, and I'd enjoy it. And Brad won't let me have a cat, the selfish prick. Don't you just hate men who don't like cats? I promise I'll spend some quality time with him. Sophocles, right?"

Pamela showed her surprise in her eyes, which made Beth smile.

"I insist. How are you getting to the airport, by the way?"

Pamela hesitated a moment, wondering where all of this neighborliness was coming from. "I called the shuttle," she said.

She made a few more protestations before giving in to Beth's insistence, then invited her inside for a quick tour of the plant population. Beth seemed to be in a hurry, so she gave her a key to the condo and thanked her profusely. She hadn't arranged anything at all with the neighbor yet, and this was a godsend, despite its origins from left field.

"By the way," said Beth before she was off the porch. "Keep this between us, okay? Brad doesn't . . . well, let's just say he's a little weird about the partnership right now."

Beth winked, her smile that of a best girlfriend sharing a secret.

"Sure," said Pamela, not really understanding—or caring, for that matter—what the request or the wink really meant. "Whatever."

Beth hurried off to her car, palming the key to Pamela's condo inside the pocket of her coat.

Pamela had already closed the door, so she couldn't see that Beth was smiling.

Brad hated it when she was late. Tonight was not the night for that, because she really wanted to send him away with a bang.

THE call that Ken Wong had been expecting came just after midnight. He was sitting on his perfectly made bed in a well-practiced lotus position, eyes closed, the back of his hands resting on his knees. Soft music filled the room from a $6,000 Bang & Olufsen quadraphonic system wired into the ceiling, playing a hypnotic Eastern chant sung by monks with agents. But his ears were tuned into the rain pelting his bedroom window, arriving on black waves of wind. As with the chant, he was able to lose himself in the sound.

The ringing telephone jolted him back to the present. He gathered himself, took a deep breath, and then picked it up without opening his eyes.

"Yes," he said.

"We are ready," said a soft male voice.

"There can be no margin for error," said Wong.

"There will be no error."

"You understand that everything I have worked for is at stake."

"Completely. We have prepared for all three of your people, as you have instructed. Especially Teeters. Some piece of work, that guy." There was silence for a few moments. Then the voice continued, "If there is nothing else, then."

Wong slipped easily to his feet and went to the window, putting his hand on the cold glass before he spoke. Lights from a cruiser crossing the lake sparkled through the storm, like diamonds dropped to the bottom of a pond.

"Do it, then," he said quietly.

The line clicked, the dial tone returned.

He stood at the window for many minutes with the receiver still in his hand, transfixed by the rain.

18

Just as Ken Wong was hanging up his telephone, as Brad was pushing himself into his wife from behind in an act of uncharacteristic creativity, as Pamela was trying to roll up her window in a parking lot to get rid of the inebriated software engineer who wanted to take her home, as Mark was catching his breath from a final bout of dry heaves . . . as these things transpired simultaneously in what would be a turning page at the confluence of their lives . . . a car pulled out of a rest stop on Interstate 10, fifty miles west of Phoenix, pressing to make Thousand Palms before midnight. The driver backed off of eighty, settling into the right lane at seventy-five miles an hour, despite the fact that other cars were taking him in the left lane. Fuck 'em. They didn't have the hardware in the trunk that he had, and their license and identification weren't as phony as a Truman dollar, either.

The driver had pivoted the rearview mirror so that he

could check himself out with just a flick of his eyes. That had happened back in New Mexico and had remained that way since. He thought of De Niro and the mirror scene in *Taxi Driver* but refrained from saying the famous line out loud. It was the new hair, the dark color, and the senator cut, shorter than he'd worn it since, well, since ever. He looked good this way, damned good in fact, sort of Italian. The Italian Stallion. The Top Wop. Al fucking Pacino from hell. All he needed were some fly designer threads, and he could stop off in LA and fit right in, get a little high, maybe get handled. Not gonna happen this trip, though. Not with the Kmart shirts and REI boots they'd given him to wear so he'd look like everyone else. Gotta fit in for this to work. Gotta be just another asshole trying to figure it all out.

But he already had it figured out. And he'd show them what was what.

He liked driving at night. Long as you stayed at the limit and your rental car was legit, which it was aside from the fake name, there was nothing to worry about. You could just cruise. These people who hired him, they were good. Real detail people. Always a plus in this business. He had worked for his share of dipshits in his time, but this was a good gig. He felt it in his bones, and that's what he trusted most.

Here on the road, surrounded by blackness, he had time to think. To go over all the details one more time, and there were a shit-load of them on this project. Time to spend the money in his mind. Shit-load of that, too. When people died and you had to clear out of Dodge afterward, maybe forever, the money had better be of the significant fuck-you variety.

He had plenty of time. He had to be up in Medford, just across the California border in Oregon, in time to check into some fleabag airport hotel and get a decent night's sleep before all the fun began. He could have gone north out of Phoenix, up I-17 through Vegas, kill a few hours and a few brain cells. But he had to be sharp on this one. He knew his limitations, and Vegas was a limitation. It was good to know yourself this way, your limits, to be equally in command of your talents and your fears. Ironic, he thought as he passed the Arizona-California state line. That's what this seminar was all about, wasn't it—knowing yourself, facing your fears.

He laughed. They had no idea what fear was. No idea at all.

But they would learn.

BOOK
TWO

RESISTANCE

19

Brad was already wide awake when his alarm shrieked. Even so, he jumped out of his skin when it went off, as if someone had hit him with a set of paramedic's cardiac paddles.

Day One. Here we are, bucko. What in the hell are you doing here?

The one seminar instruction he had quickly disregarded was bringing his own alarm clock. Good thing, because this motel room on the outskirts of the sprawling metropolis of Medford, Oregon, had no clock. Nor did it have any personality whatsoever, a telephone, a television, heat, or a view. It smelled of mothballs and unwashed bedspreads, reminding him of his grandmother's house some three decades ago. The walls were concrete blocks painted a lovely shade of gray.

He hadn't really slept. At one point during the night he had realized, in a puzzling frenzy of honesty, that it wasn't nerves or apprehension that was keeping him awake. It wasn't really the seminar at all, in a direct sense. It was the clock. He was afraid it wouldn't go off and that he'd miss his five-thirty pickup. He found this interesting, given that he didn't really want to be here. Beth wanted him to be here, and that was that.

Or, perhaps, he simply wanted to be the CEO as much as Beth wanted it for him.

Odd, being so wide awake and yet so tired. But it was understandable—his mind had been subjected to twelve hours of intellectual acupuncture. Alaska Airlines Flight 2308 departed Seattle the previous afternoon at ten after six. He had expected to meet up with Mark and Pamela at the gate, and he was surprised and somewhat concerned when they didn't show. They'd not compared itineraries, probably because all three had simply assumed they would be booked together. That, and the fact that they had basically stopped communicating with each other from the moment this seminar entered their lives.

Still messing with us, aren't they. I have a strange feeling we haven't seen anything yet.

In Medford things went from bad to worse, because he and his paranoia had some time to kill together. The instructions had been sparse yet clear: "Someone will meet you at the airport." He'd just assumed there would be a bunch of nervous people milling around the terminal. He'd even visualized himself breaking the ice, being the first to introduce himself. He'd be the first smiling face they'd encounter, and they'd remember him that way. But there was no one there. Of the eleven people disembarking, he was the only one left standing in baggage claim without a clue where he was going to spend the night.

He was paged ten minutes after the bags arrived. The airport was small enough to conduct their pagings with a megaphone, but nonetheless he heard his name and he scrambled for the one and only white courtesy telephone in the building.

The van, he was told, would be there for him in fifteen minutes.

*   *   *

BY five-thirty he was showered, powdered, and shaved, with just a swipe of cologne, Beth's favorite. He selected a pair of khakis and a polo-style shirt with a Seahawks logo on the breast, squarely in the safe middle ground between too casual and pretentious. His bags were packed and waiting next to the door, and he waited on the edge of the bed with the blinds open. The rain, which hadn't diminished during the night, was now whipping against the window in harsh sheets, sounding as if someone were tossing handfuls of kernels of popcorn against the glass.

At 5:31 he saw headlights, then the van as it pulled to a stop right in front of his room. A quick toot of the horn confirmed this was his ride, so he tossed the room key onto the unmade bed, grabbed the bags, and headed out into the storm. A young man wearing a parka was already at the rear doors, and the handoff of the bags went as if it had been rehearsed.

No one else was in the van, so Brad got into the front seat.

"Sleep okay, Mr. Teeters?" asked the chipper young driver as he got in and put the van into gear in one seamless motion.

Brad thought he detected a note of sarcasm, but maybe not. "How could I not? I mean, they certainly spared no expense on the room."

Apparently his own sarcasm was not as well disguised, since they drove in silence for nearly a minute. It was Brad who broke it by saying, "Is it kosher to ask where we're going?"

"Airport," said the driver, no longer chipper.

Brad had other questions but decided to pass the time quietly. There was no trace of the approaching dawn, and the world consisted of seventy feet of headlight beam and a ghostly landscape of hills and silhouettes, all viewed through the greasy lens of a pouring rainstorm. It was as if no time at all had passed since the night before.

Finally the van took a turnoff and headed toward a

long bank of private hangars. At one end he could see lights coming from what appeared to be an office. But what really captured his attention was what was parked in front: it was an old DC-9, painted a dull white with no markings whatsoever on the body or tail. A charter. He could see black soot on the fuselage just aft of the two engines. Parking lights were illuminated at the tip of each wing, and the door was open, though the interior lights were off.

The van stopped at the door to the building. The driver simply turned to Brad, not moving to fetch the bags this time. "Have a good week, Mr. Teeters."

Brad nodded, got out, and went around back to retrieve his bags. As soon as the rear doors slammed, the van began to move. Brad hurried the twenty feet toward the door, but to no avail; he was soaked when he stepped inside.

THE first thing he noticed was the pile of suitcases and canvas travel bags piled against the right wall. The second thing was the smell of wet fabric mixed with fresh coffee. The room was about the size of a grade-school classroom, with militaryesque green walls and a light fixture hanging in the center of the room. About twenty people were there ahead of him, maybe more, every one of whom turned to look at Brad when he entered. Most were holding coffee cups, and they seemed to be clumped into small groups, with some stragglers alone against the walls. As Brad rubbed his hands together as if to warm them from his twenty-foot hike, he noticed a table with the coffee and several trays of pastries.

Mark and Pamela approached from the middle of the crowd, smiling in a confused sort of way.

"Where the hell were you?" asked Mark. Pamela actually rubbed his upper arm in a greeting more commonly associated with old friends.

"Bates Motel. What the hell is going on?"

"Why weren't you on the plane?" asked Pamela. "We figured you'd reconsidered. Mark was already designing his new business card."

Mark grimaced to confirm this wasn't true. "What happened?"

"Nothing happened," said Brad, his forehead creasing. "I was on the plane they told me to be on. I figured *you* missed the plane. Then I realized you've never missed a plane in your life. Her"—his eyes indicated Pamela with a healthy grin—"I could believe. But not you."

"Up yours, Teeters," she said with only slight humor on her face.

"Where'd you stay last night?" asked Brad, his eyes wandering.

"Holiday Inn," answered Pamela.

"Mind games," said Mark. "Get used to it."

Brad nodded, then went to the table and grabbed a cup of coffee, surprised at how good it was. Stirring in some sugar, he surveyed the room. The door opened and closed several times, admitting dazed and confused campers like himself, thoroughly soaked. There was no discernible commonality among the group—most were in their thirties or forties, with a few obvious twentysomethings and at least a handful pushing fifty. The majority were dressed as he was: Columbia sportswear parkas and leather coats and comfortable shoes, very middle management. If this was a business seminar, then you could believe you were in the right place, but if this was the genesis of a middle-class cult, you'd swear this was the wrong waiting room. Except, perhaps, for one guy the size of a linebacker with an earring and a shaved head. Everyone seemed engaged in two- or three-part conversations, but every eye was surveying the room while they kibitzed, sizing each other up, etching inevitable first impressions. Brad wondered how many of those impressions would hold up after a day or two together.

Brad exchanged several nods and how-ya-doin' greetings with a few others, all men. Such a gesture to a woman was too often interpreted as flirting, and this was definitely not the time for that. He'd intended to be the organizer, the guy with no inhibitions whatsoever, but this didn't seem to be the time for that, either. He wondered what had brought them all there, what stories he would hear during the week, how high the bullshit pile would reach.

He eventually gravitated back toward Mark and Pamela.

"Nice airplane," said Mark, gesturing with his eyes.

"You ever been to that airplane graveyard in Tucson?" said Brad, looking out at it. "I think it was down there, until yesterday."

"Cute," said Pamela, who didn't find airplane humor funny. The three of them gazed out to where the DC-9 loomed like something from an episode of *Tales From the Crypt*, its wet hull shimmering. Brad could now see that the paint was worn off at the nose and streaked along the sides, as if someone had recently spray-painted over the long-faded lettering of some defunct South American airline.

"God help us," muttered Mark as they stared.

Just then the door opened, and a woman entered. She wore a clear plastic rain slicker that hung to the floor, as if she lived in this monsoon and had all the right gear from REI. She pulled back her hood to reveal herself as a woman of about fifty, someone who would be comfortable as a teacher or a civil servant. She carried a clipboard, and the room immediately hushed in anticipation.

She smiled as if she knew people here. She went straight for the coffee, everyone's eyes on her. She offered cheerful good mornings to all who risked eye contact. Others avoided it at all costs.

After a couple of sips, which she seemed to relish, she held the clipboard above her head and said in a surprisingly meek voice, "Could I have your attention, please?" Then she waited for the remaining buzz to subside, a silly smile fixed on her face.

"Good morning," she said, waiting for a response. When only a few people mumbled the salutation back at her, she frowned and said, "Good morning!" in a louder voice. The response was a far more enthusiastic echo.

"Welcome to your seminar. At this time you are to board the aircraft, taking only your carry-on baggage with you. We will see to your other bags. Once onboard we will have roll call and staff introductions." She paused as a slight hum rose from within the group. "If you are here with coworkers or friends or if you know someone who is here, please do not sit with them on the airplane."

Brad could sense dozens of looks being exchanged among the group. It was beginning, and social insecurity was the first order of business.

"Also . . ." she said, louder now to quell the noise, "you are on silence until further notice. This means there is to be no talking whatsoever. I advise you to get something to eat here, enough to last you until lunch. Thank you, and we'll see you all onboard in a few minutes."

Brad noticed that everyone was wearing a confused expression.

Silence? Are you shitting me?

As the group began to shuffle, picking up their handbags and buttoning their coats, a disembodied voice said, "Hot damn!" loud enough for all to hear, and everyone except Brad, Mark, and Pamela laughed on cue.

20

There was something surreal about the walk out to the airplane, which now had its interior lights on. Brad could see the pilot in his seat, a radio headset hanging from his ear, looking busy and calm, though a bit too young for Brad's taste in aviators. The wind was blowing everyone's hair as they moved toward the stairs, and you could hear it rushing around the curves of the airplane with a whining sound. The closer they got, the older the thing looked.

He paused at the top of the stairs, noticing how complete the darkness was, the sky a sheet of black without texture. There was no horizon, no sign of the morning. They were an island in space, and this was their ark.

Once inside, he saw that the seats were arranged in twos and threes. For some reason every second or third row was blocked off with a ribbon, and as the scramble for seats got under way, Brad suddenly realized why—they had left just enough seats for the group, allowing no one to sit alone. He grabbed a window on the two-seat side about halfway back. The fabric was threadbare, the armrests worn from decades of use. A few cigarette burns were visible, and he tried to remember the year they finally banned smoking on airplanes. He could also see that the side panel had been patched at some point over the years. Everything, it seemed, needed painting or replacing. A faint scent of jet fuel hung in the air, which was already circulating with a low humming sound. Other than that, it was strangely quiet, the only sound coming from the rain pounding the fuselage, sounding a bit like static from a radio.

He saw Pamela take a seat on the same side two rows ahead. Interesting how the first to board all grabbed window seats on the two-seat side, leaving the awkward task of selecting a seatmate to the second half of the boarding party. Pamela didn't glance back at Brad or anyone else. She looked angry, thought Brad, wearing her attitude like a bulletproof vest. At least she wasn't putting on airs; Pamela was simply being Pamela.

Someone stopped in the aisle. When he looked up, he saw a woman considering the open seat next to him. She was in her mid thirties, with long straight hair that appeared as if she'd just climbed out of a cold river. It was obvious this was an uncomfortable moment for her. He remembered her from the waiting room a few minutes ago, one of the loners by the wall.

"May I?" she said, silently mouthing the words.

Brad smiled. He liked to make it easy for someone who struggled with life's tough little moments. He could relate to it. "Absolutely," he said aloud.

She put her fingers to her lips, reminding him of the imposed silence, which he had completely forgotten. He smiled with mocking isn't-this-ridiculous familiarity, but she looked away as she sat down.

He divided his attention between the boarding passengers and his new seatmate. She kept her overcoat on, a London Fog or a very good knockoff similar to those worn by downtown women, leading him to conclude she was an executive of some sort. Housewives and administrative

assistants don't wear London Fogs, they wear Burling-
ton Coat Factory. He could see that her expensive linen
pants were soaked and that her stylish shoes were very
possibly trashed from the puddles on the tarmac. Her fingernails were elegant but understated, but her hands belonged to an older woman than her face would indicate.
She had dark, brooding eyes, luxurious eyebrows, and
deliciously plump lips, the pouty kind that men noticed
and women envied. Her face, however, wasn't executive
material at all. She was too tough, a bit washed-out, a
Marlboro face, trying hard to keep it together in spite of
a few rough edges. All and all, she was attractive enough,
especially, he imagined, when her hair had been sham-
pooed and styled. But there was a sadness about her, too,
some great weight on her shoulders.

Mark passed by in the aisle, duffel bag in hand, one
of the last to board. He rolled his eyes at Brad, surveying
the remaining seats. Moments later, when Brad turned to
check, he saw that Mark was seated on the aisle next to the
goombah with the shaved head, whose military coat was
open, revealing a black T-shirt that read "Austin 3:16."
If this was an executive-training seminar—which Brad
wasn't at all sure it was—then maybe this guy was an up-
and-coming manager for the WWF reporting directly to
Vince McMahon.

Brad peered forward to see that Pamela's seatmate
was an average-looking Joe. With one glance he had the
guy pegged: neither particularly handsome nor especially
plain, the kind of guy who was easy to talk to because
he was a man with no apparent driving ego, no designer
labels, no Rolex, no look-at-me accoutrements. Pamela
had her head pointed toward the window, looking out at
the storm.

The lone flight attendant closed the door, and the tur-
bines immediately began to spool up. Brad felt something
in his stomach tighten, and he noticed that the rule of
silence was very much in effect. No one moved.

Interesting. The woman who had greeted them in the
lobby had not boarded the airplane.

*   *   *

6:25 A.M.

THE plane began to roll. Everything *sounded* fine, but as
the slow taxi to the end of an unseen runway commenced,
they could already feel the wind kicking them around.
Brad could see that several quiet and unauthorized conversations were under way; for the most part everyone seemed
slightly anesthetized, lambs led to an uncertain slaughter.
His seatmate absolutely refused to notice when he looked
her way, her eyes either closed or focused on the ceiling.

Suddenly a voice pierced the awkward silence. The
volume on the plane's public address system was much
too loud, lending the voice a harsh quality that seemed to
match the conditions outside.

"Good morning, and welcome to your flight to The
Complex. My name is Serena, and I'll be your flight attendant. Our flight is only forty minutes long, so there will
be no in-flight service, but if there is anything I can do to
make you more comfortable, please don't hesitate to ask."

She paused, as if consulting a script. Brad leaned over
to catch a glimpse of Serena, who turned out to be a perky
African-American cheerleader type. She wore the uniform of
a flight attendant, but with no airline name or logo. Brad also
noticed her figure, which was that of a dancer. And as he
suspected, she was consulting some notes before she resumed.

"Before we take off, we'd like to conduct the roll.
When I call your name, please raise your hand."

For some reason the names were not in alphabeti-
cal order, so everyone had to pay close attention. Brad
watched every hand, already trying to match names with
faces, an effort he knew was fruitless. He counted thirty
passengers, including Elisa Dozono, his aloof seatmate,
who didn't look up when her name was called.

When the roll was finished, he took a risk. He extended his hand and said, "Hello, Elisa Dozono . . . I'm Brad
Teeters."

She looked at his hand, then shook it. She didn't smile

as she again touched her finger to her lips for silence. Brad smiled, though—she wasn't going to get to him—and then did the same in return, signaling his understanding.

The plane seemed to be waiting for the roll call to conclude, because within moments of the last name, the engines roared, and it wheeled sharply. Wind bucked the aircraft as it now faced down the runway. Through the window Brad could see the lights extending into the rainy blackness. After a few moments he felt the familiar sensation of takeoff thrust, pushing him back in his seat. He loved the feeling, a little-boy fascination that refused to grow up. No matter how often he flew without Beth, he always thought of her at this moment, because, when they *did* fly together, they always held hands tightly during takeoff.

As the old DC-9 accelerated down the runway, Brad could see the approaching lights of the hangar office where they had gathered. As they whisked past, he saw that all of their luggage was still piled against the wall inside an otherwise empty room.

"That's interesting," he said softly, hoping his seatmate might hear and inquire. But she didn't.

The takeoff roll was unusually long, long enough for anyone who knew anything about aerodynamics to feel a certain tightness in the sphincter. Finally—certainly somewhere near the end of this runway designed for commuter jets and crop dusters—the aircraft rotated, scooping up pressure beneath its wings. A gust of wind slammed the plane immediately, coinciding with the clanging of retracting gear, which in turn prompted several involuntary gasps. One of the loudest came from Elisa, who grabbed Brad's arm with adrenalized strength and squeezed until it was apparent they would not fall back to earth in a tumbling ball of fire. Within seconds they were swallowed by black clouds, completely eliminating any visual sensation of forward motion. There was only the roar of the two engines and the ominous creaking of a thirty-five-year-old airframe.

As the pressure of her grip subsided, Elisa finally took a breath and mouthed the word "sorry," tossing in a sheepish smile of apology. Brad was tempted to put his finger on his lips, but he patted her hand in a fatherly way and grinned. He immediately felt her withdraw from his touch and turn her eyes toward the opposite window. He didn't know if she was embarrassed because of the scream or the contact, or both.

Something in his stomach moved, and he had a feeling it wasn't caused by the sudden need for breakfast.

21

They had been in the air for fifteen minutes. The flight attendant had gone into the cockpit and not returned, and
Brad could tell from the number of craning necks that he
wasn't the only person to notice. Elisa had taken a paperback book from her purse and was reading intently, and
when she turned a page, he could see it was a *Fodor's
Guide to Costa Rica.*

Boy, is she ever on the wrong airplane.

Interesting, he thought, that she was so concerned
about the silence rule yet not the rule about bringing reading material to the seminar. Brad could see that several
more whispered conversations had sprung up, that in fact
more people were chatting than observing the rule of silence that Elisa seemed to hold so dear.

A jolt rocked the airplane, a sensation similar to a car
unexpectedly hitting a curb. Within seconds the seat-belt
sign came back on with a barely audible ping, and the

captain's voice announced the laughably obvious presence of turbulence and the immediate need for seat belts. Brad sensed Elisa stiffen, and he thought he heard her gasp and then hold her breath as she listened.

The second jolt was worse, as if the plane had collided with a cloud of black tar. The impact caused the left wing to dip sharply, and he could hear the contents of the overhead compartment shifting violently. Elisa grabbed for his arm exactly as she had before, only this time her grip remained. Brad covered her hand with his own and drew a deep breath. Nearly two hundred hops down to California and a handful of flights back east in the dead of winter, and he'd never felt a kick in the tail like that one.

The engines heightened their pitch and the plane angled back, as if climbing. But in his stomach Brad felt the unmistakable sensation of descent. There was a definite flat-tirelike sensation now, a shuddering almost as if the plane were taxiing over railroad tracks. Then the power eased back and the shuddering stopped, and for a moment everything was quiet.

Elisa was looking at Brad now, as if expecting an explanation. Her eyes were moist, and he could see her teeth gnawing at her lower lip.

"Are we having fun yet?" he offered, trying for a natural smile. He noticed how his first impression of her hardness was gone now, replaced with a little girl's innocence. For the first time he noticed tiny wrinkles around her eyes, probably caused by too much sun and perhaps too much living.

"This isn't normal, is it?" she replied, her voice low, smooth as bourbon.

"This airplane didn't get this old by not being able to handle turbulence like this. It'll be over in a minute."

She nodded and then looked out the window, keeping her hand on his arm. He could feel her fingernails through the fabric of his jacket, and for the first time since she'd sat down, he felt guilty. He checked to see that Pamela and Mark weren't able to see that he was comforting the woman with his touch, happy to see that they were both involved with their own conversations.

AFTER the first few jolts Pamela reached for the seat-back pocket in front of her and fished out an airsickness bag, holding it in her lap. She could tell that the man next to her was watching. Screw him, she thought. They hadn't spoken yet, and she'd avoided looking at him the several times she could feel his eyes on her, inviting contact.

"Can I get you anything?" he asked, his voice barely above a whisper. "Water? Maybe they have some Dramamine or some Alka-Seltzer."

When she looked at him, she saw an understanding smile, and she instantly hated herself for thinking badly of him previously. The man had a round face with pink cheeks—the word *jolly* came to mind—with a rising hairline that matched well with his short, spiky razor cut. She could envision him out on a golf course or standing in the hot dog line at a Sonics game, a guy's guy in a gentle sort of way, with no pretension. Maybe a dad, a Little League coach. He was the kind of guy that was easy to like at first blush, but she really didn't want to. Not this soon.

She instinctively glanced at his hands for a ring, but they were folded in such a way that she couldn't see the proper finger. They were thick and strong, with well-kept nails, something she always seemed to notice in a man. In fact, she'd actually put that down on her seminar questionnaire under a list of things she was attracted to in a prospective lover. Other than his hands, however, she had already decided he wasn't her type: he didn't look successful and most certainly wasn't tall enough to plug into her fantasy of love at first sight.

"I'd give an ovary for a cigarette," she said. This was an old trick: might as well wheel out the big nasty guns right away, let them see the real Pamela to avoid any temptation to like her on first impression. Not that this had been much of a problem in her life. The abrupt comment immediately defined the relationship going forward. They could either stomach her or they couldn't from the get-go. Most couldn't.

He didn't flinch. He just smiled and nodded in understanding.

Another jolt rocked the airplane as they studied each other, sending her shoulder crashing into him. She immediately grabbed the armrest with her left hand and his knee with her right, inhaling sharply. The impact was so violent that one of the overhead compartment doors flew open a few yards in front of them, and a duffel bag tumbled out, hitting a woman on the head.

"Sorry," she said, removing her hand.

"It's okay, I'm insured." He paused, as if considering his next move. Then he offered a handshake. Looking down, Pamela saw that the other hand had no ring. "Hope she is." He glanced up at the woman who had been beaned by the duffel bag, now being comforted by the guy next to her.

"Hope we all are," Pamela said, taking his hand. "Insured, I mean."

"I'm Scott Spencer," he said. "If we're going to bite the big one this morning, I at least want to know who I'm going down with."

She rolled her eyes. "Now there's a line that wouldn't fly in a bar," she said, "if you'll pardon the pun."

"You're cold," he said, placing his left hand over hers as if to warm it.

"That's what they tell me," she said, surprised that she was letting him do this. "Actually, I'm scared shitless."

Suddenly the plane pitched forward and then rocked back again, and she instinctively grabbed for the sickness bag with her free hand. Several muted screams and gasps could be heard throughout the cabin.

"Breathe," he said.

"What?"

"Breathe. You're not breathing. It'll help take the nausea away." He put his hand on her back now, just below her neckline. "Breathe deep." She could feel the heat of his palm through her sweater and her coat. She inhaled slowly and deeply, noticing the mild scent of his aftershave and the intensity of his focus on her.

The plane's engines raised to a higher pitch, then just as quickly fell to a lower level than before, as if the plane was suddenly gliding instead of climbing, almost as if they'd lost power. The landing lights came on, illuminating thousands of bulletlike tracks of rain as the aircraft hurtled through the clouds toward what everyone was beginning to suspect would be a headline in the evening newspaper.

"Let me get you that water," he said, starting to undo his belt.

She smiled through her terror. "The seat-belt sign is on."

"To hell with the rules. We're not supposed to be talking anyhow . . . so let's break 'em all."

She couldn't help but grin. "You'll fall on your ass."

"Like I said, I'm insured."

Her smile broadened. "A half hour into this thing and I meet a knight in shining armor."

"Actually I'm a territory rep for a beer distributor, but thanks anyway."

Now she held out her hand. "Pamela Wiley. Failed artist, up-and-coming creative director, committed beer drinker. And I'm going to throw up."

She raised the bag, waited, but nothing happened. She was breathing deeply, as Scott had suggested, and the nausea slowly subsided.

Just then the pilot's voice filled the cabin for the second time.

"Ladies and gentlemen, we are sixty-four miles out from the airstrip, and we've begun our descent. However, we're experiencing some hydraulic problems with the horizontal stabilizer, so we may have to circle the field for a while to work this out. And I have to be honest with you, there is the chance of a pretty rough landing. Please remain in your seats, buckle your seat belts securely, and we'll keep you posted."

As if on cue, a gust of wind T-boned the fuselage, tipping the wings to an obscene angle. Pamela covered her face with her hands, conscious of the other passengers in various states of panic. The ambient noise level in the cabin was higher now, with the engines rising and falling and nearly everyone talking animatedly to the person next to them.

Scott put his arm around her and squeezed close, his face pale, his jaw set tight. "Remind me to kill my boss," he said, his eyes straight ahead.

Pamela put her hand on his knee and closed her eyes, waiting to throw up or to die, whichever came first.

MARK Johnson had already sized up the fellow sitting next to him, although they'd not really spoken since the airplane took off. One didn't wear an Austin 3:16 T-shirt unless one wanted to convey a few messages, especially among a group of so-called executive trainees and/or self-improvement junkies. He'd also noticed a small tattoo in the soft flesh between the guy's thumb and forefinger, a crudely drawn star with little dots between each point— what that message was, he had no idea. His hands were huge, the knuckles scarred, and the nails dirty beyond repair. The only words Mark had heard him say was a mumbled "Fuckin' A" after one of the first air pockets momentarily stopped the rest of the hearts on board, a comment that was accompanied with a huge grin more appropriate to a teenager at a Six Flags amusement park. Apparently this clown was having the time of his life. Mark guessed he was a well-worn thirty, give or take five difficult years, with thick limbs that were obviously powerful underneath a layer of fat. He wore blue jeans and work boots that had seen better days. Mark was anxious to find out what he did, why he was here, and what he expected to take away from the experience besides a grudge.

Well, not that anxious, actually. In the narrow niche of people in his social circle, heavy-equipment operators and gravediggers weren't present and accounted for. Mark had seen these guys doing their thing in bars and in alcohol-fueled groups, and of all the ways you could generalize about them, one probability remained constant: guys like this usually didn't like pretty boys like Mark. And when they didn't like you, they found unsubtle little ways to let you know, to put you in your place. By themselves they were harmless, but in numbers they were unpredictable.

Mark was working up to introducing himself when the turbulence started in earnest, which changed everything. The dull monotony of a routine flight would have assured Mark that the guy's thoughts would be shallow if not empty, that a handshake would be perhaps welcomed or at least tolerated. But now, with angry mountains of clouds and the airplane about to break apart, his seatmate was on adrenal overload.

This was probably the most fun he'd had since he was paroled.

As the plane did a quick roll to one side and then back again, he turned expectedly toward Mark and said, "So what do you do?"

Mark wasn't sure he'd heard correctly, and in the awkward moment of pause the man pantomimed sign language and spoke very slowly, "What . . . do . . . you . . . do?" But he was grinning, further confusing Mark's response.

"CFO for an ad agency. You?"

"Gynecologist. Just kidding. District manager for a chain of tire stores."

Mark nodded, he hoped not too obviously. He extended his hand. "I'm Mark."

As his new friend returned the handshake with what could not be mistaken for anything other than an intention to crack a bone, he said, "No shit? Me, too. No, not really. I'm Jack."

Mark tried not to wince, either from the handshake or the failed attempt at levity. Just when he was trying hard to give the guy the benefit of the doubt, the doubt handed itself back.

"You think the pilot sounded scared?" Jack asked. "I think he's pissing his pants."

"Actually no. They train them to sound like they're always on Valium."

The airplane began to tremble, similar to the railroad-track effect they'd experienced shortly after takeoff. Only this time it continued, strong enough for the seat backs to perform a death rattle and the significant fat under the chin of the guy across the aisle to tremble in waves. The word *stall* popped into Mark's head, and he was tempted to try that one out on Big Jack just to see what would happen.

No one on the airplane spoke for a few moments as the shimmying continued. By now the nose had dipped to an uncomfortable angle, and the airplane was rapidly picking up speed as it descended. Mark knew enough about flying to recognize that this was neither a descent nor an air pocket from hell; this was an airplane falling out of the sky. They had either stalled or lost aerodynamic integrity, but whatever had happened was sending them screaming toward the ground.

He saw Jack draw a deep breath and close his eyes for a moment, just as his own stomach seemed to explode with something foul.

"We get out of this alive," said Jack without looking over at Mark, "we got to stick together." He paused, then added, "You and me, we're different."

"How's that?" asked Mark, trying not to inject anything into his voice.

"Well, me being *me,* for starters, and you being the only black dude and all."

"I hadn't noticed," said Mark. "And I'm not black."

A few seconds went by, and Mark assumed Jack had no response. Then a slow smile emerged on Jack's face as he finally turned his face toward Mark and said, "That's bullshit, my man. On both counts."

Then he winked.

Something about the way Jack turned back, staring straight ahead, told Mark this discussion was over. Which was fine with him. Besides, the airplane was shaking so loudly that it was difficult to hear anything else, and it was time to enter into a deep conversation with God. They were out of control, and a flaming, flesh-tearing, film-at-eleven death was at hand.

Yet despite the circumstances, instead of entering into

a pleading prayer for salvation or forgiveness, Mark found himself thinking about what Jack had said. That they were different, he and Jack, that they should stick together, that somehow he was down there in Jack's self-proclaimed league of losers, just struggling to get by. Perhaps his salvation resided in his ability to understand why this bothered him so, and in that he found hope: he wasn't ready to die. Not tonight.

Jack had been right. It *was* bullshit. All of it.

22

Everyone stopped talking within a few seconds after the shuddering commenced. Deafening sounds emanated from everywhere, from the trembling overhead doors, from unseen beams and bolts straining beneath the metal skin of the fuselage, from the rising and falling pitch of the failing turbine engines. Yet despite the chaos it seemed oddly quiet, as if thirty people were accepting a possible fate that they had moments earlier been afraid to look in the eye.

No one moved. No one breathed.

The interior lights blinked twice, then went out. The cabin was engulfed in a sudden blackness that seemed to have a texture to it, a tangible cloud of fear. An eerie, lightninglike strobe effect flashed through the windows as the plane burrowed through pockets of vapor that seemed to explode with white in the outside landing lights.

Brad heard Elisa softly mutter, "Oh, my God . . ." for no one's benefit other than the two of them. Her eyes were closed, and he knew she was expecting to die. He squeezed her hand tighter, realizing that he did, too.

This was it.

He'd never really considered this moment before. He'd been on rough flights before, experienced food poisoning and a bungee jump that almost went south, but death had never been an option, and he'd never legitimately faced that blank sheet of paper upon which he would be asked to give an accounting of his days. He realized his predominant emotion wasn't fear but a feeling of complete and utter helplessness. He was as angry and disappointed as he was afraid.

But the fear was gaining ground.

Somewhere in the darkness he heard sobbing, almost surreal in its softness. And suddenly, comprehending the sound, Brad realized his own throat was painfully tight. It wasn't just for his own fate but for the anonymous soul beside him, for all thirty of them, each facing his or her end in their own way. He felt lightheaded and realized he hadn't been breathing. He exhaled and quickly drew in another, holding it as well.

And then it came, the much-fabled flashing of his life, the cavalcade of regrets, the roster of unrequited dreams. Curiously, he thought of the questionnaire he'd filled out three weeks ago, realizing that perhaps that made the exercise at hand—dying—more efficient, a dress rehearsal of sorts. He thought of Beth, of the insurance policy he didn't buy, the diamond he'd skimped on because he just didn't understand, the sharp words he'd used too often, the times he'd noticed his beautiful home but not commented on it, the feel of the skin on her hip at night, the smell of her, the cute little way she answered the telephone, how he missed her on the road, how he was incomplete without her and more than fulfilled in her presence. How lucky he had been. How blessed. How loved.

Behind him a male voice was whining, "Oh God oh shit oh God . . ."

Elisa began to tremble. The sound of the raging slipstream enveloped the fuselage, which by now had surely exceeded its McDonnell-Douglas specifications for airspeed and was ready to snap off a wing. He put his arm around her and pulled her close, watching through the window as flashes of blindingly white light made the wing appear and then disappear, like a flashbulb in the forest.

He hadn't been to Europe. He hadn't swum naked in the Caribbean or stood atop a mountain at dawn to kiss the sun good morning. He hadn't read the classics or taken Beth on the Alaska cruise she'd always wanted to take. He'd been cold to his parents, arrogant to his coworkers, insensitive to his friends. It always had to be his idea, his comfort zone, his flavor of the month.

Another disembodied and tearful voice from behind could be heard softly pleading, "Oh, God, please no . . ."

God. Brad realized he wasn't sure how to ask for forgiveness. It wasn't about not believing or not going to church. He definitely believed. It's just that he didn't give his belief much square footage in his consciousness. He was too busy with the pressures of his own little realities to dwell on the academics of forever.

Looking ahead, he couldn't see Pamela's hair above the top of the seat. She was probably slouched over, her face in her hands, a posture he'd seen before in the presence of pressure. He wondered what she was going through, how the movie of her life was playing before an empty theater.

He then pivoted to check on Mark, who was sitting very still, his eyes closed. He could have been sleeping, though his face showed that a nightmare was very much in progress. He'd seen this pose before, too.

Suddenly the plane's PA system crackled to life. The flight attendant's voice sounded appropriately panicked, short of breath and battling for control through a veil of fear. It was much too loud; in her terror she was holding the microphone too close.

"Your attention . . . prepare for an emergency landing! When you hear the word *brace*, put your head down between your knees—"

. . . *and kiss your ass good-bye* . . .

"—and hold your legs with your arms. This might be

rough, so hold on." There was a pause, and then she added, "Good luck to all of us . . . and may God bless you."

The speakers cracked a few times, then went silent.

And then, as if on cue, the shuddering lessened and the nose elevated slightly. On any other flight this would be routine procedure during descent. The "flare out," it was called. Brad chanced a quick glance out the window, noticing that the darkness had given way to shades of gray. Dawn. The rain had stopped, though the ride was still unsteady and the engines uneven.

Suddenly the plane lurched to the right, the wings tipping with a jerking motion, as if the pilot was fighting to bring them back to level. Simultaneous with this, the cabin was filled with the shrieking of the flight attendant's voice over the plane's public address system:

"Brace for impact! Brace! Brace!"

Brad released his hold on Elisa's hands, seeing her lower her face to her knees after meeting his eyes for an instant. There was nothing serene about her expression. He did the same, conscious of his breath coming in short spasms.

He brought the image of Beth to his mind, and he said good-bye.

He felt Elisa grab for his hand, not wanting to die alone.

THE aircraft reared back, its forward momentum melting away with astounding quickness. Then the wheels slammed into the ground, causing the plane to bounce high back into the air, where it tilted again before righting itself. A second impact followed, feeling very much like a bad touchdown on a routine flight. The plane still rolled forward . . . they were not tumbling, not lighting up like a gargantuan roadside flare . . . they were simply slowing down, smoothly and evenly.

Reverse thrust was applied with a deafening roar, and the aircraft slowed to taxi speed.

Brad sat up and looked out the window. He was breathless, and his arms ached from the force with which he gripped the armrest and Elisa's hand. When the reverse thrust abated, the sudden quiet was deafening, as if someone had pulled the plug on a soundtrack gone awry. The first thing he saw were lights on the side of a very wet runway. The second thing he saw was the horizon, a soft pink below a ceiling of dark gray. Beautiful, really, if you looked at it that way.

They had made it. God had passed out His pillows after all.

A building, a long hangar, came into view as the plane continued its taxi. Lights were burning in an office at the end of the structure. Inside the office was their baggage, just as they'd left it, piled high against the wall. Parked outside the office was a bus.

They were back at the airport in Medford. And for a time, as others looked out and comprehended their deliverance, they were ecstatic.

7:05 A.M.

ELISA'S eyes were open now and she was running her fingers through her hair, the tension spilling out of her like water through a saturated napkin.

"You okay?" Brad asked, touching her shoulder lightly. She nodded, and her eyes smiled at him shyly.

The plane slowed to a stop, jerking slightly as squeaking parking brakes were applied. Brad could see a set of portable steps mounted on a truck moving toward them. He could also see the bus beginning to move forward, turning their way as well.

Interesting about the bus. He wondered how in the world it might be here. If this was an emergency landing, if they'd turned the plane around and returned to Medford because of a mechanical problem, then there'd be no time to call for a bus, especially at this hour of the morning. The only way a bus would be here was if they *expected* the plane to return. This also explained the luggage remaining behind in the office: they wouldn't load it into an airplane that would be coming right back within the hour.

The stairway edged up to the fuselage. The flight attendant, who had disappeared throughout the ordeal in the air, cracked open the hatch. Then she hit a switch on the wall, and the cabin lights came back on. Brad noticed she didn't look up from her task, didn't seem to care how her passengers were faring after their prolonged headlock in the arms of the Grim Reaper.

People were beginning to speak to each other as awareness of their return to Medford collectively dawned on them. The pungent essence of indignation and confusion was thick in the air.

The bus pulled to a few feet of the bottom of the stairs, its door opening. It was a sleek, high-profile luxury model with the name "Evergreen Tours" on the side, similar to the team buses from his college days. Two people, a man and a woman, jumped out and hurried up the stairs, their hair slapping in the strong wind. The woman held the elbow of the man as they climbed. The flight attendant passed them without so much as a nod as she descended the stairs and quickly got into a car that had pulled alongside the bus.

By now there were many soft buzzings of conversations springing up in the cabin. Many, Brad could tell, involved the comforting of those still upset or ill. Brad looked at Elisa, who had withdrawn a tiny mirror from her purse and was smoothing the edges of her eye makeup. She didn't seem to notice that he was looking at her.

The two people who had exited the bus entered the cabin and took a position in front of the group, both wearing dark raincoats. One was a woman Brad guessed to be about fifty-five, short and slightly heavy-set, with unimaginatively styled black hair. She could be part Native American, perhaps with a distant grandfather of Asian descent tossed into the gene pool. She inspected the group the way a teacher surveys a classroom that has just been silenced and is about to be disciplined, her eyes dark pools of calm, very much in command of her world.

Her partner was a man in his mid thirties, about six

feet tall and of slim build. His hair was one of those all-weather cuts that always looked good, but he smoothed it nonetheless. He wore dark sunglasses, which only accentuated what Brad realized were movie-star good looks. No, he was actually too pretty for a movie star, more like the guy they hire in the music videos to seduce the diva. The kind of guy who looked at home on camera next to Catherine Zeta-Jones. He wasn't smiling, lending him a camera-ready, irritated, and impatient air.

The cabin hushed as the two just looked over everyone. Brad could smell the cool morning air coming in through the open door.

The woman held up her hand, one finger extended, as if she expected the group to understand that she was calling for quiet. To Brad's surprise, it worked. Within seconds everyone stopped whatever they were doing. As they waited, Brad noticed that the flight attendant was coming back up the stairs carrying a large box.

The man spoke first. His voice was without any particular power other than the confidence with which he wielded it. The sunglasses, while out of place, added to his aura of authority.

"You have all just faced the very real possibility that this day might be your last on this planet. That you were not going to survive this flight. I wonder what thoughts came to you in those moments," he continued. "Did you pray to your God? Did you cry out for your mother? Did you deny what all your senses were telling you was happening? Did you laugh in the face of death, or at least try to? Or did your life flash before you like a movie? I wonder how the story of your life played, what the reviews were like. Two thumbs up? Two down? Split vote? Only you know."

The flight attendant handed him a piece of paper, which both he and the woman studied for a moment. Brad used the pause to glance at Elisa, who stared straight ahead at their new leaders as if Brad wasn't there at all.

Now the woman took the stage. Her voice was shrill, with a subtle rasp to it.

"But this morning wasn't the end of your days. Those

of you who prayed for a second chance have had your prayers answered. Those of you who refused to believe have been proven correct. Those of you who relied on your faith were delivered from the valley of death to the point of origin, as if time itself has been reversed and a second chance is at hand. And those of you who accepted your fate, accept this: you *all* must now consider what went through your mind this morning. Some of you will learn from it, some of you won't. It is my sincere hope that you will acknowledge what has happened to you, and that you will gain value from it."

She paused, then added, "The *rest* of your life begins *now.*"

Brad could sense that people were stirring in their seats, offering whispered asides, generally reacting to having been deceived in a way that was both dramatic and unforgettable. Tension was omnipresent, like the scent of fear.

"When you boarded this airplane," the younger man said, "you were given instructions to remain on silence until further notice. When you signed on for this program, you agreed to abide by any and all of the seminar's rules." He glanced down at his notes. "Would Tiffany Palofax, Sybil Manning, and Elisa Dozono please raise your hands?"

Everyone craned their necks to see who these three were. Brad was staring at Elisa as she sheepishly raised her hand, sensing what was next. The other two were people he'd barely noticed in the waiting room before the flight, though one of them was a knockout.

"Only three of you followed the instructions, at least until you neared the landing. Only three of you remained true to your word. The rest of you gave up on your integrity. Not only with regard to the seminar but to yourselves. I would ask you to consider how often this shows up in your life, your being out of integrity with yourself, and how you feel about it. I would ask you to consider the price of being less than honest with yourself."

Brad felt like he was back in school, being cuffed for missing a tardy bell. Both the man and the woman delivered their fire and brimstone without a crack of insincerity, as if they understood some great weight behind their words that they knew would soon be all too obvious to the team.

The woman and the flight attendant began unloading something from the box. After a moment the flight attendant took an armful of whatever was inside and began moving down the aisle, handing something to each participant.

"My name is Richard," said the man, "and my associate is Georgia. We will be the facilitators of your seminar this week, and I daresay, you will come to know us well. As we will you. That process has already begun."

There was the slightest hint of a smile on his face now, which Brad was sure was not returned from this audience. This little speech was more for *him* than for them.

"Serena is passing out materials for your week. Please write your name on the first page where indicated. In a moment we will deplane and board the bus for the ride to The Complex, which is approximately three hours south of here at the western perimeter of the Mt. Shasta National Forest. Do not open your notebooks until you are on the bus. Everything you write in your notebook, with some exceptions which will become clear to you when the time is appropriate, will be held confidential. The ride to The Complex will be conducted in silence, and you are to use the time to make your first journal entry concerning your feelings about this morning's exercise."

By now Serena had gone back for a second armload of notebooks and was finishing her distribution. Brad was surprised at how thick it was and almost opened it up before remembering he had just been instructed not to. He noticed that others had the same brush with defiance. The cover was of black padded plastic, very believable as leather. The familiar diamond logo of The Seminar was small and positioned at the lower left corner, precisely where Pamela and her design team would have put it.

Richard and Georgia whispered for a moment; then Richard said, "Your luggage will be taken care of and will be available to you this afternoon at The Complex. Have a safe and rewarding journey."

As Richard turned and ducked through the exit, Georgia added, "Ladies and gentlemen, welcome to your seminar."

23

From the Journal of Brad Teeters

This is insane. I'm on a bus writing in a book, and I don't know why. Because some clown wearing Ray Bans in the rain told me to? What's up with those sunglasses? Why would he make a choice like that, at the very moment when his credibility is most critical? Give me a teacher, not some pretty-boy refugee from Venice Beach.

I can't do this right now. Everyone else is writing their ass off, but I can't. I'm too pissed off and getting carsick. Make that bus-sick. They messed with us in a way that is unforgivable. I wonder what the others are all thinking and feeling right now. Nobody is talking, like good little soldiers. They're all writing. Bet they're pissed off, too. I certainly hope they are.

Maybe later. We'll see.

Okay, it's later. And yeah, I feel better. A little. I've been watching people on the bus, some of them writing, some watching me watch them. Other than Mark and Pamela, I've never met any of these people, but it's amazing to me how much you can tell by observation. Or maybe it's how much they're trying to say. Like the guy who sat next to Mark on the plane—what an asshole. Tattoo Boy. Why would a guy like that be in a place like this? Did somebody waste their money on him, or is he simply incapable of getting out of his own way despite higher ambitions? There's a guy with a bad comb-over (Dude! Get a clue!), a guy with a perm that looks a little like Sly Stone (he's white—Dude! Get a clue!), and a bunch of others I could comment on but won't. The class loudmouth has already announced himself—his name is Matt, and he likes the sound of his own voice. Funny how you can tell the shy ones from the truly insecure ones: the latter try too hard. The rich ones from the wannabes. White collars from blue. Cool versus dorks. How do we pick who we grace with our eye contact and who we don't? What makes some people good enough for us and others not? The way they look? Their weight? Their clothes? I have to wait and see with this bunch—I refuse to pass judgment. Even though I can't help myself.

I wonder what they're writing about me. Or if they're writing about me. He's tall, that's what they're saying. Maybe not. Do I care?

Of course I care. A lot.

Too soon to tell how Mark and Pamela are doing. I expect Mark will be just fine here, maybe he'll lighten up a bit. Smartest guy I know. I have a feeling there will be no place to hide at The Complex. As for Pamela, who the hell knows? I wish her well, but I can't call it. Pamela remains a wild card. Should be interesting.

There was a woman next to me on the airplane. She was attractive but not someone I'd be attracted to, if that makes sense. Maybe it doesn't. It's ironic, because she's the one I went through this experience with, and she's the one who tipped her hand the least. A mystery woman. I have a feeling she's been around, probably one smart cookie. I have a feeling she's here to do some serious work and anyone who gets in her way will be steamrolled. I don't intend to be that person. She will be interesting to watch.

In another time, another place, I'd wonder more about her than I feel I should right now. (How's that for honesty out of the blocks, kids?)

I miss you, Beth. Already. I really do.

Twenty minutes later. I'm supposed to be writing about how I feel, how the flight affected me. The death flight. Okay, it scared the shit out of me. I mean, we were going to die, no doubt about it. The fact that we didn't doesn't take away from the validity of the emotions we felt in those moments. If it had actually happened, nothing that preceded it would have been different. I can pretend all day that I'm pissed off about being tricked, about the fraud. God knows I was pissed off. I've been fantasizing about suing Ken Wong, or at least kicking his ass (let's get real—he'd kung fu me all the way to the emergency room). I want to hate him for putting me through this, but how can I? Because I already see what's up here, and what's up is an opportunity I don't want to squander.

This week is a gift. I know that now, but Beth knew it first She'd wanted me to come to this from the moment it came up, because she knew. God, I love that woman.

I wonder if I'll act as if this is a gift when the going gets tough? Which it will, if today's start is any indication.

Or here's a thought: maybe Wong just managed to get us all out of town for a week while he sells the place to a higher bidder. Wouldn't completely surprise me, actually. I wonder if that's because it's what I might do. Interesting thought.

All I know is that the airplane thing worked on me. If I died today, what would I say about my life? What would others say? That he was a great guy (yes), that he worked hard (worked his ass off), that he loved his wife (no question, just ask me)? But what have I really accomplished? Who am I really? Answers: not much, and I don't know. Now I have a second chance—that's what it is, no different than if the emergency had been real and we'd been miraculously saved from the jaws of death.

My guardian angel came through in the pinch, and here I am.

To be honest, this was a lot easier when I was pissed off.

24

The bus headed south on I-5 out of Medford, and within half an hour had passed Ashland and was climbing into the Siskiyous, which guarded Oregon from the influx of evil Californians. Once well past the majestic silhouette of Mt. Shasta, which they could barely see on this still-stormy morning, and somewhere north of Redding, the bus turned west onto State Highway 299. Forty-five minutes later it veered north on State Highway 3 and twenty minutes after that turned God-knows-which-direction onto an unmarked road paved during the Truman years and began a dizzy journey westward into the depths of the northern-California wilderness. Not that it would have helped anyone triangulate their location. Visibility was next to nonexistent as the bus passed through stretches of fog and mist, which gave way to a relentless rain.

For the most part the bus was quiet. Brad noticed several pairings engaged in whispered conversation over the tops of the seats, while others wrote solemnly in their journals. Some found solace in gazing out the window, and a few, like Brad, seemed to be engaged in taking an inventory of their peers. For the most part his gaze was greeted with a nod or a smile. Something changes between people when they share an experience together, and the closer that experience comes to death, the more liberal social graces become.

Pamela and Mark were at opposite ends of the bus, their faces hidden from his line of sight. He imagined Mark sound asleep and Pamela staring at a blank page in her lap, every fiber of her being craving nicotine.

One guy, however, shook his head in disapproval when he caught Brad's eye, causing Brad to look away first. As chemistry goes, they were already oil and water. He was short and stocky, mid thirties, and prematurely bald, the kind of guy who would seize any chance to shake his head in disapproval at a six-foot seven-inch all-American boy with a beacon smile. Brad remembered him from the hangar waiting room as being particularly loud, needing to be in charge. Toward the end of the trip Brad saw him hunched down in his seat talking on a cellular telephone, which of course was clearly against the rules and, just as clearly, inevitable for this guy.

At one point, as Brad took a break from his journal writing to stretch his neck, the guy sitting in the seat behind leaned forward and tapped his shoulder.

"Doug Vincent, Denver," he said, extending his hand over the seat. He whispered conspiratorially, as if they were two scouts on a campout after bedtime. Brad shook hands instinctively, then put his fingers to his lips to remind them both that a rule was in jeopardy here. It was hard for him to do, because he liked this guy immediately and appreciated his taking the risk. It was something he would do. Brad wanted to reward him with reciprocation, but not after this morning's lecture on integrity.

The guy smiled and nodded, as if he already understood.

Another guy looked at him without expression, which registered with Brad as judgment.

When Brad turned back to his journal, something made him look up. Elisa was watching both interactions from across the aisle. Was it a coincidence that she had selected that particular seat, or was he assigning meaning where there was none? She smiled her approval and nodded slightly before returning to her own work, and Brad did the same.

25

After what seemed like much more than the promised three hours, the bus finally pulled over and stopped, parked behind a panel truck that had been waiting for them. Just beyond was a massive gate, and on brick pillars flanking the entry Brad saw the logo of The Complex etched in stone.

Richard and Georgia got out of the van and walked toward the bus, holding their arms up against the sudden attack of wind and rain.

Richard still wore sunglasses as he boarded the bus, despite the fact that it was one of those days where daylight never quite penetrates the oppressive curtain of the weather. Brad noticed others exchanging looks as he boarded and realized that, unless something changed, this was going to be a week-long joke.

"Welcome to The Complex, and to your seminar," said Richard. He was standing next to the driver, speaking loudly so all could hear. Georgia remained behind on the steps. "When the bus stops you are to disembark, men to the larger brown building, women to the smaller white building. Your luggage will be waiting for you there. Claim your bags and find a bunk. You have fifteen minutes to change your clothes or shower or tend to any personal needs. At precisely eleven o'clock you are to meet inside the main hall with your notebooks, which is located in the modern building adjacent to the boardinghouses. I suggest you dress comfortably for a long day ahead. You are on silence until you disembark, at which time you are free to get to know your teammates."

He smiled, studying the group for a moment before exiting the bus.

The Complex was a fifteen-hundred-acre ranch surrounded on all sides by steep wooded hills thick with lush ponderosa and Monterey pines. There was a palpable isolation to the place, as if the outside world couldn't see in without a satellite. The lone access road wound up into the hills in a series of switchback turns that were never intended for bus travel, and once atop the crest they could see a group of buildings far below, centered on the floor of a two-mile-long, slightly ovular bowl. Roads snaked out from these structures in several directions, paralleling long fences that divided the property into a tapestry of multi-colored fields, where gangs of cattle and horses grazed. A winding river bisected the property, nourishing several dense pockets of forest. An eerie mist clung to the ground at the base of the hills.

The rule of silence reigned as the bus descended into the valley. Thirty pairs, of eyes were wide and alert, like children passing through the gates of Fantasyland for the first time. Brad felt a familiar gnawing in his stomach, a sensation he trusted rather than feared. The game was about to begin.

Once on the valley floor the bus passed through another archway with the diamond-shaped logo of The Complex mounted at its pinnacle. They had entered a gravel-covered courtyard much larger than a football field, which was enclosed on all sides by a freshly painted white corral fence. In the center was a huge equipment shed, painted a rusty red and resembling a classic barn. An old school bus, a faded yellow backhoe, and a few battered pickup trucks were parked nearby. Other scattered pieces of equipment made the place look like a salvage yard. Beyond, at the other end of the courtyard, were several mobile-home trailers joined together into what Brad assumed was an office of some sort, since all the lights were on and people could be seen moving about inside. A few cars were parked next to the gate leading to its porch. Across the way, at the end of a paved and well-lighted walkway several hundred yards long, was the only remotely modern building on the property, with stucco siding and Spanish tiles on a gently sloping roof. Brad guessed ten, maybe twelve thousand square feet. Had to be the general assembly hall. This structure had a manicured front yard laced with pathways covered by brightly colored gravel. In the center, standing eighteen feet high, was a gleaming metal sculpture—the diamond logo again.

The bus stopped in front of several wooden buildings that reminded Brad of the barracks from the TV show *Hogan's Heroes*. Between the men's brown bunkhouse and the women's white bunkhouse was a larger hall, also of weather-beaten wood, which Brad assumed was the dining hall. Covered breezeways connected all three buildings, and fresh flowers lined the walkways.

The place looked very much as he'd expected. It was summer camp. Except for the classroom building, which, with its lack of windows and austere coldness, seemed to Brad a bit like a funeral home you'd see driving through New Mexico.

PAMELA made sure she was one of the first off the bus, actually getting out of her seat and waiting next to the door before it stopped. She didn't care what anyone thought of this, because she was on a mission—she needed to fire up a cigarette, and fast. If there was a nook or cranny somewhere nearby, great, but otherwise she'd do it right here in front of God and everybody. If it was against some rule, they could go screw themselves.

A moment after she'd stepped off the bus, someone tapped her on the shoulder. She was surprised to see that it was Scott, expecting to see Richard or some new authority figure with something autocratic to say.

"You okay?" he asked, matching her stride. He put his hand on her shoulder, leaning down to see her eyes.

"Yeah, I'm fine. Nicotine fix." She offered a sheepish expression and shrugged.

"Stop," he said, putting pressure on her shoulder. His face was gentle, but his tone was insistent. He moved in front of her, placing both hands on her shoulders now. "I know what you've got in that pocket, ma'am."

Her forehead creased, unsure what to make of this. His expression had grown momentarily serious, rather than the concerned boy next door he'd been moments earlier. For a moment she felt genuinely guilty, which quickly gave way to the beginning of indignation. People who made her feel guilty were on the first page of her shit list.

He reached in his own pocket and withdrew a lighter. His expression regained its softness as he held it up and struck the flame for her.

"You don't have to run away, you don't have to sneak off and hide, and you don't have to worry what anybody thinks. It's okay to be *you*, Pamela Wiley. That's just a little advice from a new friend. Just be you."

He stood there with the flame flickering weakly in the wind. She was conscious of others moving in behind, looking at them as they passed, this movie-moment grin fixed on his face. Finally she cracked a smile, took the cigarette out of her pocket, held his hand steady, and leaned in for the light.

"I thought you quit," she said, exhaling.

"Oh, I never started. See you in a bit?"

He was already backing away, turning toward the men's bunkhouse, his expression smug. She nodded as she took in a deep drag, realizing that she was almost grinning.

Only here in never-never land would a decent-looking guy like that do something so . . . nice. Probably gay, she thought; wants to be girlfriends.

BRAD was surprised when he saw that Mark had saved him a bed. After making a nonnegotiable stop at the rest room—where a sign read: "Do Not Under Any Circumstances Drink the Tap Water"—he had resigned himself to the last available bunk.

Sure enough, Brad's bags were the only ones remaining next to the front door when he finally emerged. It was never explained how they got here before the bus, but he was getting used to the strange and inexplicable where The Complex was concerned. The building was divided into separate rooms, each containing three to six bunk beds and each connecting off a main room containing a card table, a community ironing board, and a wood stove. A water cooler and a large stash of full bottles occupied one wall. The largest wall was composed entirely of river rock, upon which hung yet another iteration of the now-familiar logo, this one carved from pine and polished smooth.

Each pair of bunks shared a small dresser. The bunk above Brad's was occupied by a heavyset fellow with bright pink cheeks who had brought his own pillow from home. They introduced themselves, and Brad learned that Tom Turner and the pillow were from Santa Clara. This was the guy from the bus who'd shot Brad a look when he was talking, though he seemed nice enough now. Next door and above Mark was one of the few teammates Brad guessed was over fifty, who introduced himself simply as Stu and didn't seem all that talkative. At least he'd get some sleep with all these Type Bs around.

The obnoxious guy with the cell phone was apparently in another room, which as far as Brad was concerned was perfect. The less he saw of that guy, the better.

Brad was stashing his empty suitcase under the bed when Mark tapped him on the back, then indicated with his eyes that he should look across the room. The guy in the lower bunk across from them had taken off his shirt. It was Jack, Mark's seatmate on the airplane. His body was covered with scars and tattoos, some of them written in Japanese. But the thing Brad's eyes could not avoid, and the reason Mark tapped him, was the tattoo on Jack's back, stretching shoulder to shoulder in three-inch letters: "REVENGE." The typeface was Gothic, leaving any medieval or satanic implications to the eye of the beholder.

Brad looked away before Jack or anyone else caught him staring. He chanced a glance at Mark, but it was too risky for them to engage in any communication, verbal or otherwise. Jack was someone it was easy, and prudent, to leave alone. Then again, thought Brad, why would anyone burn a tattoo like that onto their back if they didn't want you to notice?

After a moment Mark again tapped his arm, pointing at his watch.

26

The seats were arranged in three rows of ten. Each chair was touching the one next to it, leaving no elbow room or means of escaping incidental contact, despite the fact that the room could easily hold two hundred people. Nametags were waiting on a table by the door as the wide-eyed participants entered the hall. Ethereal flute music played softly from unseen speakers. The building didn't appear to be very old; Brad thought he could detect the unique scent of new carpet still in the air. There were no windows or wall hangings; the only decor was a U.S. flag in a corner of the room. Bright spotlights focused on the thirty chairs, leaving the perimeter of the room in shadow.

They were center stage, and it was showtime.

As he took a seat in the front row, Brad had a heightened sense of being watched. The context was different now: everyone knew who had screamed or cried in the face of death, the wise-asses and the cynics had announced themselves, and for the most part it was obvious who had come to win. It was a look in the eyes. Small talk was minimal as the team filtered in, mostly introductions and where-are-you-froms. Mark took a seat in the middle row right behind Brad, and Pamela was seated in the back row on the end.

The music faded as Georgia and Richard entered the room. Richard, yet again wearing sunglasses, stood to the side against the wall, while Georgia walked to the front of the group and folded her hands calmly in front of her. She was smiling, but not altogether approvingly; more like she knew something the group did not.

"Recently at a major university," she began, "there was an experiment that illustrates the limitations of our experiences and belief systems, and how those factors determine our success and happiness in the world, even our survival."

She then proceeded to tell the same story Ken had told him a few days earlier, about the starving monkey who died with its hand in a jar clinging to the banana. It took a moment for Brad to recognize it as the same parable, and when he did, he smiled. Wong was passing it off as a little ditty he'd simply come up with to make a point, when in fact he was parroting Georgia. Brad's smile remained fixed through the telling—over the years Wong had assumed authorship of more than a few of Brad's parables, too—and Georgia's gaze lingered on him a little too long, perhaps misinterpreting his expression.

Upon completion, and after smugly soaking up the oh-my-God reactions of her audience, Georgia stepped aside, allowing Richard to take a place in front of the group.

He, too, regarded them a moment before he spoke.

"We live in a world," Richard began, "that urges us to cling to what we know. To value that which we can see and touch. Your challenge here this week is to look closer, with much honesty and possibly some pain, to what you cling to in your life—be it job security, emotional security, drugs or alcohol, codependent relationships, fear of failure, fear of success, fear of being alone, fear of rejection, the limiting beliefs of your parents, whatever it is—and then understand why you are holding on so tight. It is also to comprehend the possibilities if you do indeed let go, and to begin to find the courage, and the means, to move to the next level of achievement and potential in your life."

Now he smiled, very convincingly, as if suddenly he was their new best friend. Brad wondered if every woman in the room was swooning, if every man felt suddenly invisible.

"But first, let's get to know each other a little better."

The smile remained. Brad could sense the group squirming. No one liked this part, even those who could fake it well were dealing with something foul and angry in the pit of their stomachs. The pause was long enough that Brad wondered if someone was expected to leap to their feet and introduce themselves, and he was just about to be the first to do so when Richard spoke again.

"If you are single, raise your hand."

About half the room put a hand in the air, though not enthusiastically or quickly. Brad checked to see that Mark and Pamela were participating, which they were.

"Thank you. Those of you who have been married and divorced, please put up your hand."

Mark counted eight hands now, several of whom were among the previous singles group.

"Thank you. Those who make over $100,000 a year, please raise your hand."

Two-thirds of the room raised a hand, including Brad, Mark, and Pamela. Pretty upscale crowd. Brad found himself feeling sorry for those with their hands at their side, one of whom included their roommate with the word "REVENGE" tattooed across his back.

"If you make over two hundred thousand, keep your hand up."

All but five put their hand down. Brad was close, and considered keeping his hand in the air. Hell, if you counted the value of his company-paid health insurance, that would do it. He was the last to lower his hand, seeing that Mark and Pamela were both watching him closely to see if he'd fudge. Mark, of all people, knew what Brad made.

Finally only two hands remained in the air for the over-half-million category. One belonged to a woman in her late forties, looking more like a women's correctional officer or a coach than a successful executive. The other belonged to Scott, who had sat next to Pamela on the airplane.

Pamela felt a little buzz starting to reverberate in her stomach. Scott didn't look the part, and he was too nice for it. Scott, all of a sudden, was too good to be true. And because of that, the seminar suddenly had a whole new agenda for her.

The drill went on for thirty minutes. It covered every conceivable and some inconceivable demographic category: self-image, criminal record, sexual preference, belief in God, attraction to someone in the room, career dissatisfaction, unsavory habits, not wanting to be there . . . on and on. No one was spared the momentary humiliation of exposure on some indictment of their humanity, affirming the biblical contention that we are all indeed sinners.

27

Lunch was uneventful, both the food and the forced social gymnastics. Silence had been lifted, but not simply for social graces. The group had an assignment to fulfill. During lunch they were to identify three people: the person among them they'd most like to have a friendship with, the one they'd avoid at all costs, and the person to whom they are most attracted to sexually.

The morning's exercise had put people in a no-nonsense mood, so any chitchat was sincere and often startlingly intimate, as if people were auditioning for the assignment lists to be created after the meal. Brad sat with Mark and Pamela, who was embarrassingly outspoken about her discomfort at having her privacy invaded in a public forum. That would certainly get her on a few lists for question three, Brad thought. Elisa sat at the same table, but other than a few smiles triggered by coincidental eye contact, she and Brad didn't have a chance to talk. But there was no question, at least in his mind, that there was an awareness under way between them, and that an interesting conversation was an inevitability.

After a while people began to break away to complete their assignment, and by the end of the lunch break the lodge was eerily silent. Names were being written down, and most people were afraid to look up from their notebooks.

Brad, however, had finished the assignment in his head before leaving the classroom. Despite having no instructions to the contrary, he eliminated Mark and Pamela from eligibility. The person with whom he believed he could have a meaningful relationship was Pamela's new friend, Scott. He was sexually attracted to Elisa, though the terminology made him uncomfortable. The person he'd most like to vote off the island, so to speak, was Tattoo Jack, though Matt and his mouth and Richard and his sunglasses were close runners-up. Nothing in the instructions said instructors were immune to bad chemistry, or from his vote.

Following lunch, while everyone was struggling with their lists, Brad went back to the assembly hall early in search of a telephone. The need to speak to Beth was urgent, and not simply because he wanted to tell her about his morning. He needed to connect, to remind himself of what was real and what was an exercise. This place was seductive, and he was committed to not being seduced, in any sense of the word.

The building was empty. Inside the front doors was a small lobby, which in turn opened up into the classroom area, though those doors were locked. The group had entered the classroom directly through double doors from the outside patio. Another doorway led into a hallway, through which Brad could look down into what appeared to be an office. Seeing no one around, he took a few steps beyond the door, just enough to peek into the office. On the desk, as he had hoped, was a telephone.

He was halfway through punching in his home number when a hand covered the phone. Brad hadn't heard anyone approach, and his heart jumped to his throat, his eyes wide and guilty.

A huge young man was smiling at him. He wore a white polo shirt, which of course had The Complex logo on the chest, the fabric clinging to a well-muscled torso. The guy was almost as good-looking as Richard—where did they get these people, central casting?

"I'm sorry, Brad, no calls are allowed from here." The smile was formal, almost daring Brad to protest. The huge hand remained on the phone, moving only to allow Brad to put the receiver back in its cradle.

"Sorry, didn't know," said Brad. He extended his hand to introduce himself. The guy was only six-one or -two, but the height difference didn't seem to influence the unique chemistry that exists between two men sizing each other up. Both men knew that Biceps Boy could kick Brad's ass, no problem.

The young man accepted the handshake but instead of saying his name, said, "Sure you did." The smile strained, but remained in place.

The handshake was painful, full of meaning. Brad smiled through it, then just nodded and left the room, wondering when he'd get the chance to talk to Beth. Besides, his lunch was suddenly not settling so well, and he needed to sit down and think.

The session following lunch was more traditional in nature, though still laced with intimidation and insecurity. The group was asked to introduce themselves one by one, using a maximum of two minutes each. Many were squirming before Richard and Georgia finished the brief instructions—there were certain criteria attached to the introduction—and squirmed even more when the two of them left the room completely with the parting comment, "You have one hour. Be sure everyone gets a chance to speak."

No one moved for a very awkward first minute, then Matt jumped to his feet. He was in the middle of explaining that his limiting belief was that he had to slow down so others could keep up with him, a problem he'd had since school, when someone yelled, "Time!" He kept going on about the challenge of patience in his life when the same voice said, "Two minutes!" He talked for another half a minute before he sat down.

As the exercise proceeded, Brad suspected most people were barely listening, too nervous not only about what they would say but how and when they would seize their moment to stand up. Soon several people were standing at once, waging battle for the next turn.

Brad wondered who would be the last to go, knowing, by God, that it would not be him.

He went fifth. His speech was efficient, announcing that his heroes were Bill Russell, Michael Jordan, and Dale Carnegie. His limiting beliefs were that he was certain that he could convince anyone of anything he believed in, which wasn't realistic and often painful when it didn't happen, so too often he didn't try. Sort of a full-circle hitch in his ego. He saved the thing he was most proud of for last: playing major-college basketball, leaving out the part about occupying the end of the bench his entire career. He was going to say something about his relationship with Beth, which was the real answer, but changed his mind, realizing he would be alone to wrestle with his reasoning later on.

Mark went somewhere in the middle of the hour. His comments were surprisingly witty, the group finding his humor dry and fresh. He spoke for less than a minute, saying his limiting belief was his fear of racially motivated judgment, which made him shy and insecure, and that he was most proud of his state of fitness, which he worked on daily.

Pamela surprised her two coworkers when she stood up shortly after Mark. It was amazing how she could summon a modicum of charm when motivated. What a waste of femininity, thought Brad. She was most proud of her ability to bring the talent out in young people, and her heroes were the great painters of the Renaissance. She paused and looked down, then finished with, "And I have too many limiting beliefs to mention here."

There was a hush as she sat down. She wasn't crying, but it was close enough to make everyone uncomfortable.

The first layer of the onion was being peeled away, and the scent of fear and honesty was everywhere. Tears had already been spilled; two women and two men had broken down, and everyone knew more were on the way.

Thirty people, thirty self-assessments. Each participant now had twenty-nine first impressions to revise, to elaborate upon, to ponder, and ultimately to act upon. Mark did the math in his head: there were 870 relationship paradigms under fevered construction, no doubt covering every square inch of the map of human psychology. And that 870 didn't even include the thirty most powerful relationships of all, the reason they had all come here, the work before them: their relationship with self.

Mark was hooked. He had reduced it all to numbers.

2:30 P.M.

A twenty-minute break commenced with the playing of "It's My Life" by Bon Jovi. Many of the group sang along, a few at the top of their lungs.

Water, fruit punch, and coffee were served with mixed nuts from a table in the foyer. A small band of smokers adjourned to the covered porch—Brad hoped Pamela would find lots of new friends there who would not be hazardous to her health.

Small talk was as easy as it gets, with everyone wearing their hearts on their nametags. "So you're in advertising . . ." seemed to be the way to approach Brad, to which he replied, smiling, "Actually, I'm in sales," and it went from there. As he chatted up his new colleagues, he saw Elisa off to the side talking earnestly with a woman, noticing a certain lack of humor in her eyes, appreciating the way she used her hands to fluidly make her points. It was a sensual movement— she'd look good doing sign language. Their eyes met, but both looked away instantly and without expression.

Eyes off, Bradley. What is up with you, anyhow?

He managed to break away from a headhunter from LA for a trip to the restroom, and when he returned to the group, there was a rare moment of solitude as he refreshed his coffee. He felt eyes on him, turning to see Elisa standing before him expectantly.

"So, my airplane hero is a basketball hero, too," she said, her smile sneaky, as if she was on to his little display of ego during his introduction. "What's it like talking down to everyone all the time?"

He grinned appropriately. "I can see right off I'm going to have to be on my toes with you," he said, injecting as much double entendre as she had.

Everything about her seemed different now, with no imminent fear of death or rule of silence to handicap their conversation. She wore a linen pants suit that said money, which wasn't the impression he'd registered on the airplane. A little makeup did wonders, taking years away. She'd been confident yet subdued in front of the group, saying that she was here to send her demons packing like she had her ex-husband. Brad was certain she'd made it onto quite a few lists from the lunchtime exercise.

"I haven't had a chance to thank you for this morning," she said. "I'm sorry I was so pathetic; it's taken me all day to get over it. My stomach is still upset."

"So are you thanking me or saying you're sorry?"

"You're not going to process me, are you?"

"Do what?"

"Process me. That's what they do here: tear into something you say, twist it into something that supposedly reveals some great truth about you, or something that's transparent about you. It's called processing. Get ready for it."

He noticed her hands again—no jewelry, great nails. "You've done this sort of thing before, I take it?"

"Yeah, but I'm back. Glutton for punishment."

"Then I can use you for advice. I won't tell anyone you're willing to hand it out . . . you'll be mobbed."

"Oh, please do . . . anything to be popular."

"I don't think that'll be a problem for you this week."

She smiled, then said, "I do believe you're flirting with me, Mr. Teeters." She took a sip of her coffee, smiling into the cup.

"Really? Maybe I'm just trying to be popular, too." He took his own sip, noticing that their eyes didn't meet during the moment. "Now who's processing who?"

The music started up from the room.

"I do want to hear about your basketball days," she said, tossing the cup into the trash. "I love basketball, especially the college game."

They started to walk in together. "Great," he said. "My place or yours? Wait, I'm flirting again . . . I'll stop."

She just smiled at him, then broke away, as if to ensure that they wouldn't sit together for the next session.

Sitting down, he noticed that Pamela and Scott were walking into the room together and that she was laughing at something he said. Good for him, he thought. Good for her, too.

28

The heavy artillery rolled out that afternoon. Georgia's presentation of the instructions seemed to be deliberately convoluted; listening to her, Brad was reminded of Strother Martin briefing the new prisoners in *Cool Hand Luke*.

Brad felt his body chemistry shifting into panic mode. This was the dreaded dyad: pairings in which each partner was to write in their notebooks their most candid first impressions of the other. Each pairing would last three minutes—long enough to completely devastate the person sitting across from you—before moving on to the next pairing, until everyone had reviewed everyone else.

There were decisions to be made here: whether to be brutally honest or simply honest, whether to go deep or stay in the wading pool, whether to risk or play it safe. The hardest part was knowing that the person sitting across from you was doing precisely the same thing, filleting you into a psychological petri dish, as well.

As fate would have it, Brad's first partner was Matt. He'd jumped in front of him with an expression that was friendly yet knowing in a let's-get-this-over-with sort of way.

Soft, evocative piano music filled the room, which was otherwise silent.

In Brad's opinion, Matt was a certifiable blowhard. It was obvious that he was hiding something under a veneer of macho and ego and that he was insecure and terrified of exposure. But when Brad began writing this down, he very quickly and unexpectedly found himself looking up at the man across from him, who was scribbling furiously. He remained motionless for several seconds before returning his pen to the page, and when he did, he found that his negative energy was giving way to an unexpected empathy.

Brad wrote that he hoped they'd make a connection during the week. He didn't know where this had come from or why, because it hadn't been his intention at all. This guy was an ass—maybe such assessments were no deeper than the moment. Maybe the only criticism worth giving was of the constructive variety. The rest was baloney, and it belonged to the giver, not the receiver.

Either that, or Brad was just being Brad: schmoozing the opposition.

All that, and there were twenty-eight others left to face.

AFTER nearly an hour the exercise was interrupted when one of the men uttered an obscenity loud enough for the entire room to hear. This was followed quickly by his getting up and storming across the room to where Richard and Georgia were observing the group, knocking over a chair in the process. It was Jason Perkins, the guy with the bad comb-over, and he was obviously angry. He had been the most vociferous that afternoon; Brad had heard him use the word *lawsuit* more than once. Brad watched the way he was acting as the discussion with the instructors proceeded, the way he swept his hand toward the room, as if he were representing them in his argument, the way they used their hands to signal that he should calm down.

Finally, red-faced and frustrated, he turned and stormed out the door, slamming it behind him.

"Please continue your exercise," said Georgia, and that was that. Apparently Jason had snapped. The button in him that this exercise had pushed had the word "Eject" on it, and he was gone.

The transitions between periods were awkward, as people moved to new chairs and new partners. There was a tendency to avoid the tough calls. Perhaps this was why Brad and Elisa didn't find themselves in front of each other for a while, and when they did, why it was so difficult to find words. They exchanged small grins as they adjusted their chairs and waited for Georgia's cue, listening to Tchaikovsky's *Romeo and Juliet*.

Brad wrote: "Got to admit, you frighten me. I've been attracted to women before . . . hell, I'm a guy, after all. But we shared something today, and I can't stop thinking about it. For a time all we had was each other, and for a time it seemed like that's all we'd ever have again. Each other. Without a word we were linked, then and there. Silly, isn't it? We didn't even talk. Amazing, how people can connect. Amazing, this thing we call chemistry. I realize it's the context of this place, where the normal rules don't apply, where we are not allowed to hide from each other and play our little man and woman games. I am happily, deliriously happily, married to a beautiful woman. She reminds me of you, actually. In another time, another life, I would be filing my approach with air-traffic control. I guess it's okay to tell you that, here in the safety of this journal. Because it's true. I wonder if it's okay, though, to feel it?"

He looked down at her notebook page, seeing that she had drawn a little flower in the corner of the box next to his name.

He felt himself turning red when he looked up to see that she'd caught him spying. She seemed flustered by this, not able to hold his eye contact as she shifted position to better shield her notebook from view. As he looked closer, he also saw that she was tearing up.

On a lark, he did something similar next to her name: he drew a little smiley face, knowing she was watching him do it.

GEORGIA called for all pencils to be put down just before the hour of five o'clock. Then, amid an ensuing buzz that bordered on protest, she instructed the group to tear out the six pages allotted to this exercise and pass them to Richard or Gary, who were circulating among them. At first a few people refused, but it became apparent that the day would not move forward until everyone complied, which they finally did when Georgia asked humbly for the group's trust.

That's what it was now, an issue of trust. The credibility of the entire seminar was on the line and everyone in the room knew it.

29

After a buffet dinner with a distinctly vegan orientation, the group was summoned to the courtyard in front of the classroom building. As Richard began his introduction to the evening's exercise, Pamela stood up and interrupted him.

"Excuse me, but I have to know something before we go on."

Brad and Mark exchanged worried looks. If anyone in the room was capable of awkwardly calling him out on his sunglasses right here in front of everyone, it was Pamela. But this wasn't her style; she was more of a one-on-one pain in the ass than someone who liked to showcase her attitude. Then again, because this was a trust issue, Pamela's second thoughts weren't all that surprising to anyone who knew her.

Richard didn't say anything. But even his sunglasses, inexplicably still worn here in the dark, couldn't mask his irritation.

"We were wondering . . . what is going to happen to the forms we turned in?"

"*We* were wondering?" repeated Richard. "I thought you said *you* have to know something."

"Well, some of us were talking and . . ."

Brad tried to recall Pamela speaking to anyone other than Scott since they'd arrived, but couldn't. He wondered if Scott was somehow behind this little show.

"So you weren't wondering, you're speaking for some others on this issue, is that right? Did they elect you their spokesperson, Miss Wiley, or are you simply stepping up to the podium on your own volition?"

The team was squirming, lots of glances bouncing around amid twenty-nine puffing clouds of breath condensing in the crisp evening air. Brad caught one from Elisa, who mouthed the word "processing" and winked.

Pamela didn't say anything. After a moment her chin began to quiver. To everyone else it may have looked like she was cracking, but Brad figured she was readying a venomous explosion that would surprise everyone.

"I asked you a question, Miss Wiley, would you like me to repeat it?"

"No." A tear appeared now, which she wiped with the back of her hand.

"Then I'd appreciate an answer."

Nothing happened. The room was still, as if time itself had stopped.

"Miss Wiley, we're not going to go any further until you give me an answer, and there are twenty-eight other people who have paid $10,000 apiece *not* to watch you position yourself as the spokeswoman for all that is just and true in an otherwise unjust and confusing world."

She was fighting back tears, making a response difficult. Brad realized he was seeing something here that hadn't occurred at the office: restraint. Some of the participants openly showed their disapproval of what they perceived to be Richard's attack, which, given Richard's combative mood, Brad thought might be a risky proposition at the moment.

Richard's voice softened, but only a little. "I submit to you, Miss Wiley, that this little program of yours isn't working. It isn't working at the agency, and it certainly isn't working in your personal life. Am I right?"

The asshole had read her file and was beating her over the head with it now.

"No," she sobbed, her eyes on her feet.

Brad raised his eyebrows in surprise, then noticed that Mark was doing the same. This was a Pamela they'd never seen before.

Richard paused, then said, "You can sit down now, Miss Wiley." He smiled at her with sudden and surprising warmth, as if he'd been on her team all along through this little soap opera. Perhaps he had.

"We have something to work on, don't we?"

She nodded, not looking up at him or anyone else, and sat down.

He raised his shaded eyes to the group. "Don't we all, ladies and gentlemen?"

THE exercise began with the group marching through the dark along a dirt road in rather ominous silence. They were headed for an area several hundred yards from the courtyard, though the blackness was complete and compromised only by a half dozen flashlights passed out for the journey. Whether caused by the silence or the darkness, Brad sensed a surreal energy sparking among them as they hiked along.

After about a half mile they entered a clearing surrounded on three sides by tall pines, opening to a canyon. The space was illuminated by spotlights mounted on the trees, and the evening's mist filled this little world with a nightmarish quality, something from a Hieronymus Bosch painting best kept in the gallery cellar. On one side of the clearing a thirty-foot vertical drop opened to the river below, whitewater that emerged from blackness tumbling over huge rocks like moguls on a ski slope before disappearing into opposing blackness. The thick trunks of two pine trees stood twenty feet apart at the edge; if one peered over the precipice, their roots were visible, extending out from the sides of the embankment. Connecting the trees was a long platform about the width of a diving board, positioned about eight feet up. To step off one side was to fall to the ground and possibly break an ankle. To step off the other side was to plummet to certain death.

It took a half hour to explain and demonstrate the exercise, with instructions having to be shouted over the thundering of the river. The group huddled close to keep warm as they listened, the buzz of Gore-Tex gloves rubbing against nylon ski-jacket sleeves providing background percussion. Each participant would step onto the platform, where Richard or Georgia would give them a quiet little pep talk, no doubt connecting the metaphoric aspects of the exercise to their life in the real world. Then they'd walk out to the middle of the platform, where they'd be blindfolded and spun in circles until they were completely disoriented. Standing erect with hands clasped against the chest, shouting out the word "falling!" when ready, he or she would fall rigid into the arms of their teammates. On the ground below the platform the catchers were also being prepped, shown how to stand with arms linked into a human basket, how to bend the knees to cushion the impact. A couple of the guys weighed in somewhere north of two-fifty, so there could be no margin for error.

Trust and integrity. The themes for the day, served with a dollop of primal terror.

The group quickly caught on to the real juice of this exercise. The team of catchers was not remotely random. Georgia had a clipboard, with the names of the catchers predetermined for each participant. They'd extracted something from the case files that made the selection of the catchers meaningful and/or metaphoric.

One woman had a thing about men, particularly strong, good-looking men. She feared them, considered them the enemy. She was the first up and had no idea that Georgia had assembled the ten best-looking guys on the ranch to be her catchers, Mark and Brad among them.

After falling, lying there in the arms of these men, she began to weep. Richard, using a soft voice right off a studio-produced relaxation tape, told her to remain still, to simply *be*, to gaze into the eyes of her teammates that had been there for her. These strapping men, these sexual predators, these human beings. Her weeping was uncontrollable, and watching her, holding her, the catchers began to weep as well.

Matt the loudmouth was caught by ten women. He was a chauvinist and a misogynist in life, and here he was with his ass in their well-manicured hands.

Jason had obvious issues with authority. So his catchers included Richard, Georgia, Gary, and several teammates who had been exposed as upper managers and leaders in their respective careers, again including Mark and Brad.

Mark's fall was delayed while the catching team tried to get organized. Richard was loud and critical, saying things like, "Come on, people, this man's life is in your hands here! Get organized and focused!" The ten contrived and confused minutes were all for Mark's blindfolded benefit. When he fell, he found himself in the arms of the ten smallest people on the property, eight women and two men.

Brad was caught by a group that seemed to have no commonality, none of whom cared that he'd played college basketball or that he was a brilliant conversationalist. People being there for each other. The catcher cradling his head was Elisa, smiling down at him through her tears, chin quivering. In the few moments that each subject was allowed to simply remain in the arms of their catchers, Brad could feel her fingers gently caressing the back of his head.

Pamela was the last to go. She had passed on her turn twice, and by the time she climbed to the platform everyone knew she was terrified. She stood on the platform for fifteen minutes listening to the instructions, unable to ignore the roar of the river below. Every time Richard asked if she was ready, her answer was always no. After a while he had each member of the catching team offer a verbal assurance that they would be there for her, but still she resisted. The team cheered her on until finally Richard called for silence, leaving Pamela alone with her resistance. "You have one minute to decide," he said. "Your teammates are soaked and tired, Pamela."

Brad thought he heard his bunkmate, Tom Turner, who was one of Pamela's catchers, mumble something that sounded like, "You got that right."

Then nothing moved.

After thirty seconds, Pamela began to cry, softly at first, then hysterically. This was something Brad and Mark had not seen before.

"I can't," she said, her voice barely audible.

Georgia walked out to the middle of the board, put her arm around Pamela's shoulders, and whispered in her ear, which seemed to calm her down.

When Georgia was finished and had moved away, Richard spoke so the whole group could hear.

"This is your life, Pamela . . . the opportunities don't come twice." His tone was soft, like a parent consoling a child upon the loss of her pet. "You get to choose. Choose in, or choose out. Choose life, or choose isolation. You have to trust someone, sometime. It might as well start here." A pause, then, "You have ten seconds."

The ten seconds came and went.

"Take off your blindfold and step off the platform," Richard said in a cold tone.

Pamela didn't move.

"Do it now. This exercise is over."

"Wait," she mumbled, her voice full of emotion. She was trembling openly now.

"Too late, Pamela," said Richard. "The exercise is over."

Scott, who was one of Pamela's appointed catchers, said, "Give the lady a break!"

"She had her chance," shot back Richard. "She doesn't need you or anyone else to help her understand what's going on here, thank you." He glared at Scott for a few moments before returning his attention to Pamela, who was pulling off her blindfold, revealing downcast eyes filled with shame.

*   *   *

ON the walk back to the classroom, Doug Vincent fell in next to Brad and Mark, who was walking quietly on his other side. For a moment their footfalls matched perfectly, each step crunching into the dirt road upon which they marched.

"You work with her, right?" A quick flick of his head indicated he was referring to Pamela, who was walking a dozen yards ahead of them, barely visible in the ambient light of the flashlights and the stars. His voice was quiet, out of respect for the moment. The group wasn't exactly on silence, but they had been urged to reverently contemplate the emotions they'd just experienced.

"I do," said Brad. "She's brilliant at what she does."

"She always like that?"

Brad didn't answer at first. Ahead, Pamela and Scott were walking together, his arm about her waist. He had been leaning close and whispering to her the entire way.

"She has a few issues," said Brad, grinning slightly.

"Ad agency, right?"

"Sort of. More a marketing agency, a lot of online stuff, but we're getting into the media."

"No shit? Small freaking world—I run a Web design development shop in Denver."

"What's it called?" interjected Mark, who hadn't appeared to have been listening.

"Hit 'n Run Media," said Doug. "Founder fancies himself a copy guy, I guess."

"Sure," said Mark, "Dan Wellington, right?"

Vincent's face went slack before he smiled. "You know Dan? Glad I didn't say anything I'd regret."

Mark shot Brad a quick look, then said, "Our owner knows him. They hang in the same circles, I think. Some sort of CEO group that meets once a month."

"Asian guy, from Seattle, isn't he? I've seen him; I think I even met him once."

Now it was Brad who glanced at Mark before he said to Vincent, "Ken Wong, of Wright & Wong. Small freaking world."

"Wright & Wong, of course," said Vincent, shaking his head.

They rounded a corner and the illuminated buildings of The Complex seemed to be on fire with light. They walked the last few hundred yards in silence, contemplating the coincidence of their bosses knowing each other, rather than their blindfolded fall into the arms of strangers.

"Just out of curiosity," Brad finally said, "what brings you here? How'd you hear about this?"

Vincent grinned, as if the question dredged up something complicated.

"Actually I didn't. This was all Dan's idea. He was here last spring and came back with his pants in a wad about it. To be honest, I wasn't all that keen on coming, but he wouldn't have it any other way. And it's his dime." He paused. "What Dan wants, Dan gets . . . so here I am."

They were near the door now. Music could be heard from inside the room. Brad's and Mark's eyes met at the exact same moment, and their eyebrows were arched in the exact same manner.

THE session lasted thirty minutes and was consumed entirely with what the experienced personal-growth junkies among them called "shares." Brad noticed that it had been the same small cast of characters who stood up in the front of the group to bare their souls all day long, and this session was no exception. Neither he, Mark, nor Pamela shared, though Brad was genuinely moved when he heard others relate how the trust fall had provided them with a breakthrough. He, too, had been moved by the experience, but not to the point of telling anyone about it. He hoped his breakthrough would come, because he was starting to worry that he was not in touch with whatever higher power seemed to be whispering into everyone else's ear.

As the group walked back to the bunkhouses, Brad saw Elisa standing near the entry to the men's building, each hand rubbing the opposite arm for warmth. From her smile and the way she held his eye contact, he knew she was waiting for him.

He tried to hide his surprise—or perhaps it was his discomfort—when he saw that her arms were now outstretched arms when he was a few feet away. The day had evolved into a hugfest of the first order, so this would not be out of school to anyone walking by. Only, perhaps, for him.

"I need a hug," she whispered—they were supposed to be on silence again—embracing him enthusiastically and holding it for nearly a minute. Brad had no choice but to return the gesture and after a few seconds, surrendered to it, enjoying the scent of her hair and the warmth emanating through her jacket.

When it appeared she had no intention of ending it in the foreseeable future, Brad said softly, "Are you okay?"

He felt her nod, but she didn't say anything. A few moments later she pulled away, and when she did, Brad saw that her eyes were moist and red.

He touched her face tenderly. "What is it?"

She looked embarrassed. "Tell me one thing about your wife," she said. "The one thing, more than any, that makes you love her so much."

Just then, a woman walking behind them toward the bunkhouse whispered, "Silence, children." They watched her depart before returning to the moment.

Earlier they'd both been part of a small group discussion in which each participant talked for one minute about their life, what was either working or not working. Brad had talked about Beth, how he couldn't remember the world before her or imagine it without her.

He pursed his lips, understanding now: Elisa was alone.

"Her fierce loyalty," he said. "That woman would absolutely tear apart anyone or anything that threatened me or our home." He grinned, picturing his wife. "She's like a mother lion, caring for her cubs and guarding her territory. God help you if it's the dinner hour and you're a giraffe who took a wrong turn."

This made Elisa smile. Brad thought another hug was at hand as she moved toward him. He froze when she put her hand on the back of his head and pulled it down toward her upturned face. The kiss was soft, and at first it seemed that's all it was, a kiss between friends, so he didn't pull back. But then the tip of her tongue pressed into his mouth, playing for a moment before he awkwardly turned away.

"Elisa . . . I can't. I—"

"Shhh." She put a finger over his mouth and smiled. Her eyes were near the breaking point, but she held the tears at bay. "I've always wanted someone like you," she said, caressing his cheek for a moment before she turned and walked toward the women's bunkhouse.

Brad watched her go, wondering if she'd turn for a parting glance, but it didn't happen.

30

The rebellious Jason Perkins was back. He was sitting in a chair in the central foyer area in the men's bunkhouse when the team returned from the debrief. A small crowd had engulfed him by the time Brad arrived, and he was telling them about what had happened after he stormed out of the session earlier that afternoon. His voice was barely above a whisper, having been reminded by one of the guys that they were supposed to be on silence. Matt muttered, "Fuck silence," and Jason went on to relate how he couldn't find a way to get off the property.

"They wouldn't take you?" asked Matt, as usual the first with a comment.

"Hell no! I asked if I could use a phone and they put me in this little office, but there was no phone book! I didn't know where to tell the operator to look . . . no cab, no bus, nothing, man! I finally got a cab company in Redding to talk to me, but they wouldn't come out here. Said they didn't even know where the hell I was."

"So basically, they wouldn't let you leave." Matt again.

"Oh, yeah, I could leave. But if I did, I was on my own; they weren't going to drive me anywhere. And there was no refund: I split, my boss's ten grand stays here. Which means, my pending partnership is in the shitter. That made me stop and think. Then this guy— you know, with the big guns?—this big asshole tells me with a shit-eating grin that it's a forty-mile hike to the nearest gas station, that it's getting dark and I'd better get moving. Unless, of course, I wanted to take the direct route, which is twelve miles to the road in the rain as the crow flies over two mountains. Said there was a cafe there, and they'd let you use the phone for free if you could still talk."

Jason turned slightly and pointed toward the hills behind the classroom building.

"Guy was in my face all day, in case I was gonna make a scene or something. I wanted to go back into the session with all of you, but they wouldn't let me. Said I needed to cool my jets. Really pissed me off. It was like Russia, man, the fucking KGB."

There was much response to that, and the volume of the grumbling was suddenly intense. Several guys called for quiet, and the group gradually hushed.

"So what are you gonna do?"

"What choice do I have? Call my attorney? Have my wife come get me? Where do I tell her to come? I'm here, the money's gone, there's no way out. Not realistically. Might as well stick it out." He paused, then added, "Maybe I'm the asshole after all. I mean, that's what they want me to think, isn't it? That it's me?"

"Welcome to the seminar, ladies and gentlemen," said Matt.

"Fact is, we're all trapped, guys," said Jason. "We're lab rats, and the only way out is a bus next Saturday. Unless you're up for a twelve-mile hike over a bunch of mountains. Deal with it."

Then one of the guys who hadn't uttered a word all

day stunned the room back to silence. Brad had noticed him, the lean look of his neck and jaw muscles, the graceful way he moved, his thick flowing hair, jet-black and wavy. He, too, had been a man of few words during his introduction—the only guy who was as invisible was his bunkmate, Tom Turner—and Brad had been challenged to write anything meaningful about him during the feedback exercise, other than he looked like he was in great shape and he hoped they'd get to know each other. Simon, Brad thought, though he couldn't pull up the last name to go with it.

"Provided we don't kill each other first," was what Simon said, not waiting for eye contact or a response as he turned toward his bunk and began to undress.

WITH the crowd of men surrounding and focusing on Jason Perkins, it was easy for one of the men to back away from his teammates without being noticed. He had intended to check his bag first thing once he was back in the bunkhouse—that's just how he works, that's just the kind of guy he is. Thorough. He'd checked it three times already today, and he'd do it again first thing in the morning when the guys were jockeying for their turn in the shower. But the Jason thing had happened as soon as they walked through the door, and it would prove to be a good diversion.

His bunk was in one of the side bedrooms off the main parlor where Perkins was holding court. He sat on a chair and slid the green U.S. Army bag from beneath a table where he'd stashed it in plain sight, where no one would think to pay attention. A combination lock held the zipper in place, and he worked at it between glances up at the door. Once it was open, he slid his hand inside and felt the arsenal of weaponry there: three handguns, two rifles, a hunting knife, six boxes of ammunition, three rolls of plastic packing tape, six sets of handcuffs, two mobile phones, passport folder with cash.

He had checked for no other reason than it made him

happy. He would sleep better for it. Happiness was indeed a warm gun. That, and the half million bucks he'd receive once he'd used it according to plan.

31

On each pillow in the bunkhouse there rested a manila envelope with the appropriate name on it. Inside were thirty familiar pieces of paper clipped loosely together. The top one was what they had predicted the others in the group would write about them during the afternoon's assessment exercise. A reminder of the gap between perception and reality. The others were the assessments themselves. They had been clipped and copied and sorted and assembled, and now they were in the hands of the assessee. No one had known that what they had written would be read by the person they were writing about. No one had suspected that their most private thoughts about the person in front of them would be shared. It was feedback time, no holds barred.

Maybe they should have suspected. Maybe that was the point.

The bunkhouse was suddenly quiet as a tomb. The

muted sounds of rustling paper were the only compromise to the rule of silence now.

MARK sat Indian-style on his bunk and quickly rendered the results into data. Of his twenty-eight critiques, nineteen were largely negative—67.86 percent, Mark calculated within a couple of seconds, rounding up. Not completely scathing, but if you had to check a box, the vote was thumbs down. Three were too close to call, and six were just slightly on the positive side, mostly about his looks.

He read everything twice. Amazing, how you could find a different take on things the second time through. The first read was not to be trusted.

His teammates thought he was aloof. That he was largely absent. Full of himself. Withdrawn. One said he was ripping his teammates off by not being present, not giving of himself. Another said it appeared that he was afraid, and wondered how he'd make it through the week since things were only going to get hairier. This writer wished him well, said it was obvious there was a talented and loving soul beneath that beautiful but timid exterior. Several commented that he was probably just quiet by nature or perhaps shy. Another said his intelligence was obvious but it was all a waste if people didn't want to engage with him, which they didn't.

One said he probably looked hot naked, preferably wet and glistening.

One, however, made him forget the others. It read: "The smart money says you won't survive the week. And I'll be there to watch you go down. Hope you get some fried chicken this week before you crack, wimp. You are alone. If I were you, I'd go home now, before things get ugly."

Mark folded this one up and put it in his pocket, rather than back in the envelope with the others. He was suddenly nauseated and was the first one in the bunkhouse to put down the materials and try to go to sleep. But he was, he believed, the last one to do so.

*   *   *

IF ever there was a situation that called for abundant quantities of nicotine, this was it. So Pamela put on her coat and went outside to a lonely bench under a spotlight next to the dining lodge. It was misting slightly, but nothing short of a typhoon would move her back inside. She was glad no one else was of like mind, because she knew what her reaction to the envelope would be.

What she read surprised her. It even pleased her, once she got past the expected but nonetheless stinging comments. "I think you like playing the bitch," one person wrote, "because you get to hide there, excuse away the hard work of being in relationships with people. It's your cowardice you need to work on, dear, not your bitchiness. And by the way you're not that good at it, either. I could outbitch you any day. But I at least try. I see a nice person in there . . . come out come out wherever you are!"

Now that's feedback, thought Pamela. Dead-on accurate, no holds barred, coated with a little saccharine hope. Good thing these were written before her dressing down by Richard, and then her fiasco at the trust fall.

She winced as she recalled some of the things she'd written. She had no idea, of course, that her subject would actually read it, so she hadn't held back. It was all a hoot, none of it meant to harm, intended only for her own entertainment during what everyone else somehow perceived as a world-shattering opportunity for emotional enrichment.

She'd hoped Scott's feedback about her would leap out of the envelope and into her hands, that his words would sweep her away to a night of wicked thoughts and peaceful sleep. They had connected so easily, and her earlier conclusion that he was too good to be true had been replaced by a sincere desire to simply be in his company. He'd been there for her tonight, not trying to rationalize her failure but rather assuring her that life would go on and that he'd be there for her all week long.

At the end of the evening he'd moved her around the side of the classroom building and kissed her, a hesitant softness soon yielding to a probing tongue and tight embrace. She'd be in his pants before Wednesday at this pace, given half a chance, and that would be just fine with her.

BRAD read through his critiques quickly. His hands were actually shaking as he began, but he was immediately put at ease. For the most part people were kind; they commented on his smile, on how he seemed to have time and a kind word for everyone. One noted his obviously cultivated conversational skills, then questioned his sincerity. "Guys like you are usually working an angle," the writer said, "and I wonder what yours is." One went so far as to say that if they were asked to elect a leader, he would get their vote. Someone else noticed how protective and soft he'd been with Elisa on the airplane. The most critical review came from someone who said they could see through his bravado, that he was as scared as the rest of them, and when push came to shove he'd still have to prove himself, just like everyone else. It ended by calling Brad an arrogant prick.

One slip of paper had a line drawing of a flower next to his name. The writing style was fluid, that of a woman who had excelled in school from the early days when handwriting was graded.

Elisa wrote: "Brad, I told you I had been to a seminar like this before, that I knew what was coming. Only half of that is true—I have been to THIS seminar before, under another name with different instructors, so they don't know who I am. And because of that, I do indeed know what is coming tomorrow. The two, however, are not connected. What I am about to say to you will seem fantastic and incredible, in the very literal sense of the word. I have no real confidence that you will act upon it. But I pray that you will. This is my gift to you. In giving it, I hope that somehow I will be judged mercifully. I know we are in a contrived environment, that everything here is a metaphor, but I cannot help what I feel toward you. This is why I'm taking this risk. You touched me today, Brad, and then you moved me. I've watched how you are with everyone, and I find myself unable to look away. You do not deserve what tomorrow promises. Maybe in another time and place, you and I might have stood a chance. God knows the chemistry is there. Your wife is a very lucky woman. I, on the other hand, am a fraud."

Brad glanced about the room to ensure that he hadn't drawn any attention to himself. Reassured, he returned his attention to the page.

"You must leave this place. Now. Today, as soon as you read this. Do whatever it takes, but you must get off this property. Pretend you are sick, or simply quit and walk away. If you love your wife as you say you do, then do it for her. There are people who want you gone, Brad, you and the others. I know, because I have been hired to be here by those people, to play a role in it. But I cannot. That is all I can say. I am not who you think I am, and this place is not what you think it is. I pray this message makes its way to you and that you will heed my warning. I also pray I do not see you tomorrow. And if I do, please forgive me, and know that I had no choice in the matter."

AN eerie stillness filled the bunkhouse as the men pondered their feedback. Brad took his shaving kit into the bathroom to remove his contact lenses and brush his teeth. Looking into the mirror, he saw that he was slightly pale.

When he opened the leather shaving kit, he found a piece of paper inside, folded into a square. As he opened it he felt the entire day coalesce behind his eyes.

"Brad, just wanted you to know how well loved you are and how proud of you I am for taking this on. You are my hero, and I will always take good care of you. Love, B."

He turned his face away from two other guys sharing the mirror. One of them, the lean and ruggedly handsome man named Simon, seemed to be watching him. In a moment when most would avert their eyes and give him some space to be alone with whatever had moved him, Simon just continued to stare, forcing Brad to look away first.

32

I don't know what's happening to me. One minute I want to be home again, then I can't wait for what they'll throw at us next.

This place is insane. It's like living in a movie—there is no comfort zone, and anything can happen at any minute. I feel like Jim Carrey in The Truman Show. *It's as if what we all think in the real world, in the most private part of ourselves, is what is spoken here. People wear sunglasses at night, and it seems to be okay.*

I'm humbled by my teammates—I've already seen men weep and women curse like longshoremen. People have stood up before the team and confessed things that would make a jaded professional cry for them; a man told us today that his wife committed suicide a year ago. A woman stood up and said that her father had molested her for twelve years growing up and that she'd never told anyone before. The whole team broke down at that one. Do I have problems? Hell no.

Pamela is off to a bad start. I can't tell if she's bucking this or if she simply can't handle it. There's a pretty good guy who seems to have latched on to her, maybe that will keep her afloat. But I still wonder if she'll snap, and when.

I worry about Mark, too. He's like the genius kid in school that skips two grades and finds himself hanging with older children who kick his ass and steal his lunch. Maybe he'll step up.

One guy, Doug from Denver, works for someone who runs in the same crowd as Ken. He was sent here against his will by his boss—sound familiar?—who, like Ken, has been here before, sometime last spring. Coincidence? I wonder. There are no coincidences at The Complex.

I received a warning to leave here, that something bad is just ahead. Was this a joke? A provocation? Don't the instructors read this stuff? Perhaps not. Will I heed the warning? Of course not. Will I remember that I was warned when it happens? That's the question that interests me now.

Everything is suspect, designed to provoke a response. I trust nothing. I am staying, though not with complete peace of mind.

God, we did some scary shit today. I think about all the ways fear affects my life. I guess my major breakthrough of the day is that I have a lot of work to do.

I can't sleep. I'm writing this with the lights out—there's enough brightness coming in from the window because it's a full moon. Of course there is, it's a movie set, and the lighting guy is good. No rain right now. A couple of guys are snoring, but I have a feeling I'm not the only one who can't sleep. Fact is, a lot of us seem to be waking up.

And it's only the first day. My God, how much more can they throw at us?

There are things I'd like to write about, people I'd like to write about, but I won't. Even so, I'm burning this book before I get home.

33

SEATTLE

11:20 P.M.

Beth parked in the visitors lot at the far end of the condo-minium complex. It was raining hard, one of those Seattle rains that sent transplanted Californians scurrying back to their roots in their Range Rovers. Nearly all of the lights in the complex were off at this hour on a Sunday night, which was why she'd waited until now to come.

Beth slipped the key easily into the lock and stepped inside, only then pulling the hood from her head. Pamela had left the light over her stove on for the week, and it was casting pale shadows into the entryway where she stood. She started to pull off her gloves, a function of habit, but changed her mind and left them on.

Her first scheduled watering day was Tuesday. Pamela said she'd give her kids a good soaking before she left, which was, of course, only the night before.

But Beth couldn't wait until Tuesday to see how Pamela Wiley lived.

She stood motionless for a few moments, absorbing the essence of the place. The first perception was one of smell: smoke-saturated fabrics of the rug and furniture that would require incineration to eradicate, a trace of cat urine, the unique odor of indoor plants. The condo was a thirty-year-old apartment conversion, and so it had no style or soul, the floor plan drawn by entry-level architects working on a tight budget.

Beth's heart froze for an instant when something suddenly moved at her feet. It was Pamela's cat, Sophocles, who had emerged from the hallway to greet his company. It rubbed up against her ankles, already purring.

Beth kicked the cat away, hard enough for it to issue a muted squeal and lose its footing on the slick hardwood floor before scurrying for cover in the living room.

Beth used the tiny flashlight on her keychain to navigate through the rooms. She paid little attention to the plants, which were certainly in abundance and legitimately in need of expert care while Pamela was gone for the week.

She started in the living room, inspecting the CD collection, noticing that the television was only a nineteen-inch portable. A rack of books received a close inspection, most of them romance novels, all hardcovers, with a few self-help titles thrown in. One dealt with addiction recovery, another with depression. Those were all in paperback.

Beth put everything back precisely as she had found it.

The refrigerator was interesting to Beth, as much for what it didn't contain as for what it did. There were three brands of beer and all types of cocktail mixers, several flavors of chip dip and salsa, chocolate-chip cookie dough, an unopened package of bacon, and six cylinders of Pillsbury pop-'em-in-the-oven cinnamon rolls. There were also two different prescriptions in dark brown bottles. No juice, no bread, no real food at all.

Our friend Pamela has a death wish, thought Beth, grinning in the darkness.

The bedroom closet was next, a tiny walk-in affair with a chest of drawers along one wall. But after a few minutes of rifling through everything she was disappointed—

nothing from Victoria's Secret, no nasty little mail-order playthings, no letters to savor, no narcotics to pilfer. The clothes were equally boring, nothing Beth would ever be caught dead in.

Pamela had forgotten the fun of being a woman. She had lost the love.

Almost as an afterthought, Pamela opened the nightstand drawer. Resting inside was a silver handgun with a black handle, and next to it was a small cardboard box of ammunition. Beth had no idea what make or model it was. Guns frightened her, in fact. Which was why she was surprised at her reaction when she picked it up with her gloved hands and looked at it more closely. Her stomach was buzzing with a sudden excitement, the kick inherent to a brief caress of the forbidden.

She touched the barrel briefly to her lips and held it there for a moment, enjoying the coolness of the metal. Then she gently placed it back into the drawer at precisely the same angle as she'd found it.

Before leaving she checked to see that the cat had ample food in its dish in the kitchen. Then, opening the door, she surveyed the neighboring windows for lights, and seeing none, slipped out and hurried to her car.

34

Monday
6:00 A.M.

For a moment all the men wanted to kill Gary, who
was referred to by some of the men as Biceps Boy, a
nickname Brad had actually introduced. When they
said there were no alarm clocks at The Complex, they
weren't kidding; they had Gary and his biceps, marching through the bunkhouse wearing a skintight tank
top and boxer shorts in what seemed like the black of
night, banging on an empty five-gallon bucket with a
soup ladle.

As the men silently went about the business of strapping on the outdoor gear they'd been instructed to wear,
someone shouted, "Goddammit!" loud enough for everyone in the vicinity to hear.

Brad turned to see that the source of the expletive was
Matt, who had his back to them and was frantically going through his suitcase, pulling things out and frantically
tossing them to the side as he dug deeper.

Finally he stood erect, drew a deep breath, and shook
his head, his face a deep shade of crimson.

"What is it?" asked Tom Turner, sitting on the edge of

the bunk above Brad, pulling on his socks. Nearly everyone had stopped to watch this play itself out.

Matt hesitated, as if he was considering not answering
the question. When the men heard the answer a moment
later, they knew why.

"My mobile phone is missing," he said. "It was here
last night, I used it to call my wife, in fact. But now it's
gone. Somebody took it in the night."

6:45 A.M.

AFTER a continental breakfast the group assembled in the
general hall. Everyone was keeping their distance from
Matt since he still seemed to be fuming about his phone.

Brad noticed almost immediately that Elisa was not there.

He asked several of the women where she was, but no
one knew. In fact, they weren't aware she was missing, and
now they, too, were alarmed.

As Georgia and Richard entered the building, Brad cut
them off.

"Excuse me . . . good morning . . . we have a missing
teammate, I'm afraid."

They just looked at him with blank expressions.

"Elisa," he said. "She's not here."

The two instructors exchanged a very quick glance.

"Elisa has left The Complex," said Georgia, as if impatient with his intrusion. They kept walking, and Brad
walked with them.

"What happened? She was a friend . . . I want to know."

Finally Georgia stopped.

"Sometimes people can't handle it here," she said. He
wondered if Georgia ever smiled. "The intimacy is too hard
on them, the degree of courage to face it too immense."

"So she's gone," he said, "just like that. She walked
forty miles back to town? I don't think so."

Georgia's face cracked with amusement before she
said, "You're wondering if this is about you, aren't you?"

"Is it?"

"I have no idea. Only you know that. I'm just pointing something out. Where else does this show up in your life, Brad?"

"Where else does what show up in my life?" he repeated in disbelief.

She almost smiled, then quickly walked away.

THEY had been told to bring heavy coats and their best waterproof gear, as it was drizzling outside. The group sat on the classroom floor in a circle, in the middle of which stood Richard, dressed for a day of outdoor work.

"Before we depart for our walk to this morning's exercise," he said, "I would like anyone here who has broken one of the agreements made prior to and after arrival at The Complex to stand up at this time."

Matt shot to his feet with an urgency that seemed to border on defiance. He'd gladly fess up to a flagrantly broken rule for the chance to get his hands on whoever took his precious mobile phone in the night.

Only a few others got to their feet right away with him. For a moment all eyes showered them with what felt like judgment, but then a few more stood as well, as if they'd thought about it and realized they were guilty of something.

After a moment about half the group was on their feet.

Richard glared at the people still sitting on the floor. "I guess the rest of you are the ones who completely honored the rule of silence on the bus and in the bunkhouse last night. Am I confused, or wasn't compliance with the rules one of the things you all agreed to? You did *all* agree, did you not?"

At that moment it occurred to Brad that the instructors had a mole installed in their midst. How else could they know who talked to whom and when?

A few more stood, including Mark this time. Brad was still on the floor, avoiding eye contact with Richard. He was thinking about the strange message he'd received from

Elisa, realizing that it was bothering him more than he thought it would.

Richard stopped in front of Jason, who was still sitting. "How about you, Jason? Didn't you agree to attend the entire program? I seem to remember a question or two about early withdrawal." For a moment it looked as if Jason might reprise his little act of the day before. But he stood up, casting his eyes to the ground.

A few more stood with him. It wasn't his intention, but suddenly Brad realized he was the only person remaining on the floor. Richard was heading his way, walking with his hands clasped behind his back.

Brad scrambled to his feet before Richard got too close. All twenty-nine remaining teammates were standing now.

Richard stopped next to Brad, looking up at his face through his shades.

"Mr. Teeters, good morning."

"Good morning."

"I'd like you to tell the group why it is that you were the last person to stand this morning."

Brad hesitated. To react too fast would smack of insolence, and Brad knew this was a time for contemplative humility. He didn't want to appear defensive or plead guilty. Let the jury decide.

"Well," he said, "I don't think I know."

"Oh, I think you do. Why don't you tell us."

Richard continued to pace around Brad in circles, his hands still behind him. It occurred to Brad that his earlier confrontation with Richard and Georgia about Elisa's whereabouts was most ill-timed.

"I wasn't sure about the question."

"Really? What was it that confused you, Brad? The part about what you agreed to, or the nature of the instructions to stand if you'd violated that agreement? Which?"

"Well, neither. I just . . . didn't stand right away."

"Perhaps your mind was somewhere else this morning?"

"Perhaps."

"But you did violate your agreements like everyone else, isn't that right?"

"Yes."

"And which agreements did you violate?"

"The rule of silence. On the bus, and last night."

He quietly prayed that Richard wouldn't inquire as to the nature of those indiscretions, because he wasn't sure what he'd say in response. Ratting out one's friends was certainly fodder for a seminar moment, and this little seminar moment was shaping up to be a dandy.

"And that's it?" asked Richard, more a statement than a question.

"Well, yeah."

Richard leaned close and spoke softly, low enough that only those nearby could hear. "It isn't working, Brad. Your bullshit is just bullshit here."

Richard walked away. But he kept talking to Brad, louder now.

"You didn't try to use a telephone yesterday, in one of the offices when everyone was eating lunch?"

Brad felt his cheeks going flush. "I did."

"And isn't that an agreement you consented to, that there would be no telephone calls other than in an emergency? Was there an emergency, Mr. Teeters?"

"No. I just . . . no. There was no emergency." He caught a glimpse of Mark, who looked away as their eyes met.

"You consider yourself a man of your word, don't you, Brad?"

"Yes, I do. I did."

"And you wouldn't break your word to anyone here, would you? We can all count on you to do what you say you'll do."

"I believe so. I try." Now he caught a glimpse of Pamela, who didn't turn away. She was enjoying this, he surmised. Bitch.

"Because you're a great guy, and you honor us in that way."

"That's right." This one had a twang of defiance in it.

"But you broke your word to yourself, didn't you, Brad? Wasn't that the real agreement we all made—to ourselves? To follow the rules here? When did you begin selling yourself out, Brad? What about you isn't worthy of the integrity of your word?"

"I—"

"You don't have to answer. Everyone, please sit down."

Brad felt a sea of eyes on him as he lowered to the floor. Thankfully, Richard drew the attention away from him with his wrap-up. Brad had been a prop, and he had played the role of the sap to perfection.

"How often do we do that?" continued Richard, still pacing. "How often do we sell ourselves short, as if we don't measure up, as if we don't deserve integrity? We start a diet, and then we break it; we promise ourselves we'll quit smoking, and it lasts a day . . . we try to forgive ourselves, but we can't. How can others trust us if we can't even trust ourselves? How can others forgive us if we can't forgive ourselves? How can God believe you when you make promises to Him, when you can't keep your word to yourself?"

He was back at the front of the room, surveying the group as if he were sending them to war. General Patton in Ray-Bans.

"Gather in the courtyard in five minutes."

Then he and Georgia walked out of the room. There was no exit music today.

THE march to the morning exercise took an hour and a half and was conducted in complete silence. Gary led the way with a blistering pace that was an irritation for most. If the idea was to tire them out, then their torturers knew what they were doing. It was an off-road hike, straight across muddy fields, over slippery fences, up and then down several forty-five-degree hills the size of an NFL stadium, unnecessarily traversing a stream and then back again to make sure everyone's feet were wet and soon numb.

They marched single file. Mark was a few places behind Brad, and Tattoo Jack was right behind him. Several times during the second half of the hike, Jack placed a hand on Mark's back and shoved him forward. When Mark turned, Jack's smile was of the up-yours variety and full of testosterone-fueled challenge. Mark said nothing, though his stare and Jack's responding taunt grew longer with each exchange.

Scott took a position right behind Pamela. He put his hand on her back from time to time as well, but in his case it was to help her up a hill or over a fallen pine tree, to steady her on a slippery slope, or simply to let her know he was there. Each time it made her smile, though she did her best to hide it from him.

There were grumblings and an occasional profane expletive by the time the group reached a clearing. Like last night's exercise site, the river bordered one side, cutting through a forty-foot crevasse and guarded on both sides by vertical rock walls laced with exposed roots. Only this time there was a network of cables waiting—some extending across the canyon, others looped up to bolts and pulleys affixed to poles or trees. Ropes were everywhere, inexplicable at a glance.

Three strangers stood next to a pole where the cables were anchored, as motionless as the trees. They were watching the group arrive, not a smile among them.

Brad felt something stir in his abdomen as he thought of Elisa and her note.

"Good morning, people," said the largest man when the group had gathered. His build was long and lean and cut from the rocks he'd obviously spent his life scaling. The other man was his exact opposite, quite short and soft-looking. The third was a woman of small stature with the most intimidating glare of all.

"Welcome to hell," the tall man said, his voice straining in an attempt to be heard over the roar of the river. He squinted for emphasis, without a trace of humor.

Brad leaned toward Mark and whispered, "I need to talk to you." But Mark just shot him a dirty look and fixed his attention on their new instructors.

The woman picked it up. "Today's exercise will be a team effort. One team. This is not about competition, it is about survival. It is not about success or failure, because failure is not an option."

The shorter man had his turn now. His voice was

squeaky and high, and several of the men had to choke back a smirk upon hearing it.

"The objective of the exercise is to move your entire team from this bank to the other bank." He was pointing across the canyon. Richard and Georgia stood there holding mugs of hot coffee while chatting with three other strangers, members of the rope crew judging from their climbing duds. Several vehicles were visible through the trees in the distance. "There will be water available, but no food other than some trail mix. You will remain here until the entire team has crossed the canyon. At that time you will be transported back to the facilities for a hot meal."

"This is absurd!" said Jason. It wasn't clear that he intended to be heard, but he picked the one moment when the wind and the water seemed to pause.

"We shall see," said the taller man. "You will have two choices today. You may elect to rappel down the near cliff, cross the river on the beam, then climb the opposing rock wall. Or you may elect to cross the river on the elevated cable you see above the canyon."

No one was looking at the instructor as he spoke. At the bottom of the canyon was a perfectly round and smooth pole, laid lengthwise across the water, which looked as if it had been freshly painted with axle grease. It sagged in the middle, meaning anyone crossing on it would have to contend not only with the issue of balance but with a bouncing movement as well. The river was about sixty feet in width, and every ten feet a vertical pole was bolted upright to the beam, presumably to steady the lucky traveler.

Above the river stretched a thin, taut metal cable, spanning the canyon some twenty feet above ground level, making the fall over the water somewhere in the neighborhood of fifty feet. To access the crossing cable, one had to climb a pole using a series of U-bolts, which were wet and undoubtedly slippery. There were actually two cables to be used for the crossing, one directly above the other, creating a gap of about seven feet. The idea was to hold the upper cable with your wet hands while shuffling along the lower cable with your numb feet.

The whole thing looked to Brad as if it had been designed by P. T. Barnum.

"Safety is our number-one concern today," said the
woman, who launched into a demonstration of the harnesses to be worn by each "crosser." Once fitted with a
harness and an assortment of straps and clamps, nylon
climbing ropes were clipped in place, which were then
looped through crampons and eyebolts solidly affixed to
one of several poles and trees. These then extended down
to ground level, where other teammates would, if theory
held as well as the ropes, have your life in their freezing
hands.

The demonstration of how to get into and secure the
harnesses and then how to man the safety ropes, called
belays, took nearly twenty minutes. It began to rain in the
middle of the demonstration, but the instructors didn't
seem to care or notice. The group was quiet and attentive,
sensing that this would only happen once.

"There is a little catch in the exercise, however," said
the shorter man at the conclusion of the demo, finally
cracking a smile that wasn't remotely infectious. "Just as
there always is in life. The catch is that members of your
team cannot elect the same mode of crossing three times
in a row. If two consecutive crossers elect to rappel-cross-
and-climb, then the next must cross the wires. The climber
after that may again elect. All of which means, some of
you will get to choose, others will not. All of you, however,
will cross the canyon, and all of you will be helping your
teammates into their harnesses and manning the safety
ropes. You will be holding your teammates' lives in your
hands today, let there be no mistake about it."

*There are people who want you gone, Brad, you and
the others . . .*

A few moments of uncertain quiet ensued, accompanied by the sound of tumbling water. Most eyes were on
the ground now.

"Excuse me," said Jason, his hand suddenly thrusting
into the air. "But if this goes down like you say, then the
last people to cross won't have anyone on their ropes."

"Then I strongly suggest you don't go last," said Matt, making a popular point, judging from the laughter. Several others began to chime in. From the worried look on their collective faces, the exercise was not starting off well at all. Which, Brad surmised, was precisely according to plan.

The woman instructor simply held her hand up and waited for quiet. When the grumbling died down, she said, "As a team, you will determine the order of your crossers before you begin. Once established, it cannot be altered. You will have three minutes to establish your order and create shifts for harnessing and manning the ropes. After that, the exercise will be done in silence, with the exception of shouting out support for your teammates during their cross, which you are encouraged to do. Any other conversation or side talk will be considered a violation of the rules, and you will have to start the exercise over from the top. You will all be responsible for suiting up each crosser, three deep behind the person in the pit. When a crosser begins on the ropes, another begins strapping in. Which means, you also must decide who does the strapping in, who does the checking, and who mans the ropes. And by the way, no person may do the same job for more than three crossers in a row."

Several hands shot up immediately. In the moment's pause, Tattoo Jack leaned over Mark's shoulder and said quietly, "Afraid yet? You oughta be."

Mark felt the blood shoot to his head as he turned to see Jack winking at him. He mouthed "kiss my ass," and Jack chuckled.

"If you violate any of the rules of the exercise," said the woman, "anyone already across the canyon must come back to this side—wading, I might add—and the exercise will begin again, in the same order you originally established. I've seen this take as long as eighteen hours, people, so I advise you to be organized and clear."

"One of *us*," chimed in the short instructor with the high tenor voice, "will do the final clearance for each crosser prior to contact with the crossing ropes. No one crosses until we clear them."

There was a pause, during which no one raised a hand.

"Your three minutes begins now," said the tallest man. All three instructors then began to walk toward the side of the clearing, where four sets of harnesses were laid out on the ground.

Brad caught Mark's eye and with an urgent expression clearly communicated once again that they needed to talk. But Mark put a finger to his lips and turned away.

PAMELA turned to Scott and gripped his arm tight enough to tell him that she was upset. Everyone was suddenly talking at once, the volume rising as the so-called leaders among them jockeyed for position.

"I can't do this," she said.

"You know," he said, "that a part of your brain hears you when you talk like that. The part that decides whether you *will* or not."

"Spare me the Tony Robbins bullshit, okay? I'm afraid of heights. Big time."

"So am I," said Scott. He shrugged. "So what do we do?"

He looked so sincere. Pamela realized that he was right without having to hammer it home. There was no real alternative to trying, so why not approach it differently than your innermost fears would have you approach it? Why cave in to a losing proposition out of the box?

"I'll make a deal with you," said Scott. He had put his arms around her and touched his forehead to hers as he spoke. "You be there for me, okay? And I'll be there for you."

"What do you mean? How can I *be there* for you when I'm already here?"

Scott pursed his lips good-naturedly. "In spirit. Moral support. Believing that the other person can do it when the person doesn't believe it themselves. Power of love, baby."

"You really buy into all this shit, don't you?" she said, trying to lighten up.

"Humor me. Be there for me, okay?"

She nodded. "And you for me, then."

He nodded and kissed her on the cheek. "Always," he said.

As he turned away she realized she wasn't as nervous as before, about the fall or about anything else for that matter. For the first time in days, she felt a sense of lightness. She watched him join in the debate over how to proceed.

She'd never met a man like this one, and if she played her normal game, she'd scare him off. So maybe today, maybe this time, she'd try something different.

For Scott. The man who was too good to be real.

35

SEATTLE

10:30 A.M.

Beth was sponge-painting the upstairs guest bathroom when she heard the doorbell. She was going for a Tuscany look, and it just wasn't clicking, so she was grateful she had all week to get it right. Pamela had done it in her bathroom, and if it looked good in that shit-hole, it would look fantastic here. Most of Brad's trips were one-day power jaunts to the Silicon Valley, so she had big plans for the week. After the bathroom she planned on gutting the attic, followed by hand-sewing new curtains in the guest bedroom and a morning or two at the health club. The last time Brad left her for several days, she'd had new carpet installed and the front yard relandscaped. God forbid he ever take an extended trip to Europe or Asia—she'd have a few walls knocked out while recovering from plastic surgery.

It sure beat the hell out of schlepping metabolic enhancers to the neighbors.

The doorbell rang again as she descended the stairs,

coffee cup in hand. After ten-thirty on a Monday morning—could be anyone. It was the wrong day of the week for the Jehovah's Witnesses—or was it the Seventh-Day Adventists?—whom, she realized upon reflection, hadn't been either witnessing or adventing all that much lately.

She froze upon opening the door, seized by a combination of confusion and familiarity. Before her stood two men wearing suits, one a stranger, the other someone she knew. She had forgotten the name but had no trouble recalling the face, a face even more handsome than she remembered. It was the young man from the seminar company, the little fireplug charmer with the wrestler's neck and the European-cut suit who had taken her to lunch to pick her brain about Brad, searching out his deepest fears and childhood issues. He was dressed the same way he was then—very GQ—and his expression was full of familiarity as he extended his hand. In his other hand was a valise from Mont Blanc that cost more than their last vacation.

The second guy, carrying a briefcase of much lesser stature, wore a raincoat over a suit from Sears. He was older, somewhere around fifty, she guessed, with a receding hairline and creased eyes from too many Palm Springs vacations. Unlike the smaller man, he wasn't smiling.

"Good morning," said the one she knew, "remember me? Thomas Stanton, from the seminar? I hope we're not interrupting."

Beth was immediately conscious of her appearance: no makeup, her hair unbrushed, and, worst of all, the fraying workshirt she was wearing, which was actually one of Brad's. The comment struck her as odd—how can someone drop by, out of the blue, and say they hoped they weren't interrupting?

"Of course I remember you, come in . . . I'm such a mess . . ."

"On the contrary, you look quite wonderful." The men stepped inside and seemed to survey the house, which thankfully was magazine-layout ready this morning, as it was every morning.

"I should have called first. This is Ellison Rainey . . . with the FBI."

Instead of shaking her hand, Rainey whipped out his wallet and held forth his FBI identification. Beth found herself studying it for a moment, conscious of her suddenly elevated heart rate. Ellison Rainey, Special Agent. Special at what?

"I don't understand . . . is there a problem?" she asked.

The two men exchanged a quick glance. "Could we impose on you for some coffee?" asked Stanton, glancing at the cup in Beth's hand. "If you have a pot going, that is."

Beth nodded, barely hearing. "I'll be a moment, make yourselves comfortable."

He smiled an acknowledgment. Rainey seemed more interested in the interior decorating than in social graces, as if he were already deep into the assembly of a psychological profile.

The family coffeemaker was nearly empty, and as she refilled it she was aware of her nerves coming to full alert, palms warm, breath short. Yeah, he should have called first. Especially if he was bringing the FBI with him. As the water began to simmer, she looked at herself in the reflection off the black enamel of the refrigerator, unconsciously primping her hair as she wondered what this was all about. Certainly not about her little outing the night before.

She eyed the telephone, filled with a sudden desire to call Wong and demand an explanation. But there was no time, and a phone call now, if detected, would seem out of place to the point of suspicion.

Impatient, she filled two cups with hot water from the sink fixture, dumped in two respective teaspoons of Folgers' finest, and returned to the living room, cups in hand.

"I'm guessing black," she said, handing one to each man.

"That's fine," said Stanton, already taking a sip. Rainey, who seemed nervous, put his on the coffee table, keeping his eyes on the surroundings instead of her.

"I have to assume this isn't a social call," she said, "and from the presence of Mr. Rainey here, that something is wrong. So please cut to it before my adrenaline count gets out of hand and I start to lose my pretense of cool."

"We do have some questions," said Rainey as he opened his briefcase to withdraw a file, which he opened on his lap. Then he removed a pen from his breast pocket and, with a flourish more appropriate to prime-time television, clicked it open.

"Is Brad all right?" she asked, her voice sharper.

"Brad's fine, Beth." Stanton was using that liqueur-smooth voice in an attempt to inject calm into the moment. Then he turned his eyes toward Rainey.

"Your husband and two associates have made an offer to buy out their employer, a Mr. Kenneth Wong, is that correct?"

Beth's eyes bounced between both men, neither of whom moved. She was suddenly relieved that she hadn't called Wong a few moments earlier.

"Yes, that's correct. What's going on?"

"Would you characterize your husband's relationship with . . ."

"His name is Brad."

"Would you characterize Brad's relationship with Wong as a friendly one? Do they hang out, drink beers after work? Or is the proposed takeover more of the hostile variety?"

Beth looked at Stanton as she asked, "What does any of this have to do with you? Something's happened . . . Brad's in trouble. Tell me, dammit!"

The two men again exchanged looks. Stanton seemed to center himself before he went on.

"Something has come up, Beth. Agent Rainey is here to try to head this off before it gets . . ."

"Before the situation takes a serious turn," finished Rainey. "If we can get to the possible root of the issue, we can—"

"What issue? You guys are really starting to piss me off here."

"We're not handling this very well," said Stanton, directing the comment to both Rainey and Beth. "I'm sorry." And again, he turned back to Rainey.

"Okay," said Rainey, closing the file on his lap. "Something *has* happened at The Complex, where your husband is attending the seminar run by Mr. Stanton's company. There's been an intruder. We have a situation unfolding, Mrs. Teeters. Your husband and the others have, for all intents and purposes, been taken hostage."

Beth brought her hands to her mouth, her eyes welling up as her breath froze in her throat. From the hallway Brad's grandfather's grandfather clock chimed. Somehow she managed to say, "Oh, my God . . ."

"Thus far everyone is fine," said Rainey. "No one has been hurt. The situation is static at the moment—"

"What the hell does static mean?"

Stanton jumped in. "It means we don't know much. All lines of communication have been severed except for a cell phone. We don't know who is doing this, or why, other than the fact that a ransom demand has been made. There are three gunmen, maybe more."

"Can't you trace the cell phone?" asked Beth.

"Stolen," said Stanton, shaking his head sympathetically.

Rainey's expression indicated he didn't appreciate Stanton's help. "We have all the standard countermeasures deployed—an experienced hostage negotiator is en route, a psychological profiler is on board, and of course we've secured the area. We've set up a command center in Weaverville, just west of Redding, and the entire resources of the Bureau are at our disposal. We're prepared to handle this, and part of that is checking into who might stand to gain from—"

"Like you guys handled Waco? I feel much better knowing that."

"We've learned a lot since then, Mrs. Teeters."

For the third time, Beth saw the two men exchange knowing glances.

"There is something you should know, Beth. Something which I think, I hope, will make you feel a little better about this. Calmer, at least. Brad and the others . . . this isn't what you'd think it is. They aren't being held at gunpoint, they aren't terrified. In fact, we believe that the participants in the seminar aren't even aware of the situation."

Beth processed this for a moment. She pictured Brad hanging upside down from ropes singing "Kumbaya," or whatever the hell they did at these things, and she almost smiled.

"How do you hijack an entire seminar without anyone knowing?"

Stanton responded. "By being very clever, I'm afraid. Imagine being on an airliner, with a criminal up in the cockpit . . . the passengers wouldn't need to know a thing, at least not at first. The hijacker takes command, negotiates with the ground, the plane very gently changes course, if at all . . . meanwhile the flight attendants serve dinner and the movie runs as scheduled. That's what's happened here, we believe. The students are being protected from the truth, for their own good. As far as they're concerned, the seminar is proceeding as planned."

Beth's tears finally made their appearance. Stanton, as if expecting this, was ready with tissue from his jacket pocket.

"There's one more thing you should know," said Rainey. "A ransom demand has been made. While we never recommend meeting the extortion demands of kidnappers and terrorists, we do believe in covering all contingencies. In this case, that involves you. And all the other families of the hostages."

"What are you saying?"

Now it was Rainey who looked at Stanton, passing the baton.

"Beth, they're asking for a payment from each family for the return of the hostages. It's not an all-or-nothing demand. Those who pay get their loved one back, those who don't . . . don't. Their words, not mine. I'm sorry."

"How much?" she asked impatiently.

"Well, that's another interesting thing here. It's different for each hostage. We think the kidnappers somehow had access to confidential files, because the ransom appears to be on an ability-to-pay basis. And pay quickly."

"How much, dammit?" Beth's voice rose an octave for this one.

"Two hundred fifty thousand for your husband's safety," said Rainey.

Beth covered her face with her hands for a moment. The men allowed her this time, understanding the overwhelming nature of the news.

Finally, Rainey said, "It's up to you, Mrs. Teeters."

Beth looked up. "What do mean it's up to me?"

"I'm saying we will do everything in our power to secure the release of your husband and the others. As far as the ransom goes, it can be a useful negotiating tool, a way to buy some time. The FBI cannot and will not supply any ransom money for you. But if you choose to turn this money over to us, we will use it at our discretion to bargain for the release of your husband, and in the event the money actually changes hands, we will do everything in our power to get it back to you. There are, of course, no guarantees."

Beth drew a deep breath and blew it out with an audible gust. "Are you completely crazy? We don't have that kind of cash lying around!"

Rainey, who was looking at his file, interrupted. "Quick-turn lines of credit, mortgages on jewelry and cars . . . family resources, friends, employers . . . according to your records . . ."

"What records?" Her voice was sharp again.

"We work closely with the IRS and other resources in matters such as this."

"And, I have to be honest," Stanton chimed in, "we provided some of this data to the FBI."

"You told the FBI my father has money?"

"We turned over our entire file on Brad, given the circumstances. We were just trying to help. I'm sorry if that offends you, but—"

"This is . . . too much. It's unbelievable. I have to think . . ."

She stood and began pacing, one hand held to her forehead.

"We—*you*—have until midnight tomorrow to respond, Mrs. Teeters. Or I should say, to produce the money—in cash."

*   *   *

SPECIAL Agent Ellison Rainey departed the Teeters house without further elaboration, promising to remain in close touch. He stressed the importance of speaking to absolutely no one about this situation. He left her a card with a telephone number—but no name, which Beth found interesting—at which he could be contacted, and assured her that she should not hesitate to do so for any reason whatsoever. Thomas Stanton remained behind to comfort and counsel Beth, having arrived in a separate car.

For the first half hour they simply rehashed what they did and didn't know. Some anonymous extortionist with no stated agenda other than profit had somehow hijacked The Complex and was holding the seminar participants hostage against the sum, in Brad's case, of a quarter-million dollars. All lines of communication had been cut off, and the road leading into The Complex had been rendered impassable from what appeared to be an explosion of a bridge. The participants were, as far as Stanton knew because this is what he'd been told, completely unaware of their peril and were engaged in the seminar curriculum otherwise undistracted. Families had until midnight the next day to turn over the money, and it would be wired to a nameless account on the island of Grand Cayman, at which time the seminar would simply run its normal course and everyone would return home as if nothing at all had happened. Those who couldn't—or wouldn't—come up with their share would find that their loved one had suffered some unspeakable fate. Attempts to enter The Complex property would be dealt with with deadly force. Stanton explained the geography of the place—in effect, The Complex was on the floor of a giant bowl, protected on all sides by steep hills—and how that fact supported the threat.

Because of past FBI foibles in hostage situations, the Bureau would be in no hurry to send in covert armed forces, especially since they didn't as yet know whom to shoot at. They would exhaust the negotiation process first and, assured Stanton, were working with some anonymous party operating from an as-yet undisclosed location. They would go all the way with the ransom payments in an effort to avoid casualties.

"When you make your calls," said Stanton, "you need to keep this confidential. This is important. Stick to the issue of the money. Do you understand?"

She nodded. She wasn't sure she did, but perhaps it didn't matter.

Beth went into the kitchen to find a pen and a pad. Stanton remained in the living room while she worked, unaware that for the entire thirty minutes she was alone, not a mark was made on the page in front of her.

36

From the Journal of Brad Teeters

Someone was injured today. I want to record everything, in case this ends up in court, because no one did anything wrong.

The beginning was bloody chaos. Everyone wanted to be in charge, voices raising, tempers flaring. I was one of the bigger assholes, in fact. I knew how we could do this. Mark and Pamela stayed back, going with the flow as usual. In Pamela's case, though, I think she's just trying to keep it together. I'm worried about her.

A lot of ideas were being offered up at once, including mine. One of the guys heard what I was saying, and he got everyone's attention and said that, unless we united, we'd fail, we'd be out here all day and night. Half of the three-minute planning period was gone, and if we didn't come up with something then, the exercise would break down. "This man has a plan," he said, and he was pointing at me. I realized I liked that, because I believed in what I was going to say. I believed in myself.

I told everyone who wanted to cross the wires to stand in one group, everyone who wanted to go down and walk the beam to stand in another, and anyone who didn't know or didn't care to stand in a third. There were seven who wanted to go down, eleven who wanted the wires, and ten who wouldn't commit. I named the seven climbers captains and told them to take one wire person and one no-commit person to compose seven teams, numbered one through seven. We d go in that order. My team would go last, because I thought we had the best chance. Each team would harness the one in front of them. The two teams behind them manned ropes. It was up to the captains to make sure no more than three crossers elected the same method. We'd make up the rest as it went down.

My team was the only one with two people. One woman left the seminar today.

There was a lot that was good. People were stepping into their fears, doing things they didn't think they could do. It rained off and on, and we were all hungry and cold and tired and sometimes pissed off. There were a lot of tears and screaming and temptation to quit. But there were no quitters today. We wouldn't let anyone quit. Jason was really angry, but the instructors wouldn't talk to him. Said he was going to leave, but by God he made it across the wires. Think he learned something about himself. Six people fell into the river, but the ropes kept them from going under. One guy just hung on to the pole, his legs in the water for nearly a half hour, crying like a baby. We all yelled out encouragement, but in the end it was up to him. That's how it is out there. That's what we all had to learn today. It's all up to us.

Mark had a rough go. He froze in the middle of the wires. He kept looking down at the river. You could see his legs trembling, which made the wires vibrate. The big asshole with the tattoos was all over him, yelling about being a pussy, until me and another guy told him to knock it off. I think he meant well, but you never know with him.

Pamela had an even rougher day. She tried to leave several times, but her friend Scott was always there for her. They have forged a strong connection, and thank God for him, because Pamela is ready to crack. She's terrified of heights, of course, but somehow it worked out that she couldn't go down the ropes because the two people before her had done that. Her friend, Scott, finally got her to climb up to the wire. He took her off to the side, and we all watched them holding each other. Not sure what he said, but she gave it a go. It took forever, but she made it across. Some of the people are getting tired of her shit. Can't say I blame them.

As for me—well, it wasn't too bad. I went down the ropes and burned my hands. I slipped off the pole and landed on my crotch, but the pain went away (I think my balls were numb from the cold), and I finally made it across. The rock climbing was the hardest part. I froze a couple of times, didn't think there was a foothold for me. But I could hear people yelling, someone saying this was my life, and I thought of Beth and just went for it. Corny-sounding, I know, but that's what it was. I'll always remember how that felt. Just going for it. Not worrying about failing or how I'd look.

Then there was the accident. A women was injured on the high wire today. One of her safety ropes snapped, and before the other ropes could break her fall, her neck slammed into the lower foot wire. She went limp, just hanging there in midair in her harness. I could tell there was trouble because the instructors just took over, literally throwing the people on the ropes out of the way. One of them went out on the wires without a harness to get her. What was sad was that the lady, Melanie, was so scared when she started. She had trouble taking the first step, and we were all yelling that we'd be there for her, that the ropes were under control. And then this shit happened. She'll never trust anyone for the rest of her life. They took her away in one of the cars, and she's at a clinic down in Weaverville getting checked. She could be dead for all we know. It looked that bad. The instructors and Richard and Georgia had a meeting right after it happened, and there were tempers flaring, I could tell. Then they yelled at us for fifteen straight minutes. I thought they'd call it all off, but we had to finish. The rest of the ropes were inspected carefully, and it all went fine from there.

Everyone is pretty upset. Especially Jason. He says he's out of here, that he's going straight to his lawyer. Yeah, right. Like he's gonna hike forty miles. I don't blame him, actually. Doesn't exactly fill one with a sense of confidence going forward.

We didn't get back here until after three. They've given us a couple hours to rest and write in our journals. No one feels much like talking right now.

I don't know what to feel. I feel alone, yet I'm surrounded by support. I feel tired, yet there's another exercise tonight. I'm also a little confused. Someone tried to warn me about today, said it was dangerous and that I should leave. That was a little frightening and confusing, but I think the person who issued the warning was just a very frightened and confused lady. I was going to talk to Mark about it, but I've decided to let it go. No point in scaring him any more than he is already.

What I'm really scared of is what's next

37

SEATTLE

5:37 P.M.

Stanton left Beth alone for the majority of the afternoon, coming and going several times, occasionally checking in without seeming to want specifics. She was happy to oblige by not giving him any.

Beth was deep in thought, obviously considering all the possibilities.

"What have you got?" he asked. It was near the dinner hour, and Stanton had been distant all day, preferring his mobile phone to her company.

Beth exhaled heavily and closed her eyes for a moment before starting in.

"We have forty thousand and change in a savings account, another thirty in a CD that I can call in early with a penalty. Same with Brad's IRA, though they say they need some kind of documentation, so I don't think that'll work. Our broker says we can convert our account to margin and that he can cut me a check tomorrow for the available credit. There's no time to sell those stocks and get the money by tomorrow, so that's the best he can do. My bank says I can pick up a check tomorrow for fifty thousand on an unsecured short-term loan, with the promise that I'll start jumping through hoops to get a secured second mortgage on the house immediately. I can always sell the cars, but I don't know what I can get. I checked the ads, maybe I can squeeze forty to forty-five out of both.

"You won't get market value," said Stanton, "especially within a one-day time frame. We can put you onto wholesale buyers, sympathetic ones, but even they will bend you over and . . . sorry. You won't get market value. Count on about seventy-five percent."

"Okay, thirty for the cars. My jewelry—"

Beth stopped, biting at her lip and turning her face away. Stanton put his hand on her shoulder and waited for the moment to pass. Finally he said, "There's a better than even chance you'll get it all back, Beth."

"This is so unfair."

"Life is unfair sometimes. We do what we have to do."

She looked up at him. "You've been in one too many group hugs, I think."

"There's no such thing as one too many group hugs, or one too many seminars, if that's what you're inferring. Truth is truth, Beth. Our seminar is about truth, about avoiding the human tendency to make up stories when the going gets tough."

She nodded and returned her attention to the list, tapping the pen on the pad for a few moments.

"Unless everything tanks, I think I've got it covered."

"I've seen this go down before, Beth. You need more resources here."

Her face instantly went red.

"Have you called your father?" he asked, his tone suddenly patient.

From the way she looked at him, it was obvious this was a can of worms. After a moment she said, "That's none of your business."

"You're right. It's *your* business. I simply asked the question."

"Damn straight."

"And how your agenda with your father stacks up against it."

Her body language softened. It was as if the truth, placed squarely on her shoulders, was a weight that pressed her back down into the bar stool on which she'd been sitting all afternoon.

They went over the list a second time, concluding that with any luck they had it covered. A quarter-million dollars wasn't all that tough to get one's hands on in a pinch.

She declined his offer to send someone over, stating that she'd spend the evening gathering documents and putting a financial statement together. She was exhausted, which was unfortunate given what she had to do next.

At the door he hugged her awkwardly, then whispered in her ear.

"I want you to think about something," he said. His grip on her shoulders was tight and his tone grave. "There's another option. Whether you consider it or not is up to you. I bring it up simply to put the entire situation in context."

"I'm listening," she said. With a slight push he got the hint and allowed her to move back.

"You are aware that Brad has a $1 million life insurance policy, with you as the primary beneficiary. You may or may not be aware that he has another $1 million policy through the agency. What you don't know, because he just did it, is that before going to the seminar he purchased a half-million-dollar term policy. All three policies have a double indemnity clause in the case of death due to causes other than disease or medical complications. That's $5 million, Beth, in the event Brad dies in an accident . . . or as the subject of a homicide."

Both of Beth's hands flew to her mouth, and her eyes popped as wide as her suddenly open jaw. She froze like that, staring at him for half a minute. Stanton held her gaze, as if to cement his sincerity.

"What are you saying to me?" she said, barely audible.

"I'm just painting a picture of your options, Beth.

There are always options, and options are the landscape of life itself. Life is nothing if not the sum of our choices."

Their eyes locked, though she could feel her vision blurring.

"I want to be alone," she said, her voice a whisper. Her stomach, which had been in a knot all afternoon, was rolling like a tumble dryer.

Stanton nodded. As he turned to go, he promised to return in the morning to accompany her to the banks and, if necessary, to hawk the cars and jewelry.

Beth watched through the blinds as he walked to his car and drove away. She remained there for several minutes, at the end of which a sly grin emerged on her face.

There were indeed options. Even more, perhaps, than even the handsome Mr. Stanton could fathom.

It was time to have another little chat with Ken Wong.

38

THE COMPLEX

6:45 P.M.

The classroom had been transformed into what was supposed to be a chapel. The lights were dimmed, and the chairs had been set up with an aisle down the middle. One end of the room had been partitioned off with curtains hanging from portable rods extending from either wall. Two sets of portable yet massive candelabras stood in each corner where the curtains met the walls, and next to them on either side were several large flower arrangements. Organ music added the crowning element to the chapel effect.

"Who died?" whispered Matt as the group filed in. No one answered, but everyone considered the question curiously appropriate.

They sat for ten minutes, listening to organ music and exchanging puzzled looks.

Finally, Richard appeared from the side door, walking with his hands folded in front of him. He wore his usual sunglasses and what several guessed to be a $2,000 suit.

He stopped in front of the group, the curtains directly behind him, studying them a moment.

"I want you to think of a child, an infant. Picture the child in your mind. Hold the child, feel the softness of the flesh, the smell of it, like scented powder."

As he spoke, the side door opened, admitting a young woman carrying a baby wrapped in a pink blanket. She approached the first row, handed the baby down to a woman seated there, then whispered something in her ear.

Richard continued. "Look into the child's eyes as she looks up at you, helpless in your arms, trusting completely. Now ask yourself . . . Does this child harbor a single dark thought? Does this child feel prejudice, does she think herself better than any other?"

The woman holding the baby passed it to the person next to her. Everyone in the room could hear it cooing softly.

"Does the child have issues with men . . . issues with money . . . issues with God? Is the child unbearably vain, insufferably selfish? Does the child have the slightest problem expressing herself? Does she fear the room full of people she doesn't know? Does she either crave attention or shrink from it?"

The baby was now passed to a hesitant Tom Turner, who held it awkwardly.

"Does she harbor fear beyond the need for the comfort of her mother's breast? Does she know jealousy? Does she lie and deceive? Can she manipulate knowingly and cunningly? Is cruelty part of her nature? Is she cold and withdrawn? Is she stubborn and spiteful? What does she know of resentment, or of revenge? What does she believe in, and what does she scorn?"

Brad watched another woman take the child into her arms, noticing that she was crying softly, the tears glistening on her cheeks as the soft organ music played on.

"Is the child politically correct? Is she stylish or plain? Is she beautiful or is she ugly? Is she intelligent or stupid? Fast, or slow? Good, or evil? Happy, or unhappy? Blessed or cursed? Lucky or unlucky? Deserving, or not? Gay or hetero?"

Richard continued as the baby passed from teammate

to teammate. Brad noticed how perfectly and slowly he spoke the words, his tone and pace smooth, his emotion genuine. Sunglasses or not, this guy was a total pro.

Several people wiped tears from their eyes.

Brad watched Pamela hold the baby, her face at first completely devoid of emotion. After a moment her chin began to quiver, and she quickly passed the child on to Scott, the two of them looking very much like a couple regarding their baby for the first time.

There was no end to Richard's narrative of the darkness of the human psyche.

"Will she be giving, or will she be selfish? Will she love her parents or long for independence? Will she embrace God or cling to cynicism?"

As Mark smiled down at the infant that was now in his arms, Brad, who was sitting next to him, noticed that no one was looking at Richard anymore.

As Mark handed the baby over to Brad with what seemed an exclusively male lack of confidence, Richard continued to reference chemical addictions, codependence, and various psychological anomalies. The child was completely content, looking up at Brad with her infant smile. He could smell her, that unique scent of innocence. Her gaze locked on his eyes as if pleading for him to listen to what Richard was saying, that her very future depended on it. As he finally handed her across the aisle to a woman whose makeup was already streaked, he felt his own emotions grip him by the throat.

When the baby reached the final person in the last row, Richard stopped, having exhausted his roster of the human tragedy. The room was silent for nearly a minute as the woman, presumably the baby's mother, took the baby in her arms and quietly exited through the side door. The organ music stopped, and the room was completely quiet.

Richard's voice was softer now, almost a whisper.

"Where do we learn these things? Who teaches us these thoughts and behaviors? How do we learn to *be*, to live? And when, I ask you, does the responsibility for the outcome change hands . . . from those who raised us . . . to ourselves? I ask you."

Richard suddenly walked from the room. The soft music continued to play, a lullaby from an old Olivia Newton-John album, written for her own baby daughter.

Brad closed his eyes and drew a deep breath, allowing himself the tears.

GEORGIA entered from the side door when the song concluded. After a moment the organ music resumed, only with a markedly darker flavor now.

"We begin as innocents, yet we die as sinners. We begin with hope and joy, yet we die with pain and broken dreams. We begin as truth, yet we die liars. We begin as equals, yet too often we die as victims."

The curtains behind her parted on cue with her last word, obviously being pulled from behind by unseen stagehands. The room filled with a collective gasp—six feet behind Georgia was a bronze coffin, propped at an angle toward the audience. A spotlight fixed on the closed lid, casting a surreal glow on the gleaming surface.

Next to it was a wide-screen television.

"As you watch this tape," continued Georgia, "I'd like you to think about your own life, and consider this: you began this journey alone, and in the end, you begin the next journey alone, as well. What you make of the time in between is your choice, and it becomes your legacy. You began as a gift unto the world . . . what gifts you leave behind are within you even now."

As the music faded away, Georgia walked to the side and departed through the door. The television screen came to life on cue, with soft guitar music that was both melodic and wistful. A title on the screen read: "Thomas Gifford—A Life."

A series of slowly dissolving still photographs commenced, first of a newborn, then a toddler, then a young boy whose face they would watch mature into that of an adult and then, ten minutes later, of an old man. Without a word of narration, the team learned that Thomas Gifford had been loved by his parents, that he'd had a brother and a sister, both older, that he'd played baseball and been in the Boy Scouts, that he'd played the trombone in a marching band and was skinny as a teenager. He'd become an architect, he'd built houses and strip malls. He'd married his college sweetheart and fathered two sons who would eventually take over his business. He'd been in the Navy and served on a cargo ship. He'd loved dogs and music and was a romantic who worshiped his wife. He'd kept his yard immaculate and his car impeccably polished. He'd believed in God and church and family and was a patriot. He'd had a roomful of grandchildren and retired with a traditional gold watch, and he'd buried his wife when he was an old man with a cane, standing alone next to a grave on a gray and windy day in the Midwest. He had lived for eighty-one years, and now he was gone.

When the video concluded, you could hear the sniffling and the shuffling as people dug for their handkerchiefs. Mark took an inventory through his own veil of emotion, noting that everyone had been moved to some extent or another. The stoic Simon, who rarely changed his facial expression, had a quivering chin. Even Tattoo Jack sat motionless with glistening red eyes.

In the silence that followed, Richard reentered the room. He walked up to the casket and opened the lid. As he did, he looked back toward the audience, as if to judge their response.

What he saw on those faces was complete and utter horror. Because inside the coffin was the dead body of a woman.

The room was still for a few heartbeats. Then Pamela screamed at the top of her lungs, commencing a human cacophony of shock and outrage.

It was Elisa. Her throat had been slashed from ear to ear, the partially crusted blood glistening under the harsh lights of the classroom. Dry, distant eyes remained open, as if pleading for help.

BOOK THREE

REVENGE

39

Seeing the audience's reaction, Richard turned to look inside the coffin for himself. Recognition took only a fraction of a second. He instinctively jumped backward, his mouth gaping open before he tripped over the leg of a plant stand bearing a huge flower arrangement.

Georgia rushed up from the back of the room and leaned over Elisa's body, touching her face tentatively before lifting a wrist to check for a pulse. The effect caused a brief moment of quiet, as if everyone was awaiting a verdict they already knew had come in.

Someone began to cough hysterically. Brad assumed they were getting sick, but he couldn't take his eyes off the macabre sight of Richard and the casket and Georgia screaming for someone to get some help.

A hand gripped Brad's arm, a woman steadying herself. She was gasping, and her sense of balance had suddenly deserted her. Matt stumbled to the double doors leading outside, but they were locked. This realization caused Brad's stomach to explode with a sudden terror. Was this simply the next act? Would there be some grand insight and growth waiting for them when this was done? No, it couldn't be. This was too real. Richard couldn't possibly be that convincing, and Elisa was much too dead.

The look on Georgia's face erased any remaining doubt as she motioned frantically to the large one-way glass panel located next to the office door, screaming to whoever was stationed there to call the police. Quickly she began to choke on her words, coughing violently, unable to scream any longer.

Pamela was hyperventilating with her head buried in Scott's shoulder, her back to the grotesque tableau at the front of the room. Others held the same pose, and the ambient noise level now rose to an extent that no specific words were audible, just snippets of confusion and panic and urgings to calm down.

Someone gasped, then coughed hard enough to vomit.

Richard struggled to get back to his feet but fell back to his knees, knocking the heavy plant stand over and sending the flowers scattering across the floor toward the rows of chairs.

Brad's peripheral vision picked up motion from the side. He turned in time to see Pamela sinking to the ground, her hands still on Scott's shoulders as her legs buckled beneath her. Her eyes had rolled back in their sockets, and her mouth gaped open. Scott tried to support her weight, but together they tumbled to the floor as if in slow motion.

Looking at them, Brad's vision began to blur. A wave of nausea suddenly hit him, like an IV injection that assaults the brain with an inevitable rush, and he felt the sudden desire to sit on the ground.

Behind him, Doug Vincent coughed and then collapsed in a heap, gagging. Sybil Manning tried to break his fall, but his weight dragged the tiny woman with the big heart down with him, and she just lay there next to him, without the strength to get back up. After a moment she appeared to simply fall asleep, using his hip as a pillow.

Within seconds, two other people began a similar descent toward the ground, as if in slow motion.

"Drugged . . ." gasped Mark, who had made his way close enough to Brad to grasp his shoulder before he fell over the backs of a row of chairs.

In front, Richard's eyes had closed, unconscious now. Georgia's eyes rolled back in their sockets as Pamela's had, then her head rolled gently to the side until she was motionless.

Brad felt his knees giving way as the room began to spin. He sank to his knees, taking this cue from the others. Those still standing wore confused and terrified expressions. Muted coughing sounds filled the room, combined with the sound of bodies tumbling, like sacks of sand being tossed onto a dike. Brad hoped he'd go unconscious before he had to throw up. He steadied himself on his hands and knees for a moment, sensing a terrible movement of the room, but then his elbows betrayed him, and he was flat on his stomach. He could smell the musky scent of the carpet. All sound was replaced with a hissing that was more sensation than auditory. He was suddenly grateful that the nausea seemed to be passing; a lot of rock stars died this way, and he always thought it would be a shitty way to go.

Just before he surrendered to the blackness, he noticed that the red rose lying a few feet in front of him was made of plastic.

40

For perhaps the most frightening moment of his life, Brad thought that he had taken Elisa's place in the box. At first he couldn't open his eyes, but his thoughts became gradually more coherent with each passing second, as if emerging from a dream. Gradually he began to gain an awareness of his body, though he couldn't shake the sensation that he was separate from it, the occupant of an inanimate shell.

Soon the shell was tingling, like an arm that has been slept on wrong when the blood is finally allowed back into its veins.

When the moment passed he opened his eyes. He was in the classroom, seated on the floor, propped upright along the wall. Propped, because his hands were bound behind him just tight enough to mean business without compromising circulation. His feet were also bound, though tighter than his hands, causing his feet to go numb. It took awhile for all his senses to align, for the floor to steady itself, and for his mind to admit that everything it saw and comprehended was the real deal now, not some image manufactured by his subconscious.

Several stark realizations arrived at once: all of the students were bound identically and propped like folding chairs against the wall. Everyone's mouth had been covered with silver packing tape. People were stirring, their eyes wide and inquiring. Some were nodding that they were okay, others were shedding tears. A few seemed to be squirming, reminding Brad of those poor little hog-tied calves at a rodeo. They had been positioned symmetrically around the room, about ten feet separating each person. Enough so that if two bound people fell toward each other, like specimens toppling over in a waxwork warehouse, their heads wouldn't touch. It was surreal, a human Stonehenge.

He took a quick inventory and saw that the instructors were not here with them. The casket had been removed as well as the chairs and the funeral props. Even the floors had been cleaned of the fake flowers and the occasional puddle of vomit. Nobody had a nametag anymore. They had been collected while they napped and dreamed of death.

Only now did Brad notice something else. Somehow, as he regained his faculties, he had not comprehended the most glaring oddity of all.

Simon, the quiet teammate with the piercing stare and intimidating presence, sat in the middle of the room. He was not bound hand and foot like the rest of them, though he was as motionless as anyone else. He seemed serene, completely at peace as he straddled a chair backward, his hands folded on the back, chin lowered onto his hands. As if he were studying a sunset. Sitting this way, his forearms looked like thick bridge cables, made all the more intimidating by virtue of an indecipherable tattoo, etched in an Eastern language alphabet. His eyes moved constantly, registering each teammate's arrival back from unconsciousness.

Two people strolled the room, both strangers, both carrying rifles. They were dressed alike, all in black, their coats slick and padded. Ski wear for terrorists. One was a tall, very heavy man with rosy cheeks, about thirty, with the kind of face that got him carded on his night out with the boys. His drugstore-blond hair was about an inch in length on the top and shaved close on the sides. He tried to look bad, in the street sense of the word, but Brad knew instantly he could take this guy if the gun and the packing tape were eliminated from the equation.

Sometimes, he reflected, men just know things like that about other men.

The other henchman was, upon closer inspection, actually a woman. Her sandy brown hair was short and flat, a bit like the early Beatles wore theirs, and the gun looked huge as she cradled it in her arms. Like Simon, her face was lean and taut.

Brad blinked his eyes firmly to clear any remaining effects of whatever had knocked them on their collective keisters.

Simon never moved, other than his eyes, which took in everything as he waited for everyone to return from the land of nightmares. His sneakers looked brand-new—he'd gone shopping for a new kidnapping wardrobe. Brad noticed that the muscles connecting his jaw to the skull just below the ears seemed to twitch, as if he could bite through sheet metal.

The bulky gunman finally nodded at Simon, who stood and began walking around the room. He moved with a casual grace, like a just-drafted NBA player strolling into a press conference. He completed one lap, meeting each set of eyes as he went. Several times Simon raked back his jet-black hair with his fingers, and Brad had the perverse realization that Beth would like this guy, or at least the way he looked: long and lean and in all probability mean as hell. The bad boy with the complicated psyche, the kind of guy women wanted to change with their love.

"You already know my name is Simon," he finally said, continuing his circular walk. The two armed flunkies had stopped at opposite ends of the room, fixing their attention on their leader. "My colleagues in our little adventure are

Morse and Fisher, and you will give them your respect, as you will me."

All eyes glanced at each of them before returning to Simon.

"What you have seen here this evening," Simon continued, "is significant if not for its meaning, then for its implications. The woman in that box attempted to betray us last night. This could not be allowed. Believe me when I say that our initial intention was not to kill her or anyone else. But having compromised that, we decided to put your very pretty friend to use as a demonstration of our commitment to our goals. Perhaps, when you've had a chance to consider your circumstance, you will learn what those goals are."

Simon stopped in front of Brad and seemed to hesitate, allowing the eye contact to penetrate. Perhaps a coincidence of timing, perhaps not.

"Learn from this: betrayal, or any form of defiance, will not be tolerated. Remember her dead face, if you must, when you find yourself considering a similar act, however trivial. If you do as you are told, the chances of your survival increase dramatically."

Brad saw that Pamela, who was positioned directly across the room from him, had her eyes clamped shut, as if trying to block it all out.

"All telephone lines have been severed, with the exception of one, which is in the office adjoining this room. That room will be our primary center of operations, and anyone who attempts to enter that space will be shot. All vehicles on the property have been disabled, with the exception of one van, parked outside, the keys to which are in Morse's pocket. Water will be brought into the room, where you will remain until this is over."

The bathroom, Brad observed, was in an alcove at one end of the classroom. He'd noticed before that there were no windows in the men's room, and he assumed the same was true of the women's room.

Simon stopped next to Matt and looked down at him. "Any remaining mobile phones on the property have been confiscated. If you have one in your possession, I suggest you turn it over at the earliest opportunity."

Fisher moved close to Simon and whispered something in his ear.

"Your instructors and the staff are sequestered elsewhere. They, like you, are safe for now, and are at risk only to the extent they do as they are told and refrain from interfering. Our visit to this little zoo will last approximately twenty-four hours. Who remains behind, and who survives, is completely up to you."

Simon stopped at the feet of Tattoo Jack, who outweighed him by about a hundred pounds. He snickered and shook his head, as if Jack had just challenged his authority with some defiant look in his eyes. It wasn't the first time in the past two days that friction had snapped between them like sparks; then again, Jack had managed to offend just about everyone on the property.

"I will not hesitate to execute anyone who gets in my way." He narrowed his eyes, the dark humor gone. "Are we clear?"

The two men locked eyes. Brad got the feeling Simon could stay that way, cold and fixed, all day long if necessary.

Finally Tattoo Jack slowly nodded, convincing no one.

"We shall see . . . won't we, Mr. Doerst?"

Then he walked through the side door that led to the facilitator's room, followed by Morse and Fisher, who had yet to meet the eyes of anyone else in the room.

8:55 P.M.

AFTER about ten minutes, Morse returned to the room. He charged through the outside doors and marched straight to one of the women sitting nearest to that door. With an odd and unexpected gentleness, he pulled away the tape from her mouth. The room seemed to gasp from behind its collective gag when he produced a knife from his pocket. He used it to slice the tape away from her ankles, then reached behind her and did the same for her wrists. He left the room without a word.

The newly freed woman sat rubbing her wrists. She looked confused, glancing between various pleading sets of eyes and the office doorway. The person next to her, Matt, made a particularly urgent sound behind his gag, and this seemed to bring her to her senses. She removed the tape from his mouth, then worked his wrists free. Matt then undid his own ankle restraints and, unlike the woman, did not hesitate to move to the person next to him to set the pyramid scheme of liberation under way.

Within ten minutes everyone in the room was free, moving about to loosen cramped limbs. Some quickly grouped off in various combinations to commiserate or weep on willing shoulders. Others walked off their stiffness; a few wept alone.

Brad was one of the last to be unbound, by Stu. As the older man was working on him—the tape around Brad's ankles didn't seem to want to give—he saw that Pamela was locked in an embrace with Scott, shaking uncontrollably.

When Stu moved on, Brad found himself alone.

Suddenly a woman to whom he hadn't yet spoken approached Brad, her face streaked with tears, her arms extended. He held her for many minutes, felt her trembling as she sobbed, and for the first time surrendered to the moment, unable to control anything at all about his world. She smelled of hairspray and freshly ironed clothes, though there was nothing fresh about her or anyone else in the room. He began to cry with her, then stopped himself, as he'd always been able to do.

He couldn't crack. He needed to be ready, in case opportunity knocked.

41

SEATTLE

9:15 P.M.

Ken Wong was deep in his evening's routine meditative state when his doorbell sounded. It wasn't your average doorbell chime—no, in this neighborhood you adorned your humble abode with useless accoutrements of the most creative variety, and one of Ken Wong's favorite frivolities had been a $600 digital catalog of animal sound effects that served as the doorbell. Tonight's random selection was reputed to be the mating call of the spotted hyena, the most vicious of a female-dominated species. When he opened his door, it occurred to him that it could turn out to be eerily appropriate.

Ken wore only a pair of loose-fitting and shimmering black silk boxers as he opened the door. His body was, by his own estimation and that of others, a close approximation of perfection, with body fat in the lower single digits, and he wasn't at all shy about showing it off, even to unidentified strangers.

But tonight's caller was no stranger. Not to his house, or to the subtleties of his martial-arts–honed body. It was Beth.

Wong stood aside to allow her entrance, trying to hide his surprise. She was dressed for a casual evening—more like beers and a ballgame than girl's night out—and as she passed he smelled his favorite perfume, Orphee, the official scent of the famous restaurant called Maxims de Paris, where they had dined on snails and smoked fine cigars during an impromptu extended weekend after an international Web-standards conference in Monte Carlo. It had been the first time they had made love, though it was much too violent and bizarre to qualify for that gentle descriptor. It also commenced their two-year affair, commensurate, not coincidentally, with the discovery that her husband had been cheating on her.

He wondered if she was still on the same two-ounce bottle of the perfume, and if she thought of him when she put it on.

"What's up?" he asked, his expression walking the line between confusion and cordiality, taking her raincoat from her after she'd removed it somewhat assumptively.

She said nothing as she turned and headed into the condo, heels clicking on the rough, smoky-gray marble slabs of the foyer. He followed her through the entry hallway, past its thousand-gallon aquarium built into the wall and containing, among other rare creatures, a small sand shark and an infant moray eel, into the great room and its two-story glass wall opening to a spectacular view of the bay and the downtown skyline. The Space Needle was framed front and center, and in the distance on nights much clearer than this he could see the lights of Safeco Field. As condominiums go, this was Seattle's answer to Trump Tower at something around $800 a square foot. The walls here, as in the entry, were of rough-hewn stone, laced with imported wooden beams and shelving. A sixty-inch HDTV screen dominated one wall, the subject of recent cover stories in both an electronics magazine and an interior-design trade journal.

Beth didn't hesitate to collapse into the folds of a plush black leather recliner, which emitted a whoosh of air as it accepted her weight.

"Get you anything?" asked Wong, still standing in the entry. The question was equal parts hospitality and sarcasm.

"Yeah, as a matter of fact," said Beth casually, as if she were ordering a drink. "How's a half million dollars in cash sound?"

Wong sat on the matching couch, which wrapped around a built-in stone table. He selected the end farthest away from his guest, picked up a remote control, and punched a button. A fire popped into existence in the huge fireplace along the two-story sandstone wall opposite the screen.

"Okay," he said, "talk to me."

"You didn't say anything about any ransom money," Beth said. Wong had told her about the use of a great deal of cash in some of the seminar exercises, as much as a half million dollars, he'd said. And while this had certainly captured her imagination, the notion of that money coming from *her* hadn't been part of her thinking.

He leaned forward, brow furrowed, a hand grasping each knee.

"Perhaps you should start at the beginning."

Beth drew a deep breath before beginning, as if she had to tap some deep well of patience to comply.

"Two guys came by today, one from the seminar company, one flashing very impressive FBI credentials. Precisely what you said would happen. They're claiming everyone at the seminar has been taken hostage."

"Of course," said Wong. "That's what I told you they'd say."

Beth narrowed her eyes, shifting uncomfortably. "What I can't figure out is *why* you told me. I mean, the way I figure it, you ripped me off. The kidnapping angle is supposed to be the family's learning experience, their own little mini-seminar, so that when their loved one comes home all safe and sound, they'll understand what they've been taking for granted, blah blah blah. Isn't that what you said? Except I knew it was coming, and any benefit of that experience went out the window."

He shrugged at her. "You said to tell you everything. I know better than to cut you short when you want something."

"You didn't mention ransom money."

Wong stared for a moment before he said, "Perhaps I didn't rip you off, after all."

Beth grinned suspiciously, shaking her head slowly in disbelief.

Wong's face gradually softened into a sheepish grin.

"They knock on your door with the kidnap story and scare the bejesus out of you; they leave you hanging for a day or two, see how you're doing, what you're going through. Then, depending on the person, sooner or later they pull the plug on it and give you their story, make you face what you really feel and believe in your life. Then they leave you to sort it all out by yourself. Make you come to grips with your relationship with money. It saves marriages, changes lives."

Beth shook her head. "There's more to it now, isn't there, Ken?"

Wong got up and began to pace, his eyes on the imported oriental wool throw rug over the imported marble floor. She'd seen this a million times and knew he was processing data and options with incredible speed and insight.

Their eyes locked for a moment before Wong sat back down, shaking his head disgustedly. "They're fucking with me," he said.

"What's this have to do with you?" she asked.

"It was only supposed to be a quarter million, not five hundred. They knew you'd come to me for the money. Think about it—five hundred thousand on one-day notice. They know more than you think they know about your connection to me. They knew you'd come here. That's part of it, you and me. And now I'm faced with a dilemma, aren't I? It's me who has to decide who I trust, what I believe in, and what I'm willing to risk."

Beth bit at her lip and gazed out the window. She started to say that he was dead-freaking-right on that count, but he continued before she got it out.

"They're giving me a little seminar of my own," Wong added.

"That's absurd."

A shadow of a grin played over his face, a memory perhaps. Then he looked at her. "Don't sell these people short. They're capable of anything and very good at what they do. They have resources, an international network of talented people committed to the work. They believe they're changing the world, one mind at a time."

"Sounds like a bad tag line. What do you believe?" she asked.

A distant ship's horn broke the silence, and both of them stared out at the blackness that stretched into the horizon.

"I'm still working on that one," said Wong.

The horn sounded again.

"What if it *is* a scam?" said Beth. "Maybe someone who knows their game decided to cash in for real."

"Nothing is real at the seminar," said Wong. "Except what you feel and how you respond. That, and what you learn from the experience. That's all very, very real."

"Then you don't have anything to lose, do you?"

Beth got up and walked past him, out of the room into the hallway leading to the entry foyer. Wong followed.

Beth was slipping her arms into her coat when he arrived in the arched doorway. He leaned against the cave-like wall and watched, the lights of the aquarium casting a warm aqua glow over his skin.

Beth looked at him and said, "You're going to come up with the five hundred grand, you're going to give it to me, and I'm going to give it to them. If this is real, you've just saved Brad's life. If it's part of the game, then you risk nothing. Maybe we all learn something from it."

"That's a lot of cash on very short notice."

"Deal with it. I need it by ten."

She opened the door, started to leave, then stopped. She turned around and went to where he stood.

When she was directly in front of him, she shoved him back against the rough rock wall. For an instant he thought she was playing—this was a familiar move, part of their dance not so long ago. His mind raced, filled with contradictory hopes.

He winced when his bare skin touched the cold stone. With one hand she pinned him there by the chest, while the other went to his crotch and grabbed both of his testicles in a grip that was firm beyond playfulness.

She allowed him to see the resolve in her eyes before speaking.

"I still own these," she said, her voice barely above a whisper. "Which is why I was wrong a few minutes ago when I said you have nothing to lose."

She leaned close, and the scent of her perfume returned to fill his senses.

"What else haven't you told me? No more surprises, no new little games. Tell me all of it, or you lose these."

She squeezed, and he cried out. He knew he could put her down with one quick move, but she was right about what she owned and what he could lose if he did. Instead he took a few deep breaths and swallowed hard, realizing he'd misread the moment. He wasn't sure if he was relieved or even more alarmed.

"I haven't told you about Mark," he said.

FIVE minutes after Beth's departure, Wong picked up the phone and punched in a number from memory. After a beep he left a message: "This is Wong. Someone call me as soon as you get this. It's urgent."

He hung up and went back into the great room, standing at the window. He rested his forehead against the cold glass as he tried to figure out where he might possibly rustle up five hundred thousand in cash by ten in the morning.

42

THE COMPLEX

10:51 P.M.

The sound of the door opening jolted everyone to attention. Morse burst through with his gun leveled, followed by Fisher, who looked much less comfortable with her role as an enforcer.

The two hours the team had been left alone had been chaotic and unproductive. Most were consumed with various incarnations of primal fear, crying, and looking for ways to express their outrage. Some believed the entire thing was a ruse, resulting in more than one argument, the worst of which—between Matt, who believed, and Tattoo Jack, who didn't—had to be quelled through physical intervention. Scott had been the first to step between them.

Brad spent most of the time quietly going over alternatives with Mark, Doug, Stu, and a few others. Some of the ideas were both courageous and desperate: charge their three captors with teams of five guys each, taking whatever casualties were necessary and inevitable; boost someone up through the hanging ceiling tiles in the hope there was a roof exit. Others were insane: call Simon's bluff in the hope that Tattoo Jack was right, that this was all an exercise of some sort. If they were wrong, they might just get someone killed in the process.

Mark had the best idea: to let Simon play his next hand, at which time they would reconvene their informal counsel and see what could be done. For now they had no alternatives, no way out of the room, and their only hope was acquiring information, which they hoped would be forthcoming.

Pamela never moved from Scott's side. They huddled alone in a corner of the room, whispering occasionally. Judging from her fetal-like position on Scott's lap, Brad feared she was on the edge of losing control. The terror of their situation, coupled with nicotine deprivation and the loss of control, had rendered her nearly comatose.

At one point, however, Scott left her alone and came over to where Brad and the others were gathered. He squatted down Indian-style—it occurred to Brad that the guy had probably been a catcher in younger days—and listened for a few moments.

"Listen, I want you guys to know something," he said, glancing warily at the two-way glass panel next to the office door. "If you need me, if you have a strategy, count me in. Whatever it is, if you need an able body, let me help."

"How is she?" asked Brad, motioning with his eyes to the corner, where Pamela appeared to be sleeping.

"Not good."

Brad just nodded, suddenly loving this man.

That was the moment a fierce banging on the door ended their commiseration.

"**MOVE** to that end of the room," said Morse, pointing as he strode across the floor, obviously a man with a purpose. He had banged on the door before entering to warn a group of people who had settled in close to it. Brad wondered if anyone else noticed the pitch of his voice, high and scratchy. Were it not for the gravity of the situation he would have laughed.

"On the ground," said Morse, using the barrel of his rifle for emphasis.

At that moment Simon strolled into the room, his hands pocketed as if he were cold, or perhaps bored. He dragged a chair with him and positioned it in front of the group, now huddling on the carpet. He sat on it backward and ran his hands through his hair and studied them, in no hurry to begin.

"Who the hell are you?" said someone from behind Brad's vantage point. A woman.

"Who I am is not important," Simon answered.

"You said you'd tell us what you want," said the same woman. It was Sybil Manning, who had proven herself to be among the most outspoken and opinionated of the group. Her emergence as the first voice of outrage surprised no one, including Simon.

"You're not afraid of anything," he said, amused at her tone.

"Of course I'm afraid," she said with disgust. "I'm sitting here with a psychopath and his two lackeys and have no idea why or for how long."

"It's all very simple, really," said Simon. "You are being held hostage against the payment of a ransom by your families or employers. If that money arrives before midnight tomorrow, you get to go home and write a book about this. If not, you get to go home in a box. Nothing more complex than that."

He allowed this to settle in, and it was deathly quiet while it did.

"The FBI—I assume it's the FBI—is already in contact with your families, who as we speak are probably cleaning out every conceivable resource available to save your sorry asses. There's really nothing you can do here, so my advice is to relax, try to get some sleep. There's a long night and day ahead for all of us."

Brad found himself looking down, not sure if this was fear or defiance.

"You, Teeters," said Simon sharply.

Brad looked up.

Simon smiled. "You're quite the big man, aren't you?"

Brad wasn't sure if this was a challenge or an insult. Simon seemed to read his confusion and continued.

"I mean, you manage people, you're cool under pressure. No offense intended."

"None taken," said Brad, though his narrowed eyes betrayed that he was lying.

Simon grinned. "That's good. It is hereby your job to keep your friends safe. You are responsible for their lives. Something goes wrong in here, it's your ass first."

A voice from the rear of the group said, "You're fucking crazy, man."

Simon's smug little smile vanished instantly.

No one moved.

Then Simon grinned again, as if he'd thought it over.

"You're testing me now," he declared, glancing about the room. For the first time his face was flushed with emotion, like a parent tired of being patient with a belligerent child. "I was hoping for something a little more dramatic, something that would require me to demonstrate the consequences of resistance, but this will have to do."

He stood up, kicking the chair to the side, the sudden violence causing everyone to gasp and shrink back a few inches.

"Who said that?"

No one moved. Many looked away as he scanned the room.

"I will ask one more time. Who said that?"

"I did." Sybil Manning stood up. Everyone knew it hadn't been her, including Simon.

He smiled. "Morse!"

The big man lumbered quickly to Simon's side. Simon surveyed the group, squinting slightly.

Then he pointed directly at Mark.

"Take Mr. Johnson outside and shoot him in the back of the head."

A collective gasp seemed to emanate from the group

as Morse charged forward into their midst. Mark tried to get to his feet, but Morse put a size fourteen Doc Martens boot into his chest to put him back down.

"I didn't say shit!" Mark seethed.

Suddenly Tattoo Jack yelled out, "I said it! Try that on me, asshole!" He started to make a move toward Morse, but Fisher took a few quick steps in from the flank and cocked her rifle in his face, freezing him in his tracks.

For a moment no one moved. Then Simon said, "Too late." He nodded for Morse to continue.

Morse outweighed Mark by at least a hundred pounds. He grabbed a handful of collar and began dragging Mark toward the door, despite his kicking and swinging wildly. Brad and Scott sprung to their feet simultaneously, Scott in the lead. But before they could get near Mark, Simon sprung from his chair and, in a move that would have played in slow motion on a movie screen, swept Scott's legs out from under him. Before Scott hit the ground, Simon had him in a choke hold.

Brad froze in his tracks.

Simon was grinning. And now everyone in the room knew why: he was a martial-arts master of some kind, unchallengeable by anyone in the room.

"Stop this," yelled Brad. "We get it, alright? Don't do this!"

Scott's face showed pain, perhaps the fear that his neck might very possibly be broken in the next moment. Pamela started to rush in, already crying hysterically, but was stopped.

Morse had the still-struggling Mark close to the door. A few men and one woman rose to their feet as if to intervene, though there was hesitation in their intentions now. Simon gave Scott's head a little twist to head them off, and the resulting squeal did the job.

Morse kicked the double outside doors open and pulled Mark through. It could have been a father hauling a delinquent son out back to the woodshed, only this licking had far darker consequences.

Simon released Scott and got to his feet. Scott remained

on the floor, rubbing his neck. Pamela came to him now that Simon had stepped away.

"Don't let anything like this happen again," said Simon, pointing at Brad. Then he shuffled toward the other door leading into the office. His hands were pocketed again, and he was whistling.

Moments later, the sound of a gunshot froze everyone.

43

Morse released his grip on Mark almost as soon as the doors dosed behind them. He quickly grabbed Mark from behind by the belt, using the grip to maneuver him to a point halfway along the walk from the door to the gate. Mark was conscious of the cold night air, which instantly heightened his awareness. Morse released him with a shove, hard enough to send him to his knees. Mark's heart pounded inside his chest, yet his thoughts were strangely clear. Perhaps it was adrenaline on both counts, counteracting the narcotic depressant effect of terror.

Or that he hadn't given up. In a moment with no seeming alternatives, there was no time to think, nothing to consider or evaluate. There was only the instinct to survive.

He had fallen onto the pathway that led from the bunkhouses through the sculpted yard to the classroom entrance patio. The pathway was lined with river rock, each slick stone the size of a softball.

A glance back at his captor revealed that Morse was inspecting the chamber of his rifle and that he was focused on some task there. The barrel was lowered and pointing to the side. A much too confident and casual pose. In that instant of recognition Mark's instincts found a confidence of their own.

There was a six-foot gap between them.

Without looking down Mark grasped the first rock his hand encountered. In one motion he used his other hand to push himself back up, pivoting as he raised it up. Morse sensed the motion, but before he could level the gun, Mark's forearm struck the barrel, sending it and the weight of Morse's upper body to the side. Milliseconds later the rock crashed against his temple. He stumbled back against a stone bench, losing his balance and tumbling over it onto his back.

As he fell, the rifle discharged, sending the round into a black sky.

When Morse gathered himself and looked out across the courtyard, he saw Mark's silhouette, sprinting past the gate into the parking lot.

Morse brought the butt of the gun to his chin and squinted down the barrel, bringing the sight to bear on the dark silhouette disappearing into the night.

He lowered the rifle and bit at his lip. He watched a moment longer, until Mark had completely disappeared from view, before he turned and hurried around to the back of the building.

44

Tuesday

12:21 A.M.

Twelve miles, as the crow flies.

This was the all-consuming thought as Mark ran out of the courtyard, across the parking lot, and down the strip of dirt road, barely visible in the dim moonlight, which tonight was diffused by a thin mist. He'd expected to hear the crack of a rifle shot, but he knew he was safe when he reached the central parking area. He took note of the office trailers, all dark, and wondered if this was where Richard and Georgia and Gary were being held. He actually slowed his pace, remembering there were phones there, but then he recalled Simon telling them that the phone lines had all been cut.

Twelve miles. This was what they had told Jason when he was trying to leave the ranch. It was forty miles of road, or straight up over the hills as the crow flies, twelve miles to a road and a cafe. He had to decide now, literally on the fly. The lives of everyone could depend on what he chose.

He sprinted down the road, veering right past the stables, then vaulting a fence to cut through a meadow toward the hills, precisely in the direction Jason had pointed.

He had been spared. The plane had gone down, and he had been bumped to the next flight. The governor had phoned in a pardon. The meaning of it all was less important than the elation of it, combined with a sudden sense of purpose. The realization was like an adrenaline rush, and it fueled each soggy step toward salvation.

It took him half an hour to reach the far end of the valley, about a mile and a half to the north. There were fences and shallow ravines and a few modest rock embankments, but there were no rivers or impossible vertical walls. He rested for fifteen minutes, momentarily safe in the knowledge that the buildings were out of his line of sight. When his mind started to manufacture sounds, he got back on his feet and began his ascent to freedom.

It took another half hour to climb to the top of the hill. He went straight up the side, stopping every hundred yards or so to catch his breath wherever a stump or rock offered him cover. The fear-fueled sprint away from the buildings was taking a toll on his legs now. He never looked over his shoulder toward the valley until he'd crested the summit. Once there, he fell to the ground and allowed his heart rate to return to sanity, conscious of a burning in his lungs that was exacerbated by the cold air. His legs and particularly his feet were numb and throbbing now, but he'd made it. It was time to rest, assess the situation, survey what faced him on the other side.

He climbed on a large rock, sensing an eerie feeling of disequilibrium. A layer of clouds hung less than a hundred feet above him. They were moving, rolling like waves at a beach. He closed his eyes, hoping the dizziness would pass.

It didn't. Whatever had drugged them was still in his system, weighing him down as surely as if he'd had a backpack with a tent and a week's worth of provisions. He realized with some surprise that he was desperately tired.

He should be back there, with them. Fate had intervened, and fate demanded to be repaid. The price would be summoning help, no matter what the toll on his mind and body. But he would be of no value to anyone if his body betrayed him.

The cloud cover seemed to descend around him. Where below there had been mist, now the clouds hugged the very peak upon which he rested. There was nothing to see to the north where he was headed, not even the silhouettes of hills against a skyline. Nothing. When he looked back, he saw that the clouds had obliterated the buildings from his view, as well.

He was in limbo, lost in space, with no reference point. All he had were Jason's angry words: twelve miles, a road, a gas station, a cafe.

His ankle was suddenly throbbing in pain. Maybe it was the shift in blood flow, or the release of the pressure on his ankle as he rested. He'd tripped over something that his eyes hadn't detected in time, but the echo of the gunshot still rang in his ears, and he'd been incapable of feeling pain. Until now.

The more tired he became, he realized, the more often something like that would happen to him. Each step in the dark tempted fate.

He had to rest. Just for a while. Perhaps until dawn, when he could see each footfall. When his head would be clearer and he had a chance.

He slid from the rock to the ground at its base, noticing that his legs had stiffened, and that his ankle protested when it again supported weight. Lying on the ground at its base, he'd use the rock to shelter himself from the biting wind. Each breath hung in front of his face—he estimated the temperature at about forty degrees, and it would only get colder as the night wore on.

So tired. So frightened.

He closed his eyes. Just, he told himself, for a few minutes.

45

When the gun went off, the team had frozen in what would have been a Pulitzer-worthy photograph, twenty-seven gaping mouths, all eyes fixed on the door. A few people could be heard sobbing, and soon many groups had formed to share shock and grief. One joined hands in quiet prayer, led by Sybil Manning.

Some chose solitude, especially the men. Stu, perhaps the oldest among them, sat cross-legged with his eyes closed in what looked like a meditative pose. Tom Turner was prone on the floor on one elbow, wide awake and watching everything closely. Even Matt had nothing to say now. Brad sat alone against the wall with his head lowered and his eyes held closed with the thumb and forefinger of one hand. No one saw his tears.

An hour later the outside doors swung open. Morse entered carrying two huge water bottles by the neck, one in each hand. Fisher held the door for him, her weapon lying awkwardly across her arms like a child carrying a length of wood. In one hand she held a bag of paper cups.

The room was eerily quiet as everyone watched.

As Morse was putting down the bottles, Pamela suddenly shook herself loose from Scott's arms and charged, shrieking something unintelligible, her fists held high. Fisher saw it coming but seemed unsure whether to advance or raise her rifle to blow her away. Pamela got in a few significant blows to the back of Morse's head before Scott reached her and pulled her off. When Morse turned, ready to defend himself, Scott threw Pamela behind him and held up his hands, palms forward, as a sign that it was over. The two men locked eyes as the moment played out, steam dissipating from an overheated engine, before Morse shook his head in disgust and stormed away.

Brad couldn't believe what he'd seen. Pamela, of all people, wouldn't in his wildest dreams be a candidate for suicidal rage. Funny what love can do, he thought. He remembered when it had moved him that way, too, and wondered what had happened over the years, the softening of the edges, a millennium of water rushing over rocks.

Funny, he corrected himself, what this seminar can do.

1:46 A.M.

PAMELA was trembling as Scott led her back to their little corner of the room. He held her in his arms, rocking back and forth as one would a wailing infant, waiting for it to pass. It took several minutes for her breathing to return to an even pace.

"I can't do this," she said, the words muffled as she spoke into the crook of his arm. The skin there was slick, wet with her saliva and tears.

"You can, and you will," said Scott, stroking her hair now.

Suddenly she raised her head, and a moment later shrank back, as if some dark new realization had jolted her back to reality. She stared with wide, confused eyes.

"What do you want from me?" she said, loud enough for others to hear. Several people turned their heads but quickly turned back to their own manner of coping.

"I want you to get a grip," he said. "You can't change this. You can only change *you*, how you respond."

"Spare me the seminar pabulum," she said. Spittle flew from her mouth as she spoke. "I'm not some fucking project for you to work on while you're here!"

"No, you're not." He looked away, biting at his upper lip, obviously stung by her comment. He held the position, fighting off words he might regret saying.

"Then why me?" she asked, her voice only slightly softer. "There's twelve women here, and you glom on to me like I was some kind of fucking catch. I don't understand what you're doing to me!"

She started to tremble again, the last words choked with tears.

"Pamela, listen. I didn't sit next to eleven other women on that airplane when we thought we were going to die. I didn't have eleven other honest conversations about my life and my fears, and I didn't receive eleven other unconditional acceptances in return, okay? And as long as we're being so freaking open and honest with each other all of a sudden, I didn't kiss eleven other women . . . and I don't have eleven other chemical attractions that I have absolutely no control over, other than to acknowledge this one and reach out and hope that my friendship is returned in kind."

He struggled to remain in control of the moment.

"Don't do this," he said, his voice softer. "You always do this."

"You don't know me," said Pamela, barely audible.

"I know you. You're me. Something good comes within close proximity, and if it's big and real enough to pierce our defenses, then we look for a way to shoot it down before it gets too close. Sound familiar, Pamela? We can't see the good in anyone else because we can't see it in ourselves." He paused, his eyes descending with the tone of his voice. "I just wanted this to be different. I wanted *me* to be different."

She started to speak but stopped herself. She just stood there, caught between her truth and his.

"If you want to be alone," he said, "that's your choice."

He got to his feet slowly, pushing on his knee for leverage like an old man, and began to move away.

"Wait!" she said before he got ten feet. This, too, caused several heads in the room to turn.

He turned. Her arms were extended, and her face had completely lost the battle with emotions. He returned to her, and after embracing motionlessly for over a minute, they resumed their position on the floor, leaning quietly against the wall, arm in arm with her head on his shoulder.

Waiting.

2:25 A.M.

DOUG Vincent plopped down next to Brad against the wall, startlingly close. Brad felt it more than he heard it, and realized he must have been asleep. The ensuing adrenaline jolt made him queasy for a moment, and he drew a deep breath to knock it back. He was surprised to see that two other men were with him, sitting on the other side. One was Derek, a serious-minded guy from Las Vegas with pitch-black eyebrows as thick as a carpet sample, and the other was his bunk buddy, Stu.

"You okay?" asked Vincent. Brad hadn't spoken or interacted with anyone since Pamela's aborted attack on Morse.

"No. But I'll make it. You?"

Doug ignored the question and launched into the reason he had come over.

"Derek and I were talking, and guess what. He works for a corporate events and exhibits company, sort of from your world."

Derek smiled nervously, and Brad pursed his lips, nodding in acknowledgment.

"Turns out," said Doug, "that he and his boss"—he turned to Derek now—"hell, you tell him."

Derek leaned across Doug to speak in conspiratorial tones. Next to him, Stu leaned even farther away from the wall to remain a part of this.

"My boss sent me here, like yours did, and like Doug's did. So we were comparing notes about our companies and all. Turns out my boss and Doug's boss know each other."

"Which means," said Doug, unable to stay quiet, "that his boss knows your boss. They're all part of that same little CEO group of theirs."

"Bunch of assholes," said Derek. "Flying off to Maui and Cancun on the company dime once a month to trade secrets and buy each other hookers. It sucks."

"It's their dime," said Brad.

"Yeah, and it's my profit-sharing," said Derek, "which makes it my dime."

"So what's your point?" said Brad. He was digging for more, rather than challenging anything he'd heard.

"Then we're talking to Stu here," said Doug, "and guess what again?"

"His boss knows those guys, too."

"Knows them?" said Stu, slightly incredulous. "Hell, one of 'em is in our office once a week. That is, when they're not all together in Aspen or Orlando."

Brad nodded, and for a moment all four men processed what they'd shared.

Doug broke the silence. "You said you'd made a buyout proposal, right?"

Brad nodded.

"And that he wasn't crazy about the idea. Mad as hell, you said."

"At first."

"Me, too," said Derek. "Not exactly a takeover bid, but close. He signed a letter of agreement when I came on board six years ago that I'd be an equal partner after five years. He's been ducking me for a year now, saying we'll get to it. Come to find out he's entertaining buyout bids from the outside—we're talking ten, twelve million—and I'm sitting here with zero equity and a letter he claims is invalid because it wasn't witnessed and written on a bar napkin, which it was. He's trying to fuck me, the bastard. I've filed a suit, which means he can't fire me or he's in shit up to his elbows. Then all of a sudden, right in the middle of all of it, he's interested in my personal growth and sends me to this seminar."

They exchanged suspicious, nodding looks.

"My man wants me out," said Stu. "He's young, early thirties, thinks I'm an antique. There's no way the little puke can fire me, no just cause, and he's smart enough to know he'd have my lawyer crawling up his ass if he tried. He's asked me to consider early retirement, even made a pretty decent offer. I told him no way. I love what I do."

"What is that?" asked Brad.

"I'm in finance, venture money mostly—executive vice president in charge of operations," said Stu, who was in his early fifties. "Basically, I run the show while he's off with your boss and their bosses, spending our profit-sharing while we shovel their shit. I've tried to talk to him about it, tried to boil it down to a return-on-investment thing, but all it did was piss him off even more that I'd get in his sandbox. Basically, the guy hates my guts, mostly because he's stuck with me."

After a moment of quiet, Brad said what they were all thinking.

"Basically, he wants you dead."

That triggered another moment of silence, each man nodding silently.

"Like his boss wants him dead," said Brad, nodding toward Derek, "and his boss wants him dead," nodding toward Doug.

"And your boss wants you and Mark and Pamela dead," said Doug.

46

4:40 A.M.

A few managed to fall asleep, using each other's torsos and legs as pillows, some reclining arm in arm. The lights had been dimmed, and any conversations were in hushed tones, imparting an essence of a library after hours. Or perhaps a mortuary—the distinct context of death was at hand, sucking the energy from the room like an embalmer's appliance.

They made the rounds in pairs, Brad with Doug, and Derek with Stu. They got right to the point: who sent you here, why, and would they have anything to gain if you came home with a tag on your toe? In the end they discovered two more executives from small firms whose founders ran with the Ken Wong crowd and who stood to gain something significant if they never made it home. That made eight people with direct connections to the CEO group, all of them significant thorns in their boss's side.

They also determined that each CEO had, like Ken Wong, attended this seminar in the past year.

There was more. Two members of the team were currently parties to high-stakes lawsuits against major corporations, one woman had a divorce case going that involved a prenuptial agreement offset with a gigantic life insurance policy, and there was a lawyer who had convicted a union official with mob connections and who had sworn vengeance upon the grave of his dearly departed mother.

Twelve out of twenty-nine people. And that didn't count Elisa, whom someone obviously wanted dead, or any connections that were too subtle or indirect to unearth at this point.

Coincidence? None of them could be sure. It was too outrageous to consider seriously, yet too obvious and convenient to discard. They were huddled in the corner of the room farthest from the office window, sitting in a circle on the floor as they went over it again and again.

"Then what's up with the ransom?" asked Derek. "If they wanted us gone, why ask someone to pay for getting us home safe and sound?"

"A diversion," said Brad. "Something goes wrong, we all go boom, and it looks like a kidnapping fuckup."

"And nobody looks under the right set of sheets," said Stu.

"I don't buy it," said Doug. "I don't buy any of it."

Several moments passed, as they had when any provocative idea surfaced.

"Maybe it *was* the CEO group," offered Stu. "But maybe they're on the level, one of them went through the program, put the others through. They had some kind of personal breakthrough while they were here, realized who butters their bread. They got together afterward and decided to sponsor their core executives, whether we wanted to come or not."

They thought about this a moment, then Derek shook his head, saying, "Not my guy. The only breakthrough he had this year was quitting drinking after totaling his Jag."

"Fact is," said Brad, "it doesn't really matter. Knowing who's behind this doesn't change anything. We're here, it is what it is."

Doug Vincent suddenly got to his feet. "Maybe not," he said. He started to walk away.

"Where are you going?" asked Brad.

"To find out," said Vincent without turning around.

THEY watched Doug Vincent march up to the office door and pound on it with his fist. After a moment the door opened. It was Morse, who immediately shoved Vincent back, then stepped into the room and closed the door behind him. He held his rifle with one hand at his side, something no hunter or soldier would do.

The room stopped its collective heartbeat and listened.

"I'm calling your bluff," said Vincent.

Morse's face contorted into a confused mess, as if he'd just heard the most outlandish statement of his life.

"Are you crazy, man?" he finally said, bringing the rifle to bear on Vincent's chest.

"Yeah, I am. So are you." Vincent took a step toward Morse, allowing his chest to touch the muzzle of the gun. "You're bullshit! This is all bullshit!"

Morse seemed at a loss for words.

"C'mon, fat boy! Right here, in front of everybody!" When Morse didn't shoot, Vincent turned to the team and said, "See? Look at this . . . it's all bullshit!"

Just then the door opened. Simon strode into the room and without hesitating shoved Morse out of the way, taking his place in front of Vincent, whose face quickly drained of its bravado.

"What's the problem here, Mr. Vincent?"

"The problem is, I don't believe any of this."

"That's unfortunate. But it doesn't change anything. And it doesn't necessarily have to get you killed."

"No? How about we take you and fat boy here down, right now? Maybe that would change something, eh?"

Simon smiled, and if anything, seemed to relax rather

than tense for battle. He just stared Vincent down, waiting for him to make his move.

"Come on, show me something! Where are the instructors? Where's Mark's body? How do we know you aren't just a seminar trick, just another airplane going down? I'm calling you out, right here, right now!"

"Morse!" barked Simon. The big man didn't move. "Go get them, bring them here."

Morse nodded and went through the door. Fisher remained at her post, rifle at the ready.

Simon spoke to Vincent now. "Fat boy, as you call him, allowed your friend Mark to get away, I'm afraid, so there's no dead body to see. I hope the bodies of your instructors will satisfy you. And I hope, for your sake, that Mark gets lost somewhere in the hills with the bears and the snakes."

Brad felt his body tense. He was immediately filled with a palpable elation: Mark was alive; he was out there, running through the night. He shot a look toward Pamela, who had heard this and was suddenly alert. She nodded back at him. In that instant he was reminded of their connection and was strangely warmed by it.

The door opened. Richard and Georgia were slowly marched into the room, guided by Morse, who had a hand on both of their collars. They were blindfolded with the same tape used on them earlier, and their hands were bound behind them. The sight of Richard without his sunglasses seemed odd, adding to the weight of the moment.

Morse gave Richard a violent shove, and he stumbled to the floor. Georgia was left standing there alone, teetering slightly in her bondage.

"Believe," said Simon. Then he turned and went back into his office.

Morse waited a few moments after the door had closed. Then he advanced on Vincent, placing the muzzle of his gun under his chin. His grin was ugly as he said, "Believe *this*, motherfucker."

Then he wheeled and pointed the rifle toward Georgia. The blast sent her reeling until her back slammed against the wall. She remained there for a second or two, already dead, then slid down, leaving a grotesque red streak on the wall in her wake.

Among several screams, Pamela's was the loudest.

Morse took a firing position, waving his rifle in an arc to warn anyone who might consider a charge. Fisher did the same, though she didn't look as confident about it.

Then Morse went to where Georgia was lying. He grabbed a fistful of the fabric of her shirt and dragged her toward the outside doors, which Fisher quickly opened for him. The doors slammed closed, leaving them alone once again.

After a stunned moment, several people rushed to remove the tape from Richard's face and wrists.

47

When Tiffany Palofax removed the tape from Richard's eyes, a collective gasp seemed to fall over the room. One of his eyes was blank and stared straight ahead, while the other drooped and flicked from face to face. This man who had been blessed with the looks of a Greek god had a glass eye. Even in the midst of their peril, the seminar moment was not lost on anyone, because everyone in the room had harbored critical thoughts and assumptions about the sunglasses prior to now. Brad wondered when it would have come up in the regular curriculum, certain that it would.

Richard had been drugged with something more potent and enduring than whatever had been served to the rest of them. He'd just seen his partner cut down in cold blood, and it understandably hit him harder than the others.

Ten minutes after Georgia had been shot, Richard emerged from under the veil of the drug to share what he knew. But before doing so, he dug his sunglasses out of his pocket and put them on, conscious that everyone was watching him do it.

He and Georgia had spent the previous hours in a darkened storage room only slightly larger than a closet. Since they were gagged, they were not able to speak, and they'd received no visits from their captors other than a brief check-in from Fisher to verify they were still breathing. He didn't know the whereabouts of Gary or the rest of the staff.

After a while he seemed energized again, breaking character from his cold and distant seminar-guru persona as he fielded questions about himself and the seminar program for which he worked.

Brad asked if he remembered Ken Wong or any of the other CEOs, hoping that something from his recollection might shed more light on their theory. But Richard wasn't sure—a new group came through here every month, each of them unique, each full of high-powered businesspeople looking for more meaning to their lives. After a while, market share and return on investment proved itself to be nothing more than a game, ultimately impossible to win. Soon, many, if not most of them, realized that the real meaning of their lives resided elsewhere.

Then someone asked him how he got here, and the group fell silent, listening. He spoke softly, with the anesthetized energy of a man who had just lost someone he loved. Richard, who was in his early forties despite looking much younger, had been around since the heyday of what was called the human-performance industry, the legacy from which this very seminar had been spawned. He confessed he'd done them all: EST, Lifespring, PSI, Anthony Robbins, Actualization, Dale Carnegie, even a dance in a maroon sarong with the Rashnishies as a teenager. The church of his childhood had failed to provide answers once a few adult realities kicked in, and he'd been searching ever since. He'd walked on fire and jumped from airplanes and been screamed at by every flavor of self-proclaimed guru that came down the pike. Basically it was all the same stuff, and to some extent it all worked. It worked because it was truth. A dangerous truth, perhaps, but truth spun and tailored to the style of the particular mortal man trying to immortalize himself. Lives changed, people grew, cynicism melted away in favor of love and enlightenment. Some even discovered God in a refreshing new way, as Richard had.

It was hard, Richard said, to finally look truth in the eye and not see God there. The harder you looked, the clearer His face became.

"If this turns out ugly," he said to no one in particular at the end of his reverie, "it will mean the end of everything. Everything we've worked for, the entire personal-growth industry, will be history. All we'll have left is organized religion and politics and a few books by M. Scott Peck and Deepak Chopra." He paused. "God help us."

Hearing this, it occurred to Brad that there might be something to think about here. Maybe this wasn't a bunch of renegade CEOs trying to get rid of the people who threatened them at all. Just maybe this was something bigger and much more impersonal. Somebody—a church, a disgruntled graduate, a self-proclaimed warrior of God—was out to quell an entire movement. And as it had been since man had been recording its history, the means toward that end included the slaughter of innocents who just happened to be in the way.

Then again, it was just as likely to be good old American greed: ransom for profit.

God help us, indeed.

48

6:05 A.M.

Mark awoke gradually, the line between his dreams and the emerging morning proving to be a moving target. It was the rain that finally brought him around, and the first thing he realized was how cold he was, and how hungry. Then, when he slowly got to his feet, his legs and especially his ankle reminded him of everything that had happened. A pang of realization kicked him in the stomach, and he knew that what he thought was hunger was something else.

He glanced at his watch. The clouds had retreated to a higher altitude, and there was an ambient glow emanating from the east, allowing him not only to read the time, but to triangulate his position.

Twelve miles. On a normal day that would be six hours, eight hours tops. Today, in this environment, he was looking at a full day. Considering that he really had nothing more to go on than the casually pointed finger of a pissed-off man, maybe longer.

Twelve miles.

At best he'd covered a half mile, probably less.

He had to get moving.

It took awhile for his body to get loose, and he knew enough to do some stretching before he really put it into high gear. The last thing he needed now was a muscle pull or, worse yet, a tear. Going slow, however, was a trade-off with his comfort level. It was cold, and the sooner he got moving, the less the chill would torment him.

At first he walked, and when his legs stopped screaming, he tried to run. Before long he discovered a middle ground. It resided somewhere between running too hard and simply giving up because of the pain, and with the discovery came hope. He'd found this zone through trial and error, running and climbing in spells that left him breathless and unable to move for many minutes. Very quickly those brief respites became unbearable, as his body cooled and the sweat-soaked clothing sucked the body heat from his skin. By pacing himself he could move at a steady pace, climbing to the next crest, resting for a few minutes, then descending into the shadows of a ravine.

He found peace in the half-light of the predawn, and this surprised him. At the root of it was the knowledge that he was invisible, that he could move through the brush and across the occasional clearings unseen. He could hide from everything here, the truth of what he was running from, the fear of what he might find ahead.

Or worse, not find.

And so he ran and climbed, climbed and ran. Not hard, but steady. With a purpose that made it easy, even rewarding, to go on.

49

The Complex

8:10 A.M.

Everyone had stopped talking long ago, retreating to private little hells to play back the movies of their lives.

In his solitude, between moments of intense writing in his journal, Brad found himself noticing how the group seemed to separate during the silences. Tattoo Jack sat alone along the opposite wall, his head buried between his knees with his hands clasped behind his neck. He hadn't moved in a long time; Brad assumed he was sleeping. Either that or he was lost in a state of grief, or perhaps fear, that no one in the room could either fathom or give him credit for. Tom Turner was similarly withdrawn and had watched the screaming and the shooting with a calm that bordered on apathy. Pamela and Scott sat Indian-style near the office door several yards out from the wall, leaning in so their foreheads touched. They had been whispering to each other nearly nonstop, and Brad wondered what had filled their plates so lavishly. Once in a while Scott would stroke her hair, and occasionally they put their arms around each other and slowly rocked to and fro, as if one of them was humming to the other. For a while three people had huddled in a corner, looking around conspiratorially to see that no one could listen in. Several pairings lined the walls, talking on and off, mostly just sitting with their eyes closed. Richard had sequestered himself in the farthest corner from Brad, occasionally glancing around the room as if to evaluate selected individuals. A few still wept, a soft sobbing, usually into a convenient shoulder. Several people lay flat on the floor and appeared to be sleeping.

The lights remained dimmed, adding to the somewhat ironic sense of peace in the room. It was certainly light outside by now, but there was no way for the morning to penetrate the room, where it remained an eternal night. But perhaps the most bizarre element of all was the music that Simon had piped in over the speakers: soothing, even loving, the light melody of a flute. In the dim light it transformed the room into a dreamlike netherworld, the Epcot Center of confinement.

Time passed slowly, and with excruciating clarity.

STU again nestled against the wall next to Brad.

"I just wanted to tell you something," he said when Brad looked up.

Brad nodded his consent to go on.

"In that feedback exercise," said Stu, "the one where we wrote about each other, I said you were an arrogant prick. That was me. I'm sorry I did that. I didn't mean it, I knew I didn't mean it when I wrote it."

If you only knew how right you are . . .

"A lot of us are counting on you," said Stu, averting his eyes slightly.

He got back up, patting Brad on the knee before returning to the solitary space along the wall he'd claimed for the night.

Brad's thought, watching him go, was that he wished

he could tell Mark the same thing. That he was sorry for what he had written about him in the feedback exercise, for all the times he had taken him for granted, or simply not taken him at all.

But Mark was gone. He was somewhere outside, running through the rain.

At least that's what he wanted to believe.

A shiver snaked down Brad's spine, the gravity of this situation suddenly hitting much closer to home. He pictured Beth, imagined cradling her warm body in their bed, going to sleep with his hand resting on the crest of her hip.

I'll take good care of you. . . .

He hoped she would forgive him his frail humanity, the complex contours of his ego, his fits of childlike neediness, his occasional self-absorption. He hoped she would remember him without lingering regrets, because in his very male imperfection he truly did love her perfectly.

50

Seattle

9:33 A.M.

Stanton materialized on Beth's porch just before nine. He wore yet another designer suit, this time under a plush navy wool overcoat and a white cashmere scarf that, in her mind, made him look like a European homosexual. She had trouble keeping a straight face as she opened the door.

"Did you sleep?" he asked.

"What do you think?" Beth wore a soft pastel lime linen pants suit more appropriate to a luncheon than a morning of intrigue and crime.

She handed him a cup of coffee after he took off his coat.

"Has anything changed?" she asked. "This all seems so odd . . . someone kidnaps my husband, holds an entire training facility hostage, and then everything just stops, everyone goes home to dinner, like this was all some nine-to-five routine."

"Believe me, the FBI has been up all night, as have our people. Nothing's changed. We have been assured the hostages are doing fine, that in fact they have no idea anything is wrong. Our instructors are very cool under pressure."

"Right," she said, pursing her lips. Beth had noticed how Stanton seemed to disappear into a wistful reverie when he talked about his seminar.

"This will all turn out fine," he said, touching her arm. She pulled away gently. "Are you ready?"

"I'm going alone," she said.

"I don't understand. We can help you. We have contacts and—"

"I don't need your contacts."

"Now I really don't understand."

"It's handled. I called someone."

Stanton's eyes widened. "You called your father?"

"Who I called is none of your business."

He squinted at her, as if trying to peer behind the crumbling facade. "Is something wrong, Beth? You're different. A bit of a chill today."

"You want the truth?"

"Of course. I deal in the truth."

Beth bit her lip for a moment before starting in. "I think you're full of shit. You and Special Agent Dumbshit . . . I think it's all a crock."

Stanton raised his eyebrows and tilted his head, like a puppy trying to understand.

"You want more?" asked Beth.

Stanton nodded, eyes wide.

"I think this is some kind of seminar thing you're doing, trying to pull me into it. All this talk about my father and me, Brad's life insurance . . . you're trying to push my buttons. And Ramey's about as believable an FBI agent as I am a supermodel."

Stanton gritted his teeth, as if this feedback stung. "Don't sell yourself so short," he said. "Or him, for that matter." He grinned, but quickly went back to business when he saw that Beth wasn't in the mood. "I'm sorry you feel that way. But that doesn't change anything. Your husband is a hostage—that's the hand we've been dealt, whether you like me or if Special Agent Rainey's approach is effective or not. I can leave, if you want . . . we'll keep you informed, roll the dice on the money. Your call, Beth."

Their eyes locked, though Stanton was better in the moment than Beth. His expression was as cold as stone, while Beth was nodding slightly, barely holding back her thoughts. Finally she said, "I can't risk my husband's well-being on a hunch that might just very well be paranoia. But I'm going by myself. You go do whatever you want; I'll be back in an hour with the money."

Now Stanton nodded, though a proud grin was emerging.

"There's one more thing," said Beth, who was in the process of putting on her jacket. "I'm going down there with you. To Weaverville. I want to be there when it's over."

Stanton just stared, very well trained at the art of concealing his thoughts.

"I'm not sure we can do that," he said.

"Oh, you'll do it. Because if you don't, I'll know I'm right. Game over."

She held the door for him, glaring to emphasize her determination to do this her way. Looking back at her, Stanton realized she was used to just that.

She got into her car, parked in the driveway. He got into his, which was parked at the curb. He waited until she had backed out and had driven out of sight before picking up the mobile phone. His hand was shaking slightly as he punched in the numbers from memory.

"**SHE** wants to what?"

Mrs. Pratt's voice was loud enough to bring pain to Stanton's ears.

"You heard me correctly. She's a controller, very much in need of being close to the action, if not in command of it."

"So she's on to it, then."

"Not exactly. Very suspicious, but she's covering her bases. Really rather remarkable, the way she's moving forward despite her cynicism. I say we keep her going. If we pull it now, her feelings of fear won't be validated, only her feelings of paranoia. We reinforce the wrong thing if we pull before she really feels like she might let her husband down and be a widow because of it. Let's have her sweat it out."

"What am I supposed to do with her once she's down here?"

"Put her on hold. Leave her alone with her thoughts."

There was silence on the line. Stanton checked his watch; he needed to call the pilots and notify them to expect another passenger.

"We've never gone this far before."

"Should be interesting."

Another pause. Then, "All right. Make sure Rainey understands what's necessary from him to play this out."

"I'll take care of it."

The line went dead. Stanton turned up the radio before calling the pilots. One of his favorite songs was on, and there was always time to stop and smell the music.

51

10:02 A.M.

"Hi Beth!" The receptionist at Wright & Wong knew Beth well, though she had started working here after Beth's departure from the company. A few years of company picnics and Christmas functions qualified them as bona fide acquaintances, though her expression today was more surprise than pleasure. The smile quickly gave way to an inquisitive set of wrinkles on her forehead.

Beth smiled back. She never liked the woman, probably because she had sucked up to Ken Wong in a way that, if it ever came down to choosing sides, made her Brad's adversary.

"Ken's expecting me," Beth said, the plastic smile barely in place.

"Actually, he's not here. He got called out of town suddenly."

Beth glanced at her watch, feeling something in her stomach kick up its heels.

"But," the receptionist continued, "he said to send you up, that your package is there waiting for you."

Beth tried not to smile too enthusiastically and hurried toward the elevator.

An athletic bag sat on Ken's chair. After checking to see that nobody was likely to barge in, Beth tore open the zipper. Inside were bundles of hundreds. Without holding it above the top of the desk, she quickly counted one of the bundles; there were fifty in each bundle, or five grand. Then, leafing through the bag with her hands, she counted the bundles. There were one hundred of those.

Five hundred thousand dollars.

She couldn't stop herself from smirking as she zipped the bag back up, slipped it under the shoulder strap, and hurried toward the elevator. When the door opened a few minutes later, she consciously wiped the grin away and tried to appear casual, issuing a small wave of farewell to the receptionist. But the woman was on the phone and didn't look up.

Once in her car, she unzipped the bag again, taking fifty of the bundles and transferring them to a large plastic Kmart bag, used the previous Christmas for a purchase of stuffed animals for her two nieces. Then she drove a few blocks away, stopping on a deserted street between two tall buildings. She got out of the car, put the Kmart bag containing the money into the trunk, then got back in and drove away.

BETH made one other stop before heading back to meet up with Stanton. It was a small detour, but there was no way she could head down to the ranch to confront this situation without handling this one last piece of business. She needed to pay a little visit at Pamela's condo. The plants would be in dire need of water, and Sophocles would be done with his stash of Friskies.

And she needed to pick up a few things for the trip.

On the way back home she noticed that her hands were

shaking. She wished she had a cigarette, actually checking the glove box for one. She often indulged her secret little habit when Brad was out of town, and now was as good a time as any.

52

Beth looked out the window of the FBI Gulfstream and watched the gridwork of Portland sliding smoothly beneath them, some thirty-one thousand feet down. The air today was without a wrinkle, and the small jet was quieter than any commercial airliner she'd ever been in. A glass of wine was making the journey even calmer, though the availability of spirits on an FBI aircraft made Beth consider her cynicism even more seriously than before. But she could afford a little cynicism now, and she was prepared to play this out. Rainey sat across the aisle reading a book about loving relationships—an interesting choice for an FBI agent working a ransom case—while Stanton was engrossed in a whispered conversation using the plane's cabin telephone.

They had been waiting for her when she arrived, and actually smiled when she parked the car in the garage and emerged with the athletic bag. She went inside the house without waiting for them to join her, and after a moment's hesitation they followed her in.

She left the bag on the kitchen counter while she went into the bedroom for a few minutes, and when she returned carrying a small suitcase with her provisions for the trip, Rainey was counting the money.

He looked up, a strange expression on his face. "This is amazing," he said, as if he'd just discovered another Dead Sea scroll.

She grimaced and shook her head. "I'm sick to my stomach," she declared, glaring at the money bag.

"We'll take good care of this," said Stanton. "In most cases we get it back."

"You mean the FBI gets it back." Her eyes narrowed.

There it was. Stanton tried to hold her gaze, but the unspoken hung between them like smoke from a bomb going off. She had him now. Or at least, she had everything she needed to move forward with what was beginning to feel like a viable plan, whether he bit down on this hook or not.

The plan had begun to coalesce soon after Wong had told her about Mark, how he was at that very moment lost in the woods, running for his life.

"Of course," he said, finally looking back at her.

"Worst-case scenario," offered Rainey, who seemed clueless to this entire little exchange, "we get your husband back, and the money takes a little longer."

"Worst-case scenario is Brad coming back in a bag," said Beth, popping three pills and chasing it with a full glass of water. When she was done, she looked up and said, "When do we leave?"

The two men exchanged a quick glance. "Right now," said Rainey. "The plane is waiting."

Her expression indicated this confused her.

"You didn't think we were driving, I hope," said Stanton, trying that smile again.

"I don't know what I thought." They were both staring at her, and it occurred to her that if Brad's life was in their hands, he was in bigger trouble than she thought. "I still don't."

Stanton held out his hand toward the door in a "shall we?" type of motion.

"I hope we can earn your trust," he said as they went outside. He carried the bag with one hand and gently guided her with the other hand on her back as they walked toward their car. It was a Ford sedan, which would be a good fit for the FBI. Especially if that's what you wanted someone to think.

Now, less than an hour later, she was riding in a Gulfstream V jet supposedly operated by the FBI, heading to the smallest town in central California, as far as she knew, to see what would become of her husband. She hadn't cleaned out their bank accounts or otherwise destroyed their credit, as she initially thought she'd have to, and she'd had a bit of fun twisting Wong's balls, figuratively and literally, in arranging her own financing. Amazing, the power that men handed to their women on a sterling-silver platter—gold-plated, if the woman preferred it that way. Two hundred and fifty thousand of Ken Wong's dollars were safely stashed in the back of her BMW, and the possibility of her ending up with the other two-fifty wasn't yet out of the question, depending on how things went down. Neither side had tipped their hand at this point, everyone was sticking to their story. If this was really a K&R—the term Rainey had used earlier for kidnap and ransom—then she was doing all she could do for her husband. She hoped she'd get him back in one piece. And if somehow it all went to hell, there would be $5 million in insurance money to help her get back on her feet.

On the other hand, if this was a seminar ruse or perhaps an elaborately staged extortion scheme, well, it wasn't her money at risk, was it. If some of Wong's money got misplaced in the process, he wouldn't be in a position to do much about it.

She was covered on all sides, no matter how it turned out. That was why she was here, on this airplane. To stay in the game, keep her options alive. To simply hand over the money and sit back to wait for a phone call would be to relinquish control. And control had always been something she cultivated. Something she required.

Beth felt underneath her for her purse, just to be sure, before settling back into the plush leather seat. She lifted it an inch off the floorboard, feeling the weight there, and smiled. She took a luxurious sip of the cheap cabernet, holding it in her mouth until it stung the soft flesh beneath her tongue.

There were twelve hours left until midnight, and there were still plenty of options to explore, none of them with any significant downside.

53

THE COMPLEX

2:10 P.M.

Panic was setting in, exacerbated by hunger. It had occurred to many that Simon had abandoned them, which presented its own set of problems, since there was no way out of the room. The place was built like the prison that it had become, with bolted doors impervious to even the most motivated of human attacks. And since the outside world would not expect to hear from anyone at the ranch until Saturday, the prospect of their impending independence from Simon and company wasn't the best-case outcome they had been praying for.

It had been eerily silent during the many hours they had waited, with the exception of constantly shifting combinations of conversations and commiserations. Brad spent several minutes with Pamela and Scott, checking in just to see how she was doing. He came away more worried about her than before; she seemed almost euphoric in her new coupling with Scott, clinging to him the entire time like a schoolgirl. She wouldn't trade this for the world. But it was a recipe for heartbreak, Brad believed, because this wasn't reality, it wasn't life, and in the real world Scott would see the real Pamela and run like hell.

At one point, about two hours earlier, Matt began shouting and banging on the outside doors, trying to get someone's attention. When that didn't work, he switched to the office door, a gesture that was met with heartfelt disapproval from the team, fearing Simon's retribution. A little later Tattoo Jack, as if to dare Simon's retribution, had stood on someone's shoulders to push one of the ceiling tiles aside. He'd asked Brad to help him, and when Brad declined, confessing that he thought it was a foolish risk, Jack called him an asshole and moved on to the next tallest man. Standing on the man's shoulders, he'd hoisted himself up through the opening in the tiles and into the gridwork from which the ceiling was suspended. But he was up there for only a few minutes—they were long minutes, however, since the team feared this would be the moment of Simon's return—coming back with the news that there was no roof hatch to be found and that none of the metalwork holding the ceiling in place could be pried apart without tools. The idea had been to produce some lengths of metal for use as weapons. It was that very notion, actually, that inspired the meeting to which Brad was about to be summoned.

Brad heard his name being called. He looked up to see six or seven men sitting together along the wall, situated a few yards down from the office window. It was the one place in the room where anyone observing them from within the office would not have a clear line of sight.

Stu was urgently motioning him over.

Brad got up and began to pace, which several people were already doing, stretching their legs after hours on the hard floor. He strolled to the end of the room, then toward the wall, where he hurriedly joined them. Scott was also present, having left Pamela alone for the first time since the ordeal began.

"We have an idea," said Derek.

Stu jumped in, which Derek didn't seem to like, though he said nothing. "There's a four-by-six mirror in the bathroom," he said, casting a quick glance toward the office glass. "Someone goes in there and uses a boot heel or a fist wrapped in a shirt, whatever, and smashes the hell out of it. We take the biggest shards of the broken glass, we conceal them under our clothing. Then, when the opportunity presents itself, we jump the bastards. Cut them to whatever extent we need to take the rifles away."

All of the men were looking at Brad, as if his approval was required to move forward.

Brad nodded thoughtfully, not wanting to rain on this parade with his opening volley. But the nod was the only thing he could think of in the way of encouragement, and it was fading quickly.

"So how do you keep from cutting off your fingers when you strike with the glass?" he said.

"Thought of that," said Derek. "You wrap your hand in fabric, an article of clothing."

All eyes shot to Brad for his response.

"So we just all sit here without our shirts waiting for them to come back, and when they do, hope they don't notice."

"Thought of that, too," shot back Derek. "We're all wearing shorts, right? At least, I hope to God. One by one we use the bathroom, take off our shorts and stuff them into a pocket or down our shirts. Then, after the mirror is shattered, we go in again one by one, taking out a shard of glass as a weapon."

"We do the same in the women's john," chimed in Doug. "Between the two mirrors, we should get enough big pieces to do some damage."

Brad nodded, genuinely trying to find merit in the idea. He was moved by their sincerity, the boyish enthusiasm they seemed to have for their scheme. Hope was perhaps more important than common sense, at least at this point, and he didn't want to be the one to poke holes in their new little balloon.

"Have you seen that man fight?" asked Brad. "Did you

see the way he kicked Scott in the head? He knows some shit, guys. Shit you don't want to mess with, I promise you."

"I know some shit of my own," said Tattoo Jack.

"He can't take four or five of us," said Derek.

"Four or five of us with sharp glass," chimed in Scott. He nodded toward two other men, Tom Turner and a guy whose name didn't surface in the moment. They nodded back, as if to reassure him that they believed.

"Maybe you're taking your nomination as our safety supervisor a little too seriously," said Jack.

Brad drew a deep breath and closed his eyes. He knew they were counting on him for a major role in the plan. He was arguably in the best shape of the bunch, the most athletically gifted, other than Mark, of course. The idea of coming at Simon with a wedge of broken mirror held in a hand wrapped up in his Jockey shorts wasn't his idea of hope.

"We need a diversion," said Stu.

Brad snapped his attention to Stu, realizing they'd thought this through in some detail before calling him over. He wondered why.

"What for?"

"We need to draw him out. Jack has an idea."

All eyes shifted to Jack, whose countenance was all grim business. "We do it twice. The first to see if he'll even come out. If he does, we do the mirror, we load up, wait awhile, then do it again and hit him. We end it there."

"Wait a minute," said Brad. "What the hell are you talking about?"

"A fight," said Jack. "Scott and I get into an argument, and that argument will escalate into a fight, right here in the room. I don't think he'll just sit back and let us kill each other, do you? He'll come in, break it up, make a scary little speech, and go back to whatever the hell he's doing in there. Then we'll know. Later, the fight resumes. He comes back, pissed off and maybe a little careless, and we take him."

"While the fat guy just watches."

"Simultaneous attack," said Stu. "All three of them."

Brad nodded, but not approvingly. "Risky," he said.

Jack didn't like this, rolling his head back in disgust. "Of course it's risky. What are you, a pussy? You think anything we do isn't going to be risky? You want a free pass, Teeters? Fuck you."

"I'm not your problem," said Brad with surprising cool.

"Don't bet on it," said Jack.

Brad smiled, knowing this would piss him off even more. "He might do something radical the first time he comes out. Make another example of you."

Jack's eyes narrowed to slits. "I'm already responsible for one example. I can handle him."

"Right," said Brad sarcastically.

"I can handle you, too, big man," said Jack.

This was getting out of hand, and Brad knew it. He also knew in that instant why Jack was so intent on being the diversion. It was his way to step up, his way to atone for what he'd done that had ended up with Mark being taken outside. Knowing this, it was easy to keep his cool in the face of the man's aggression toward him.

Looks were exchanged, no one sure where this was going.

"You in, or not?" asked Jack, still looking directly at Brad.

Brad didn't answer. He met each set of eyes boring into him, torn with indecision.

"Defining moment, Brad," said Scott.

Brad felt the heat swelling in his cheeks, felt his heart pounding in his chest. It was a familiar sensation, borne of what was, in some ways, a familiar dilemma. He was torn between his heart and his head. His heart wanted to support their plan, be part of it, help make it happen, and feel good about himself for contributing. His heart wanted to stick it in Jack's face. But his head told him this was suicide, at the very least putting his hand in dire jeopardy of being sliced open, at the worst inviting Simon's fury and wrath.

"He's a pussy," said Jack, his voice venomous. "Maybe we start the diversion right here, him and me."

"That's not a bad idea," said Derek. "A little realism."

Brad looked up, having now been called out.

"I'm in," he said, smiling right at Jack. "Either way is fine."

54

It had taken Mark all day to travel just under three miles. The first couple of hours had yielded steady progress, his ankle cooperating with only a dull hum of pain, with an occasional scream to remind him it was still there. The weather was his most formidable enemy now, alternating between a light mist and periods of showers that turned the ground to mud and made the rocks too slick to safely use as handholds as he climbed. His clothing was soaked through, and the chill had permeated to his lungs, which responded with a nagging little cough.

When the cough became oppressive, he'd rested for about an hour just before noon, and it was then that his legs stiffened and his ankle turned the corner from bad to worse. He was at the bottom of a gully, surrounded by steep brown hills, and he found himself suddenly dealing with a new level of fear, the very real possibility that he might not find the road he was looking for. And that if he didn't, he just might die. There was nothing out here, absolutely nothing, and with the cloud cover obscuring the sun he had only the vaguest notion of his direction.

He licked rain from some leaves in an attempt to hydrate himself.

In the first hour after this rest, he estimated he'd covered only a quarter mile. Ahead of him was what seemed like a vertical rise of several hundred feet, the steepest he'd encountered yet. He considered an alternative path, literally walking around it instead of over it, but the hill extended in either direction as far as the eye could see. He'd picked what appeared to be the lowest point to reach the crest. He had no choice.

He was well past halfway up when the soft ground gave way to a riverbed of lava rock. It looked as if huge black stones with porous surfaces had been dumped from the crest by a fleet of trucks, tumbling down and gathering on themselves before reaching the critical mass necessary to stop any farther descent. The hill was about forty-five degrees in pitch, and the rocks were slick with wet moss.

He was well into this portion of the climb when his foot, clad in a Reebok running shoe with a web rubber sole, slipped from its hold. This, in turn, caused him to crash face first onto the rock he was scaling, the jagged edge of which protruded sharply. Under the full weight of his body and his reaction to the impact, his hand slipped off, and he rolled to the side, bouncing against a large boulder before landing in a shallow crevasse between two smaller rocks.

The fall had knocked the wind out of him. He remained motionless for several minutes before the pain began to localize. Whatever had been wrong with his ankle was now a full-blow sprain—it had swollen to the point where he could not see or feel the wide knob of ankle bone on either side. But the real dilemma now was his chest. Judging from the pain that resulted from drawing a deep breath, Mark quickly concluded that he'd broken a rib. Each deep breath brought on a reflexive cough, which caused a stabbing pain in the side of his rib cage.

He remained there on the rocks for another hour, frozen with indecision. His first impulse had been to simply wait. Sooner or later, for better or worse, the situation at the ranch would resolve itself and someone would know that he was missing. They'd come for him. He'd be easy to spot here, either from another ridge by someone with field glasses or from a helicopter.

But that could take a day or two, perhaps more. The seminar wasn't over until Saturday, and that might be the first time anyone from the outside would be expecting contact from anyone at the ranch. Anything could happen to him in that span of time: he could die from exposure, he could die from internal bleeding if the rib had punctured something, he could die from an escalating cough that just might rip out his lungs.

Or he could die from guilt, knowing he'd given up. That his teammates might have had a chance had he persevered. The knowledge that he'd done nothing would kill him slowly over the years.

He got to his feet, suddenly nauseated. After several deep and extremely painful breaths, his head cleared, and he took his next step.

55

WEAVERVILLE, CALIFORNIA

4:10 P.M.

Forty-four unmarked and convoluted miles to the southeast of The Complex, a woman in a Lincoln Navigator pulled into the lot of a small motel with an adjoining coffee shop. She got out of the vehicle, flipped up the substantial fur collar of her coat to block the biting wind, and hurried into the coffee shop on fashionably heeled boots.

Inside, the only occupied table entertained three people—Special Agent Ellison Rainey of the FBI, Thomas Stanton, and Beth, all of whom had arrived at a nearby airstrip on a $30 million private jet less than two hours earlier.

"I'm sorry I'm late," she said, shaking hands with the men, then with Beth as Rainey introduced them.

"Beth Teeters . . . Patricia Pratt." They shook hands.

"Has something happened?" asked Beth, struck by both the height and beauty of the woman. But it wasn't her looks that intimidated Beth and, Beth presumed, every other woman who got this close. It was her aura. The

$4,000 coat and the $1,200 Fendi boots and the jewels and the confidence of the filthy rich. If they told her this woman was with the FBI, Beth would laugh in their face and call the bluff right here. In fact, though, they hadn't told her anything at all, only that Mrs. Pratt was coming.

"I've been told you are the woman in charge," said Beth, walking a line between cordiality and impatience.

"You've been told correctly, and I hope you'll tell me everything else they've said about me," she said. Her smile didn't fit the moment; this was cocktail-party chitchat.

She quickly sensed this incongruity in Beth's eyes and shifted gears.

"I'm sorry, this is no time for attempts at wit, however lame. How are you holding up, Beth? We can get you something, if you want."

"I'm okay. I just want to talk to my husband."

"That's impossible, I'm afraid. The lines to The Complex have been severed—"

"I know that," said Beth, immediately regretting her quick edge. "I was being rhetorical. Tell me, if you would, what it is you are in charge of here. Please."

Mrs. Pratt shot the two men a glance, as if to say she wasn't expecting someone with Beth's moxie.

"I run the seminar company. I own it, actually. With Thomas's help, of course."

Beth moved her eyes between the woman and Stanton, and then it clicked.

"He's your son."

Both of them smiled sheepishly, and the resemblance was even stronger now.

Rainey jumped in. "We're working very closely with Mrs. Pratt to understand the property layout, as well as the nature of the situation. She's been very helpful."

"I imagine you're a wreck yourself," said Beth, softening just a touch.

"How perceptive of you," answered the older woman.

"Forgive me . . . I mean, you don't look stressed out . . . in fact, you look like you're waiting for your limo to take you to Rodeo Drive."

Mrs. Pratt smiled. "Now there's an idea." Then her entire countenance changed, a shift toward gravity. "Frankly," she continued, "I have news. Not good, I'm afraid. I'd originally come here this morning to meet you and offer my condolences, but I got a call from the ops center, and there's been a development. Might as well tell you now, no sense holding onto this stiff upper lip any longer than necessary."

All three leaned in, the men in particular. Rainey had been writing himself a note, but he put the pen down and focused on Mrs. Pratt.

"There's been a death at The Complex."

"Oh, my God," whispered Beth, an involuntary reaction. "It's not—"

"No, your husband is fine, as far as we know."

"Who was it?" asked Stanton.

"The family hasn't been notified," she answered coldly without looking at him.

"So when these so-called updates come in . . . how does that work?" asked Beth, her eyes narrow now, almost suspicious. She could feel the heat of Stanton's eyes on her.

"We are in direct communication with the man doing this," said Mrs. Pratt. "He calls at irregular intervals, wanting an update on the money. We wait, we answer, that's how it goes down."

"And who is he?"

"We can't say," said Rainey. "I assure you, his name would mean nothing."

Beth closed her eyes. It was important to maintain the illusion of panic, of her teetering on an edge. It was easy, because she was indeed nervous, unsure how this would turn out, and what would be required of her as it did.

"The FBI is doing everything they can," said the elegant older woman, reaching her hand out toward Beth's shoulder.

"Your money has been wired to the Cayman account," said Rainey. "Most of the others are in, but there's a few that are, shall we say, delayed. We have the suspect's assurance that the hostages will be free upon confirmation of the required deposits, and we are negotiating his transportation off the property."

"His *what*?" Beth wasn't sure she'd heard this right.

"He's asking for a way out of this, of course. Why extort the money if you don't plan on getting away to spend it?"

"But you're not going to let him—"

"We're focusing on getting your husband and the others out of there," said Rainey. "That's our objective. Everything else, including the money, is just going through the motions, moving things forward. Our only position is to comply. If we don't—"

"She's justifiably upset," said Mrs. Pratt, not liking Rainey's tone.

"Let him finish," said Beth. "If we don't *what*?"

"Then we risk a worst-case scenario outcome."

Everyone was looking at Beth.

"Which means what?" she finally said.

Rainey glanced at Mrs. Pratt. "The kidnapper carries through on his threats."

"And those are?"

Rainey and Mrs. Pratt exchanged a look. "I think you know," he said.

Beth's gaze drifted out the window toward the bank of five-story pines that surrounded the parking lot of the little cafe-motel complex. It was pouring rain.

"I'd like to go to my room," she finally said after drawing a deep breath.

"Of course. Thomas?"

"And I'd like a car. While I'm here. I can't just sit in a room and wait."

Both Rainey and Stanton looked quickly at Mrs. Pratt, and Beth could tell they hadn't anticipated this one. Mrs. Pratt, however, kept her eyes on Beth, the moment hanging heavy, as if Beth had asked the unthinkable. Finally she reached into her purse and pulled out her keys and slid them across the table.

"Take mine."

"I must ask you to remain in town," said Rainey. "So we can reach you if something breaks."

Stanton stood and helped Beth to her feet. When she got to the door, she stopped and turned back to the woman in charge.

"I hope your attorney is as sharp as the way you dress," she said.

They watched her go, then stared at the door for a moment.

"What do you think?" asked Rainey, his eyes still on the door.

A tiny smile came to the woman's face, though her eyes grew distant.

"I think this will all work out to her satisfaction," she said. She focused her attention back on Rainey as she stood up, towering over him as she buttoned her expensive coat. She narrowed her eyes and added, "See that it does."

56

THE COMPLEX

5:06 P.M.

Brad would have much preferred the role of Jack's opponent in the staged fistfight over what they had in mind for him. He had been right about his self-assessment as one of the most capable men in the group, and because of that he had been selected to be in the first wave of attackers armed with a shard of glass from the bathroom mirror. When that fateful moment arrived, Jack and Scott would be available to help out but would be unarmed, given that they would already be scuffling with each other. Can't have them rolling around on the floor with a spike of ragged glass in their pocket. The first blow needed to come from the strongest arms in the room, and that meant Brad, Doug, and Derek, with a few others right behind them.

He had no role whatsoever in the dress rehearsal. Jack and Scott would begin their little dance, and they would see what Simon would do. Brad still feared their production might not make it past this opening-night performance—which was precisely why they were doing it this way—but he had to admit to himself that his adrenaline output was on overload. However far-fetched it seemed, this was better than sitting around without a clue.

Richard had not been omitted from the plan entirely. He still seemed to be operating at half speed, dozing off between fond reminisces about Georgia—it was clear that he had looked up to her as a mentor as well as a treasured friend.

While they waited—Jack and Scott wanted some time to plan and choreograph their little tiff—Brad went into the bathroom to check out the mirror. It was huge, much thicker than he anticipated, solidly bolted to the wall. Looking at it, he wasn't at all sure the thing could be broken without using a piece of metal as a bludgeoning device, which they didn't have. It also occurred to him that, when the blow was delivered, it would make a terrible racket, and no one had considered how to mask it from Simon's ears. Perhaps another diversion.

He would cover that base with the men after the first phase had played itself out.

Everyone took their places, strategically positioned for quick access to the point of the scuffle. It would go down ten feet in front of Brad, with Derek right next to him. Doug was directly across the room, creating a crossfire when they charged. The other men would sweep in from all four corners of the room, taking out Morse and Fisher, whose position during the chaos was an unknown variable at this point.

But for now, of course, they would simply wait, and watch.

It commenced with a screaming match. Scott was on the floor with Pamela, as they had been all day long. Jack stood in front of them, and to anyone looking on it appeared as if they were simply having a hushed conversation, which had also been happening all day long.

Then, Jack seemed to snap.

"Just get the hell away!" yelled Scott. It was the first time those not involved in the plan—over half the team—

had cause to look, and they appeared appropriately alarmed.

"Fuck you, man!" Jack kicked Scott in the legs. When Scott tried to get to his feet, Jack pushed him back down to the floor and pointed his finger. "You stay down, little man, you hear me?"

Scott fired out toward Jack's legs, hitting him at the knees. Jack doubled over on top of him, grasping him in a sort of reverse upside-down bear hug before they fell to the side as a single unit. They appeared deadlocked like this, neither man allowing the other to escape as they rolled and squirmed to the center of the room.

It was a clever gambit, mused Brad, because no punches could be thrown this way. It would be difficult to fake a fistfight, and this had to be convincing. So they wrestled instead of boxed, locked together like hockey players in a brawl, and each of them was giving it all they had, not really faking anything at all.

The most violent aspect of the moment was their screaming. Both men yelled muffled obscenities from within their hostile embrace, punctuated with grunts and moans. Pamela screamed with outrage for them to stop— Brad wasn't sure if this was in the script or not—and her voice was piercing, enough to cause a woman sitting next to her to cover her ears.

Morse was the first to crash through the office door on the other side of the room. He had a handgun instead of a rifle this time, which he promptly fired into the ceiling directly above the point where Scott and Jack were engaged. A surreal rain of ceiling tile dust showered down on them like a gray lunar snow.

Morse kept coming.

Scott and Jack either didn't hear the shot or didn't care. They continued to grapple violently, arms and fists now swinging wildly yet relatively harmlessly.

Brad felt a chill shoot up his spine—this was too good, too convincing. Their rage had found an outlet, their fear a voice, and they were venting it with all they had. The ancillary sounds of confrontation were the most intimidating of all: the thumping of knees and heels onto the carpet, the guttural expulsion of air from their lungs as they lunged, the friction of their clothing straining and tearing. He was sure they'd planned it all just this way, but it was nonetheless hard to watch, because they were the good guys and they were punishing each other with reckless abandon.

Morse kicked at the twisting duo. Fisher had entered the room now, taking a position several yards away, rifle ready. Morse kicked again, and one of the men screamed at the impact. The two combatants fell apart, their faces scarlet with rage. Jack was bleeding from his forehead, and it streaked his face into a grotesque masque. The sight of blood would convince even the most skeptical onlooker that this was real.

And then dress rehearsal went to hell. Whether it had been planned or if Jack had simply been overcome with rage was a question that would never be resolved.

Jack, who had risen to his knees like a supplicant about to pray, shot forward in a dive toward Morse's legs. The bigger man kicked out defensively, catching Jack in the head, stopping him cold. Morse flipped him over, then stepped across so that he was straddling his body from above. Then, to the horror of everyone in the room, he brought both hands to his gun, execution style, pointing it down at Jack's chest, and fired.

Jack's body jerked and seemed to lift off the floor at the impact. Morse didn't flinch. He waited a few seconds, holding the pose, then fired again.

Morse quickly wheeled and leveled the gun at Scott, who was still on the ground and slinking back as fast as he could. Morse had assumed the firing position on reflex, and Brad realized he'd underestimated this guy from the beginning. He was trained at this, and one had to assume good at it.

Another gunshot shattered the air, a more subdued "pop" than the one from Morse's gun. It came from the office door, where Simon now stood. He was pointing a handgun toward the ceiling, where he had just blown another hole in the soft tiles.

Everyone froze.

"Put the guns down," he said to Morse and Fisher, both of whom reacted slowly, as if confused by the command, almost as if they were now among the captives.

Morse put his gun at his feet. Fisher saw him do it, then did the same.

Simon went to Fisher, keeping his eyes on Morse to make sure no second thoughts emerged. Then he placed his own gun on the ground next to hers.

A terrible, wet sound issued from the downed man, and his body shuddered. A pool of blood was seeping into the carpet beneath him. Seeing it, Brad couldn't help but believe Tattoo Jack had just died.

Simon put both hands in the air, like a criminal showing the police that he's unarmed. He moved to the center of the room, where he turned in a circle, shifting eye contact as he did.

"You want a fight?" he asked of everyone.

Then his eyes fixed on Brad. "Do *you* want a fight?"

Brad tried to hold his gaze, but couldn't.

Simon didn't wait for an answer. He shifted his attention to Derek, who was next to Brad on the floor. "Do *you* want a fight?" Derek didn't look away as he shook his head.

Stu was next.

"How about *you* . . . do you want to fight me?" Stu didn't as much as twitch.

Simon moved a few yards away, glaring at the women, until he came to Jack on the floor. He put the tip of his shoe on Jack's hip and pushed. The body had stopped moving.

"*He* doesn't want a fight," said Simon, still looking down at Jack.

He turned, looking directly at Scott now.

"How about you, Scott? Do *you* want a fight? Right here? Right now? You obviously like to mix it up, how about you and me? Come on, let's have a little fun!"

Scott had crawled to the side of the room and was being comforted by Pamela, whose chest heaved as much as his. He just stared back at Simon, and it wasn't clear whether he was intimidated or considering the offer. What was clear was that he looked like he'd been on the losing end of a run-in with Stone Cold Steve Austin and wasn't up for another round with anyone, much less someone of Simon's ability.

The room was quiet, the moment consumed with Scott's defeat as he turned his eyes away. But they had all seen what Simon could do. Every man in the room was thankful it wasn't him being called out.

Simon shook his head in disgust and began to pace. "Anyone who wants to play hero, here's your chance. Take me on, right here, right now, and if you put me down, you go free. Everyone. No strings. You all just walk out of here."

He pointed toward Fisher and Morse and said, "If I go down, you'll let them all go. No interference. If I go down, it's over, and you clear out. Are we clear?"

Morse nodded. Fisher didn't respond.

"Do I have your word?" demanded Simon. When both of his lieutenants nodded, Simon turned his attention back to the group.

"Come on, people!" he shouted, his anger showing through now. "There's my gun—somebody make a move! Who's the hero today?"

The room was filled with that awkward stillness that surrounds a public humiliation. Simon continued to turn in circles, a victorious boxer in the middle of the ring, wearing a happily mocking expression of disbelief on his face. As he moved, he stepped over what was now certainly the dead body of Tattoo Jack, his shirt torn at the neck, the letters reading "REVENGE" visible across his upper back.

Brad thought Simon looked high, their first glimpse of the real psychopath behind the quiet, brilliantly in-control criminal facade.

As if he was reading Brad's mind, Simon shot over to him. "How about you, Teeters? Mister large and in charge—why not step into it, one time, *step into the fear*, as they say at these little psychobabble campouts." He paused, shaking his head sadly. "But you won't. Every cell in your body is screaming at you to retreat, to find a back door, to talk your way out of this like you think you're so damned good at doing . . . am I right, Brad?"

Brad held his gaze this time, prompting Simon to grin as he backed to the middle of the room once again.

The grin instantly vanished. "And tonight, if you're alive tonight, you'll be alone with your cowardice once again, won't you, Teeters?"

Simon held his gaze as he shook his head slowly. Brad looked away and closed his eyes.

"You disgust me," he said. "All of you. My guess is, you disgust yourselves."

He moved to the center of the room.

"Anyone!"

Everyone looked away.

"Look at you! No one willing to put it on the line! A room full of . . ."

It was then that someone from behind said, "Fuck you, man."

57

Simon spun, just as every eye in the room snapped toward the person who had spoken these suddenly profound words.

Tom Turner was on his feet and was taking off his shirt. His body was surprisingly muscular—Brad hadn't noticed anything about the guy until now, except his seeming absence from every critical moment they'd experienced—and, to everyone's surprise, revealed several large scars on his abdomen and back. Wounds of some kind. Those a vet might bring back from the battle line, forever unexplained.

"And a hero comes along . . ." said Simon, positioning himself between Turner and the middle of the room.

Turner had removed his shoes and was advancing cautiously, never taking his eyes off his adversary.

Without taking his eyes from his approaching opponent, Simon pointed his finger in Morse's direction and said, "Anybody interferes, you shoot them. If I go down, it's all over."

Morse happily retrieved his gun. Fisher did the same a moment later.

"Let's dance," said Simon, grinning at Turner now.

A chill shot up Brad's spine when he saw how Simon's presence had instantly transformed into something cold and businesslike. All the sarcasm and parody of mentorship had vanished, replaced by steely-eyed concentration. His knees seemed to morph into springs, his movements suddenly serpentine, almost balletlike. His hands came up to waist level, open palms facing inward, fingers delicately separated. He seemed to float laterally, shadowing Turner's more awkward, boxerlike feints as he began to bob and weave.

"Kick his ass," said a woman across the room from Brad. It was Tiffany, an extremely attractive woman who hadn't said much since they'd arrived, but always seemed to be smiling. Until now. Tiffany Palofax, it seemed, had had enough of this. Other voices joined hers, and suddenly it was a barroom brawl.

Turner made the first move, a lunging roundhouse right from a million roadside taverns. Simon ducked under it, smoothly dropping to his hands before swinging his legs in an arc a foot off the floor, clipping Turner's legs out from underneath him. As Turner stumbled forward, bracing with his hands against the impending impact with the floor, Simon somehow sprung back to his feet, and with what seemed to be a seamless continuation of the move, glanced a kick across Turner's face. Not a killer blow at all. Seeing it, Brad had the impression Simon was toying with this guy.

Turner rolled to the side from the blow, landing on his back on the floor. Blood was running out of his nose into his mouth, dripping onto the carpet. Simon could have advanced, but he held back, watching the man bleed. Brad now knew he was drawing this out.

Turner froze a moment, spitting blood, feeling his face in disbelief. Finally he struggled to his feet with Rockyesque fortitude and assumed the same posture as before, though now he wiped at his nose with his wrist.

"Time to die," said Simon, his countenance suddenly cold. "Last chance, hero man . . . you want out? We can shake hands, go back to being chickenshit hostage and psycho kidnapper. I don't know about you, but I find that shit boring, don't you think?"

Neither man moved for a moment.

"I'll even sweeten it for you," said Simon, slightly amused by Turner's resilience. "I'll let you walk out of here . . . straight through that door, right now. Just give it up, and you're home, man."

A final grin, malicious and thirsty, appeared on Simon's face for the briefest of moments. Then it vanished, his face again intent on something conclusive.

"Or you can go for it," he said, "save everyone's ass. Your call, hero man. Moment of truth."

Turner, holding Simon's gaze, shook his head and grimaced. He wiped at his nose, then spit something bloody onto the carpet.

"Fuck you," he said, his voice a whisper.

"Good man," said Simon. A moment later, he made his final move.

58

Simon's move on Turner was so fast and efficient that it defied the naked eye. It was a sweeping takedown in which Turner, despite an honorable attempt at his own driving tackle, appeared to have his legs kicked out from under him, and while momentarily airborne was flipped, mounted, and driven into the carpet face first. How he avoided having his back broken was the part the eye couldn't comprehend, but it was clear after the brief flashing of limbs and spinning torsos that Turner was flat on the ground with the air knocked out of him and that Simon was sitting squarely on his back. His knees pressed on Turner's rear deltoid shoulder muscles, thus cementing the man's face to the carpet fibers while completely incapacitating his arms. Simon was leaning forward as he implemented a choke hold around Turner's neck with one arm, while the other hand rested against the temple. Clearly, Simon could snap Turner's neck at any moment.

But instead, Simon seemed to revel in the moment, in allowing everyone to see what he had done. Turner's face was bright red, as if the choking process was already well under way, and his eyes were clamped shut, etched into slits of pain.

"It's all over," said Simon, his voice gentle now. The room was quiet, with more than one fist stifling a cry or a badly timed expletive. "You will remember this moment and this man for the rest of your lives. Because he is the only one among you with the courage to step up and the integrity to see it through to its conclusion."

Simon's eyes swept the room. This time no one looked away, and he seemed to make eye contact with specific individuals, his gaze burning deep.

"Learn from him," he said.

And then, in the pause between disbelief and hope, everything changed.

Music suddenly filled the room, just as the double doors leading outside opened wide. It was over-the-top glory music, an Olympic theme, perhaps, or the title track from one of the Rocky movies.

Several people appeared from outside and walked into the room. None of them were known to the participants— Stanton, Ellison Rainey, an elegantly dressed woman they assumed to be Mrs. Pratt, who until now had been a faceless legend. They stopped ten feet from the door, positioned so everyone could see them clearly.

A moment later another woman strode through the door. It was Georgia, very much alive. With her was Gary, Biceps Boy himself, who hadn't been seen since this whole business started.

Just then Tattoo Jack rose from the dead, the front of his shirt soaked red with fake blood. Without looking at anyone, he moved to the newcomers and stood next to Georgia, turned to face his teammates.

Elisa materialized from the darkness outside, wearing a ski coat and a shy smile as she walked into the room. She caught Brad's eye long enough to make sure they connected before she looked away, searching for other eyes to meet.

Simon released his grip on Tom Turner and joined them, as well. Morse and Fisher came with him, standing at his side as they turned to face the group. Fisher was crying softly, though her smile was radiant and proud.

Turner remained on the floor, rubbing his neck, his confused eyes wide as he looked up at the people who had assembled there and were looking back at them.

Strangest of all, the newcomers, Georgia, Simon, Elisa, and all the others were clapping their hands in applause.

THE overwhelming response of choice was to weep. Among them it assumed a wide variety of forms, couplings, and levels of intensity, and even those who continued to deny tears felt the need pounding at the back of their eyes, as joy collided with residual anger, relief shared the stage with regret, and doubt and confusion competed for airtime with a sense of calm certainty. Who-you-really-are was looking who-you-thought-you-were right in the eye, and it didn't blink, nor could you look away.

And so you wept.

The victory-lap song continued, and when it ended it started up again immediately. The newcomers and resurrected guests were sharing hugs all around, and there was a general feeling of euphoria mixed with shock, not unlike the brief moment of relief they had experienced on the airplane after it landed in one piece a few days earlier in Medford.

They had been saved. They had been renewed.

For the most part the hugs were as brief as they were intense, as if the room were suddenly one large reception line that had to keep moving. Those on the inside of the ruse used the moment to whisper something personal to nearly everyone who had been subjected to it—reassurance that hesitation and fear were normal and nothing to be ashamed of as long as you learned something from the experience. Reinforcement was offered for courage demonstrated and restraint applied, congratulations were given for surviving what was, for the mind at least, the jaws of death. Each person was alone with what they knew to be their ledger of personal truths, the accounting of their emotions, thoughts, and regrets in the dark hours of their impending doom.

Tom Turner, the hero of the day, remained strangely unmoved. It was as if the rage he had summoned to cross Simon's line in the sand was too immense to simply evaporate in the midst of all this suddenly liberated love. Nearly everyone expressed their admiration and awe at what he'd done, a few added their heartfelt thanks. He said nothing in return, overcome by what most assumed to be a boiling stew of relief and humility and pride that would sort itself out later on.

Scott and Pamela greeted people as a unit. They accepted others into their embrace, never letting go of one another no matter who came to them to share the moment. Several people commented on how happy they were for them, wishing them well going forward as a couple, if that's what they chose for themselves. At that moment, there was no question it was.

Brad's tears emerged when Elisa put her arms around him and squeezed, burying her face in his chest. He could feel her subdued sobs, and he wasn't sure if it was because of the moment or because of what they had shared. When she pulled back, he started to say something, but she put her finger against his lips to quiet him. She smiled like an angel who already knew the answers, held his tear-filled eyes for a moment, then moved on to the next survivor, leaving him to comprehend that he had always been alone with the script, that she had never really been here at all.

Suddenly one of the end walls began to pull back. It folded in five-foot sections into compartments now open in the longer walls, revealing another adjacent room about half the size of the classroom. This space was furnished with a half-dozen large round tables filled with place settings and fresh flowers. At the far wall was a seafood buffet manned by servers dressed all in white, the scent of shrimp and lobster simmering in garlic and herbs already luring the team forward. They had not eaten in thirty-six hours, and this was their reward.

Brad ate alone, observing the celebratory feast from a self-imposed distance. He was filled with an uneasy feeling that he suspected was the specter of his own hesitation during the crisis, exacerbated by the contradictory emotions caused by Elisa's return to life and her revelation as a shill.

It was only then, completely consumed with himself, that it occurred to Brad that amid all the relief and diffused anger and coalescing enlightenment, Mark had not returned to the room.

BOOK FOUR

REDEMPTION

59

On silence again. People are sick from eating too much rich food after such a long period of hunger, and lobster in creme sauce certainly qualifies as rich. But we were warned about this before we sat down to eat and, once again, were left to live with the consequences of our choices. The seminar is always under way. Lucky for me I didn't eat that much. Then again, my stomach was already in knots.

There's a lot going on. We've been sensitized, we are at the peak of our ability to feel, and to whatever extent we don't feel anything is the extent to which we have already died, checked out. It defines the work we have ahead, the needed growth. Then again I can't and shouldn't speak for anyone else. That's part of my problem back in the real world, isn't it—I'm as much in need of personal growth as anyone here. I've certainly learned that much.

I'm worried about Mark. I know him, and he's not in his element out there in the woods. I can't imagine they'd leave him alone for that length of time, but they assure me he's fine. Better than fine—he's having his own seminar, custom-tailored to what he needed. I asked Richard about it, and he said not to worry, to come see him later and he'll show me how they're handling him. This, I gotta see.

I'm trying to get my head around what has happened. People are not who I thought they were, things were not as they seemed. Maybe that's the entire point. Tattoo Jack isn't a thug with an attitude problem; he's someone who's dedicated his life to helping others grow. Elisa isn't a needy soul in search of human contact; she's a cold-blooded psychological terrorist with a loving heart. Simon isn't the devil; he's Caine from that old TV show called Kung Fu, *a master teacher. And Tom Turner isn't the quiet, standoffish guy we all thought; he's a quiet, standoffish role model, of all things. You never freaking know.*

Someone asked Georgia what would have happened if Turner had not called Simon out when he did. She said the pressure for someone to step forward would have escalated gradually, becoming a more obvious solution as time went on. In the morning, when the airplane arrives, and if no one had stepped up by then, they simply would have called it off at the climax of a mock-up mass execution that would have rocked the world of everyone involved. No class has ever reached that point, she said.

As for the airplane, it's coming anyway, first thing in the morning. Skydiving, of all things. Weather permitting, of course, and it's supposed to clear up. Matt said that of course it's going to clear; these people have a direct line to God. Maybe he's right. In any case, jumping out of an airplane suddenly doesn't seem so scary anymore.

No, shit like that is easy. It's understanding why you used to think it was terrifying that's the hard part. That, and looking back at everything you've missed because of your fear.

Beth would love this. I have to think of a way to get her down here.

60

WEAVERVILLE, CALIFORNIA

6:40 P.M.

Beth hated everything about the shit-hole of a motel room. She'd taken Mrs. Pratt's Navigator around town for a little spin and an early dinner—reconnaissance, actually—but Weaverville was only slightly larger than a freeway rest stop, and it didn't take long. It was a waiting game now. One window sported drapes made from what looked like yellowed sheets no longer fit for the beds, and the place smelled of ammonia tub and tile cleaner. And of course, the television didn't work. But it was finally dark outside, which was one of the things she was waiting for to put her plan into action.

The fact that they'd left her alone only served to convince her that her instincts were right on the money. And to proceed with her idea.

Then, unexpectedly, someone knocked on the door.

It was Rainey, a soaked raincoat draped over his shoulders.

"Is something wrong?" she asked, stepping aside for him to enter.

"No, no, there's not. Everything is status quo. We got another payment wired to Cayman. There are only three left, I think. There's a problem with one family, but we're working it out."

Rainey's eyes were nervous, never alighting on one point in space for more than a moment or two.

"Have you heard from them?" Beth asked. When he seemed confused, she added, "The bad guys? Any word on Brad or the others?"

"Nothing. Our man is one tough cookie, I have to be honest with you."

"Man? I thought you said there were three men."

"We're not sure how many there are, actually."

"But there's only one you talk to."

"That is what I meant, yes." He was squirming, and she was enjoying being the reason. "We need your help, I'm afraid. Do you happen to have a photograph of your husband with you? In your purse perhaps?"

"Why?"

"Do you have one?"

Her look was suspicious as she sat on the bed and opened her purse. She fished out her wallet, then put it on her lap and didn't move.

"Something has happened, hasn't it? To Brad."

"Not that I know of." He gestured toward the purse with his hand. "Please?"

She squinted at him. "You need a picture because you don't know who someone is, and they can't tell you who they are because they are dead, or perhaps just unconscious. You need to identify someone. Am I right?"

"We need it for the file, Mrs. Teeters."

She squinted at him. "You're not telling me something."

He didn't argue. He just stared back at her.

"I deserve to know."

He nodded sheepishly, his eyes darting around the room. "The picture, Mrs. Teeters. Please."

She stared a moment longer, then opened the wallet

and took out a photograph of her and Brad in formal wear sitting at a dinner table.

"It's just a precaution," said Rainey, taking the photo. "In case we . . . need to identify any of the hostages. We're soliciting pictures from all the families."

"Your story smells as bad as this room."

"I'm sorry."

He nodded respectfully, then quickly left.

They were good, she gave them that. Just the possibility that something had happened to Brad smacked up against the cold steel wall of her resolve like a warhead. What if this was real? What if her husband was really looking down the muzzle of a rifle, no doubt thinking of her and praying to the God he'd never been able to convince her to take seriously? What if she couldn't see the forest for the tall trees of her own agenda?

She sat on the bed, staring at the wall, considering it all.

Then it suddenly occurred to her that the FBI, better than any agency on the planet besides the CIA, could hit up a DMV in any state and have a driver's license photo faxed or e-mailed anywhere on the planet, all in about forty seconds from the time of the request.

She was back in the ball game, sitting in a box seat with her resolve.

6:59 P.M.

BETH waited several minutes after Rainey had departed before she made the call. She drew a deep breath as she listened to the ringing through the handset, steadying herself. This was it, the moment of no return. Everything would be different if she didn't hang up.

"Weaverville Police. How may I direct your call?"

"I need to talk to an officer," she said. "A detective, I think."

"What is this in regards to?"

"It's kind of complicated, actually."

"May I have your name, please?"

"Certainly. My name is Beth Teeters"—she injected a subtle shot of emotion into her voice here—"and I think someone may have kidnapped my husband."

61

THE COMPLEX

8:29 P.M.

Based on how hard it was raining now, Brad didn't buy the theory that the skies were going to clear by morning. The distance between the bunkhouse and the seminar offices—three adjoining trailers and a porch—was only two hundred yards, but by the time he got there, running full out, he was soaked.

He was nervous about this visit. It was a peek behind the curtain, and he wasn't sure he wanted to know. While the facade had been removed from the curriculum, there was something comforting about flying coach instead of sitting in the cockpit. Like seeing the kitchen of your favorite restaurant, sometimes it's better not to know.

Richard answered the door, which was of the sliding glass variety. The interior of the trailers was surprisingly pristine and businesslike, like a downtown insurance brokerage office, with computers and new carpet. The walls were crowded with framed motivational posters showing a

variety of eagles and golf courses situated on rocky shore-
lines, each offering a provocative tag line about challenge
and courage. Georgia was on the telephone, Mrs. Pratt
and the young guy with the thick neck were stooped over
a desk looking at some papers, and Gary was working in
front of a computer.

Richard shook Brad's hand as if they were just meeting,
which Brad found a little odd. The others didn't look up or
otherwise acknowledge him, which he found even odder.

"How are you doing?" asked Richard in his best
bedside-manner voice. His cocked-head look of concern
tipped Brad off that the question related to the afternoon's
turn of events, which Brad had taken harder than most.

"Bottom of the barrel," said Brad, then quickly added,
"nowhere to go but up."

"You're very present, very engaged," said Richard,
putting his hand on Brad's shoulder.

"That's an understatement."

Richard smiled, signaling a transition in their conversation. He guided Brad by the elbow to the computer station where Gary was sitting, taking a position behind his
shoulder and leaning in.

"Run the transponder," he said to Gary. As the muscular young man tapped at the keys, Richard turned back
to Brad.

"Mark has leadership issues," said Richard. "He's de-
pendent on a structure to thrive because he believes he is
unable to function outside of one, to be a leader of self. He
believes he is not worthy of leadership; at the same time he
challenges the competencies of those who lead him. Our
objective is to prove those assumptions false."

The screen changed to a graphic image of a map,
which Brad quickly realized represented the ranch. He
spotted the entrance road and the group of buildings, the
river winding through the property and the surrounding
relief lines of the hills. The image of an airstrip could be
seen to the west. The ranch itself was relatively small in the
center of the screen, with the map showing miles of terrain
all around.

To the north of the buildings, about ten miles away, a green light was blinking.

"That's Mark," said Richard, putting his finger on it.

Brad looked up, his expression posing all his questions.

"When Mark was taken from the building under the guise of being executed, he was given the opportunity to escape, which he seized. He did very well with that, in fact. You may remember—as he was being led outside he was held by his belt from the rear. He was, in fact, having a transponder attached at that moment." He reached to a shelf on the wall behind the computer and produced a small device about the size of a nine-volt battery. It was a square piece of metal with a clip on it, black in color. Richard began to affix it to Brad's belt as a demonstration.

"The signal is picked up by satellite and transmitted here, where it is cross-referenced against a GPS program and displayed here."

Brad shook his head. "You've known where he is the entire time."

"We do indeed." Then to Gary, he said, "Zoom in."

Gary tapped a few keys, and the image shifted to a tighter view. The green light still blinked, but now it was easy to see his specific location relative to the hillside over which he was traveling.

"Amazing," muttered Brad.

"Back out again," said Richard, at which Gary tapped more keys, causing the image to return to the original view.

Richard touched the screen again. "He's looking for this road—here—pressing northerly at less than one-half mile an hour because of the hills and the inevitable wrong turns. Once he reaches the road—*if* he reaches the road— he has a fifty-fifty chance of choosing the right direction, in which case he'll come upon the café, where Gary or someone from our staff will be waiting for him with a change of clothes and a hot meal."

"Which is why I was absent from the exercise of the past day and a half," said Gary without looking up.

"What if he chooses wrong?" asked Brad.

"Then we pick him up." Richard checked his watch. "He

has until oh six hundred hours tomorrow until we pull the plug. Either way he goes, he benefits from the experience."

Brad just shook his head again, picturing Mark out there, soaked and exhausted, blaming everyone he could think of.

"These numbers," said Richard, pointing to a window in the corner of the screen in which several numbers were displayed, "show us his pulse and breathing rate. Again, if we see a problem, we go for him."

"My God," said Brad.

"Besides being a little uncomfortable, he's never been in any real danger since he left the property," said Richard, staring at the screen like a proud father stares at his son's trophy case. "It's taking him a little longer than normal, but he's doing fine."

"This is amazing."

"It is, isn't it? Your tax dollars at work. This technology was developed by the U.S. military for covert antiterrorist operations in Beirut. It's expensive, but worth every penny. You might ask Ken Wong about it when you get back."

Richard's grin was mischievous. He even winked.

Brad nodded, realizing he was in far more competent and professional hands than he could have imagined. All of it, from the crash simulation to the illusion of a kidnap scenario, had been choreographed and implemented with military precision. He wondered how much of the seminar was, in fact, the offspring of a military mind.

"Are we good?" asked Richard, eyebrows raised. He wasn't referring to their technology or creativity, he was asking how Brad felt.

Brad nodded. Together they headed back to the door.

"It's good that you were concerned," said Richard. Again, he extended his hand for Brad to shake.

Outside, rushing through the rain back toward the bunkhouses, Brad passed Tom Turner on the path. He smiled, but Turner barely looked at him as he trotted past, moving with labored movements. Perhaps he was sore from his altercation with Simon that afternoon, which would be understandable. He was wearing a huge parka, one Brad hadn't noticed him wearing prior to this. Brad turned and watched, seeing that Turner was heading toward the office trailers, too.

Brad wondered why. Especially where Turner was concerned, because the guy had demonstrated no emotion or opinion since they'd arrived.

What seemed oddly out of place was rendered ordinary here, so Brad let it slide. He was more concerned with a new piece of the puzzle, something he wished he had asked Richard about when he had the chance.

He wondered how Mark knew anything about a road, much less the direction in which to find it. Then he remembered it had come up the other night when Jason returned in a huff from his brief attempt to leave the ranch. Jason had even mentioned a cafe. As far as Brad knew, this was the only time it had come up. Now, recalling the night of the conversation, it seemed oddly contrived, as if Jason was making sure this information, otherwise peripheral to the issue at the time, was clearly presented.

So they would hear him. So that Mark would know.

62

This time, when someone knocked at the seminar office door, everyone looked up. They had been expecting Brad when he arrived earlier, had even seen him coming up the walkway. But they weren't expecting anyone else to come calling after that, and anyone who had any business in the office was already here. These trailers were out of bounds to the students, so if one of them came knocking, it was cause for concern.

Richard answered the door again. When he saw that it was Tom Turner standing there, his heavy parka soaked and reflecting the light, he thought he knew what this was about. Turner had just experienced perhaps the most intense moment of his life, and he needed to talk. This was not the time, but he would say something to the man that showed he understood and that he would be there for him tomorrow. He would urge him to go back to his bunk and write it all down, assure him that it would all look different tomorrow.

"Thomas," he said, not making a move to let the man inside. Despite the hour and the knowledge that his cover had been broken, his sunglasses remained in place.

"I need to talk to you," Turner said.

"You're on silence, Thomas. I'll talk to you tomorrow. You have a lot to write about in your journal. It's not every day you discover who you really are."

Turner seemed nervous, glancing back over his shoulder toward the bunkhouse. Circles of rain were visible streaking under the lights that hung from poles in the courtyard.

"Something's happened," he said. "With the men. You need to know."

Richard smiled patiently. "Not tonight. We're having a meeting."

"I need to come inside," said Turner.

"Thomas, I really must insist . . ."

Turner opened the parka and extracted a thick-barreled handgun from his belt, pointing it directly at Richard's chest.

Richard stared at the gun without expression, showing no fear. He had seen a lot of things from a lot of spanking-new heroes in his time at The Complex but never anything like this. He backed away from the door, allowing Turner to step inside.

The others had been looking on, and were already shrinking back toward the rear wall as Turner stepped in, closing the door behind him.

"You," he said, pointing the gun at Gary, "unplug all the telephones and bring them here." He indicated the center of the floor at his feet with his other hand. When Gary seemed to hesitate, Turner fired the gun through the back wall of the trailer.

It was then that the first real jolt of fear hit them. Because short of a muffled thud, barely discernible from the rain pounding the metal roof of the trailer, there had been little sound when the gun went off. Turner was using a silencer, which was something your average street criminal or handgun hobbyist gone postal would not have access to. Only a professional used equipment like this.

Gary moved quickly, unplugging the four telephone extensions in the trailer and tossing them at Turner's feet.

"Mobile phones," said Turner.

Stanton produced a mobile phone from his jacket, and Mrs. Pratt dug one from her purse. Both of them tossed the units to the floor.

"Where is Georgia?" he asked.

No one answered, but Turner noticed that Richard's eyes flicked toward the window involuntarily.

"Where are the others?" His tone was even and calculated. Not the tone of a madman or someone simply confused beyond reason. This was the tone of premeditation.

"There are no others," said Stanton, his own tone defiant. His mother touched his wrist lightly to signal the need for restraint.

"Simon, Morse, Fisher, Jack, all of them."

"They're gone," said Richard. "Their work here is done. They left right after dinner. Listen to me, Tom, we can . . ."

"No." Turner held his free hand up to signal quiet. "We can't. Where is the money?"

Richard and Mrs. Pratt exchanged an immediate look, and the others traded similar looks a moment thereafter.

"Listen to me," said Richard. "There is no ransom. That's God's truth."

Turner nodded, as if he understood Richard's position. Then he fired a bullet into Stanton's upper leg. The impact sent him spinning in a manner not unlike the way Simon had sent Turner spinning earlier, only this time there was a crimson spray in the air, trailing the arc of his fall and splattering his mother's face.

"That may or may not have just severed his femoral artery," said Turner. "You have only minutes to find out. Give me the money now, and you can call for help. Fuck around with me, and we'll all stand here and watch him bleed."

Mrs. Pratt was silent as she sank to her knees next to her son. One hand was already on his leg in an attempt to compress the wound, while the other was under his head, holding it off the floor.

"Get it," she barked without looking up.

Richard opened a cabinet next to a desk and withdrew a large satchel. He opened it up and tilted it so that Turner could see that it was full of several smaller bags, including an athletic bag. With one hand Richard opened the athletic bag so that Turner could see that it was full of many bundles of cash. When Turner nodded, Richard tossed the satchel to the floor at his feet.

Turner looked at his watch.

"Lie down on the floor," he said, motioning with the gun.

Richard didn't move. The others, who had started to comply, saw this and hesitated, waiting to see what would happen.

"Quid pro quo," said Richard. "Let me make the call."

Turner seemed to grin, his gaze locked on Richard's.

"Defining moment, isn't it?"

"Yes it is."

"Good man," said Turner, just before he brought his other hand up to the gun and pulled the trigger. The bullet struck Richard squarely in the center of his forehead, propelling him against the wall, which was now coated with a geometrically perfect array of his blood and tissue. His sunglasses spun through the air as if in slow motion, landing on the floor, the lenses splattered with flecks of blood.

Turner didn't hesitate. He pivoted, keeping both hands on the weapon, and fired at Gary, who had risen to his feet and was advancing. The bullet went through his throat, moments before another entered his temple cleanly, taking the other side of his head with it into the back of an upholstered chair.

Mrs. Pratt instinctively tried to squirm for cover but was unable to get to her feet. She was backing away crab-style, using her hands, but slammed into the leg of a desk. Turner was on her instantly, pointing the gun at her head.

She closed her eyes. She felt nothing, dead before her head bounced off the carpet.

Turner fired one more shot, this one into the back of Stanton's head to finish the job. Then he went through Richard's pockets until he found a thick ring of keys.

With the rain still pelting the top of the trailers, there were no sounds to be heard, either here or certainly not two hundred yards away at the bunkhouse, where people were just now turning in. They were going skydiving in the morning, and they needed their rest, especially after the ordeal of the past two days.

Tom Turner turned out the lights in the office before he closed the doors. His parka was wrapped tightly around him as he hustled along the path toward the neighboring trailer, where he knew Georgia would be sleeping, and where he'd put a bullet in her brain without her ever opening her eyes. Then he'd go back to the bunkhouse to join his teammates. He'd stash the heavy satchel under his bed, and no one would have a reason in the world to ask what it was.

He was their hero, after all.

63

WEAVERVILLE, CALIFORNIA

9:45 P.M.

Beth's call to the local police had been frustrating at first because she couldn't get past the department receptionist, who fancied herself an investigating officer instead of a phone jockey, forcing Beth to go over the story twice. When Officer Bryon Garvin finally came on the line—after Beth was on hold for five minutes—she had to start from scratch yet again, and by now her tone was impatient.

She told him that her husband had enrolled in a seminar being held a few miles from here, and asked if he was aware of the program. He said that he was indeed and asked what the problem might be. She explained that they had come to her with their story about a kidnap and ransom, claiming to be FBI. But there were holes in their story and in their credibility, so she called the Seattle office of the FBI to check it out. She said they seemed noncommittal but wouldn't confirm that the agents were, in fact, on the level. She told him about the ransom money—specifically mentioning a quarter million dollars—and how she'd demanded that she be brought down here to be closer to her husband when the storm blew over, and that without hesitation they'd flown her here on their private jet and stashed her in a seedy motel, leaving her to worry herself sick. She was calling, she said, to verify that there was such a crisis under way at the ranch and to verify that her money was in safe hands and that her paranoia was, in fact, just that. And she added, because she was scared, coming here had been a mistake.

Garvin listened without interruption, other than an occasional clarifying question. Beth assumed he was taking notes, and she couldn't tell from his tone whether he was taking them seriously or not. He asked where she was, asked for the spelling of all the names she'd mentioned, promised to get back to her after he checked a few things. He also made her promise to stay right where she was until he got back to her.

It had gone exactly as she'd hoped. Better, in fact—Officer Garvin called back ten minutes later to tell her he was on his way over.

10:36 P.M.

OFFICER Garvin arrived just a little under an hour later. He was a wiry little man, the uniform fitting him too loosely, but he looked like he could take care of himself if push came to shove. He was about forty, with a neatly trimmed goatee, something Beth had never seen on a police officer before. Small town, different policies, she decided. The guy was probably the local barber in his spare time. Worst thing that ever happened in Weaverville other than speeding tickets, she surmised, was an occasional fishing-license violation and perhaps a beef or two at the local watering hole. She imagined the entire police department, all four of them, waiting with bated breath for Garvin to return from this particular call.

Beth sat on the bed in her room, Garvin in one of the chairs. He wanted to hear it all yet again, taking more notes as he listened. He rarely looked up as she spoke, and avoided any facial reaction. Finally, when Beth was finished, he looked up with a strange fog in his eyes, as if he'd just bitten into a lemon.

"Well, I think I know how to handle this," he said.

"Did you call the FBI?" she asked, sitting forward anxiously.

"I did. I'm afraid I didn't get anywhere with them, though, or with the state police. I assure you, if there was a hostage situation anywhere near here, we'd know about it first."

"So you're saying this whole thing is a fraud," she said, her voice fragile. "They're trying to rip me off."

"I don't think anyone's trying to rip you or anyone else off here. But I think I do know what's going on," he said. "What do you say we take a little drive out there and see?"

"To The Complex?" asked Beth, trying not to sound as excited as she felt.

"Why not? If the FBI is there, they'll stop us and we can get some real information. Maybe from your boy Rainey himself. If not, it'll put your mind at ease."

"The hell it will."

"At least you'll know your husband is safe."

"What about my money? Is that safe, too? If this is a scam, it might be dangerous."

Garvin smiled patiently. "You're in good hands, Mrs. Teeters." He stood, adjusting the heavy belt with its myriad of guns and radios and handcuffs and other paraphernalia. "Shall we go?"

Beth nodded and got up to fetch her coat.

64

THE COMPLEX

10:54 P.M.

With the rule of silence in effect and the dual residue of the rich food and the day's emotional roller coaster lingering, many of the team had turned in for the night. A few still wrote in their journals, a few others lay in their bunks staring at the ceiling, Brad among them. The more time he had alone with his performance of the last two days, the more uneasy he became. Pamela and Scott were sitting outside, huddled on a bench in the breezeway that led to the dining hall, casting the rule of silence to the wind. Like Brad, Pamela was worried about Mark, and despite Brad telling her about the transponder and Mark's safety, she needed Scott's reassurance more.

No one had the slightest awareness that the lights in the office trailers had gone dark.

Tom Turner rushed through the door, his eyes wide with urgency.

"Gentlemen—everybody up! Assembly in the classroom in three minutes!"

He repeated the instruction as he moved quickly through the bunkhouse. As the men began rousting themselves, he hurried to the door of the women's bunkhouse and yelled the same to them.

No one seemed to be particularly surprised or annoyed. Here in this place, the unexpected had become routine, and after what they'd just experienced, this was just another chapter in the book of their week.

The entire team was inside the classroom in the three minutes Turner had specified. Everyone except Turner, that is, though no one seemed to notice his absence.

He was back in the bunkhouse, making sure everyone had complied with his instructions.

After walking through both bunkhouses twice and taking a quick spin around the buildings, including a peek inside the dining hall, Turner went back to his bunk. He slid out the satchel he'd taken from the office trailers and opened it up. There were sue separate smaller bags and sacks inside, each containing loose bundles of cash. He had been told that anywhere from three to eight of the families would turn over ransom money, and six would do just fine. He didn't know what the other two families would do, and he didn't care. That was somebody else's problem now. There was well over $1 million here, though he was in too much of a hurry to be precise. A million was enough for now.

A chill shot up his spine. He felt giddy, light-headed even. He hoped he wouldn't have to shoot anyone else, but if he did, that was fine. This was business, and business was good right now.

He checked to see that his gun was fully loaded. Two other handguns were tucked into a holster now strapped over his shoulders as he walked out of the bunkhouse toward the classroom, where his teammates were waiting.

It was time for the real seminar to begin.

65

NORTH OF THE COMPLEX

10:57 P.M.

From the beginning, Mark hadn't been naive about how long it would take to hike twelve miles over unfamiliar terrain in the rain. His only compass had been the pointing hand of an angry man, and with the pitch of the hills he'd climbed and the loss of any visual reference point, any number of wrong turns could have unknowingly turned eight miles into twenty. What he hadn't anticipated were the injuries. His ankle was numb, a blessing, but it was also stiff. When his weight landed on it wrong, a pain shot up his leg as if something hungry had just bitten it off. The cough in his chest had stabilized, but it occasionally caused him to retch; earlier he had coughed so violently he vomited bile, forfeiting body fluids he could ill afford to lose at this point. This, of course, reminded him of what he was now sure to be a broken rib.

Every inch of him that wasn't numb from the cold was screaming at him in agony. He used to enjoy hiking, but he vowed to take up an indoor sport from now on. Bowling sounded good.

He'd been on his own for nearly nineteen hours, and he had no idea where he was.

He'd paused at each crest, scanning the horizon for lights. In some ways the darkness had been helpful, because any lights in the distance would mean the possibility that he'd found the road or the café, or at least something that connected to civilization. But the pain had forced many rest stops, most of them longer than the actual periods of moving forward.

He was resting atop a ridge when something in the distance caught his attention.

A flash of light. Maybe a shooting star low in the sky. The clouds had parted in places, revealing a dense pattern of stars that on any other night would have captured his imagination. Perhaps that's all this was, this illumination he thought he saw—his imagination.

He saw it again, about a mile out. It could have been headlights on a road bending around a hill, cutting off his line of vision. It had been moving fast, like a vehicle on a highway rather than a four-wheel drive on an unpaved and unnamed road. He strained his ears to hear something, but his hearing was as numb and shut down as his sense of touch.

This could be it. The road that would lead him to the cafe that would lead him to the telephone that would be his and his teammates' salvation. Or perhaps he'd miscalculated and was back at the ranch itself, having simply gone in a giant circle.

He pictured Brad and Pamela. A wave of emotion hit him unexpectedly, filling him with resolve. He was all they had now. That is, if it wasn't already too late. He'd never felt this alone, and suddenly admitted to himself how alone he'd always been. Perhaps that could change, should he survive. Perhaps that would be the good that, in a moment of reflection, he would conclude had been borne of this experience.

He watched for ten more minutes, but the lights didn't return.

With no other options, he hurried down the embankment in front of him, some of the distance covered sliding on his backside in the mud. Once off the ridge he was again navigating on instinct and memory.

There were two major hills between him and the point where he'd seen what he chose to believe were those headlights, and he knew that every minute counted now. Because he knew he might not make it through another frigid night.

WEAVERVILLE, CALIFORNIA

11:00 P.M.

THE first place Beth and Officer Garvin went after leaving the motel was the Weaverville police station. It was, in fact, adjacent to the Weaverville City Hall, sharing a parking lot and a view of a Wendy's and a Shell station. He'd told her to stay in the car, as he'd only be a minute. Fifteen minutes later he returned and suggested she come inside where it was warm. Some of his earlier phone calls had been returned, and he needed to talk to some people before they ventured out to the ranch to see for themselves. There were also some bugs being worked out with superior officers, including waking the mayor with the possibility of a kidnap situation, in which case the FBI would indeed need to be called in. The FBI, it seemed, was a political football one did not want to fumble.

Half an hour later—Beth was thankful for the coffee and magazines in the waiting room—Garvin was all apologies and charm when he finally emerged from the door leading to the offices where this negotiation had taken place.

"That took some doing," he said.

"We're still going up there?"

"Oh, yes. I don't mean to alarm you, but the FBI hasn't heard about any of this, and they're a little curious. Nobody up at The Complex is answering the phone, but that's normal for this time of night. Not that we ever have to call, but it stands to reason. Wouldn't hurt to drop on by and check it out."

"They wouldn't answer if someone had a gun to their head, either."

"Oh, quite the contrary. In that case they'd want to make things look as normal as possible. So they'd have someone answer the phone and play nice."

"In that case you just contradicted yourself. You said nobody would answer this time of night."

Garvin smiled. They were walking back out to the car, the night air refreshingly crisp, like a cold washcloth applied to a throbbing headache.

"That's right, that's what I said. The mayor says they'd answer, so something must be up, and guess who has rank here. When in doubt, check it out."

"I like when-in-doubt-call-for-backup better."

"Oh, but you see, there is no backup. Tonight there's only me. Me and this."

He patted the gun tucked into his leather sheath. Next to Garvin's slight frame it looked reassuringly huge.

66

THE COMPLEX

11:06 P.M.

The team waited with the doors wide open, wondering where Richard and Georgia were and why they had been summoned here. Silence had been abandoned in favor of a series of subdued conversations to pass the time, an exchange of how-are-you-feeling check-ins offered in the warm context of mutual survival. They had made it through the storm together, and nothing was worth their adrenaline now.

Turner appeared in the doorway. Without looking at anyone he pulled the double doors closed, then reached into the pocket of his heavy parka and withdrew a set of keys. He could sense the room hushing behind him as he tried one key after another, finally finding one that slid into the dead bolt cleanly. When the bolt was set, he turned to see that all eyes were fixed on him and that the room was silent.

"If you would gather in the center of the room," he said, "on the floor, please."

The people moved without hesitation or expression. Tom Turner had risen above their rank that afternoon, and everyone just assumed that in doing so he had taken on some new responsibility. He was now their leader by default, and there was no reason not to comply.

When they were on the floor, Turner took a position between them and the door, remaining standing. He put his hands behind him in a George C. Scott-as-Patton pose.

"A situation has come up," he said, his face deadly serious. "What I'm about to tell you is all too real, not more seminar bullshit. You won't want to believe me, especially after everything they've put us through, and you'll try to find a way to conclude that you are being once again provoked. As Richard would say if he were here, you'll be making up a story that suits you. I assure you, this is not bullshit."

He waited, seeing that several of the faces looking back at him were grinning, already in doubt. We'll see who's smirking in a few minutes, he thought to himself.

"Where is Richard?" asked the most predictable source in the room, Sybil Manning.

Turner ignored the question, narrowing his eyes.

"Part of the regular seminar curriculum involves your spouses. Not all of you, but a select few, depending on your marital and financial situation. While we've been here getting the shit scared out of us, some of your spouses have been approached by people pretending to be the FBI. Your spouses have been told that this seminar has been commandeered by extortionists who are demanding they pay a considerable ransom in exchange for an assurance of your safety."

Turner allowed himself a moment to enjoy the response. These candy-ass pukes with their network marketing businesses and their pending partnerships and their disintegrating marriages . . . they could all kiss his tattooed ass in a few hours. For their sake he hoped they didn't piss him off in the meantime.

He pulled the gun from his parka. A collective gasp swept over the group, which inched backward along the floor.

"Just cut the shit, okay?" It was Scott, already getting to his feet, his face full of disgust. "We're tired, we're confused enough already, and this isn't going to work tonight, okay? Don't fucking insult our intelligence by asking us to buy into another illusion." His eyes left Turner and scanned his teammates. "Am I right?"

The group voiced their collective support. In response, Turner cocked the gun and leveled it at Scott, silencing the room.

Scott grinned. "Right, like I'm buying this. Now you're going to blow me away, is that it? Let's not wait all night to get to it then, okay? I'm calling you on your shit right now, right here, hero man."

Scott stepped over Pamela's legs and began weaving through the people toward the front, where Turner was standing.

Turner fired. Scott felt the bullet slice through the air a few inches from his ear before he heard the explosive sound of the gun itself. The wall behind him showed a clean black hole, from which chalky dust was already wafting into the air. The room seemed to resonate with the echo of the blast; its occupants were frozen in the moment, unsure what to believe.

Pamela reached up and grabbed Scott's belt, yanking him back to her. He resisted, remaining on his feet as he used his hands to pry hers off him, the way an out-of-control teammate fights off the restraining hands of his teammates

"What is this?" he demanded.

Now it was Turner who smiled. "You know and I know," he said. He let a few moments pass. Then, for the benefit of the others, he said, "Ask him if he's a shill."

All eyes went to Scott, but he didn't move.

Turner smiled. "What's it gonna be, hero man?"

Half a minute passed.

Finally Scott said, "I'm not buying it. Everything we learned today was about believing in yourself, about stepping into fear. You took your shot today, and look at you now. All my life I've been watching guys like you step up. Now it's my turn."

Turner was already shaking his head. "Don't do it, man. I'm not shitting you."

"Neither am I," said Scott. He began walking forward.

Turner brought his other hand up to the gun. "Stop now!"

"Nothing to it," said Scott, stepping over the last person who might block his path.

Turner fired. The bullet hit Scott squarely in the center of the chest, the impact lifting him off his feet, pushing him backward. When he landed, he was sprawled over Brad's legs, facing up, with his head on Pamela's lap. He looked up at her, his eyes already glassing over. Her face was splattered with blood from the exit wound sprayed on those who were sitting behind where he had been standing. Pamela's mouth was open, a guttural whimper coming forth as she touched the wound with her fingers, as if to see if it was real. She brought red fingers up to her face and squinted at them. When she looked back at Scott, who was already dead, she saw his eyes and knew. They all knew now. This was different than what they'd seen earlier, the theater of their deception. There was no mistaking what had happened here.

Turner remained in his firing posture, ready to do the same to anyone who attempted an advance. The room was full of screams, but only briefly. While Turner hadn't moved, the distance between him and the others had increased as they shrank back to the wall, leaving Pamela out front, still holding Scott's head in her hands, her face buried in the nape of his neck, trembling as she sobbed uncontrollably. Brad was behind her, holding her steady but not attempting to pull her away. As he did this, he glared at Turner, his restraint barely winning the tug-of-war with his rage.

"Real bullets, people," said Turner. "No more audience plants making you believe in what you see. You can believe everything now. Test me again and you'll learn that lesson the hard way. Life sucks, then you jack—that's my fucking life philosophy, and I'm the guy with the gun, right? I've got the money, that's all I came here for. Stay put, stay quiet, and I'm out of here in the morning. That's it. That simple."

He grinned, deliberately trying to provoke outrage. While he sensed it just below the surface, no one stirred.

"It's all bullshit," he said, shaking his head disapprovingly as he lowered his hands and the gun. "Take the fucking money and run—that's the only reality."

He backed toward the door, retrieving the keys from his pocket. This time he had no trouble finding the right one, which he used on the dead bolt. He opened the door, slid outside, then locked it behind him.

67

Forty minutes after Beth and Officer Garvin pulled out of the Weaverville police station parking lot, they were descending the winding road that led into The Complex. In the dark all Beth could see was a brightly lit group of buildings in the dead center of the bowl, but in the driving rain it was like a flashlight dropped in a pool, and nothing else was visible. A fresh buzz started up in her stomach, part apprehension, part excitement. If nothing else she'd probably get to see Brad tonight, and to her pleasant surprise that was the biggest butterfly of all. All of this was for him, after all.

Then again, that might not happen. They'd meet with some seminar employee, chat for a few minutes about how things are going, explain that they'd had a report they were checking out and how sorry they were to bother them at this time of night. They'd be reassured that everything was okay, they'd be thanked for their diligence and told that it felt good to know the law was watching out for them, then they'd drive home to explain it all to the mayor, who would undoubtedly be disappointed as hell.

This would be precisely how she would play it if she were holding a group of people hostage in this situation. She'd feed the bloodhound they'd sent to the door a tasty piece of steak laced with a sedative that would put the whole issue to bed.

She wished she could see more of the place. This was where her husband was rearranging his attitude and perspective, including about her. Perhaps because of that she felt connected just being here, like a parent visiting their child's school for the first time.

They came to the group of lighted buildings after driving on level ground for a mile or so, which were arranged around an egg-shaped space the size of a stadium parking lot. Most of the buildings appeared old, appropriately camplike, arranged in a circle around a large courtyard. On one side were several trailers, all dark, and on the other a handful of buildings that were obviously bunkhouses. The largest building, however, was much newer than the others, looking more like a church or school. Strangely, it had no windows, an attribute lending it a somewhat sinister air.

When they pulled into the central parking area, she saw a man standing at the end of the pathway leading from this modern building. When they got closer, Beth noticed that he was wearing a heavy parka with the hood up to shield him from the rain, and when they stopped a few yards in front of him, she saw that he was short and stocky, with a bad complexion.

"Stay in the car," said Officer Garvin as he put the vehicle in park, switched off the engine, and opened his door. Beth noticed that he unlatched the leather flap that held the gun in place in its holster. He did it with a bit of a flourish, as if he wanted her to notice this little act of bravado.

"**Evening**," said the man, mustering a smile.

"Evening," said Garvin, accepting the man's handshake. "Richard around tonight?"

"No, sir," said Tom Turner, peering over Garvin's shoulder at Beth. "He and Georgia left things in my hands tonight, I'm afraid. Can I help you?"

He had been sitting in one of the chairs on the bunkhouse porch, where he could see the classroom building clearly and stay out of the rain. He'd been counting the money when he saw the headlights approaching and had worked up this scenario as his first line of defense. When he saw the car turn into the courtyard and that it was a police cruiser, every hair on his body stood on end. Quickly he zipped the satchel closed and took it back inside, stashing it under his bunk. While there he checked his weapon, making sure the safety was off.

He drew a deep breath, then went outside to stand by the gate leading to the classroom. If the local police knew anything at all about this place, they might just buy his line.

His second line of defense was in his pocket.

"Mrs. Pratt?" said the officer. "Her jet's over at the Douglas City airport, so I figured she'd be here."

"Not that I know of," said Turner. "She hasn't shown up this week, actually."

Garvin looked around before saying anything else, taking in every building with what Turner thought to be an analytical, even a suspicious stare.

"And you are . . . ?"

"Turner. Tom Turner."

When they shook hands a second time, Garvin knew Turner was nervous.

"You're one of the students?"

"I am."

"And they left you in charge, you say?"

Turner nodded. "Leadership thing, I guess. My turn on the hot seat. I don't know where they are, really. To be honest, we don't have a clue where they go when they leave us."

Garvin nodded. He looked at the bunkhouses. "Everyone asleep?"

Since the lights were still burning at this hour, in which case nobody would be asleep, Turner sniffed out the baited question.

"Hardly," he said, mustering what he hoped would be perceived as a complicated smile. He flicked his head toward the classroom and said, "All-night session. What's going on?"

Garvin smiled. "I know how it is. I took this class two years ago myself . . . quite the mind-fuck, if you don't mind my saying."

Turner felt his muscles relax slightly.

"Well put," he said. "What's the situation? Can I help you with anything?"

Garvin chanced a quick glance back at Beth, then quickly back to Turner. "She wants to talk to her husband."

Turner nodded slowly. "Gee, I don't know . . ."

"Happens every once in a while, actually. Richard usually sends the husband or wife out, lets 'em kiss and hug, and the worried spouse goes away satisfied that everything is okay."

Turner looked beyond Garvin to the car, the hand in his pocket resting on the handle of his gun.

"She's afraid he isn't okay?"

Garvin smiled, guy to guy. "Something like that."

Both men turned and looked at the car, then quickly away.

"If you're in charge, then you can make it happen, am I right?" said Garvin, his smile condescending.

Turner pursed his lips, unsure. He thought a moment, then shook his head.

"I don't think I should. I mean, this is my responsibility, and hell, for all I know this is a test of my leadership integrity, just another illusion. You're probably an actor from the Bay Area like the others, and she's . . . hell, she's probably Mrs. Pratt's niece or something. Nope. No way. Not on my watch."

Garvin grinned sympathetically. He'd been here, of course, so he knew. "I see your point. But I'm afraid this is for real."

Turner nodded, knowing that it was.

"Who is it? Who's she want to see?"

"Brad Teeters."

Garvin couldn't see Turner's reaction, which was a

fresh jolt of adrenaline. When he was hired for this job, he had been given a list of names, people to whom he was supposed to give special care—some tender, some not so tender—and one of them was Brad Teeters. And because Tom Turner didn't believe in coincidences, he was suddenly very much on the spot.

He squeezed the handle of the gun in his pocket.

Just then the police car door opened. Beth Teeters got out and was walking toward them.

BETH was never any good in moments like this: when she was out of control, and the subject of discussion she could not hear. She saw the men look back at her several times, saw the nervous tic in the parka guy's body language. Exacerbating this feeling of unease was the fact that on the drive out here Garvin had been chatty as hell, all small talk and flirtatious banter, when he should have been pumping her for information about her allegations. By the time they'd arrived, she'd concluded Garvin was not taking her seriously, that he was yanking her chain, and that she'd need to be on her toes.

Then again, she didn't need for him to take her seriously. Not yet, anyway. She simply needed him to be here.

Now, however, while she was very much on her toes, she felt it might be going south. She had to take things into her hands right now, or it would blow up in her face.

She pushed open the door and got out.

"Excuse me," she said, already striding toward him.

Both men turned. She noticed they shot each other a quick glance as she arrived at their side. The rain was a dull roar, so their voices were louder than normal.

"Hi . . . I'm Beth Teeters, my husband—"

"Brad, of course." The man extended his hand. "I'm Tom Turner. We've heard a lot about you."

Garvin said, "This is the woman who, how shall I say this, is worried about her husband."

The man nodded and smiled. "I see. He hasn't called you, and you're concerned, am I right? He should have told you that he wouldn't have a chance to call. This was made clear to him in his instructions. I'm sorry. He's doing just fine. Exceptional, actually. He's a very special man, Mrs. Teeters. But of course, you already know that."

"I'd like to see him, if I could."

The man smiled. "I'm sorry, that's impossible."

"No," said Beth, "*I'm* sorry, but I've come all the way from Seattle on an FBI jet on the report that something is very wrong here, a report from your own people, I might add, and I'm not leaving until I see Brad."

The man nodded, seemed to be considering something. Beth's nerves began to sing: he should be confused if not slightly outraged, demanding clarification—*an FBI jet, you say?*—insistent that things here were fine. He should be reacting to what she'd just said, asking questions, feigning surprise, demanding clarification. But instead of any of these he was just standing there thinking about it, and that just didn't add up.

"We're having a group exercise—"

"At one in the morning?" asked Beth. She glanced at Garvin, who only nodded, clueless. As if to say, hey, it's your show.

"We don't wear watches here at The Complex," he said. He pursed his lips, then said, "Let me check . . . I'll see if I can pull him. But only for a minute. He's actually leading the session himself, you see, and this will be very disruptive. He's a marvelous leader, your husband. You must be very proud of him."

"Right now what I am is very concerned about him," she said.

Turner tried to smile, but it was as phony as a presidential apology. He was thinking that if this was anybody other than Brad Teeters, he'd play hardball and say no. But there was something more to this than met the eye, and the best play was to take the chance. The fact that Teeters was untouchable meant that someone connected to Teeters was at the heart of the play, and that made him nervous.

"All right, I'll get him. But only for a minute. Wait here, please."

He headed down the wooden pathway toward the windowless building, his pace slow and awkward, as if he was tired. Or as if he was buying time.

"**WHAT** do you think?" she asked Garvin, keeping her eyes on the man as he retreated toward the building, which now looked to Beth a bit like a mausoleum.

"I think you should have stayed in the car like I told you to," he said.

"What did he say? I mean, you two were standing here shooting the shit . . . he must have said something."

"I don't think you want to hear it."

"If you had $250,000 of your money on the line here, wouldn't you want to hear it?"

"Okay . . . he said you were lying. That this was an excuse to see your husband."

"He said that?"

"I have no reason to be untruthful with you, Mrs. Teeters. He said it happens all the time. People miss their spouses—men, mostly—they get suspicious for all kinds of reasons, and they come up with all sorts of schemes to get on the property to see for themselves. Some just show up, usually pretty pissed off. The money thing is a new one, he said, and a pretty good one at that. He got quite a kick out of it, actually."

She watched the man stop at the door, saw it open, watched him go inside.

"And you believe that's what this is?"

"I'm not here to judge, Mrs. Teeters, I'm just here to help."

"Well you can add me to that pretty pissed-off list," she said. She decided not to say anything more until Brad came out.

Everything was going perfectly.

68

Brad heard the key in the lock, saw the door open, watched Turner come inside and head directly to where Pamela was being comforted by Tiffany Palofax and Sybil Manning. Scott's body had been taken to the far corner and covered with jackets, but the mound of fabric had remained the focal point of the room.

The group fell back against the wall as Turner entered the room. Brad noted that Turner hadn't locked the door behind him, that he'd simply swung it shut as he stormed in. This realization also caused Brad to acknowledge a distinctly different flavor of respect for authority among them now. Somehow, after facing and surviving Simon's transparent threat of death, the proximity of the real thing carried a whole new dimension of fear. Defiance was gone this time, replaced by silent resignation.

Turner went to where Pamela and the woman were huddled. He pushed Tiffany and Sybil to the side and grabbed Pamela by the arm, hauling her to her feet. Then, to Brad's emerging horror, Turner dragged her to where he was sitting, leaning against the wall directly opposite the outside doors. He stopped in front of him, Pamela hanging from his grip as if she'd collapse if left on her own.

"You," he said to Brad, "on your feet, big fella."

Brad obeyed, suddenly nauseated and dizzy.

"Come here," he said, as he began dragging Pamela toward the doors across the way, walking backward slowly as Pamela stumbled along. He held the barrel of his gun to Pamela's head as he went.

Once at the doors he jammed it inside her mouth. She cried out and gagged simultaneously, but he kept it there as he strengthened his hold on her arm and looked Brad in the eye.

"Listen to me, because everyone's life depends on it. You hear what I'm saying? You fuck with me, she dies, they all die, then your wife dies. Are we clear?"

Brad showed his surprise on his face, prompting Turner to go on.

"She's outside," said Turner, indicating the direction with his head. "Your fucking wife . . . she's with a policeman."

This news was so out of context that Brad couldn't respond.

"I don't know how you got word to her, or even if you did, but know this: you're going to get rid of her, you're going to do it quickly, and you're going to do it with a smile so that she goes away relieved instead of worried. Are we clear?"

Brad shook his head quickly. "Time out—we're not remotely clear. How did—"

"Maybe you can tell me when you get back in here and I see taillights."

Brad looked behind at the group for help, but everyone was motionless. Turner was speaking in low tones, and Brad doubted anyone could hear them clearly.

Turner tugged Pamela closer to him. "You'll tell your wife that you are fine, that you are having the time of your life. You'll seem confused that she's here, but you'll be appropriately happy to see her. You'll listen to her story, and you'll laugh when you hear it, but not condescendingly so because you're a nice guy and you are sensitive to her feelings. She thinks you've been kidnapped, imagine that shit, but somehow she's here and you're here and now she's confused, ya know? You'll tell her that it's all part of the seminar curriculum and that you neglected to warn her that she might get involved in some way. Her and the other spouses. *Capisce?* Tell her it's all a big fucking misunderstanding. You'll diffuse this situation, and then you'll return to this room and convince me that she is going away happy, no longer suspicious and very embarrassed. It's all about taillights, Teeters. Give me taillights, and your little friend here can go back to pissing her pants, and I'll leave you alone."

Turner raised his eyebrows as if to question Brad's understanding. The two men locked eyes, Brad balancing the shock of this sudden development with the clarity of Turner's instructions.

Brad finally nodded.

"We cool?" asked Turner. He opened the door slightly, and Brad could see two people standing next to a police car. He took a deep breath, trying to steady his nerves. Then he nodded again.

"Do it," said Turner, pulling the door wider, flicking his head toward it.

69

12:31 A.M.

When Beth saw her husband approaching, she sprinted up the wooden path to meet him. Over the years she had learned to jump into his arms and kick her feet as he snatched her up, bringing them eye to eye for whatever expression of affection that was appropriate to the moment.

He smelled musty, in need of a shower. She could feel him crying softly as he held her. This reaction startled her and in a moment's resolve, strengthened her, too.

He put her down and then touched her face. Beth reached up, using her thumb to wipe a single tear from his cheek.

"Can we have a minute here?" she asked Garvin, who had followed her down the path to greet him.

The police officer nodded sheepishly as he backed off.

"God, it's good to see you," he said when they were alone.

"I don't know where to start," she said. "You look . . . so tired."

"We don't get much sleep around here. This is all very intense."

"But you're okay? Nothing is wrong?"

Brad stole a look back at the building. "They told me you were upset, that something happened, that you think there's something going on here."

A flash of indignation appeared in her eyes. "That man, the one from the seminar company that took me to lunch that day to talk about you? He showed up at the house two days ago. He said—"

Brad held up his hands. "Stop. Listen to me. Don't say any more, okay?"

"But, Brad . . ."

"I can't know about that," he said, "and I don't want to know about that. Listen, I know it's hard to understand, but whatever it was, it's all part of this . . ."

He used his arm to indicate the entire ranch. "It's one of the exercises, and it involves you. I don't know what it is, but they said it would rock your world. All the spouses are going through the same thing and . . ."

"But they're not *here,* Brad! I am! I can help you!"

"I know, but listen, I don't *need* any help . . . they probably didn't expect you to—"

"They flew me down here, okay? On a fucking FBI jet! Do you hear me?"

"Beth, please . . ." He put his fingers on her lips. "It'll ruin it for me if you tell me. I don't know what happened, and I don't care—just let this run its course, okay? Please, do this for me, for us. You have to trust me. Trust that I'm doing the right thing here."

She had to be sure.

"They've got our money, Brad."

"I said stop!" His tone was sharper now. He took a deep breath, her words slicing into his mind.

It was the pause, the way he looked at her, that told her what she needed to know. Brad was clueless about the money. It was all an outside job. Her seminar, not his. Maybe, just maybe, she could make this work.

As Beth processed these thoughts, what Brad was feeling was pride. His wife was a fighter, a take-no-prisoners woman of action. They had come to her for money, and she had been a pit bull, insisting that she be allowed to see for herself. And here she was, where no other spouse or even the FBI had been allowed to stand.

"How are Pamela and Mark doing?" she asked. When he didn't answer, when his eyes narrowed, he confirmed what she suspected.

They embraced again.

"Beth." Garvin had stepped forward and was now touching her shoulder. "They're waiting for him. I shouldn't have brought you out here. As you can see, everything is fine."

Brad kissed his wife very gently. "It's okay, sweetheart. It'll be okay. Whatever they said and whatever you think, just relax, go with it. I'm okay. I promise. Everything will be fine. I'll be home in a few days."

She looked at Garvin and said, "A few more seconds. I'll be right there."

He backed off, heading for the car.

Beth pulled Brad close, pressing her lips to his ear, speaking very softly.

"Listen to me, listen very carefully. I know what this is. Don't ask how, just listen. When he asks for people to go with him, you go. Do you understand me? Whatever it takes, make sure you're one of them who goes with him."

He started to pull away to ask what the hell this meant, but she held him so that her mouth remained close to his ear.

"Do you promise?"

He nodded. "I promise . . . but—"

"Trust me. I love you . . . you have to trust me."

Now she backed away, holding his arm loosely with both hands, letting it slip through her grip until their hands met. They exchanged a final squeeze before their fingertips parted, his expression confused.

He nodded slightly.

Then he turned and walked quickly into the building without looking back.

*   *   *

SHE watched him go in, then stood quietly as she stared at the double doors for a moment. She turned and looked up at the massive metallic statue to her right, looming over the courtyard. The clouds had parted slightly, and she could see the moon perfectly framed inside the diamond silhouette of the statue, casting splinters of misty light in all directions from its gleaming chrome surface. It looked as if it might clear up by morning.

But instead of thinking about Brad, she was thinking about someone else. She was thinking that the moonlight would help Mark see in the dark as he stumbled through the forest, still in search of the road.

Or so Wong had told her.

When she turned, Officer Garvin was standing at the door to the car, holding it open for her.

She knew everything she needed to know now. It was time.

70

WEAVERVILLE, CALIFORNIA

2:04 A.M.

"There's something you should know," said Officer Bryon Garvin as they drove back to town. Unlike the ride out, this trip had been in silence until now, the headlights casting a surreal cone of illumination into the rain-streaked blackness. The windshield wipers were, as they had for Bobby McGee and Janis Joplin in that song, clapping time, but there was no hand holding or singing on this trip. Just the wipers and the hum of the tires cutting through patches of standing water on the road.

Beth almost grinned at the irony of his statement. There was something *he* should know, that's for damn sure. Instead, she just turned her head so that he could see she was listening.

"I knew there wasn't a kidnap and ransom situation when I took you out there," he said.

She just nodded.

He glanced over and grinned sheepishly. "I've been

through the course. I know all about the kidnapping thing. They vary it a little every time, depending on the needs of the students. They study those profiles to death, you know, and they create certain situations for certain people."

He paused, giving her a chance to respond, which she didn't.

"It's a very effective exercise," he said. "It changed my life . . . changes a lot of lives. I bet your husband will say the same."

She stared straight ahead now, feeling him steal another glance at her.

"We work closely with the seminar group all the time," he said, "and most of the department has been through the course. Hell, the whole town has been through it, including the mayor."

"Village of the fucking damned," muttered Beth.

"'Scuze me?" he asked.

"Nothing." No chance he'd know the movie, anyway.

They drove in silence for another minute before Garvin started up again.

"When you called in earlier . . . well, of course I knew what you were talking about, but I didn't. I mean, I'd never heard of a ransom angle before, and no one had ever come to town asking to be taken out there, either. So I checked it out. We couldn't reach anyone out at the ranch, but the mayor—been a good friend of Mrs. Pratt's for years—he told me they've started involving the spouses, that they select a few couples from each seminar and put them through the ransom routine. Said that someone showing up on our doorstep about it was inevitable and that I should play it out, let you discover it for yourself."

"Discover what for myself?" she said with a low, even tone.

"What your husband really means to you. Your marriage. Your relationship with money. How you respond to fear and the sudden appearance in your life of a significant threat to your well-being."

"Oh, just that," she said. A moment later, "You people

have a lot of nerve messing around with people's lives that way. You could get sued. Or worse."

"I don't work for the seminar," he said defensively.

"Maybe you should," said Beth, staring straight ahead. They drove for a few minutes in silence.

"I apologize if I have contributed in any way to your anxiety," he finally said. "I just wanted you to know—this was all for your own good, that I was just trying to help."

She allowed a few seconds to pass before she said, "I'm going back to Seattle in the morning. Tell Mrs. Pratt thank you for the use of her car. I'll leave it at the bus station."

"Bus stops at the WinCo, at nine," he said.

"It'll be in the lot," said Beth. "Keys under the mat."

Nothing more was said until ten minutes later, when the squad car pulled into the tiny motel parking lot. Mrs. Pratt's Navigator was one of only three vehicles there, and Beth breathed a sigh of relief upon seeing it.

"God bless you, Mrs. Teeters," said Garvin as Beth opened the door and got out.

She ran toward her room without looking back.

Once there, she noticed that he remained in the parking lot until she got the door to her room open. But instead of going in, she walked back out into the rain toward him. His window was down by the time she got there.

Her face was different now. Softer, showing the stress of the evening.

"How long are you on tonight?" she asked. "In case I need to talk to someone."

He smiled. "I'm on till six," he said. "Don't hesitate to call. That's normal, you know, after it sinks in and all."

She nodded, issued a barely perceptible smile, and hurried back to her room.

SHE waited thirty minutes. She spent the entire time sitting on her bed, never taking off her coat, the curtains open and the lights off. She stared out at the road, which was the main drag in Weaverville. Not a single car came by the entire time.

Finally, when it felt right, she got up, went outside, and fired up the Navigator.

She headed west, back toward the ranch.

71

THE COMPLEX

3:09 A.M.

Brad returned from his brief reunion with Beth to find Pamela already safe in the arms of Tiffany and Sybil. Turner had watched the whole thing from the doorway, and upon seeing that Beth and Garvin were indeed getting back into their car, he'd released her and allowed the women to take her back to the corner of the room.

When Brad came back inside, Turner motioned with his head for him to move away from the door. Brad was surprised the man wasn't interested in a debrief of some kind, but he didn't say a word and seemed uninterested in Brad from that point forward. Turner remained next to the door for less than a minute, peering through as the police car departed. Then he opened it, stepped outside, and closed it again. The sound of the dead bolt quickly followed.

*   *   *

3:51 A.M.

BY now a few people had somehow managed to fall asleep, as much from exhaustion as from any ability to set their predicament aside in their minds. This would be their third straight night in this room, and even Brad, who was as keenly aware of the situation as anyone, could feel the need to close his eyes. Some of the men—Matt, Derek, Stu, and a few others—could be seen engaging in what appeared to be a lively debate, and on one occasion Matt motioned for Brad to join them. But Brad wasn't interested in covert plans or armchair heroics right now. He just wanted to be left alone, to make the time pass in silence. Any more ingenious schemes could get them all killed, and Brad wanted no part of them.

The sound of the key in the lock was almost gentle this time. Turner came in, still wearing his heavy parka, with one hand buried deep in a pocket, where the gun was surely waiting. He motioned for Brad to come toward him, as well as several others. Anyone, in fact, who was still awake. In less than a minute about half the group was sitting on the floor in a semicircle around Turner, reluctant disciples all.

"I thought you'd want to know what's going to happen," he said. "I have no interest in any more violence, you have to believe me."

That much was true. He was sent here with a list, to make sure certain people wake up dead and bring back a shit-pile of money, but fuck that. There was enough money involved, and the exit strategy was already in place. He'd just disappear with it. Honor among thieves, my ass, he thought. Do your own fucking dirty work.

"I want out of here as much as you do," he continued, "so here's what it looks like. At dawn the skydiving plane will land. No one on the outside is aware of our little situation, so it'll arrive as scheduled. I need four people to come with me to the airstrip. The rest will stay here, locked in this room until someone comes and lets you out. The four who come with me, providing I get off the ground without incident, will be free to go get help. That's your job, to make sure that happens. I figure it's a day-and-a-half walk out of here, easy, and by that time I'm history. Everybody stays dry, a little hungry, but safe. Any questions?"

Surprisingly, there were none.

Turner allowed a tiny smile to break his otherwise serious countenance. "You want to know what they had planned for you? What Simon was going to do if I hadn't stopped all the bullshit when I did? He was going to tell you that the ransom money he was demanding from your families hadn't arrived and that he was going to shoot one hostage every hour until it did. He was going to tell you that the means of choosing who got shot was going to be a question. If you answered yes to the question, you went into the shooting pool. You answered no to the question, you got immunity, so to speak. You know what the question was? Question was—do you believe in God? Imagine that shit? You say yes, maybe you get clipped. You say no, you're safe. They called it the Judas game, deal with the fucking devil. Get this—know where they got the idea? From that Columbine school shooting: those jackass kids played the Judas game, blew away a beautiful little girl who had the guts to say what she believed in, even with a gun to her head. That's your fucking seminar, ladies and gentlemen."

He watched the eyes of the group, most of which were cast down at the ground. "There'll be no Judas game today, kids. I don't wanna go there. So you decide who goes and who stays, no bullshit games. Easy deal—best hikers come with me, the rest stay here. But while you're at it, you might want to think about what your answer would have been if Simon had asked you that question. Or worse, if I had."

Turner paused, his own eyes drifting. His voice was lower as he added, "I know I have."

He turned and went back to the door. "I'll come back in an hour. Have it figured out."

He left, bolting the door behind him.

*   *   *

4:11 A.M.

EVERYONE went back to their respective locations along the wall the moment Turner closed the door. The most interactive thing that happened was a quick exchange of glances, a sharing of relief and acknowledgment. Matt caught Brad's eye, pointing at him with a sort of silent military hand language, then pointing at Derek and at Sybil Manning, who undoubtedly could outhike them all. Finally he thumped his own chest and held up four fingers, the communication now clear. All three of the other parties to it saw that they had been included, as did several other people who were not. Matt had just assembled Turner's hostage party without a word.

Brad took his position across from the door. There was comfort in routine, and where you sat and who you sat with was all they had to work with. Brad sat alone. Like everyone else, the Judas game played at the edge of his thoughts.

Brad tried to push it away. In his heart he knew what he would have chosen. What he didn't know, and had the awareness to recognize, is what he would have done in the moment. No man can know that until the moment arrives.

Instead he thought about writing in his journal, which he'd had the presence of mind to bring when Turner summoned them to the room just before midnight. He'd already recorded the new turn of events, though briefly and without his usual personal take on it all. He wondered if there would be time for that, or if he'd have anything to say if there was.

After about ten minutes of trying to fall asleep, Brad realized he needed to use the bathroom. When he went inside, he saw that the mirror had been shattered and that there were no significant shards of glass remaining on the floor.

72

TWELVE MILES NORTH
OF THE COMPLEX

4:25 A.M.

The moon had come and gone periodically, and in the brief interludes of illumination Mark could see the outline of a sea of surrounding hills. Even when he was resting on top of one, the dark relief of bordering crests against the sky's milkier shade of black made him acknowledge the vastness of his isolation. He almost preferred the pitch-darkness of complete cloud cover. He had lost all direction now, and his legs were failing. Hope had grown fleeting and more fickle with each passing hour; it came now only in brief flashes that were quickly swallowed by the endless dark in which he swam.

He was walking slowly over level ground when his knees buckled and he fell, face first. His impulse was to run, accelerate into the fall to break it, but his legs churned in space, touching nothing. He tucked and rolled, the world in a tumble dryer, landing on rocks.

After a moment he realized he was lying in ice water

and that he couldn't breathe. He remained motionless for several moments, strangely comfortable. The rocks were smooth to the touch, alive with energy. He could hear the rushing sounds of the water as it washed over him, and he knew he'd fallen into a stream.

This was as good a place as any to die.

He laughed out loud at this thought. It was maudlin, disgusting. Dying was not an option. That's what the seminar people would want him to say, and by God, he believed it now.

He rolled to his side, took a deep breath, and placed his palms on the riverbed to push himself to his feet. Then he crawled through the water to the bank, catching his breath. This was bad. It was already near freezing, and in wet clothes he'd not last much longer.

He took a few steps, but his legs were still numb. He sank to his knees, then his hands.

His heart began to pound. It wasn't ground at all beneath his palms. It was pavement. Cold and hard and smooth, slick to the touch of his fingers.

The road.

73

If you are reading this, then I am dead. It is just prior to dawn on Thursday, and this will be my final entry in this journal. In less than two hours we will know if Turner is a man of his word or a man with no soul, a certifiable sociopath. Simon was an enigma, a contradiction, a nightmare, a visionary, a leader, a teacher, a trickster. Most of all he was a catalyst.

Turner, on the other hand, is simply a criminal. Nothing deeper than that.

For me, the hardest part now is not knowing what Beth was really saying, her comment about our money being taken, about her knowing what is happening and sending in help. Wondering if I'm doing the right thing, working with her instead of against her, never really knowing, waiting for the other shoe to fall. As it is in life. Somehow we've managed to adapt to our cluelessness, to go on without knowing the reason we are here. We rationalize our ignorance by inventing religions or falling back on atheism, which has to be the chicken exit of all time. If only we could kid ourselves as well when it comes to things that count less, yet cause us to burn inside.

Only one answer remains. Faith, with courage. That's all we can understand, all we can truly ever know for sure. Our faith must sustain us, or we have nothing.

Not sure where that came from, but it's important. I'm glad I wrote it down.

Which is the higher thought: to confront one's death without fear or without regret? I think it is the latter, because the former is always a lie.

This is what I have learned today.

I know what I must do. And to be perfectly honest, I'm scared shitless.

74

TWELVE MILES NORTH OF THE COMPLEX

5:14 A.M.

The hard road had resurrected each and every nerve in Mark's ankle. His limp was severe as he trudged along, the agony of each step rendering all the other aches and pains he had acquired during the past twenty hours mere inconveniences, including the broken rib. He had learned how to breathe with quick, shallow inhales, allowing him to avoid triggering the cough that felt like a knife penetrating his side. And yet, despite it all, he walked briskly. It was the only way to stay warm. His clothes had dried to a sticky texture, like a dishrag left in a vegetable crisper overnight. He had to keep moving or he would die.

His initial elation at discovering the road had been quickly replaced by indecision. He had no idea in which direction he would find the cafe that Jason had mentioned, or if it existed at all, for that matter. Certainly someone would drive along at some point, but it was almost dawn, and that might not happen for hours. Even then, there was no

guarantee that they would stop and pick up someone with
his appearance at the moment—he wasn't sure he would.
Better to stumble across the elusive cafe, which would have
a phone. So he chose a direction, what he thought was east.
His only rationale was that the interstate was somewhere
to the east, probably an hour away, and the only thing to
the west was the Pacific Ocean, at least a hundred miles
off. Then again, where one opened a cafe in the middle of
nowhere wasn't exactly an exercise in demographic science,
and he realized he might as well flip a coin, which he didn't
have. So he simply chose.

He had walked for over an hour, covering less than a
mile at this pace, when he saw a sign. He picked up his
pace, and when he got there he saw that it had only one
word on it: "FOOD."

He picked up to an even brisker, more painful pace.
A hundred yards ahead the road curved gently, making it
impossible to see what awaited him beyond the bend. After about fifty more yards, however, he was sure he could
sense that the trees around the corner were slightly illuminated, as if from a nearby building.

"Mark!"

He was so excited that he almost didn't comprehend
what he heard.

He stopped. The voice came from a wall of dense veg-
etation at the side of the road.

"Mark!"

This time he was able to pinpoint the source of the
voice.

He went to the side of the road and paused. There was
an opening in the bushes; a large black vehicle had backed
in there.

He squinted. Someone was standing at the open driver's door, motioning frantically for him to approach.

"Mark! Hurry up!"

Mark limped closer. The only ambient light was absorbed by the trees, and all he could see was a silhouette.

Of a woman.

When he was a few feet from the front end of the car,

his heart froze. This was the last person he expected to see out here.

Beth.

His jaw dropped open.

"Hurry up, get in!" she said as she came to him to help.

"What are you . . . my God, are they alive?"

"Just get in where it's warm. I'll tell you everything."

She helped him into the passenger side, his lower back aching with the motion and angle required to settle into the soft seat. He felt a sense of emotion wash over him, realizing it was over.

"My God, you're soaking wet."

He was trembling. She touched his face—it felt like a window in winter.

"We have to hurry," said Beth as she buckled in. Then she turned to him. "I'm going to ask you to do something for me, Mark. It won't make sense, but please just do it so we can get out of here before . . . while we can. I'll explain everything, but for now just do as I ask."

Mark nodded.

"Take off your belt."

"Do what?"

"Just take it off. Please."

It was painful because of his rib, but he managed it, handing it to her when he was done.

Beth took the belt and examined it closely. Mark saw her smile after a moment, then use her fingernail to pry something away from the leather. She held it up to the dome light.

A tiny black square, about three-quarters of an inch wide and thin as a nickel, with a clip affixed to it.

"What is it?"

"Radio transponder," she said.

"My God—" muttered Mark.

She pulled out onto the road, turning in the opposite direction of the cafe, which in light of the transponder discovery made perfect sense. Mark had a million questions, but for now he was simply relieved it was over, and the heat blowing from the dashboard was ecstasy. Beth was obviously intent on getting them out of there, and she would explain when the moment suited her.

Finally, though, after several minutes, he could stand the silence no longer.

"How did you know . . . I mean, how did you find me out here? And the belt . . . I don't understand."

Beth didn't look at him. "Ken told me," she said.

"Ken Wong? You're shitting me . . . *our* Ken Wong?"

"I'll explain everything," she said. Finally she smiled as she reached out a hand and set it on his knee, squeezing reassuringly. "It's all right now . . . everything is going to be fine. It's all over."

He'd never really liked Beth all that much. He thought her a phony and a social climber. But he had to admit, her smile this morning was that of an angel.

Amazing, he almost said out loud, how easy it is to be so wrong about someone.

THEY drove in silence for a minute before Beth lowered the window and tossed the transponder out. Mark started to ask, but there was something about the way she didn't look at him, didn't offer an explanation, that made it easy to remain quiet. The angel had her reasons, and he was too tired to question anything that resembled a higher power this morning.

75

THE COMPLEX

6:00 A.M.

Turner's four appointed hikers—Matt, Derek, Sybil, and Brad—sat near the door in anticipation of his return. Derek was lobbying for an attack once they were on the road to the airstrip, and he flashed a spike of mirror-glass to make his point. Matt had one, as well, and they were trying to talk Sybil and Brad into arming themselves, too.

"Right, and someone gets shot," said Brad. "As soon as we move, the gun goes off, someone gets shot."

"It's an acceptable risk," said Derek.

"It's not a risk, it's a freaking certainty," said Brad.

"I agree with Brad," said Sybil.

"Then it's an acceptable certainty. One of us gets shot, the rest are saved. With any luck it will be a flesh wound."

"Tell that to Matt's kids," said Sybil.

Matt, who had been silent on this issue, nodded as if he hadn't thought of that.

"I would think," said Derek, looking at the group

along the wall as he spoke, "that one would have a new perspective on courage after this week."

Brad exchanged an unbelieving glance with Sybil, who shook her head.

"I would think," said Brad, "that one would have a new perspective on common sense."

"Give the testosterone a rest, Derek," said Sybil. "We go with him, he leaves, we get help, no one gets hurt."

"I like those odds better," said Matt. To make his point, he removed the spike of glass from his jacket pocket and tossed it to the side of the room. It broke into several smaller pieces when it hit the wall.

All three stared at Derek, inviting him to do the same. He thought a moment, then shook his head. "I'll honor your wishes on the attack, but I'm keeping the glass."

Just then they heard a key entering the dead bolt from outside. The lock clicked and the door burst open. Turner had kicked it open so he could survey the area near the door before entering, seeing the four of them on the floor ten feet in front of him. His gun was drawn, anticipating a possible ambush. He entered cautiously, checking both flanking walls as soon as he'd crossed the threshold.

The others sat against the walls, watching. Pamela was lying in Tiffany's lap, her eyes closed, apparently asleep. They looked exhausted, perfectly willing to be left behind.

Turner approached the group of four, knowing without asking that they were the ones that would accompany him. He spent a moment looking them over, then spoke directly to Brad.

"I knew it'd be you," he said.

Brad just nodded, not sure what to make of this.

"Stand up," said Turner, speaking to all of them now. He looked them up and down, taking his time.

"Turn around."

They all complied. If he decided to do a pat-down, Derek was a dead man. Long seconds passed, until finally he commanded them to face him again.

"You will not talk," he said. "You will not step out of line as we walk. I will be behind you, and I'll shoot the first one who breaks this agreement for any reason whatsoever. If you have to piss, do it now. Leave everything you have here—that includes purses, backpacks, notebooks, or jackets that you do not intend to wear. Are we in agreement?"

They had already attended to these details. Brad had stashed his journal in the ceiling, standing on Derek's shoulders to move a tile aside.

They nodded, each of them having their turn looking Turner in the eye.

"Why not just leave us here with the others?" asked Sybil.

"Because shit happens," said Turner, stepping back toward the door. "In which case, I need something to trade."

Then, to the surprise and alarm of everyone, Turner walked past them into the room, heading for the corner where Pamela and Tiffany were resting. He knelt down, touching Pamela's face. She didn't move, as if she had no idea who he was.

"Gift of life, sweetheart."

He stood, still looking at her. "Tell your friend Mark the same thing. Gift of life."

Then he returned to the four who would accompany him, still standing next to the door. As he passed, and without looking, he said, "We're outta here," motioning for them to file through the door.

Once outside, Turner slipped a backpack over one arm and picked up a large canvas satchel. He used his other hand to hold the gun. Brad thought he looked heavy and sluggish, carrying too much weight while constrained by the thick padding of the parka. He'd get off one shot, then he was easy pickings. Brad noticed that Derek saw it, too, recalculating their agreement as their eyes met.

Turner smiled. He shook his head, as if to say, don't even think about it.

The cold instantly penetrated their clothing as they marched in silence. It was still dark outside, though a barely perceptible edge of light was visible at the crest of the hills to the east. The clouds had cleared in large part—it would be a good day for skydiving.

76

WEAVERVILLE, CALIFORNIA

6:05 A.M.

Officer Bryon Garvin was putting on his coat to go home when the telephone rang. He had already told his relief, a thin young officer in his first year named Cal Vaughn, all about his night with Beth Teeters at the ranch. Like Garvin, Vaughn was a recent graduate of the seminar. Instead of laughing, he responded to the story with empathy and the hope that Beth and Brad might find their bliss going forward. They were like two priests swapping confession stories over their second glass of wine, at once giggling at the absurdity while offering their sincerest prayers of mercy.

"Garvin," he said, picking up the phone hurriedly. He'd tried to fend off the call, citing that his shift was over, but when he was told by the department receptionist that the caller was Beth Teeters, he didn't hesitate.

Beth's voice was even more urgent than her words, completely spent in a losing battle with her emotions. It came from that place where words were poor substitutes for a depth of fear better expressed in shrieks and tears.

"Oh, God, you have to get out here now . . . they're dead, in the trailer . . . oh, my God, please—"

Her voice trailed off, and he could hear her heavy, uneven breathing.

"Beth, slow down—"

"There's so much blood . . . he's killed them . . . please, God, help me—"

Garvin was signaling to Vaughn that something was up.

"Beth, are you alright?"

The breathing, but nothing else.

"Beth! Can you hear me? What's happening?"

"You've got to come," she said, her voice barely audible.

"I'll come . . . where are you?"

"In the courtyard. Hurry, please, God, hurry—"

"Listen to me, Beth . . . stay on the line, talk to my partner. I'm leaving now. Do you understand? Are you able to stay where you are without risk?"

"No. He might come back—"

"I'll be there as fast as I can. Stay on the line."

He heard the sound of movement, of hands wrestling with the phone, perhaps dropping it. He couldn't tell if she was using a mobile phone or a fixed line, something he usually prided himself at being able to discern within moments.

"Beth! Don't hang up—"

The line clicked and a dial tone returned.

Garvin stared at Vaughn for a moment, his expression intense.

"Yeah?" said Vaughn, eyes wide.

"Looks like something's up at the ranch."

Vaughn grinned. "Something's always up at the ranch," he said.

"I don't know. I don't like it. I'm going up there. See if you can find Mrs. Pratt and ask her if she knows anything about this. Call me if you hear."

"You want me to come?"

Garvin grinned. "It's called *backup,* and no, I'll be

fine. She just needs an anchor, something to hold on to while it all plays out."

"Just another shitty day in woo-woo paradise," said Vaughn as Garvin was heading out the door.

"We'll see," said the officer, but to himself, since he was already out the door.

77

THE COMPLEX

6:12 A.M.

Beth sat in the Navigator, alone now. She was parked on the access road a quarter mile down from the courtyard complex, and she could see the lights of the buildings, all of which were on. She was still slightly hyperventilated from her breathless performance with Garvin, which had ended with her holding the mobile phone in both hands and twisting, as if she were wringing out a towel. She hadn't planned that, but it must have sounded like chaos on Garvin's end of the line, and that was the idea.

Chaos. Pure, unmitigated terror. It fit the essence of what Garvin would find when he arrived. Having seen it with her own eyes, she understood what it was.

Wong had told her about the trailer and its computer with the transponder satellite connection, and she wanted to check it to make sure Mark was still out there, so she could pinpoint his location in relation to the road and the cafe. Finding Mark was critical to success, especially since she'd put this into motion before Wong told her he might, in fact, be missing in action when she arrived. Wong had gone through it all in detail, and he had been spot-on with his instructions on how to access the program and read the data.

But there was far more than data waiting for her inside the trailer.

What she didn't expect to find were the dead bodies of the four seminar people. The trailer was supposed to be empty at this hour—that's what Wong had said, too—and upon approaching it on foot it certainly appeared to be. She'd brought along the necessary tools to smash a window and enter from the rear, out of the line of sight of the bunkhouses. That's precisely what she did, and all was going according to plan until her foot slipped on the floor, encountering something wet. The room smelled acrid, like animals lived here. She reached down with her hands, removing her glove to allow her fingers to explore, and encountered a carpet soaked through with moisture. She could see the computer across the room with its one green eye, and she discerned the outline of the monitor in the scant ambient light. She hadn't planned on taking the risk of turning on a light. But when her foot slipped, she also tripped over something, and an alarm went off in her head. So, after checking with her hand, she'd moved toward the door, tripping again along the way, feeling for the light switch. Along the way she stepped on something with a crunching sound.

When the light came on, she barely subdued her scream. Her system seized up, completely frozen with fear. Movement was impossible because her mind, the tool of that movement, had been sucked down into hell.

The first body she'd tripped over was that of a muscular young man, lying in a pool of blood that had expanded to envelop him on all sides within a six-foot circle of gore. Closer to the door was what was once a good-looking man, were it not for the charred hole in his forehead and the missing rear third of his skull. The wall behind him was dripping with a satanic abstract in crimson, flecked with pieces of bone and brain tissue. On the floor next to him was what she had stepped on a moment ago—a pair of sunglasses.

To her left was the body of Mrs. Pratt, and next to that, as if he'd tried to crawl to her side, was the body of her son, Thomas Stanton. Unlike the others, his eyes were still wide open, as was his mouth, fixed in a silent cry for help.

Beth stood motionless for several minutes, trembling, fighting to keep from screaming. She kept her eyes closed for several minutes, unable to look.

Finally, though, she summoned the same strength of will that had brought her here in the first place. Focusing on the computer, placing it at the end of a tunnel with black walls, she put the glove back on and went to it. The first touch brought the screen back to life, and she was pleased to see that it was already on the transponder program. She leaned close, familiarizing herself with the details of the map. There was a blinking green light to the north, and she saw that it was positioned right on the line that denoted the road, twelve miles from the center of the ranch.

She had to hurry. It was imperative she intercept Mark before he reached the cafe. If she didn't, if they found him before she did, it would be the end of everything.

Now, an hour later, Beth was back on ranch property. The business with Mark had been put to bed, all of it having gone better than she'd hoped. Easier, too, especially after what she'd just been through. He was walking down the center of the road toward the cafe, wobbling like a drunk trying to find his car. The look on his face when he saw her was priceless, and it moved her. She'd saved him, after all, and that fact would connect them forever.

She looked at her watch, snubbing out the cigarette she'd allowed herself in this moment of pause. Who could blame her, after what she'd seen, after what she'd accomplished.

If Wong was correct—and he had been correct about

everything thus far—the jump plane would arrive promptly at seven. Brad would be there, the money would be there, and the world would shift on its axis.

If Garvin hauled ass, he'd arrive right about then, too.

78

Silence made the tension all the more palpable as the five of them trudged along a road soggy with mud. Turner remained five yards behind, positioning the four of them shoulder to shoulder, having them link their arms as if they were walking down the aisle of a church. If an arm came unlinked, the gun went off, or so the story went. The sky was a bizarre smear of parting clouds whose edges were illuminated by the first hint of dawn. The sounds of the march were equally bizarre: five sets of slopping, sucking footfalls without unison or rhythm, the gasps of labored breathing, the brushing of denim and slick nylon on pants and coats.

Sybil Manning was humming what Brad recognized as the theme from *The Bridge on the River Kwai*. He wasn't sure if this sprang from her heart or her rebellion, a melodic fuck-you to Turner, but in either case it made the trek surreal, even light.

He made a note to try and hire this woman if they got out of here alive.

Brad forced a more analytical layer of thought over his observations. He'd made a point of checking out the exterior of the building when they came out. There were no dead bodies tossed aside, nothing remotely out of the norm. Looking toward the hills, there were no lights or other evidence of anyone close by. They were truly alone, which strengthened his resolve to let Turner leave without incident, without Derek trying for one last moment of seminar glory.

They walked for thirty minutes, a distance Brad judged to be about a mile and a half. They'd exited the courtyard and headed east toward the steep hills that boxed them in. Once there they turned onto a perimeter road that circled the entire property. After about a mile they turned back into the center of the ranch, through a gate, and headed toward a small building that was easily identified in the emerging light as an old wooden airplane hangar.

They stopped in front of the hangar, which was black from decades of weather and had missing planks along its walls. Turner instructed everyone to move apart so that each person was more than an arm's length from anyone else, unable to touch. Then he made them lie on the ground, facedown, telling them to remain silent.

Brad lowered himself gently to the ground, feeling the pain of fatigue in his legs and hips. Derek was right next to him, and their eyes met as they assumed the position. Brad wondered what he saw there, if perhaps Derek was as much a threat as Turner.

He didn't know exactly where Turner had gone. With his face pointed into the mud, and with the scant light, he could be anywhere, at any angle.

It took only a few seconds before moisture began soaking through Brad's pants, delivering a stark chill that permeated his entire body. Other than the occasional cough or the rustling of someone shifting their position slightly, it was completely quiet.

The sound of the arriving dawn was a whisper.

Fear breeds in the silences, Brad concluded. Without diversion, it consumes all thought, feeding on reason and hope, hungering for more.

Minutes passed, too many to count accurately.

And then there was a muted buzzing, barely audible at first, wafting in on the uneven rhythm of the wind.

An airplane.

79

6:51 A.M.

Officer Garvin turned onto the final leg of the single-lane, hard-packed dirt road that led in and out of The Complex, heading for the courtyard and its surrounding buildings. His heart leapt to his throat when, thankfully, he saw Beth jump out from behind a tree into the beams of his headlights, frantically waving her hands. They were about a hundred yards from the gate, and with one glance it appeared the area was completely—and because all the lights were on, eerily, as well—deserted.

Garvin jammed the car into Park and got out. Beth ran into his arms as if she were his long-lost daughter. Garvin immediately realized she was trembling.

"How'd you get out here?" he asked.

Beth pointed behind them, another hundred yards back, toward the black Navigator parked alongside a bank of bushes, barely visible if one wasn't looking for it.

"Mrs. Pratt's car," she said. "I got scared, so I hid it there."

"Are you okay?"

Garvin mustered all the sincerity he could. He'd seen some traumatized seminar people in his day, but nobody quite like this. He wondered what they'd done to her to make her react this way.

Now she pointed in the direction of the trailers.

"They're in there," she said.

"Who's in there, Beth?"

"The bodies. Four people. All shot to death. It was . . . horrible."

Beth buried her face in his chest, the trembling worse now. Garvin squeezed, as if this might help. He smiled as he waited a moment for the tremors to subside. In a few days she'd look back on this, and in addition to wondering how they did it, she'd thank them, as well.

"Let's go have a look," he said.

"I'm not going back in there," said Beth, looking up at him as if he'd made a poorly timed pass in a bar.

"That's fine, I'll go in. Let's do it."

He began walking, keeping his arm around her.

"Tell me why you're here," he said. "You said you were going back to Seattle in the morning."

"I lied. Fucking arrest me."

Garvin smiled, all parental patience. "If what you say is true, you'll have to answer that question sooner or later."

Beth nodded, as if she'd already accepted this truth. "I didn't buy that guy . . . what was his name, Turner? I didn't buy his act. And when Brad came out, he was different. Scared. Hiding something. A wife knows . . . I know. I just came back, to see more of the place."

They took a few steps in silence, halfway there now.

"What made you look in the trailer?" he asked.

"I was looking for somebody to talk to. Nobody was in the bunkhouses, and the students were in the classroom, and I didn't want to barge in, so I went to the trailer. Figured I'd wake somebody up, ask some questions. I didn't know it was an office, I figured that's where they stayed. So it made sense."

"And what happened then?"

"The door was open. The lights were off, and I thought that was kind of weird. I knocked, nobody answered. I opened the screen door and stuck my head in, yelled. When nobody answered, I turned on the light, and that's when I saw them."

She stopped, covering her face with her gloved hands. They were fifteen yards from the trailer door now. The lights were all on, just as she'd left them.

"You wait right here," he said, his stomach betraying the facade of cool he'd shown to Vaughn earlier. "You okay?"

She just nodded, keeping her hands over her face.

"I'm just going to take a look, I'll come right back. Don't move."

After a moment she parted her fingers and watched him approach the trailer.

He'd drawn his weapon, stopping short of the door. He put one foot on the stair, leaning forward as he peered in. She knew he could already see the first body and its backdrop of symmetrically arrayed blood spray on the wall, which had dripped down like melting wax.

He stopped, pulling his radio from his belt. He said something she could not hear, mumbling, perhaps, then stepped inside.

In the perfect stillness of the morning, interrupted only by families of birds and a soft wind through the trees, Beth thought she could hear the sound of an approaching airplane.

OFFICER Garvin didn't believe what his eyes were telling him was real. They were screaming it, in fact, and yet he remained unconvinced. Perhaps he was too recent a graduate of the seminar program, which, combined with his experience in dealing with students and confused family members, served to make him suspicious of what appeared to be true, especially here. Or maybe it just made him cynical. Nothing was ever as it seemed on the ranch, and the twists of perception and meaning often had multiple layers to their deception.

But he'd be damned if the back of Richard's head hadn't been blown clean off and if Mrs. Pratt's face wasn't as devoid of life as the statue in front of the classroom building.

A sense of panic swept over him slowly, starting deep in his gut and working outward, just now reaching the innermost layers of his skin, which was suddenly crawling. He'd withdrawn his radio upon seeing Richard on the floor, but he hadn't used it yet. He was speechless, standing in the middle of the trailer, turning a slow circle, taking in the bodies one at a time, his horror growing with each passing moment that they didn't move, didn't sit up and grin and say, "Gotcha again, Garv!" A part of him clung to hope—these people were incredibly good at what they did; he'd seen them create miracles of theatric deception for the benefit of their students—but it finally dissolved in a wave of ice-cold acid now running through his veins. There was a smell, unmistakable, something he'd first encountered when he went hunting with his father as a kid, the scent of death strapped to the top of the car. Suddenly he felt light-headed, and his stomach lurched. The liquefied remnants of the donut Vaughn had brought into the office this morning and the vile coffee with which he'd washed it down spilled from his mouth, plopping into the thick pool of blood still seeping from Stanton's upper leg.

He coughed, spitting out the last of the bile, clutching the edge of a desk for balance. Without taking his eyes off of Thomas Stanton's vacant stare, he brought the radio to his face and with a deceptively calm voice said, "Twenty-two, over."

The radio cracked back in a female voice, "Twenty-two, over. Go ahead, Bryon."

"Bernie, call the mayor. Tell her we have a situation out at the ranch. Then call the state police and tell them to get a homicide team out here ASAP. Over."

"Come again? Over."

Garvin drew a deep breath, fighting back another wave of nausea. When he spoke, his voice was stronger, a touch of irritation in it now.

"Tell them somebody's killed four people. Tell them Mrs. Pratt and her son and Richard and Gary are all dead as sin. They've all been shot to death."

His voice cracked with this last comment.

Bernie said something else, but he didn't hear it. He'd lowered the radio as his eyes filled with tears, and he allowed himself a moment to be alone with it, with them, before he was Officer Garvin again and the shit hit the fan with a crack of the bat that would echo in these parts for decades.

BETH hadn't moved, just as Garvin had instructed her. When he came out of the trailer, it was with renewed purpose, his gun holstered, radio in hand. Beth saw immediately that he had gone pale. Beth read traces of a myriad of emotions in his face, all with one glance, and knew that this was going to work. Garvin was the man, at least until the cavalry arrived, and he would do what he had to do to protect her and save her husband's life.

"Listen," she said, pointing toward the sky.

He frowned, not understanding.

"While I was waiting for you to get here, I saw five people leave the building and head down the road. That way."

Garvin's eyes took in the road, his expression revealing the struggle to understand.

The sound of an airplane was unmistakable now. Something old and big. When he looked up, to the east, he saw lights blinking in the sky.

"Airstrip's that way," he said, not taking his eyes away from the lights.

"I think one of them was my husband," she said, grabbing his arm. "We have to help him."

"I've called this in, the place will be swarming in minutes."

She looked back up at the sky. The airplane had turned and was descending, two large landing lights suddenly appearing like alien eyes.

"We don't have minutes," she said.

He nodded, realizing she was right.

80

Brad raised his head, saw the blinking red navigation
lights as they moved along on what he knew would be
the downwind leg of the approach. The sound was clearer
now, filling the valley as it bounced between the hills in a
confusing directional illusion. It was a thick sound—Brad
guessed a twin engine aircraft, definitely older. Not as
heavy as a DC-3, but something from that era and of that
same general profile.

The plane banked left and executed a short and steep
final. Upon turning Brad saw the landing lights come on,
two streetlamps bouncing down a hill directly at him.

The airplane touched down and decelerated quickly,
the engines roaring as the propeller blades reversed pitch.
The sound was an ugly anomaly against the soft rustling
of morning, and it split the ears to hear it. The airplane
came to a complete stop on the runway, which Brad assumed to be a dirt strip. Then, after a moment of idling,

the engine revved as it began to taxi toward their position.

It stopped twenty-five yards away from their position. The engines shut down, the sounds gradually diminishing in pitch and intensity until a numbing quiet returned to the valley. In contrast to the engines, the quiet was stark, almost frightening in intensity.

A voice, whispering but projecting. Turner.

"This is it. Don't fuck up now, kids. Keep your heads down and your yaps shut."

Brad heard footsteps, saw something in the periphery of his vision. He raised his head slightly, seeing a figure—Turner—walk toward the airplane. His hands swung free, meaning he'd concealed the gun and set down the satchel. Meaning, in turn, that he'd return for them before he boarded the airplane to leave.

Brad heard rustling next to him, then voices. Derek and Matt were whispering something to each other.

The door to the airplane swung open. A single figure appeared in the opening, shaking Turner's hand. Brad had no way of knowing if this was an ally of Turner's or simply the unwitting pilot. If it were the latter, the guy might be used to bizarre sights on this stop, people lying facedown in the mud, awaiting instructions. This was the seminar, and all bets were off.

Something deep in Brad's stomach twisted, and he realized his heart was pounding.

He could also hear muted fragments of conversation coming from the plane. He half expected to hear gunfire as the pilot was taken out of the equation, but there was nothing. Only the sound of two birds disturbed from their love nest in a nearby tree. It would be too convenient that Turner could fly an aircraft of this age and size. He'd need the pilot today, who could fly at gunpoint as well as not. The question was, would he need *them* once he was ready to depart.

Brad had been right about the airplane's age, though he didn't recognize the model. It had a double-fin tail that rested on a small wheel, casting the fuselage at a steep angle as it rested on the main gear, the nose pointing to the top of the distant hills as if it yearned to return to the sky. He thought of a television show he'd watched as a kid—*Sky King*, he thought—and wondering if this was the beginning of the fabled flashing of his life before his eyes. He hadn't given that show a single thought in over thirty years.

Four minutes passed. An eternity when one is lying in a puddle, unsure of what's next.

81

Beth and Officer Garvin were positioned behind the massive trunk of a fallen tree, five feet in diameter and resting some thirty yards from the hangar building, off to the side of the access road. From this angle they had a clear view of the airplane, and of the foreground where four people were lying on the ground, facedown, unmoving.

Officer Garvin rested his rifle on the tree, which had been sawed off at one end many years before. They had driven along this road before abandoning the squad car two hundred yards behind their current position, deciding on this when they saw that the airplane had stopped its taxi and was feathering the engines, which would result in silence in the valley once again. They couldn't risk anyone hearing the vehicle, so they proceeded on foot, Garvin grabbing the rifle from the trunk as they left. He'd ordered Beth to remain in the vehicle, but she wasn't having it, and there was no time to argue the point. He could tell this was a woman used to winning her arguments, and besides, she could help him decipher who was who among the five silhouettes in front of them.

They walked briskly but with stealthy discretion. Garvin used his mobile radio to quietly update Bernie back at the office as to their status, telling her to inform the state police to proceed covertly, as any noise might result in the execution of hostages. He didn't wait for a response, stashing the radio as they arrived at the fallen trunk, both of them falling into place behind it.

"What's he doing?" asked Beth in a whisper. The man in the airplane appeared to have drawn a gun and was turning the other man, presumably the pilot, so that his back was to him. Then he took something from his pocket and appeared to be using it to bind the man's hands behind him. When he was done, he shoved the bound man to the floor of the airplane and closed the hatch. He returned to the people on the ground, which from Beth and Garvin's point of view meant he was coming straight at them.

Beth flinched, but Garvin put his hand on her shoulder.

"He can't see us," he whispered. "He doesn't know we're here."

"What are you going to do?"

Garvin didn't answer. Beth wasn't sure if it was because he didn't have one or if he was lost in concentration. He was obviously nervous, as evidenced by his constant surveillance of the hillside and the access road for the arrival of reinforcements. This was something you didn't train for in Weaverville, California, and it showed in Garvin's eyes.

"Oh, my God," said Beth. "That's Turner."

Garvin squinted, first at her, then at the man, who was now carrying something in his hands, a bag of some kind, over to the airplane.

"You're sure?"

"That's him. I recognize the walk. That's Turner."

"I'll be damned," whispered Garvin, barely audible.

"He was bullshitting us. It was him all along."

Garvin chewed on that for a moment. "I thought it was odd the instructors weren't around."

"I get the feeling nothing seems odd around here." They were whispering like pals hunkered down in a duck blind, waiting for first light.

"You got that right. How do you explain your husband, then? Why didn't he just run, or better yet, why not tell us what was going on right there, when he had the chance?"

"He did, in a way. Like I said, I never bought into what he was saying—I think he was telling me something. That's why I came back. My guess is, he couldn't just turn on the guy, probably someone inside with a gun rammed down their throat. Brad had to come back without a feather ruffled or people would die."

Garvin nodded, liking that theory. "Your husband is one cool dude under pressure," he said.

Beth started to answer, but suddenly felt Garvin twitch, followed by his arm on her shoulder again. He'd seen something, and this was his quiet way of alerting her.

One of the men on the ground was slowly rising up onto his knees. From the way he moved, it was obvious he was doing this on the sly, without attracting the attention of the man stashing something aboard the plane. The others were moving, too, but they remained on the ground, as if they were saying something to him, pleading with him, it seemed.

As if, thought Beth, they were trying to stop him.

82

7:21 A.M.

Seeing Turner standing at the airplane talking to the pilot, Brad was suddenly overwhelmed with an urge to get to his feet and run. Turner may or may not have been a crack shot with a pistol, but at this range he liked his odds, no matter how good the guy might be. It was the consequences of success that worried him more. What Turner might do if Brad ran, betraying his trust, however perverse. The others might run, too, but then someone would surely catch a bullet in the back, precisely what Brad had hoped to avoid when he talked Matt out of using his shard of glass.

Someone, one of the others, was obviously thinking the same thing.

"Listen to me," said Matt, straining for volume while maintaining his voice at a whisper. "We could run, disperse, take off in different directions. He can't get us all—chances are we'd make it!"

Brad glanced over at the airplane, saw that Turner had

taken his gun out from under his parka. He pointed it at the pilot, who had raised his hands defensively and was backing away, deeper into the cabin. Turner said something, causing the pilot to stop and turn around, at which point Turner took something out of his pocket—it looked like handcuffs—and used them to bind the pilot's hands behind his back. When he was finished, he shoved the pilot to the cabin floor and closed the door.

"Here he comes," said Brad, risking being heard to make his point. "Stay where you are! We'll be okay. Don't screw this up! Everyone just be cool!"

Turner blew right past them without even looking. He went to the edge of the brush, picked up his backpack and the heavy satchel, and began carrying them to the airplane, again passing without a glance or a word.

"Matt?" It was Derek, trying to shout and whisper at the same time. "Next pass. You with me on this?"

Turner opened the hatch and stowed the bags inside. He remained there, saying something to the pilot, leaning inside to do so.

"You stay right where you are!" said Brad, not subduing his voice now. His heart was racing at an incredible pace, causing his ears to ring and his breath to come in short gasps. It was unlike anything he'd felt on a basketball court, and he wasn't sure he could control his limbs if the need to flee became necessary.

"I'm going for it," said Derek, "before he turns back."

Derek slowly rose up to his knees, pushing himself to his feet using his hands, remaining in a crouch as he started to move forward.

"Fuckin' A." It was Matt, who suddenly did the same thing.

Turner spun around, seeing the two men coming for him.

And a third, the tall one, right behind them.

"**SHIT**," muttered Garvin. The first guy was on his feet and moving forward, creeping but picking up speed. A second guy had done the same thing and was a few feet behind them and closing fast. They ran stooped over, like ninja assassins approaching a wall in a martial-arts movie.

Garvin pressed his cheek to the rifle and squinted down the barrel.

"Oh, God," said Beth, her voice now merely air through her mouth.

Brad had sprung to his feet, and was right behind the others.

"**No!**" screamed Brad, not holding back now. His advantage was that Derek and Matt were trying to sneak up Turner's ass as he leaned into the airplane, and this put a governor on their speed. Brad, on the other hand, was running full out, a sprinter out of the blocks, already fully erect and striding with six-foot seven-inch basketball legs, a fast break of infinite consequence.

Turner sensed them before he saw them, crouching as he spun. His first shot was wildly off target, corrupted by the spin and his sudden rush of adrenaline, hitting the hangar wall near the roofline.

Then, however, he comprehended something that caused him to hesitate, because it made no sense. It was perceived and processed in the nanosecond dimension of the mind's chemistry, but it was clear and laden with meaning. The guy bringing up the rear, the tall one, had caught up to them and was driving his head and shoulders into the back of the number-two guy, pushing him forward with such force that the two of them fell onto the churning legs of the lead guy. The tall one—this was Brad, he now realized—had the presence of mind to reach forward as they fell and wrap an arm around the lead guy, bringing all three of them to the ground in a nasty tumble worthy of the NFL. In the fraction of a second that this consumed, Turner saw that the first guy had brandished a long shard of glass in his hand, which he had intended to plunge between Turner's shoulder blades within the next half second.

Turner felt his rage, his adrenaline hit, felt it coursing through him, colliding with reason. It didn't matter who cov-

ered who, or for what reason, or who had promised what
to whom or had changed sides in the name of survival or
even honor. And because none of that mattered—he was
nothing but a fucking criminal after all, and he was in a corner now—he raised the gun and took a few steps forward
toward the men, who were now sprawled over the ground,
dazed and confused. In the background the woman was getting to her feet, but not to run—she was heading for them,
to help if she could.

Turner paused, unsure who to shoot first.

"**Now!**" cried Beth at the instant Turner seemed to pause, his
gun leveled at the churning whirlwind of limbs on the ground
that was the men trying to untangle themselves and find their
feet, which would be their only defensive hope.

Garvin didn't hesitate and in the aftermath would never
be completely sure if he'd heard Beth's cry or not. He squeezed
the trigger, and a deafening pop exploded next to Beth's face
as Garvin bucked from the force.

Ten feet in front of the airplane, Tom Turner's knees
seemed to buckle, and his head visibly whipped back with a
force sufficient to snap each and every cervical vertebrae in
a linebacker's neck. He remained upright for an eternal moment—something everyone who saw it would never forget
and often describe—before falling slowly backward, like a
headstone tipped over in a midnight prank. There was a snap-
ping sound when he hit the cracked pavement, a wet thud
that was unmistakable.

The other image that Brad would never be able to leave
behind was the silhouette of Tom Turner's head against the
rising sun, which had minutes earlier emerged from behind
the hills, masked by a high, thin cloud cover. It seemed to explode with a Zapruder-esque surrealism, concurrent with the
sound of a rifle report from somewhere behind the hangar.

And he would swear, but only to Beth as they talked softly about it in the dead of night, that Turner had been looking
right at him when it happened.

83

The efficiency of the California State Police was a sight to behold. You'd think they did this twice a month, like wedding planners, coming in and sorting out over twenty different accountings of what happened, comforting the terrified and disarming the angry, whisking away the dead with understated brevity while capturing it all on tape. The first patrol car arrived less than ten minutes after Tom Turner discovered the consequences of his own personal Judas game, and within thirty minutes the property was crawling with official vehicles and very serious men and women wearing latex gloves, while helicopters hovered overhead and emergency personnel served vitamin B-12 shots and muffins.

They were ten minutes into the forensic process before someone went inside the darkened trailer next to the gruesome murder tableau and found Georgia dead in her bed, a bullet hole in one temple, the other temple splattered across a wall.

During that ten minutes, Garvin and Beth had emerged from behind their fateful log to embrace the survivors and assess the situation. After assurances that everyone was fine, Garvin left Brad and Beth to themselves while he took Derek, Matt, and Sybil back to free the other students from the classroom. They retired to a bench in the hangar building to regain their composure, spending the first few minutes simply holding each other. Beth was appropriately tearful, and when Brad got around to asking her how she knew to tell him to go along with Turner, she put her finger on his lips and told him they'd discuss it later. She made him promise to keep this aspect of his experience to himself as the onslaught of interviews commenced, that she didn't want to complicate what was about to happen, and he had no problem with this. She had just saved his life and that of his teammates, and he owed her whatever corner-cutting she needed. Around that time Garvin returned to bring them back to the courtyard, which was already being set up as a sort of command central for control of the crime scene.

There were several teams at work simultaneously. One crew worked the office trailer, which was of course off-limits to everyone. They'd get to Georgia's trailer soon enough, for now simply leaving it cordoned off with yellow tape. Another worked the airstrip, and a third wandered about the property looking for absolutely anything out of the ordinary. At the courtyard, one station administered medical care, though little was needed other than to comfort the pervasive nausea and diarrhea, and another distributed food and coffee, while trauma specialists began the process of counseling and generally offering a shoulder upon which to cry. A checklist was developed, and each participant was required to provide their core data—address, phone, Social Security, and a brief overview of what brought them there—and some were already being debriefed in general, especially those who offered eyewitness accounts of specific incidents or felt they had a theory to contribute. All who wanted to speak were heard, and all would be involved in further in-depth debriefing over the coming days.

Like a post-game celebration following a champion-
ship, there were heroes to be worshiped. Officer Garvin
told the story as humbly as he could, stating that when
he received Beth's call, he got out there as fast as possible,
trying to balance his knowledge of the seminar's tactics
with the nagging feeling that something had indeed gone
wrong. Elsewhere, Derek and Matt were hailed as victorious warriors who had summoned courage beyond reason
to stare down Turner and force the moment, all without
the knowledge that Garvin was in the wings with a rifle
and a bead on Turner's forehead.

And unknown to everyone, Brad was quietly celebrat-
ing his own emergence from behind a curtain of fear that
had ruled his life since he was a child. He had followed his
heart, and he had been right. Had he followed his peers he
would have been dead. Someday soon, he told himself, he
would share it with Beth, but for now he was content to
be alone with it. Let Derek and Matt and Sybil have the
spotlight. They knew, too.

One of the first things Brad did upon returning to the
main area was inquire about Mark. None of the officials
seemed to know anything, and he told the story of Mark's
exile to the woods as part of a seminar exercise over and
over to anyone from the outside who would listen. But
there was nothing they could do, and they remained constant in their confidence that he would turn up. It was
nearly impossible, they said, to remain lost in these parts
for too long, given the network of roads and the availability of aerial surveillance should the need arise. It didn't
make him feel any better about it, but he at least accepted
that there was nothing he could do about Mark until later.
Hopefully, he would walk out of the woods on his own,
pissed off and completely blown away at what had happened while he was gone.

Beth was one of the first to be questioned. She had a
long session with Garvin and one by herself, both times
speaking to the same team of senior detectives, a man and
a woman who looked like they should be in a prime-time
show from David Kelley. They wanted to hear it from sev-

eral angles: how she came to be here, the seminar's ransom scheme, the money—which they'd confiscated in the airplane, with the frightened but unharmed pilot—her trip to Weaverville and dealings with Mrs. Pratt, her call to the local police and Officer Garvin, their visit to the ranch, and most of all, her decision to return here later during the night. Beth never sensed they were doubting her; indeed, they seemed to appreciate the sheer volume of information she was providing, all of it residing at the heart of the case. She was, they said, their star witness, and they assured her she would spend many more hours telling her story and answering questions.

Through it all Beth never mentioned Ken Wong. She was assured her money was safe and that it would be returned to her in a few weeks.

Brad was not surprised to see that Pamela was perhaps the most in need of counseling and medical attention. She spent an hour with two separate doctors, one of whom tranquilized her with a mild sedative, which seemed to help. By eight-thirty she was eating a muffin and chatting with people and because of that was allowed back into the courtyard to mill about with the others, who were encouraged to pack their things in anticipation of the arrival of a bus, which was en route to take them back to Weaverville.

It was, predictably, a hugfest of the first order. Pamela was the recipient of the most heartfelt expressions of remorse for her loss, which she returned with a heart full of gratitude. From within her grief there grew a seed of fulfillment, the knowledge that she could love and be loved, and the hope that she just might be able to put her life on a different course after this. She had fallen in love here on the ranch, and however contrived the environment might be, the pain of her losing Scott in the manner in which she did was nothing short of debilitating. And yet here she was, touching and being touched, loving and being loved, the center of attention.

Brad, in particular, had come to her with his heart on his sleeve. She decided right there that she would work with him and for him, that he was the only choice to run the company they'd built together, and together they'd conquer the world. Without his saying so, she knew it was he who'd engineered the final outcome of this drama, and this alone made her see him in a new light. Things would be different now, for all of them.

One of the best and most unexpected hugs of all came from Beth. They embraced in the walkway leading from the bunkhouse to the dining hall and remained that way for many minutes as Pamela wept, people passing by on either side as she tapped into a well of grief and tears she thought she'd exhausted many minutes and many conversations ago. She was genuinely touched by Beth's concern, and the years of chill between them made the moment all the warmer, because Beth knew every page of Pamela's book and still she was here. She encouraged Pamela to let it out, to tell her all about this man who had swept her off her feet, this hero who fell before their love found its wings, before it could become legend.

"Can I talk to you?" asked Beth when Pamela seemed to have regained her composure.

"I thought I've been talking your ear off," said Pamela, already confused.

"I'd like to talk to you about Brad," she said, not at all crowding the request into Pamela's self-agenda of the moment. "I'm worried about him . . . I need to hear about his week, get some context for what he's feeling."

Pamela nodded. It made sense, however ill-timed.

"Let's meet for lunch early next week."

Beth made a face. "Can we do it now? Meet me, say, in ten minutes?"

Pamela thought this seemed odd, but she was as loving and giving as she'd ever been at this moment, and consented happily.

"Meet you?" Her confusion was showing in her expression now.

Beth suggested that they rendezvous by a clump of trees a way down the road, away from the hubbub and the eyes of the others. To be honest, she didn't want Brad to know they were talking about him, she said, so she asked if Pamela would keep it to herself for now.

She said she would, and Beth kissed her cheek before she walked away.

84

Pamela had trouble breaking away. The support was an onslaught, ice water poured over a fresh burn wound, and she reveled in it, completely content to be the woman in black today. Finally, though, there was a break in the action as people got serious about their packing, so Pamela drifted to the edge of the courtyard and walked down the road to meet Beth. The sun was out for the first time all week, and it felt wonderful on her bare arms as she carried her sweatshirt in her hand, wearing only a T-shirt now.

"Pamela!"

Beth stepped out from behind a tree, using the trunk to obscure any view from the courtyard. Her smile was radiant. She wore a leather waistcoat and gloves, apparently not as appreciative of the sun as Pamela was today.

"Let's walk," said Beth, taking Pamela's hand. They were like schoolgirls. Then she added, "Let's smoke." She pulled a package of menthols from her pocket.

Pamela grinned, but more from confusion than humor. "I didn't know you smoked," she said, taking one from the pack Beth was holding out to her. Beth was proving to be quite the surprise today, indeed.

Beth held the lighter for her, then used it herself.

"So tell me everything," she said, resuming the walk. They had headed through the clump of trees and were completely hidden from sight from the courtyard.

"A lot has happened," said Pamela, grateful for the nicotine. "You literally had to be here."

Beth cast a glance over her shoulder. "Brad seems, I don't know . . . distant."

"He's been through a lot. We've both been through a lot."

Now Beth reached into her purse and pulled out a thin bottle. It was a fifth of Southern Comfort.

"Present for Brad," she said. "But I think you may need it more. Hell, I need it more." She grinned, the schoolgirl again. "Where can we go to be alone? I want to hear everything."

Pamela thought this was interesting, because she had several bottles of Southern Comfort identical to this one in her cabinet at home.

"We should get back," she said. "They'll miss me . . . us, I mean."

"They'll be here all day," said Beth, holding out the bottle, raising her eyebrows in proffered temptation.

Pamela took it and took a long, gratifying pull. It had been a long, long week in more ways than one, the absence of this being one of them.

Pamela looked around, situating herself.

"I know a place," she said. Then she smiled before taking another long pull, breathing heavily when she lowered it from her mouth.

PAMELA led Beth to another clump of trees several hundred yards beyond the courtyard. Once in the trees they came upon a clearing bisected by a river. There were two huge trees near the bank, which was a significant drop-off to the rushing water below. A wooden platform about three feet wide had been built about seven feet off the ground between the two trees. The dirt in front of it was worn and bare, as if it experienced heavy traffic on a regular basis.

"What is this place?" asked Beth.

Beth watched as Pamela looked up at the platform. She saw her chin begin to quiver as she stared, which she did for several seconds before answering.

"Hell," she said.

And then she told her everything.

Pamela noticed that Beth seemed distracted as they talked. Or more accurately, as she talked and Beth listened. They climbed up the steps—boards nailed to one of the trees, actually—to the platform, where they sat to talk and drink the rest of the sweet whiskey. She told Beth about the exercise that had taken place here, how she had failed it and herself and her team so miserably. She told her about the other exercises, the written feedback, and how the instructors had betrayed the team by distributing the contents, about the river crossing and the accident, about Richard and Georgia and how they were on her ass constantly, pushing her buttons, never letting up. She touched on how well Brad was doing, how he had gained the respect of the team and, she hoped, a newfound respect for himself, which was something he needed to work on in her opinion. She talked about the moment that Simon took everything over at gunpoint with Morse and Fisher, about Mark's execution that turned out to be an escape, about the killing, the torment, the long silences in the room. And finally, about how Tom Turner stepped up and called Simon out, and how everything changed from that point forward.

Through it all she threaded in her relationship with Scott. How they had come together on the airplane, how she had resisted him at first, but over time grew to appreciate his attention. He was unconditional with her, she said, the first man to ever be that way. His own flaws were endearing to her because they were so simple and sweet. Here was a man who didn't pretend to perfection and who needed her to make him whole, yet seemed so unconcerned with his own issues as he focused on helping Pamela with hers. She talked about how she felt when Scott had been injured in that first fight with Simon. And then, if it was possible, she said she was sure she had fallen in love with him. It was something real and it was powerful. And for a change, it wasn't connected to sex, though that was right around the corner because their chemistry was scalding hot. Scott had taught her that she could love, something on which she'd given up. More important, though, he'd taught her that she could *be loved*, a notion she'd abandoned longer ago than she could remember.

When she saw him murdered in cold blood, she didn't think she could go on. She'd never felt such pain, such emptiness. It had made her physically ill, and all she wanted to do from that point forward was die herself. It was beyond comprehension, and the suddenness of it, in combination with the suddenness of her feelings for him, was an unthinkable torment. An irreplaceable loss.

Beth had allowed Pamela to consume most of the liquor, and it made her sick instead of high. It also made the story rewarding to tell, because Pamela held nothing back, not even from Beth, a woman for whom she'd never felt any friendship or attraction. Two tigresses stalking the same plain—they had never clicked. Until now.

"I can't imagine how you feel," said Beth, seemingly more focused now that it was all out. She had listened, but she had also been looking around constantly, shifting nervously on the platform.

"No, you can't. You're so lucky, Beth. I hope you know how lucky you are."

"I do. I'm so sorry, Pamela. It must be horrible. Like you want to die."

Pamela stared at the ground. "Yes," she said, the wave of emotion returning again. All resistance to it was gone; it had a clear pathway to her eyes.

There was a moment's pause before Beth said, "Wong thinks you might just be the best choice as Wright & Wong's new CEO."

Pamela looked at her and laughed, shaking her head. "I don't think so," she said, looking down at her feet swinging freely beneath them.

"Neither do I," said Beth, suddenly reaching into her jacket pocket.

Pamela didn't feel the bullet as it tore through her brain, sending a baseball-sized projectile of brain tissue and bone splattering against the opposite tree. Her body fell to the side, and as it started to slip from the platform, Beth scrambled backward to allow room for it to do so unobstructed.

Pamela hit the ground with a dull thud, already dead.

Beth flipped herself over onto her tummy and lowered her feet, dangling a moment before lowering to the ground. Moving quickly, she placed Pamela's gun into her hand to establish a clean set of fingerprints, then raised it up a few feet before dropping it back to the ground, as if it had fallen from the platform with the body. She had placed the barrel an inch from Pamela's temple before pulling the trigger so that the powder burns would be congruent with a self-inflicted head wound.

She took off her leather gloves and began working them onto Pamela's hands. They were, in fact, Pamela's gloves, taken from her condo at the same time Beth had taken Pamela's gun. Not that anyone would notice this detail, but details were what would make this work. What they *would* notice was that there were powder burns here, on these gloves worn by the victim, again congruent with a self-inflicted wound.

Beth checked the platform to see if there had been dust or dirt, anything that would indicate that two people had been sitting there instead of one. The wood was clean; the only trace left was a smear of blood and tissue left when Pamela's head slid off the platform as it fell.

She checked the area, her heart pounding. The sound had been muted by the trees, a modest pop that she doubted could be heard back at the courtyard. And if it had been heard . . . well, they'd discover the body sooner or later, and in either case the conclusion would be the same.

Pamela had just spent the past two hours telling everyone just how devastated she was because of Scott's death.

Poor Pamela. Poor heartbroken, emotionally ransacked, lonely, alcoholic, basket-case Pamela.

BOOK FIVE

REQUIEM

85

Two Days After The Seminar

Gradually, over the course of the next two days, the students were allowed to go home. They were bused back to Weaverville and put up in the same motel where Beth had stayed, fed deli sandwiches and Kentucky Fried Chicken, and by the end of the second day there were only a handful remaining, Beth and Brad included. They had been required to go over it again and again, detail by detail, facing different combinations of police, FBI, profilers, and anonymous note takers, and the story never wavered from its center. They had been prodded and provoked, as if there were holes in their story that needed reconciliation. One of the officers asked if they wanted an attorney to be present during questioning, but Beth protested that that would not be necessary and demanded to know if any of the other witnesses had been presented with this option. All of them had, she was assured; it was merely a formality, nothing into which she should read implications.

It was on the airplane home that Brad finally got around to resurrecting the topic of how Beth knew what she knew. How she had known that Turner had taken the group hostage for real. How she knew he'd require that several people accompany him to the airstrip as insurance or that the airstrip was even part of his plan in the first place. How and why she made him promise he'd be among this group. And most important to Brad, how she managed to come up with $250,000 in cash on such short notice.

Beth sat quietly as he listed the things he wanted to know, watching him get worked up. He was obviously uncomfortable here in coach next to the window, where he usually sat so that he could rest his head against the wall during the flight. He was too tall to lean his head back onto the seat, because to do so required that he slouch down, in which case his knees impacted the seat in front of him. He had about an inch of slouch room, if that. To make today's flight all the more tortuous, the asshole in the seat in front of him had promptly slammed his seat into the fully reclined position as soon as the wheels lifted off the runway, causing Brad to sit even taller in the seat. No wonder he had an edge today.

"Are you finished?" she asked, a patient smile on her face.

He paused, then smiled back. When she said this, he knew she had a response already tied up in a neat little package, that he was in overreaction land. He realized he was flushed, but this had been kicking the back of his mind for two days. He'd not wanted to fill the already emotionally charged space between them with any shadow of his doubt, but now he had to know. Before the back of his mind collapsed.

"It's not what you think," she said.

"Just tell me what it *is*, then," he replied.

Beth adjusted her position in the seat, facing him more squarely. She lowered her voice, leaning in as she spoke.

"I knew about the kidnapping because Ken Wong told me. I knew about the airstrip because Ken Wong told me that, too. And I was able to come up with the money because he gave it to me."

"Wong funded the ransom?"

"He made me promise not to tell you. I expect you to cover me on that."

Brad nodded slowly, amazed at what he'd just heard.

"Why would he do that?" he asked.

"Because he's a seminar graduate himself," she said. "You've been so full of your own shit, your resentment and your fear of him, that you haven't stopped to notice that he's a changed man. That's why he sent you guys down here. Not because he was up to something. Just because he wanted you to experience the same growth he'd experienced."

Brad shook his head, recalling the conversations that had preceded this trip.

"You went to Wong for the money," he said, needing clarification. Their infamous history hung between the words of his question.

"I went to Ken because I was scared and confused. My God, strangers show up at our door demanding a quarter million dollars—what do you expect? I was upset, so he told me what was going on. If you ask him, he'd tell you I dragged it out of him, but that's a moot point. He told me about it all because of my reaction, and that was the point all along: to make me realize what I have, to put it all in jeopardy. He gave me the money because he knew what would happen to it, there wasn't any risk at the time. He'd get it back at the end of the week; that's how the program worked." She paused, watching his eyes. "That's how I knew."

Brad nodded. He stared out the window for the next few minutes, and she kept her eye on him the entire time, practically reading his mind as he went over it from every angle.

She also knew what was next, and was ready when he asked.

"There's something I still don't get," he said. "Color me stupid here, but I'm a traumatized man sitting in coach with some asshole's seat under my chin."

He said it loud enough for the guy to hear. She smiled and nodded for him to go on.

"You say Wong told you about the kidnapping and gave you the ransom money because you were upset."

"That's right."

"But he was talking about Simon at the time. About the seminar exercise. He couldn't know about Turner, because Turner hadn't happened yet."

Beth blinked, her gaze steady. "Go on," she said.

"So how could you know Turner had taken over, that he would go to the airstrip, that he'd need people to go with him? And why would you make me promise to be one of them?"

Beth took Brad's hand into hers. "Because I wasn't talking about Turner when I told you that. I was talking about Simon. I had no idea what had happened, Brad. I was talking about Simon. I thought you were swimming in a bizarre seminar exercise, and I wanted you to step up, take a risk. I wanted you to grow, because I knew what Simon was going to do, and I wanted you to be in the middle of it and not hang back in the crowd."

"You thought we were still with Simon."

Beth nodded.

Brad closed his eyes and drew a deep breath. It all made sense now, in a madcap movie sort of way.

"I was taking care of you, sweetheart," said Beth, squeezing his hand. "I'll always take care of you."

Ten minutes later, having not moved a muscle since their last words, Brad said, "If you thought it was Simon, if you thought it was a seminar exercise . . . then why did you come back?"

He had spoken the question without looking at her, but now he turned his eyes and held her gaze. Beth kept her breathing even.

"Because I had a feeling," she said. "Because I love you."

Their eyes remained locked for a few more seconds. Then Beth put her head on his shoulder, and they flew the rest of the way to Seattle without exchanging another word.

86

Four Days After The Seminar

Mark Johnson's broken body was found by a Boy Scout troop after a four-day search that had confounded the adult authorities. It was lying under a highway bridge at the bottom of a canyon with eighty-foot vertical rock walls. Ellison Rainey, who had played the part of an FBI agent in the ransom exercise targeted at Beth Teeters, as well as two other couples, surfaced soon after the investigation started, corroborating Brad's story about Mark and the transponder, as well as Beth's story of the ransom scheme and all that connected to it.

It was concluded that Mark had reached the road at the point at which the transponder was found, still operating as it lay among some decaying leaves on the ground. They surmised that he had rested here, and perhaps while lying on the ground the transponder had somehow worked loose from where Morse had clamped it to his belt in the minute before Mark's escape.

Once he had rested, they surmised, Mark then made a fatal decision. According to Rainey, it wouldn't have been the first time a student-runner had turned the wrong way as they reached the road in search of the cafe, but not without the transponder. Mark had walked six miles down the road in the wrong direction, finally coming to the narrow bridge that spanned the canyon and the raging river below. For reasons no one would ever know, this was where he fell to his death, his body hideously broken.

One theory posited that he'd jumped from the bridge, that the demons he'd encountered during his solo had pushed him to the edge and shown him a solution there. But this was never the accepted explanation. The authorities preferred to believe he fell to his death accidentally, perhaps in an attempt to get down to the water to drink.

No one would ever know that after picking up Mark near the cafe and driving him six miles in the other direction, Beth had stopped the car on the bridge that morning. It was here that she pulled Pamela's gun from under her coat and pointed it at Mark, ordering him to get out. In his confusion he seemed to accept her explanation that the seminar exercise was not yet over—she had smiled and winked as she instructed him to get out of the car at gunpoint—and that she would explain later. Mark played along, too fatigued to protest or question what seemed to be yet another twist in the game. She'd walked him to the railing and asked him to look out to the horizon, where the sun was emerging over the hills. She'd suggested that he pray, and it was then that she swung the butt of the gun with all her might against the back of his head. As he fell forward, it was an easy task to help his forward momentum to the extent that he tumbled over the railing, falling end over end to the rocks below. A sufficient impact, she was certain, to mask a sharp wound on the back of his skull.

Beth got back into the car and drove directly to the ranch, parking the Navigator several hundred yards up the road. It was then that she called Officer Bryon Garvin, who she knew would come to save her.

87

Seven Days After The Seminar

It had been a week of incredible pain and confusion. Detectives on the case had spoken with both Brad and Beth every day without exception, sometimes at their house, sometimes via telephone, twice in sessions with the FBI in a downtown Seattle office tower. Brad commented that he was beginning to feel like a suspect, a sentiment echoed by Beth.

Ellison Rainey was proving to be the catalyst in moving the investigation from utter confusion to a snapshot of best intentions gone wrong. The part the authorities were having trouble pegging was Tom Turner himself. Simon, which wasn't his real name, had been located and, after lengthy interviews, cleared of any connection to the incidents that occurred following his departure from the ranch. Like Rainey, he was able to corroborate those portions of the story the authorities seemed to have trouble swallowing.

Turner, it turned out, was an ex-con from San Diego with a rap sheet of previously undistinguished convictions, including burglary and assault, involvement with a fraud scheme targeting retired schoolteachers, a notebook full of traffic violations, DUIs, and a couple of possession charges. To move from this league to what he tried to pull off at the ranch made no sense, not without any evidence that linked him to the seminar. His enrollment seemed to come out of nowhere, and it remained unestablished how he had even heard of the program in the first place. His papers had simply arrived, with a $10,000 certified check, drawn on funds which had magically appeared in his checking account the previous week as a cash deposit, with no known source or explanation. The conclusion was that he had been hired for the job, but again there was nothing to go on here except the experienced logic of the detectives drawing these conclusions. He lived alone, had no friends, moved in shadows. He had been unemployed for six months prior to the seminar, other than a network-marketing scheme he'd enrolled in that thus far had yielded a total of ninety dollars in commissions. There was no way or no reason to track his movements in the weeks prior to the seminar, no phone records, no trips on commercial carriers, no way to determine whom he might have met with on this or any other business. Until something broke, it appeared the case was destined for an open file, but not one that would be ignored or soon forgotten.

Of course the press swooped in, misrepresenting the facts through implication. As sensationalism goes, this was the golden ring, and they were determined to wear it in their collective navel. They tried to paint the tragedy as a fringe encounter group gone haywire, and for the entire week it had been headline news on all the networks. The Internet was abuzz with theories, mostly concocted by tens of thousands of seminar graduates from this and other programs, who were equally divided between defensive support of the human-performance industry and explanations for what had transpired.

The coverage served to drive Beth, Brad, and Ken Wong underground. Wong was simply unavailable, rumored to be in Scottsdale after lengthy interviews with the FBI, who had assumed ownership of the case because of the alleged impersonations involved. He never once mentioned the money, and when it was pointed out that he'd withdrawn cash during the week of the seminar in the amount of a half million dollars, he was able to document that he regularly wagered that amount or more in Las Vegas over the course of a weekend and that this was precisely where he'd gone the very day Beth picked up her money. When his paper trail validated that claim, he and Beth fell off the map relative to the issue of who funded whom, which was considered to be largely irrelevant anyway.

Wong had yet to ask Beth about the cash, and she had yet to mention it to him.

Beth insulated Brad from the press, who called hourly with requests for interviews, including a $50,000 offer to appear on *Extra* to tell his story. Two weeks later they would see Derek on that very program, telling the world how he had charged Tom Turner with a shard of glass while the man was preparing to kill the pilot and escape in the airplane, rendered with all the humility and sensitivity of the seminar graduate that he was. No one at the network thought to check if Turner was indeed a pilot, and Brad's name was never mentioned on the air.

THE hardest part was the funerals. Pamela's was first, held on Friday in a funeral home in Renton, where her parents still lived. The press had converged on the site, and Brad had to be escorted to and from the building by security personnel hired by Wong, who flew back to town for the service. In a gesture of goodwill and in Pamela's memory, Beth offered to adopt Pamela's cat, Sophocles, a tidbit that made the evening news after someone in the office leaked it for a $500 finder's fee.

After a thorough investigation, the Weaverville coroner concluded that Pamela Wiley's death was caused by a self-inflicted wound from a gun registered in her name, the context of such an act being supported by the circumstances of the week before her death and the testimony of people who knew her. One of those who testified at the coroner's hearing was Beth Teeters, who told the coroner that Pamela had mentioned not wanting to live another minute without Scott, this comment coming less than an hour before she disappeared from the courtyard that fateful day in California. The coroner thought it odd that Pamela would bring a gun onto the property and then not mention it to anyone during what she assumed was a hostage situation, but when no one had an explanation that seemed to contradict suicide, he let it go. It was spring in Weaverville, and the fishing season was upon them.

Mark's body was cremated following a state-mandated autopsy. His memorial service was held in a park overlooking Elliott Bay, presided over by his brother and some cousins with guitars. Again the press tried to crash the party, but this time Wong's security forces preempted their presence with roadblocks at the gate to the park, leaving them to settle for helicopter footage shot from five hundred feet while hovering over the water.

Brad had trouble getting out of bed the entire week, doing so only to meet with yet another investigator or take one more official phone call. Beth remained at his side the entire time, rubbing his back and his cramping legs, bringing him tea and biscuits, running him a bath several times a day. By Sunday he'd gotten his appetite back, so she prepared his favorite meal of filet mignon and baked potatoes with a Caesar salad, and that night they made love for the first time since the tragedy.

Afterward he wept, apologizing for the lack of manly countenance. But this time it wasn't about Mark and Pamela and the seminar, he said. Tonight's tears were for her, for the way she loved and cared for him, for how she'd stood beside him through it all, from the moment he left home to the point at which she knew in her gut that something was wrong and that she had to intervene. She was his hero, he said, and the weight of his blessing was what had moved him to tears tonight.

She simply stroked his head and told him that she'd

always take good care of him, no matter what.

On Friday of the following week, on Brad's first day back at work, Ken Wong announced his retirement, naming Brad as the new CEO at Wright & Wong. It was a bittersweet announcement greeted with polite but respectfully subdued congratulations and a memo from the bank pressing him to recruit and hire a new CFO as soon as possible, else their credit line would be put up for review.

What wasn't publicized was a five-year majority-position buyout option as part of Brad's mid-six-figure compensation package, the details of which included the changing of the beneficiary on a preexisting insurance policy on Ken Wong's life that put sole ownership of the agency in Brad's name, should anything happen to Wong prior to the conclusion of the contract period.

BETH had, of course, begun mapping out a strategy from the moment she'd put Brad on the airplane. She had no idea at that time that Wong would make it easy for her to get on the property, but her antennae were up for any opportunity that might put Brad in the driver's seat for the CEO race. In her mind she likened it to standing behind someone at a blackjack table with a wad of money in your hand, watching every deal and every hand and counting the cards as the deck played out. If you knew what you were looking for, the count told you everything you needed to know, and if you were good, the dealer never knew you were there. You could never be sure if the count would go your way, but that was fine because your money wouldn't be on the table until it did. When the count got high enough—something that depended on one's tolerance for risk—you put your money down, confident of your chances. That's how you walked away a winner. The risk, however well managed, would always be part of this universal equation.

Beth had never approved of the prospect of a partnership between Brad and his two coworkers. He was CEO material, and only Ken Wong's ego stood in the way of that rightful inheritance. She knew better than anyone how Wong felt about Brad's success and the significant underlying talent that created it. Brad could do things Wong couldn't do. He could make clients sit up and sing. He could convince project teams to work miracles. Wong's company had been built on what Brad brought to the party, because every party needs a catalyst and a spark plug, no matter who pays for the hors d'oeuvres. Wong despised Brad for it and clung desperately to his only leverage over him, that being the power to control Brad's compensation and position.

Beth imagined that, when the initial buyout conversation had popped up, with her coaching Brad every step of the way, Wong had harbored serious thoughts of murder. She'd never completely bought into the details of Peter Wright's suicide, but no one had ever come close to tying it to Wong, and despite their intimacy he'd never come close to hinting that he'd been involved. She never considered asking him about it, fearing there would be no turning back from that point, and his friendship was serving her well, regardless of the truth of Peter Wright's passing.

But she had a feeling. The man, when crossed, was capable of anything, including murder.

The one thing she did learn from Peter Wright's death, however, was that suicide was tough to disprove, especially when all the details pointed toward that conclusion.

But all that had transpired before Wong went down to California to attend the seminar, which had been recommended to him by several of his CEO pals. He certainly came home from that experience a different man. A kinder, gentler Ken Wong, someone with different priorities and a repentant eye toward eternity. In Beth's mind, however, the notion of Ken Wong being capable of murder had simply evolved—or devolved, as it were—into something much more humane, a catalyst for something else entirely. Wong would kill the part of his ungrateful employees that didn't understand. He would send them to his seminar, they would be put through an emotional ringer the likes of which they couldn't imagine, and they would be saved.

They, too, would be born again—not in the classic Christian sense of the cliché, but in a more universal way. They would become enlightened, as he had. Only then would the buyout proceed.

Beth, however, had other plans.

88

21 Days After The Seminar

Rich Dobson answered the door wearing a terry-cloth robe over sweatpants and slippers. His home, a three-bedroom, ultra-contemporary design adorned with abstract, multi-colored neon sculptures on its exterior, was on a hillside in Bellevue overlooking Lake Sammamish, in a gated community teeming with high-tech money possessed by people with parents under fifty. He'd only been in the place for a few months, which to those who knew him was perfectly timed with his sudden emergence as a big producer in the network-marketing organization in which he worked. Big money in nutritional supplements, and Rich was good at what he did. He lived alone, though he was known to host overnight visitors on a frequent basis. The buzz on Dobson was that he batted from both sides of the plate, a rumor that gained momentum due to the fact that one of his beloved neon sculptures bore a startling resemblance to an erect penis. He was careful to keep his personal life a closed book among his downline, but the rumors had survived that effort.

Beth had him pegged as a player from the moment she laid eyes on him, though she had no idea at the time how useful her perception would prove to be.

"Beth!" exclaimed Rich, genuinely surprised if not excited to see her at this hour. He had been watching Jay Leno in bed and was just nodding off when the doorbell rang. In addition to the hour, his surprise stemmed from the fact that Beth had never set foot here before. To his knowledge she didn't even know where he lived. That, and the fact that they'd agreed to be incommunicado for at least six months, enough time to let the thing boil over, made him wonder what the hell was going on.

Especially since it was only three weeks after the fact.

Beth smiled at him, appropriately sheepish. He was not unpleasant to look at—that much hadn't changed in the weeks since their last face-to-face. That was the meeting where it all came together, where money had changed hands. Fifty grand then, another fifty a week later, when he gave her the details of whom he'd hired and how it would all go down. She still owed him another fifty, but that wasn't due until their six-month hiatus had run its course. Turner was to have taken his cut from the money lifted at the ranch, but of course things had taken a different spin.

"You didn't buzz in," he said, referring to the security gate.

"Nice night for a walk," she said, her smile acknowledging the lie. It was raining, and she carried an umbrella. This, and the fact she lived nowhere near here, made it certain that this was going to be an interesting visit. She was dressed for a night out with the girls: leather pants, tight black sweater top with a faux-fur lining at the neckline. Her comment implied that she'd left the car in one of the several parking spaces near the gate and walked in, when in fact she wasn't lying at all. She'd parked half a mile up the road in the lot of a busy all-hours Safeway store, where no one would notice or remember the car, which she'd borrowed from a girlfriend just to be safe, claiming hers was in the shop, which, conveniently, it was.

He stepped aside, allowing her to enter. She took off her coat and handed it to him, grinning rather stupidly, he thought.

"To what do I owe this unexpected and highly risky pleasure?" he asked, putting the coat over a statue in the entry foyer rather than hanging it up. His face wasn't hiding the fact that he was uncomfortable with her here.

"I've been drinking," she said, "and I'm still thirsty." She played the tip of her tongue over her lip as she said this, and in that instant he knew what this was about. High time, too, after all they'd been through, and without the big payoff, at that.

The house was dark, but the lights of the lake and the homes that surrounded it filled the space with a decidedly romantic ambiance.

"Nice," she said as she looked around. "I'd heard, and I'm not disappointed."

"You'd *heard*? From whom, might I ask?"

"You have an adoring downline," she said, acknowledging that almost all of the people who worked under him were women.

"Scotch?" he asked from the bar.

"Fine."

"Why are you here, Beth?"

"Can't a lady call on a gentleman?"

He handed her a glass, then sat down in a plush leather chair. "Titles that don't apply to either one of us, I'm afraid."

"Ouch," she said, still standing as she inspected some small statues on his mantel. "To ex-cell mates," she added, raising her glass to him.

He didn't smile as he raised his hesitantly in response.

"This is dangerous," he said, not needing to elaborate.

"Maybe. Danger is good sometimes. Don't you think?"

She saw the intrigue in his eyes, the way he shifted, as if a jolt of wet electricity had just been shot into his groin. Men were so easy, once you knew where the pressure points were, where to bury the blade when the moment came.

She put her drink on the bar and sat down on the arm of the chair. He looked up at her, grinning, as if he knew what was next. She took the drink from his hand and, as she put her leg over him to straddle his body, turned and placed it on the table next to hers.

Then she put both of her hands on his face, holding it firmly as she kissed him. It was a rough, hungry kiss, her teeth pulling at his lips between thrusts of her tongue.

When she pulled back, she saw that the same grin was in place.

"Where's Mister Beth tonight?"

"Sacramento." This much was true—it was Brad's first business trip since he'd been named CEO. She'd told him on the phone she was going out with a girlfriend tonight, not specifying which one, and she'd told her girlfriend she needed a car to run some errands, not specifying what they might be. She'd bought a late movie ticket downtown with a credit card, then snuck out the side entrance and driven straight here.

They kissed again, and this time she maneuvered her pelvic bone directly over his and began to move with deliberate intent. After a moment of this she pulled back, then reached behind and picked up his glass.

"You kiss like a woman," she said, nibbling at his mouth.

"I'll take that as a compliment," he said. He returned the thrust of her hips with sharp little movements.

"Drink for me," she said, holding the glass to his lips at a steep angle. She watched as he drained an inch of Scotch in one pull, happy to indulge her thirst for decadence.

He couldn't taste the Rohypnol—more commonly known as the street's best date-rape narcotic—that she'd discreetly dumped into his drink. She'd scored it from some kids in front of a club downtown who liked the look of the hundred-dollar bill she'd waved in their faces. After five minutes he was drowsy to the point of slurred speech, and five minutes after that, with his sweatpants around his ankles and Beth hard at work in his lap, he was sound asleep.

*   *   *

HE awoke with no memory of walking under his own power into his bedroom. Specifically, his walk-in closet. Awareness came gradually, as if surfacing from a deep dive on a dark night. His first realization was that he was sitting on the floor with his legs straight out in front of him and that he was unable to move his hands. Then he saw that his ankles had been cuffed together. In that instant he recognized the feeling around his wrists and knew that they, too, were cuffed, attached in front of him to an O-ring, which was part of an elaborate leather body harness. The position was convenient for touching oneself but little else. Both sets of handcuffs were familiar, because they were his. His heart began to pound when he realized that he was wearing women's black nylons. Those, and the harness, were from his special drawer, which he now saw was open.

These, too, were rumors running rampant within his downline. Several of the women had been right here in this closet. He was famous, about to become infamous.

When he tried to lean forward, he felt the slip-noose tighten around his throat. It was a devilish little item he'd purchased online from a Swedish sex catalog. When you leaned forward, the noose tightened to the desired tension and would remain that way until one leaned back again. That left one's hands free to do whatever else came to mind in this state of oxygen-deprived bliss.

In front of him was a thirteen-inch television sitting on a small stand. It was sitting on top of a VCR, which was playing a tape of two men with goatees exactly like his, both wearing gear strikingly similar to what he was wearing, engaging in an enthusiastic sequence of unnatural acts. The sound was on, and he could hear cheesy background music and the deep baritone moans and monosyllabic exclamations of the actors, who were deeply committed to the integrity of their roles. On the floor next to him was a metal ashtray with a burning stick of hashish. A bag full of it was on the floor nearby, and next to that was the key to the handcuffs, just out of his reach.

Beth appeared at the doorway to the closet. She had put her coat back on and was wearing a pair of black leather gloves, as if ready to depart.

She smiled, leaning against the doorjamb as she crossed her arms. The woman at the sales meeting, the one with too many Brandy Alexanders in her, had been right about everything. It was all here, just where she said it would be.

"What the hell is this?" he asked, realizing in that instant that he was both breathless and slightly nauseated.

"I'd say self-induced sexual asphyxia," she said. "But what do I know?"

"This isn't funny." He tried to struggle, and with that movement realized that she had inserted something into his anus. That, too, he assumed, had come from his drawer.

"I'd be careful," she said. "If you fall to the side, there's no way to straighten yourself back up. This is a very nasty little habit of yours, Rich."

He stared at her, trying to read the moment. It occurred to him that there was a chance she simply wanted to play. But he couldn't be sure if the coldness he was sensing was part of that game, or something far less playful.

She came into the closet and knelt next to him. She picked up the hashish cigarette and put it to her lips, taking in a long drag and holding it with closed eyes. Then, as she slowly exhaled, she put the stick between his lips and held his nose with her other hand, forcing him to inhale the smoke.

"That's a good boy," she said, breathing the words. She put the reefer back onto the ashtray. "Now, how *does* this work? Let's see . . . you lean forward—"

Beth grabbed the front of the harness and pulled him forward harshly. The leather strap pulled itself taut through the O-ring on his collar, and his windpipe was instantly and completely constricted.

"This is where you touch yourself, isn't it?" She grasped his penis with her gloved hand. To both of their surprise, it grew hard in her grasp.

"Very nice," she cooed. "And then, when you can't take any more—"

She pushed him back to an upright position, and he sucked in a desperate lungful of air.

"—you relieve yourself of your suffering. What I don't understand is, when do you come? When you're down and can't breathe or at the moment you lean back?"

Her raised eyebrows looked sincere. Then her smile ruined the effect, revealing only a cruel delight in her power.

"And what happens if you fall to the side, or if you pass out with your weight too far forward—might be fatal, I think. This is a very dangerous hobby you have here."

If this was a game, then she was playing it very, very well.

"Stop," he said, his chest heaving as if he'd just run a fast break. "What do you want from me? You want out of the back end? I can do that. I'm happy with what I got. We're square, okay? Done deal."

"Damn, Richie boy, you're one sick puppy, you know that?"

Her hand was still on his penis, stroking it rhythmically. Once again it occurred to Rich that this was her game and that maybe he should just relax and enjoy it. As edge play goes, this was way out there where he liked it.

"You enjoy this, don't you?" he said, testing his theory.

"I'll like it better when you're dead," she said. At that moment she pulled her hand away, and Rich Dobson realized he had been wrong. "You're the last connection, Rich, and I hate loose ends. Besides, your guy fucked up. People who were supposed to die didn't die, money that was supposed to disappear didn't disappear."

"You did all right," he said. "Your man got the top spot, all your money back . . . you got what you wanted."

"You're right," said Beth as she stood up and moved behind the bound man. Then she leaned down, putting her knees on his shoulders. "Beth always gets what she wants."

Gradually, she began releasing all her weight onto her legs, forcing him forward. As she did, she grasped the leather strap leading up from his neck to the hangar rod, pulling as hard as she could. She watched the two men on the television for a full minute, holding the strap taut, pushing Rich's upper body forward toward his knees.

"I want you to know," she said, "that I wiped down the glasses. And I put one of them back, just to be tidy."

She felt him struggle briefly, heard a muted sucking sound from his throat, then a few seconds later, he convulsed. His head thrashed violently in all directions, then, in an instant, it hung straight down.

She remained that way for six minutes, until the tape had reached the end and the automatic rewind function had kicked in. She believed in being sure, and six minutes was surely enough.

Rich Dobson was found dead in his closet by his cleaning lady two days later. He hadn't shown up for a downline meeting the next day, and he'd blown off several meetings with prospective players. The coroner considered it an open-and-shut case, publishing her findings as "death by cerebral hypoxia resulting from compression of the carotid arteries by ligature strangulation." Other details were not made public, but it was a short leap to a plethora of unsubstantiated rumors and hearsay. The downline was on fire that week. The investigation included interviews with several friends and lovers, all of whom confirmed Rich Dobson's long-standing interest and participation in the practice of sexual asphyxia, both with partners and without.

Beth Teeters was never interviewed. She had resigned her spot in Dobson's downline some five weeks earlier, and her name never even came up on the investigation's radar screen.

89

Ken Wong's hospice nurse was a six-foot-eight-inch African-American man named Rashod. He greeted Beth like an old friend because Ken had told him to expect her and, from the look on his face as he shook her hand as she entered Ken's condo, perhaps a bit about her as well.

He showed her into the great room overlooking the lake, where Ken's hospital bed was set up.

"You want anything to drink?" he asked.

Beth shook her head with an expression that said thanks anyway.

"Shod," said Ken, "can you give us some time here? She's here to grant me my last wish, and I don't want you getting all hot and bothered." His speech was sluggish and the volume half of what normal conversation required.

The big man chuckled and shook his head, looking at Beth in a way that acknowledged Ken's spirit, even here at the eleventh hour.

"Sure. I was gonna run up and get some things anyhow." He looked at his watch. "I'll be fifteen minutes, twenty tops. That okay?"

Wong nodded feebly. He was wearing tennis warmups, lying on top of the bed covers. He'd lost about thirty pounds, twenty-nine of which were never there to lose in the first place. An IV hose snaked out from the sleeve of the warm-up, connecting to a bag hanging from a stand at his bedside. The morphine dosage was controlled by a bright-blue electronics box, with a digital readout. The box emitted a soft beep every minute or so, as another drop of mercy was allowed to course into Ken's body.

Rashod smiled at Beth and said, "You take care of him, okay? He complains, slap him around a little."

"I promise," she said, watching him leave.

When he was gone, Beth sat on the edge of the bed. She had on jeans and a sassy little jacket, and her hair was pulled back and tied with a black ribbon.

"You look good," he said.

"You look like death warmed over," she said.

"Still sensitive, as always. How's Brad?"

Despite his announced retirement six months earlier, Wong had hung around the office on the pretense of mentoring Brad, maintaining his office in the process. He was, after all, still the sole stockholder, and it would have been bad form indeed for Brad to protest his presence. Ken left the company for real three months after that, on his doctor's orders. The pancreatic cancer that would soon kill him had been discovered ten months earlier, when Ken had gone in for a laparoscopic gallbladder removal after complaining of lower-back pain and fatigue. The doctor had noticed an abnormally inflamed lymph node and removed it, and the ensuing tissue analysis had returned the verdict of inoperable pancreatic malignancy. The prognosis had offered up a year, tops, and that was proving to be accurate.

Everything that had happened had been precipitated by this diagnosis. Like sitting in an airplane falling out of the sky, priorities suddenly change.

"Brad's okay. He'll get used to the pace. Right now he's pissed at you."

This made Ken smile. "He should be pissed at you, ya know."

"I take care of my men," she said. As she did, she stroked his leg lovingly, acknowledging their past. He put his hand on hers. His touch was weightless, indicative of his waning strength.

"But you didn't ask me here to talk about Brad," she said, pulling her hand away.

He nodded, his energy shifting. "You stole from me," he said, narrowing his eyes.

"I like to think of it as my little partnership share," she said. "For all we've been through together. For what I *know*."

"You don't know jack. And I want it back."

"Whatever for?" she asked, getting up and going to the end of the bed. "I mean, I've heard you can't take it with you. But hey, what do I know?"

Ken drew a deep breath, which obviously wasn't pleasant for him.

"Why do you think I arranged for you to participate in Brad's seminar like that?" he asked, struggling to sit up a bit. "For the fun of it?"

She smiled. Not with affection, but with sarcasm. "Because you love me," she said, "and wanted to save me from my evil ways."

Ken shook his head. "I want my money back, Beth."

"Of course. I need more time."

"I don't *have* more time."

She smiled again. "I know."

"I can undo it all, you know. Talk to people."

"So can I," she said, playing with the tips of his socked feet. "That's why you won't. I'm sure Peter's family and a few nice folks at the IRS would still love to hear how you had me doctor the books."

"None of that matters anymore," he said. "What matters is what I know. And I know I can't let you get away with this."

Beth's eyes narrowed, as if she was growing tired of the joust.

"I know what you did," he said.

"You're paranoid. Delusional."

"I know what I know."

"For a guy with his insides rotting away, maybe you shouldn't be trusting your gut feelings right about now."

"Brad would have become the CEO without what you did. You should understand that."

"I don't know what you're talking about. You're stoned on this shit."

"But you had to be sure, take matters into your own hands, like always."

Beth placed her palm on his cheek. "You should calm down. You're getting all worked up."

"It's funny," said Ken, moving her hand away. He stared out over the water for a moment before continuing. "You look at things differently in this position. Things you've discounted all your life suddenly have meaning."

"You've found God. How nice for you."

"He found me, is more like it."

She stared at him, and he had to look away.

"You know," she said, "I had a feeling this is what you wanted to see me about. Too bad, too. It could have all just . . . ended."

Beth opened her purse and took out a pair of scissors.

"What are you doing?" said Wong, his voice suddenly energized.

Then she withdrew two small bottles of Smirnoff vodka as she approached the side of the bed where she had been sitting. They were those shot bottles found in hotel refrigerators, the kind alcoholics lovingly hide in their luggage. She used the scissors to cut a small slit in the plastic bottle of morphine on the IV stand.

"We have to hurry," she said, as much to herself as to him.

Ken started to sit up, struggling, but Beth put him back down with a firm hand to the middle of his chest. Then, moving quickly, she poured one of the bottles into the IV pouch. She dropped the empty on the floor, then used her teeth to open the second bottle, pouring it in as well.

Ken's breathing was suddenly strained, and his eyes showed a new terror born of understanding. Again he tried to sit up, but even this action drained him, and another hand to his chest—this time more around his throat, actually—quickly quieted him.

Beth put the scissors on the nightstand. Then she took her hand and pushed Ken's arm, the one with the IV, flat onto the bed, just before she sat on his wrist with all her weight. Leaning sideways, she checked to see that she wasn't suppressing the flow of fluid through the IV line, which she wasn't.

Ken started to struggle, but he was no match as Beth leaned her weight across his upper body, holding the opposite shoulder down with her other hand. In doing so, her face was inches from Ken's.

"Good boy," she whispered.

Then, with her right hand, she reached out and started punching a button on the IV control box. The readout had shown a setting of "7"; she kept punching until it read "20" and would go no higher. The beeping sound increased in frequency to every few seconds or so.

"I don't want you to suffer. Just go with it, sweetheart. Just fly."

She watched his face closely. It wouldn't take long at this rate.

"You've done a lot for me," she said. "I want you to know how grateful I am. We are all grateful to you, you know. You've changed all our lives."

His eyelids were heavier now, his breathing slow and deep. "Beth—"

"Shhh," she mouthed, putting a finger to his lips. "I'll take good care of you," she whispered.

About a minute later his eyes fluttered, and then they closed. His breathing maintained its pace, though the inhales seemed deeper and more labored.

Beth sat up, taking a moment to fluff Ken's warmup top. When she moved off his arm, Ken made no effort to free himself of the IV. He was asleep now, very peaceful in his repose.

She smoothed the fabric on his sleeve. Then she dug a handkerchief from her purse and used it to wipe down the bottles and the scissors. She took each item and pressed Ken's hand around it several times, taking care to spill a little of the vodka between the nightstand, the bed, and the IV stand. Then, as an afterthought, she put a bottle to his lips and poured a small amount of vodka into his mouth. When she saw that he swallowed it reflexively without a struggle, she did this several more times. After that she stashed the scissors and the bottles in the drop drawer, as Ken might do in this hypothetical situation, to avoid Rashod seeing them right off the bat.

Then she bent over and kissed him on the forehead, letting her lips linger for a moment as she felt her eyes swell with tears.

It was finally over. Everything she had ever wanted was happening.

She went out to the kitchen to wait for Rashod's return.

First she would tell him that Ken was asleep. And then, breaking out her best smile, she would chat with him for ten or fifteen minutes before confessing that she was worried about his patient. That she and Ken had shared a tearful good-bye and that Ken had insisted that she leave him alone, that he was tired and wanted to sleep. Frankly, she would say, she was worried about him, he had sounded crazy and defeated.

And later, after he'd gone through his obligatory motions and made his obligatory calls, Rashod would hold her as she wept and tell her that this happened all the time, that sometimes patients just take matters into their own hands. Ken Wong had been that kind of man. He went out his way, on his own terms.

90

ST. SPIRIDON ORTHODOX CATHEDRAL SEATTLE, WASHINGTON

204 Days After The Seminar

It had been one of those services in which people got up to speak of the dead, and it had taken nearly two hours to accommodate everyone who so chose. Brad had been one of the first to stand, speaking from his place in the pew, his comments brief and heartfelt. As the new CEO of the company Ken had cofounded, it had been his place to speak for the employees in honoring a man who had created so much for so many.

"It has been said," he began, standing in the pew, "that the only minutes that count in a basketball game are the final ones. The rest are an inevitable exchange of the ball, shots attempted, some made, some missed . . . you lose the ball, you steal it back . . . the crowd loves you, the crowd hates you . . . your defense isn't effective, your offensive timing is off, then it all clicks again . . . you work hard, you get tired, maybe you get hurt, maybe you don't . . . you sit out awhile, but you always come back to the game. Until that final two minutes it's all just a scrimmage, and none of it counts for anything if you don't play hard and execute, learning from your mistakes as you go, so that you find yourself in a position to win when those final two minutes arrive."

He looked down at Beth, saw that her chin was trembling as she looked up at him. She smiled bravely, perhaps with pride in her eyes. For a quick moment he flashed on the journal he'd kept at the ranch and all the things he'd said about her and to her in it. The journal had arrived via FedEx several weeks after he'd been home, thankfully to the office instead of his house. He wasn't sure who at the ranch had attended to such details, who was left that would know. But it happened, and in the reality that is the seminar, anything is possible.

Brad had read through the journal one final time, then tossed it into a Dumpster behind a grocery store on the way home that night. He didn't need it around to remember all that he had learned. All he had to do was look at his wife, and all of it was new again.

"Ken Wong was my teammate, and for over three quarters I envied him the ball, resented playing under the boards while he was the shooting guard. But then we took a timeout, he and I, and we looked at the game plan again, through tired but fresh and hungry eyes. The game was on the line. And just when it counted, when those two minutes were ticking away and everything was at stake, he gave the ball to me. In fact, he pulled himself off the court, trusting us with the playbook, letting us run."

Brad paused, waited for his throat to relax, then continued. He felt Beth squeeze his hand, and when he looked down at her, she beamed up at him, full of pride.

"He was my coach. And in the end, my friend. The game ball will always be on the mantel of my heart, and the signature on it is his. It belongs to him."

He sat back down. There was silence, punctuated by the rustling of shifting bodies, the clearing of a throat, a shallow cough.

And then, the sound of someone clapping.

Beth. Always and forever, Beth.

DEADLY FAUX

1

DIVISIVENESS—Our two-party system has turned into a frat-house brawl. One nation under God is now just a schoolhouse poem . . . it's more a vitriolic let-them-eat-cake versus all-for-one-and-one-for-all cage match. Meanwhile, the middle is getting whiplash, which is no longer covered by health insurance.
—*Bullshit in America*, by Wolfgang Schmitt

PORTLAND, OREGON
October 2012

Don't get me started.

No one with a modicum of sense—and please, just shoot me if I ever actually use the word *modicum* in an actual conversation—could blame me for being pissed off about things in general. The airlines want a hundred bucks to change from a flight with a waiting list to another flight that is only half full, and thirty bucks to load your bag. One commuter line wants a hundred dollars for a carry-

on. Thank you for flying Trans Sphincter Air. My HMO
announced their annual 45 percent rate hike on the day a
pro athlete I once admired got busted—again—for beating
up a hooker and his wife on the same day, which earlier
had brought us the news of a senator's tweeting his junk to
yet another hooker. The IRS wasn't buying my deduction to
The Society for the Prevention of Cruelty to Copywriters,
one of which I once was. Reality television hadn't gone
away, nor would Britney or Lindsay Lohan or The Donald,
who continued resisting a sign-off on the restructuring of
his hair.

Grease was no longer The Word. Bullshit was.

Far beyond the boundaries of my claustrophobic little
world, the Democrats wanted us to forget that half the
working population, which was shrinking, is on the public
dole. Meanwhile, the Republicans wanted us to overlook
the fact that, among all those senators and congressmen and
governors with right-leaning tendencies and greasy palms,
not to mention dropped drawers in low places, a guy who
looked like a blowup doll and with no memory was the
best they could come up with for the next Presidential race.
That someone could actually be named after a catcher's
glove. And because of a book and a movie, half the planet
actually believed that Mary Magdalene lived out her days
as Mrs. Jesus H. Christ, while the other half—including
those with rags on their heads and bombs under their
vests—are still quite convinced that God is on their side.

At least Saddam and bin Laden were dead, with no
bounty of vestal virgins anywhere on their eternal horizon.

Bring the boys home? Not that simple, Sparky.

What's a thinking man to do, give Newt the vote? I
don't think so.

In my case, the answer was sanity itself. In my
abundant spare time I wrote a column for a liberal local
weekly—I'm no liberal, by the way, but it was the only
paper interested—titled Bullshit in America. Somehow

calling it out for the consideration of my thinking brothers and sisters made it all the more tolerable. Maybe people would realize they are not alone in their frustration at being jerked around.

There remains no shortage of material.

Then, just when I thought I was safe from the stench of my own indignant cynicism, the next chapter in my heretofore vanilla but suddenly very strange existence was about to be unleashed.

Or, perhaps better said, *unhinged.*

After one dance as an undercover facer for the Feds, a chin for hire, the last thing I ever thought I'd do was once again take up arms as a designated seducer of women at the behest of someone with a badge. A strange destiny indeed for good cheekbones and a few years modeling underwear for the local metropolitan daily.

My name is Wolfgang Schmitt, and I'm here to confirm the rumor that shit really does happen.

MY dear, sweet, institutionalized mother looked at me and said, "I *love* your new show!"

Which, had I been some talking-head movie reviewer on local-access cable—almost got that gig back in the nineties—would have been sort of sweet. But I was a happily unemployed advertising hack who had just come into a buttload of under-the-table federal money—I'll explain *that* later—so my smile was at once forced and sad.

My mother thought I was Chuck Woolery with shorter, cooler hair.

She wasn't the first person in recent memory who thought I looked like a game-show host, but she was the only one who could attribute that fine opinion to Alzheimer's. Okay, maybe the resemblance was there, but I preferred the occasional George-Clooney-meets-Owen-

Wilson comparison I used to get in bars. We were sitting in what had once been a bedroom in a Victorian mansion overlooking the Willamette River—which no one born east of Idaho has ever pronounced correctly—but was now a private nursing facility that charged five grand a month for round-the-clock apathy and food with all the charisma of car wax. The first thing I did with the aforementioned money—earned via the seduction of a billionaire's wayward wife under the threat of being audited to hell and back—was move my mother out of the state-funded hellhole into which I had originally, and naively, deposited her in the hope that someone wearing a starched white uniform would give a shit.

That notion proved to be an airball. This place was about as therapeutic as the funeral home it had once been. But that was about to change. I had an idea, and I had the cash.

"I'm not on television, Mom."

"Oh, did they cancel you? Who do I write to?"

"I'll look it up for you. For now, besides that, you seem happy today."

Maybe if I told her she looked happy, she'd buy it. My mother was constantly smiling, a trait I'd hoped would endear her to the staff until I remembered this was Planet Dementia. She wore a sweatshirt with the words *My Grandma Can Beat Up Your Grandma*—purloined when the woman in the next room died with no relatives willing to pick up her things—over a baby-blue flannel nightgown and fuzzy purple Barney slippers. The sweatshirt and the slippers both hid an excruciating irony: my mother had no grandchildren.

As her only child, that was, of course, my fault.

According to the staff here in hell's little waiting room, from time to time my mother believed she was on a cruise ship. And that she was the cruise director. One day I arrived to find her leading a geriatric line dance in the foyer to the tune of "Achy Breaky Heart," everyone wearing robes and black knee socks. After forty-nine years of living with a man whose favorite word was *goddamn* and whose idea of a family vacation was going clamming in the rain, I didn't have the heart to tell her otherwise. The day my father died, seven lost years earlier, was the first day she forgot who either one of us was.

The universe is funny that way, trading one purgatory for another.

I visited my mother three times a week. We no longer had the past in common, so there wasn't much to discuss, this being a blessing for both of us in many ways. Since I could not impose the needs of my recently broken heart on her motherly sensibilities, I found myself trying to convince her that the captain and crew really liked her and that, yes, those new folks on *Hollywood Squares* really couldn't hold a candle to Paul Lynde and his dead cronies. Somehow Whoopi Goldberg in the center square just didn't cut it for Mom. The meaninglessness of the banter had given me a chance to look critically at the accommodations, and the closer I looked, the less I liked what I smelled. A faint scent of urine always greeted me upon arrival. Sometimes there was spilled food and what I feared was vomit on her bedding—it wasn't easy to tell the difference—and that blue flannel nightie never seemed to get a day off. The staff assured me that laundry was a daily exercise and that it was taken quite seriously, and oh, by the way, that urine smell was my imagination. This was not true, however, of the crumbs that accumulated on the floor in the corners of her room, luring the occasional undiscerning cockroach.

I don't think they liked me all that much, actually.

The administrator was quick to flash his certificate of compliance from the state board of nursing home auditors, but frankly I didn't appreciate his attitude. He reminded me of that guy who married Liza Minnelli, the one who looked like an exhumed extra from the *Dawn of the Dead* and got another few minutes past his allotted fifteen sound-bite minutes when Michael Jackson died. If someone had told me the guy running my mother's nursing home was a holdover from the old funeral home days, I'd have bought it.

I should have checked her out of here weeks ago.

Then one day Mr. Formaldehyde sought me out to announce that, with deep regret, he was closing the home. I had a month to find my mother a new ship in which to cruise. Something about unreasonable regulatory pressures for sanitary upgrades—his look told me he thought I might have had something to do with that one—and the increasingly hostile and unfair reimbursement policies of those bastard Republicans politicizing Medicare. He casually mentioned he hadn't been able to find a buyer, adding that the building required significant capital improvements and that, frankly, none of it penciled out. Cheaper, he said, to shut the doors. It was at that very moment, as I visualized the aforementioned pencil penetrating the membrane of his inner ear, that a lightbulb with the wattage of a Tom Cruise smile illuminated my near-term investment strategy.

And so, being the good and newly moneyed son that I was, I decided to buy the place.

CPSIA information can be obtained at www.ICGtesting.com
Printed in the USA
BVOW08s1007031213

338021BV00001B/31/P